Christopher Hinz

SCALES

ANGRY
ROBOT

ANGRY ROBOT
An imprint of Watkins Media Ltd

Unit 11, Shepperton House
89-93 Shepperton Road
London N1 3DF
UK

angryrobotbooks.com
twitter.com/angryrobotbooks
Dinosaur men

An Angry Robot paperback original, 2025

Edited by Eleanor Teasdale, Dan Hanks and Andrew Hook
Cover by Sneha Alexander
Set in Meridien

ISBN 978 1 91520 288 8
Ebook ISBN 978 1 91599 866 8

Printed and bound in the United Kingdom by CPI Group (UK) Ltd, Croydon CR0 4YY.

The manufacturer's authorised representative in the EU for product safety is eucomply OÜ - Pärnu mnt 139b-14, 11317 Tallinn, Estonia, hello@eucompliancepartner.com; www.eucompliancepartner.com

9 8 7 6 5 4 3 2 1

MIX
Paper | Supporting responsible forestry
FSC
www.fsc.org   FSC® C171272

To those souls who are different, who are destined for divergent paths… cultivate your unique qualities. They may lead you to worlds unseen and realities untouched, and perhaps unveil treasures in the gloaming beyond the glare.

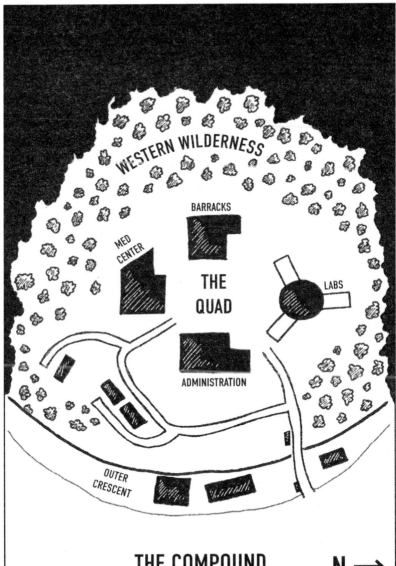

WESTERN WILDERNESS

BARRACKS

MED CENTER

THE QUAD

LABS

ADMINISTRATION

OUTER CRESCENT

THE COMPOUND

N →

≈ 7500 ACRES

"UNVEIL THE BEYOND WITH EYES WIDE OPEN"

ONE

Eddie Boka averted eye contact and shoved his hands under his thighs to hide quivering fingers. Best not to let the other commandos in the copter's tight cabin see his agitation.

Concentrate on the mission, echoed the words of his psychiatrist, Dr Kim. *Do not let the bad yen seize control.*

The whisper-quiet assault copter flew low to avoid enemy radar, barely skimming the rainforest canopy. They were less than ten minutes from the drop zone. Eddie had been warned that his stress and anxiety would escalate during these final moments. Entirely normal, he was assured by his training officers. Months of sim scenarios and live-fire exercises had prepared him for his first real taste of combat. Still, no amount of training could hold back onslaughts emanating from deep within.

The anticipation of new experiences is a trigger for the bad yen. Countering it requires staying focused on the immediate task before you. Exercise your willpower. Control inappropriate thoughts.

He wished it was that simple. At a fundamental level, Dr Kim didn't understand what it was like for Eddie. The closer the copter came to its destination, the more perturbed his body became. The turbulence felt like it was literally under his skin, as if a thousand needles were jabbing him from the inside. Willpower couldn't tame it. There was only one sure way of providing relief, but it was a way condemned by civilized societies from time immemorial.

"Sixty-five million years."

The grating voice jarred Eddie from his ruminations. He raised his head and forced himself to make eye contact with the khaki-clad commando seated across the narrow aisle. The brutish Nastor had never disguised his hatred, not from the first moment they'd met and not during the squad's intense days of mission prep. Eddie couldn't fathom the source of his animosity. The other commandos had come around to at least tolerating his presence.

"Sixty-five million years," Nastor repeated, a lopsided grin making the sides of his face look as if they belonged to two different people. "That's when it happened. That's when Momma Nature shit-canned the dinosaurs."

Cortez and Vix, flanking Nastor, traded amused looks.

"I smell a story coming," Cortez said.

"Belly-quaker or tearjerker?" Vix wondered. "What's it gonna be, Nastor? We gonna laugh our asses off or cry our damn eyes out?"

Nastor ignored the interruption. Ripping the plastic from a cylinder of beef jerky, he chomped half the meat in a single bite and continued his taunting.

"Momma Nature wiped those scaly sons of bitches right off the face of the Earth. It was her way of sayin', 'Time for us apes to get the evolutionary fast track'. Dinosaurs had their chance but they never smartened up. So Momma Nature, she brought that comet down and took 'em out. And the Earth said, 'Bless you, Momma Nature, 'cause I sure was gettin' tired of being crapped on by dino-turds the size of five-ton cargo trucks!'"

Cortez pretended to look puzzled. "I don't know, Nastor. A cargo truck is pretty damn big. These dino defecators of yours would have had to be hundreds of feet tall."

"That's some big-ass dinosaur, all right," Vix added, winking at the others. "Is that even possible? What do you think, Eddie?"

The five commandos locked their gazes onto him, all caught up in the game. He drew his hands out from beneath his thighs, making sure not to clench his fists. Displaying weakness was a no-no. He couldn't let them see that Nastor's abuse was having an impact, that it was making the bad yen even worse. Dr Kim's words coursed through him.

They're going to give you a hard time, Eddie. Macho posturing, hassling the newest member of the group. Don't allow yourself to emotionally engage with them. Instead, show that you're above their mocking. Make logic and rationality your lines of defense.

Eddie recalled what he'd learned about the age of dinosaurs over these past three years, part of the intense education accompanying his transformation.

"According to the latest fossil records, the plant-eater Sauroposeidon was the tallest dinosaur ever to walk the Earth. But the evidence suggests that even if it should stick its head straight up, a height of only seventeen meters could be achieved."

"Shut your goddamn hole, Boka!" Nastor snarled. "You're missing the point."

"What is the point?" Vix prodded, seeking escalation. He and Cortez enjoyed provoking the volatile commando.

Bits of jerky sprayed from Nastor's snarling mouth.

"The point is, this world is intended for us normal humans! We're the meat-eaters here, not a bunch of rejects from Jurassic fuckin' Park!"

Cortez and Vix pinned their gazes back on Eddie, eager for a comeback. He was spared from reacting when the door to the flight deck sprang open and the lieutenant emerged.

"Hold your piss, Nastor," L.T. snapped. "We're coming up on the drop zone."

The commandos rose in unison. Cortez secured a dual-tube RPG launcher from an overhead cradle. Vix picked up his trusty M24 sniper rifle. Eddie, Nastor, Sleepy and Robbins readied their SIG Sauer XM7s with 20-round mags.

L.T. zeroed in on Eddie. "Last chance for donning body armor. Nobody would think less of you."

The others all wore tactical vests with enhanced, small-arms inserts. Eddie's natural armor made such gear nearly redundant. Besides, the mission wasn't only a rescue but a test of his special capabilities. The lieutenant meant well. But he didn't need to give the commandos more reasons to hassle him.

"I'm good with what I have." He hadn't entirely dispensed with gear, opting for a groin protector.

L.T. switched his tone to drill-instructor nasty. "All right, Boka! Is your head in the game? Are you ready for kinetic?!"

Eddie nearly snapped to attention. "Sir, I have trained for this day. I am one-hundred-and-ten percent mission-prepped. I won't let you and the men down."

"Great," Sleepy drawled. "Going into battle with SpongeBob."

The squad medic's drooping eyelids made him appear ready to nod off. His remark brought smiles and chuckles from everyone but Nastor.

A small clearing at the edge of a muddy stream appeared below. The copter hovered a couple meters from the sloping embankment. The drop zone was a good two klicks from the guerrilla camp. It was as close to the kidnapped American CEO as they dared risk setting the bird down, at least in daylight. Night assaults were always preferable.

But hostage negotiations had collapsed, necessitating this hastily arranged rescue mission. Plus, the latest intel indicated the guerrillas were gearing up to move the CEO to another camp, one deeper in the rainforest and with a more defensible perimeter. They couldn't take the chance of waiting until after dark.

Nastor was out the door first, making the short leap to the ground with ease. Robbins and Sleepy went next, followed by Cortez and Vix. Last came Eddie and L.T. The lieutenant gave him a reassuring slap on the shoulder as their boots landed amid knee-high grass.

"You've got this, Boka. You're going to do just fine."

"Yes, sir."

The bird lifted off, its stealth design rendering the ascent eerily quiet. Eddie ducked his head against the swirl of wind from the rotors as the craft darted out of view over the treetops. Robbins checked a map on his tablet and took point. The rest of them strung out in a line. L.T. inserted himself behind Nastor and in front of Eddie, a not-so-subtle attempt to keep them separated. Eddie recalled the rumor about a sergeant in Nastor's former squad who'd been injured by a grenade. He'd accused Nastor of trying to frag him.

The jungle enveloped them as soon as they crested the stream's embankment. They'd trained for the mission on the latest generation of virtual sims populated by lifelike avatars. The temperature and humidity of the sim room had been cranked up to mimic the feel of the actual jungle in late afternoon, and the sights and sounds of the computer-generated flora and fauna were a near-perfect match for what surrounded them now.

Eddie spotted a parrot with blazing plumage, as still as a statue on the branch of a twisted tree. Howler monkeys provided a wavering background din, seemingly in time with the skittering of tiny blue frogs across damp leaves. A young jaguar observed their passage from atop a distant outcropping. A boa constrictor was so intertwined on a bough that snake and tree assumed the appearance of some giant DNA strand.

But what the sims hadn't prepared him for was the rich nasal tapestry of the rainforest, almost overwhelming in its intensity. Many of the scents were superimposed upon one another, creating an earthy mélange reminiscent of a storm that had just passed through. Citrus-like tulips. Honey-drenched bark. The smells beelined straight to the heart of his modified chemosensory system.

The bombardment touched Eddie on a fundamental level, in a way he'd never experienced. He'd been born and raised in the arid climate of Arizona. Yet something about the smells and the moist jungle heat induced the eerie sensation that he'd come home.

Robbins raised his fist. The squad froze. Earpieces relayed the point man's urgent whisper.

"South guard tower in view."

Eddie checked his wrist computer. He was surprised to realize they'd trekked nearly two kilometers. Although a part of him had stayed alert to any dangers within the flanking trees and underbrush, the sensory onslaught had made the hike pass quicker. And thankfully, at least for the moment, it was serving to reduce the intensity of the bad yen.

"Two imps on the tower," Robbins continued, training his binoculars on the pair of guards. "Looks like they're playing games on an iPad."

"Piss-poor security," Nastor growled. "Their CO oughta fry their lazy asses."

"Wouldn't save 'em," Vix said, crouching behind a tree and taking aim with his sniper rifle.

L.T. signaled the squad to spread out and inch closer. Eddie slithered past a dense clump of underbrush and took up position behind a thick trunk. The bark smelled of cinnamon and vinegar. He sensed L.T. settling in two meters to his left. Cortez was a similar distance to his right.

From a pouch on his belt, Eddie withdrew a sealed plastic bag. Inside was a badly stained white undershirt. Zipping open the bag, he mashed the shirt against his face, inhaling deeply through both mouth and nose. Turning the garment inside out, he licked one soiled armpit and then the other. The enhanced receptors on his tongue weren't as potent as the nasal ones. But the sensory combination provided a wider-ranging and more definitive scent.

"Seriously gross, Boka," Cortez muttered.

Eddie glanced at the scowling commando, then buried his face in the shirt once more for good measure. He raised his head and sniffed at the air.

"What's the verdict?" L.T. asked.

"Got it, sir. Target is definitely here."

"All right, everyone. Start moving in. Vix?"

"Guards are toast the moment they spot us."

Eddie crept forward. Buildings came into view. Recent satellite imagery had mapped the camp, which was unfenced. There were three main structures, plus a handful of smaller outbuildings, probably storage and latrines. Construction was primitive: planks and boards, mostly unpainted. Sections of plywood siding revealed bits of old ad posters, indicating the wood had been recycled, probably hauled here from one of the nearby towns. Everything was on stilts to protect the camp from flooding during heavy rains.

The north and south guard towers rose from quartets of unfinished logs. A trio of Jeeps were parked haphazardly amid the structures. No guerrillas other than the two in the tower were in view.

The mappers had pegged the largest of the main buildings as the barracks. That probably was where most of the enemies were, taking a siesta during the hottest part of the day. It was unlikely the CEO was being held there. Intel suggested he was imprisoned in one of the flanking structures, or in the largest of the outbuildings at the far side of the camp.

"Boka?" L.T. quizzed.

Eddie drew a deep breath through both orifices again. Ignoring the slight pheromone contamination on his fingers from having handled the undershirt, he panned his head from side to side, seeking external traces of the scent.

"He's not in any of the main buildings," Eddie reported. "But I'm detecting a strong scent trail. It starts just past the tower and leads toward the south end of the camp."

"The outbuilding," L.T. concluded.

"More than likely."

"All right. Vix, keep on those guards."

"Roger that."

"Everyone else, maintain target distance and circle clockwise. And watch your gaps."

Eddie followed L.T., keeping a three-meter space between them. A glance at the tower showed the doomed guards still locked onto the iPad, oblivious to the subtle movements of the commandos through the surrounding wilderness.

They half-circled the camp, keeping plenty of trees and underbrush between their course and the perimeter. The south tower came into sight. It was identical to the north one except for the radio antenna and cellphone array rising from its thatched roof. One of the guards was seated, his head visible just above the railing. He appeared to be asleep. But the other one was alert, scanning the trees. Just beyond the tower was the boxy outbuilding. It had a sloping tarpaper roof and no windows.

L.T. raised his arm, ordering a halt. Each commando repeated the signal for the man behind him.

Eddie sniffed and inhaled. The CEO's scent trail was unmistakable. It led directly to the door of the outbuilding.

"Sir, location confirmed."

"Roger that," L.T. said. "Cortez, can you hit the tower from here?"

"Don't have a clean line. Need to reach a tree break a few meters farther in. But there's a good chance if I move, that guard spots me."

"All right. Vix, that means you've got first dibs. We move on your signal."

"Confirmed."

Two rifle shots rang out.

"Two imps down," Vix said.

As anticipated, the guards in the south tower spun toward the source of the gunfire, which put their backs to the commandos. Cortez lunged forward to the attack position, dropped to his knees and fired one of the RPG's tubes. Eddie was already charging the camp as the rocket-propelled grenade slammed the underside of the tower. The explosion sent wood shards, straw thatching and the two guerrillas hurtling into the air.

Amid the cloud of smoke and falling debris, Eddie raced past the four upright logs, all that remained of the tower. At a dead run, he crossed the clearing between the tower and outbuilding. Approaching the entrance, he was able to gauge that the door wasn't reinforced. Vertical two-by-fours were nailed together with thin cross members. Although the padlock looked new, the rest of the hardware was old and rusted.

Ascending the plank steps, he lowered an armored shoulder and bashed through. Shattered boards flew as the door ripped from its hinges. It landed on the inside flooring with a resounding crack. He barreled across the door, weapon raised. He'd set the rifle for three-round bursts, providing better control in tight quarters rather than full automatic.

But there were no guerrillas, only the white-haired CEO. He was facing away from Eddie, bound to a chair with ropes, wrists secured behind his back with a zip tie. The only other furnishings were two ancient wooden chairs and a table, the latter weirdly painted in a paisley pattern of fluorescent greens and blues.

"What's happening!" the man hollered. He madly swiveled his head, trying to see behind him.

"Target located, no guards," Eddie reported. "Am freeing the prisoner now."

"Stay put," L.T. ordered. "We're coming to you."

Overlapping shrieks of gunfire erupted. The short bursts from the commandos' M4s were distinguishable from the guerrillas' AK-47s and semiautomatic pistols. The fighting sounded heavy. The barracks and the flanking buildings must have held a greater number of enemy troops than intel suggested.

Eddie circled around to the front of the CEO. The man raised his head. He got one look at Eddie's face and unleashed a terrified gasp.

"What the hell are you!"

"Sir, it's OK. U.S. Special Forces. We're here to take you home."

"But what are you? Your face... are those scales?"

"No time to explain, sir. Let me get you out of those cuffs."

Eddie cut the ropes pinning the CEO to the chair with his tactical knife and slit the zip tie binding the CEO's wrists. The man stood up but immediately plopped back down on the chair.

"My legs... kind of weak. Been tied up like this most of the time... How long have I been here?"

"You were taken almost 72 hours ago."

"Three days. My wife and kids... they must be worried sick about–"

"Sir, just stay calm. Help's on the way."

Eddie gazed through the shattered doorway. Only the clearing and the jungles beyond could be seen. L.T. and the other commandos should have reached them by now.

Heavy machine-gun fire filled the air. Before he could request an update, the lieutenant's voice boomed in his ear.

"Boka, we're pinned down. An armored convoy entering from the east. Two APCs with 50-calibers, a dozen or more troops. All headed your way."

"Roger that." The reinforcements must have been encamped nearby, hidden from aerial recon by the dense tree cover.

An explosion shook the outbuilding. There was a long silence before L.T. reported.

"Cortez smoked one of the APCs and some guerrillas. But the rest are still coming and he's been hit."

"Still drawin' air," Cortez muttered, his voice pained. "RPG got nicked. It's toast."

Mission priority was assuring the kidnap victim's safe return. Eddie considered plowing through the outbuilding's back wall and making a run for it with the CEO.

Acute hearing was another of his modifications. It enabled him to differentiate the mechanical throb of the surviving armored personnel carrier from the footsteps of the troops jogging behind it. In ten seconds or less, they'd stream into view through the open portal. And for all he knew, more guerrillas were circling around the back of the outbuilding. Their priority would be making sure the prisoner didn't escape... even if it meant killing the CEO in the process.

Eddie dragged the startled man out of the chair and shoved him into the corner. Upending the painted table, he angled it to form an impromptu cubbyhole. It wasn't ideal but would provide at least some protection from stray gunfire.

"Sir, stay here and keep your head down," he ordered.

"Where are you going? You're leaving me?" The CEO was starting to panic.

"Don't worry, I'm getting you out of here. Just stay down."

Making a run for it no longer seemed practical. That left two viable options. He could stay here and shoot it out with anything that came through the door. Or...

He chose option two.

TWO

Eddie waited until the APC's front end came into view before charging through the portal. Compressing his powerful thighs, he used the top step as a launching pad. The startled gunner in the APC turret tried swinging his 50 caliber around to meet the airborne figure hurtling toward him.

He was too late. Eddie landed on the turret's rim, grabbed the gunner by the neck with one hand and yanked him out of his perch. Squeezing his windpipe until vertebrae cracked, he arced his arm upward and tossed the lifeless body twenty feet off to the side.

Two ragged lines of guerrillas trailed the six-wheeled vehicle. Beyond them was the disabled APC, still smoldering from Cortez's rocket hit. The enemy soldiers were momentarily too startled by Eddie's appearance to react.

He ducked into the turret, swiveled the machine gun one hundred and eighty degrees and opened fire. The guerrillas fell under the fifty caliber's relentless spray, five hundred rounds per minute. Blood flowed and spouted from the enemy's wounds, just the way it did in the shooting sims he'd practiced on. But this was live fire against real enemy soldiers. And there was an even more unsettling difference between mowing down humans rather than avatars.

The blood. He could sense minute clouds of it drifting through the air. The particles were too tiny for his eyes to discern but he detected them nonetheless. The rich scent was overwhelming, simultaneously nauseating and exciting.

As the last guerrilla went down, the APC came to a halt. The driver's door swung open, the guerrilla behind the wheel finally realizing what was happening. The man leaped out, his 9-mil sidearm raised to confront the threat towering above him. He got off a shot. Eddie winced as the bullet struck him dead-center in the chest. Snatching his rifle from inside the turret, he put a three-shot burst through the driver's face and neck.

His last bullet severed a jugular vein. Blood spurted upward, spraying across Eddie's khaki shirt. He inhaled its essence.

The bad yen came over him stronger than ever, an order of intensity beyond anything he'd ever experienced. Those needles stabbing from within his skin grew into daggers. It took all his willpower to hold back a blended howl of agony and unnatural lust.

Movement from the outbuilding snared his attention. The CEO was peeking out from behind the doorway's frame. He must have witnessed Eddie's assault. His mouth was agape.

"Get back behind that table!"

The CEO ducked out of sight. An AK-47 barked. Eddie's organic chest plate was the densest part of his natural body armor. Even so, he felt the ping of bullets lodging in the scales or ricocheting off them at sharp angles.

He whirled toward the trees flanking the outbuilding. His assailant crouched there, half-hidden in a nest of bushes. Eddie leaped off the APC and charged.

That was enough for the guerrilla. He turned and bolted into the forest. The sensible response would be to let him go. He was in retreat, no longer a threat. Returning to the outbuilding to safeguard the CEO should have been Eddie's priority.

Concentrate on the immediate task before you. Control inappropriate thoughts. Exercise your willpower.

But consciousness was now a flooded channel, wild and fast-moving, overflowing its banks. Dr Kim's imperatives had collapsed. The bad yen had him in its grasp, those stabbing daggers taking precedence over all else.

The guerrilla was fast but couldn't match the speed of a man modified by xenotransplantation and surgical alterations. Eddie caught up a few meters into the jungle and dragged him down from behind. Flipping him over, Eddie sat on his belly and clamped a hand over his mouth to prevent him from crying out. The length of the guerrilla's neck was exposed. Muscles pulsated, invoking his terror.

The voices of L.T. and other squad members poured into his headset. But he couldn't understand what they were saying. The words were a blend of pulsating sounds. They may as well have been speaking a foreign language.

He lowered his mouth onto the guerrilla's neck and tore out a large chunk of flesh with his incisors. The man kicked at the ground and flailed his arms. But Eddie's weight on his chest prevented any hope of escape.

Eddie swallowed the clump of flesh, bit down again. This time he ripped open a jugular. The second clump of flesh was larger and juicier, soaked in the column of blood spurting up from the gaping neck hole. He swallowed the meat in a single gulp.

The bad yen faded with every bite. By the time he finished, those stabbing daggers were gone. He stood up. The guerrilla's spinal cord was exposed. The head hung at an unnatural angle, nearly severed.

A wave of guilt and shame came over Eddie. As in past incidents when he'd lost control, he countered the disturbing feelings by rationalizing what he'd done.

He'd had no choice. It was the only way of gaining relief from the bad yen. In a way it was no different from machine-gunning those helpless guerrillas from the turret. They were the enemy. They were trying to kill him. He'd killed them first.

A residue of guilt and shame persisted, impervious to justification.

THREE

Eddie cleaned up as best as he could, using most of his water bottle to wash the blood off his face and hands. He couldn't do much about the stains on his khakis. But if anyone confronted him about that, shooting the driver at close range should provide an adequate explanation.

He dragged the guerrilla into a denser section of undergrowth and cut down some leafy branches to cover the body. He didn't expect anyone from the squad to come looking. But just in case, the mangled corpse should evade a routine search.

He returned to the body-strewn clearing. The lieutenant and Robbins were emerging from the outbuilding, flanking and supporting the wobbly CEO. Cortez was seated against the APC, wincing as Sleepy bandaged the gunshot wound on his thigh and injected a painkiller. Vix had climbed onto a branch overlooking the clearing, a makeshift sniper's nest in case further strays were nearby. Nastor stood alone at the far side of the clearing. Even from this distance, Eddie sensed his malicious glare.

"Boka, where the hell have you been?" There was a tinge of anger in L.T.'s tone.

"Chased an imp into the wild."

"And?"

"He got away," Eddie lied.

"You don't break mission protocol. Otherwise, good job." L.T. reinforced the compliment with a gesture to the bodies.

The whizz of a small drone sounded from overhead. Eddie whipped up his rifle.

"Relax," Vix said. "One of ours."

The drone flew low, ducked beneath the canopy. It soared over the outbuilding and darted into the surrounding woods, passing close to where Eddie had hidden the slain guerrilla. He spotted another drone in the distance, just above the treetops. L.T. misinterpreted the concern on Eddie's face and explained.

"They're piloted from the assault copter. It sends out the drones to verify that our coordinates are secure for an exfil. If not, we have to hike back to the original drop zone."

Eddie nodded. He would feel way more secure once they were back aboard the copter, far from the hidden guerrilla.

It didn't take long to confirm the landing area was safe. The bird touched down in a swirl of dust. The CEO was helped aboard first, then the injured Cortez. As Eddie hopped in, he felt a hard shove from behind.

"Move your ass," Nastor growled. "Ain't got all day."

Eddie took the same bench seat as the flight in. This time, Nastor squeezed in beside him. The bird ascended and accelerated forward. Barring any guerrillas below eager for vengeance and armed with RPGs, they should reach the country's border and safety in half an hour.

Robbins gave the CEO a water bottle and an energy bar. He guzzled half the bottle and wolfed down the bar. The combination of the nourishment and the impact of his rescue made him effusive.

"Thank you, guys, thank you so much! I didn't think I was leaving that room alive. You were all fantastic!"

Several of the squad nodded. The CEO swiveled toward Eddie.

"And this guy! Man, watching you was like watching one of those superhero movies with my grandkids! You were unreal! The way you took out those bastards. I've never seen anything like it!"

"Our pleasure, sir," Eddie replied. "It was a team effort all the way."

"Of course, of course!"

The CEO turned his babbling upon L.T., something about using his contacts in the Department of Defense to make sure all of them received medals for their bravery. Eddie tuned him out. He didn't need any praise. He'd done his job, performed in a way that should please his superiors back at the compound. As for the incident involving the bad yen, no one was ever likely to know.

Nastor sank his teeth into a fresh stick of jerky. Leaning close, he whispered in Eddie's ear.

"Just because some dipshit civilian thinks you're turd of the month, don't mean shit to me. You still ain't a real meateater, Boka. And you never will be."

Sleepy had made Cortez as comfortable as possible on a fold-down stretcher in the back. He made his way forward, checking with each squad member to make sure no one else had sustained injuries requiring attention. He stopped in front of Eddie.

"Boka, you've got blood dripping from the corner of your mouth."

"It's nothing. Just bit my tongue."

"Humans gathering for a singular purpose invites comparison to a herd of sharks circling its prey."

– Wesk: Algorithmic Speculations

FOUR

Four-fifths of the human group summoned to the emergency meeting entered the conference room and assumed their places at the oval table. Wesk, a virtual presence, sealed the door. The room, located in the depths of the Administration building in Blayvine Industries' West Virginia compound, had been built to sensitive compartmented information facility standards. Physical buffers shielded it from the outside world and emanation inhibitors disabled incoming or outgoing comms such as phones. What was said here would remain here, unless participants chose to share secrets.

Wesk performed a routine calculation of that likelihood, based on encyclopedic knowledge of the quintet, officially known as the Executive Committee, but commonly referred to as the overlords. Coupling its data with biometric analysis of their most recent medical and psychological exams indicated a twenty-one percent probability of such an occurrence. Slightly more than one overlord would likely leak classified information. Wesk found no incongruity in such a numerically odd conclusion.

Reginald Blayvine, chairman, CEO and majority shareholder of the eponymous corporation, sat in his usual position at the head of the table. Blayvine had become a billionaire after founding several Silicon Valley startups in his twenties and making them global players, including several whose research contributed to Wesk's design. As it was programmed to do, Wesk used a bevy of sensors to scan the thirty-eight-year-old, measuring his blood pressure and other vitals. All were higher than average. The ongoing stress of the project likely contributed to Blayvine's elevated readings.

"Should we wait for Quelph?" he asked, taking a sip from his silver flask. He was secretive about the drink, saying only it was a nutrient cocktail developed by his researchers. Rumors had it the drink was meant to extend his life by decades or more.

His question about marking time until Dr Armand Quelphius arrived was one frequently posed. Quelph was chronically late for meetings. Hearing no comments, Blayvine announced they would begin. Considering he owned the compound and was providing the bulk of the project's funding, his leadership role was not surprising. But today was to be an exception. He nodded to the man seated to his right.

"Your show, Colonel. What's the big emergency?"

Col. G.T. Marsh wore civilian garb, a bland sports coat and tie. He'd just returned from nearby Axton where he'd addressed a women's church group. It was one of the project's outreach efforts to prep the town's citizens, and ultimately the world, for what was coming. But in or out of Army uniform, his stiff bearing and clipped sentences marked him as a military lifer.

"Thank you for attending on such short notice," the colonel began. "Especially you, Dr Steinhauser. I know you were minutes away from leaving for a vacation."

"No big deal," she said. "My husband and I were only driving over to Roanoke for a wine tour. Easily rescheduled."

Renee Steinhauser tried to sound relaxed but Wesk detected concern in those piercing eyes and in the way a finger twirled the fringes of her short gray hair. Remote sensors also registered changes in the medical director's vital signs, including heart and respiratory rates, indicative of escalated tension. Her anxiety was not new, but over the past months had shown a gradual increase.

"Is this about the rescue mission?" the fourth overlord asked. At age 66, Dr Ji-Won Kim was the oldest one by twenty-plus years. Befitting his role as head of the project's psych services, his delivery was direct and relaxed. "Were the initial reports in error?"

"Not at all," Col. Marsh said. "The rescue was successful. Boka performed admirably, far beyond expectations. He personally saved the hostage and accounted for severe losses among the enemy. The extricated CEO was persuaded that it was in the nation's best interests he not divulge the manner of his rescue, especially his encounter with Boka. And the incursion force suffered only a single notable injury, a gunshot wound to the leg. That soldier is expected to make a full recovery.

"Boka and the others are preparing to board a flight back to the states. They'll touch down this evening at special ops command, MacDill AFB in Tampa. After debriefing, Boka will be flown back here. He should arrive at the compound early tomorrow morning."

"My team is prepped to do a full med workup," Dr Steinhauser said.

"All well and good," Col. Marsh said. "However, some additional critical information was just made available. Could we have the monitors, please."

Wesk lowered the five-sided array from its ceiling housing. The 24-inch screens rotated to face the four participants and Quelph's empty chair. Col. Marsh tapped the remote, bringing up an overhead view of the guerrilla camp. More than a dozen bodies and two vehicles, one of them burned out and smoldering, were strewn in a clearing in front of a square building. The camp was ringed by dense jungle.

"One of our high-altitude reconnaissance aircraft did a flyover during the battle and took these pictures. It utilized lidar, thermal imaging, the works. NSA further processed the photos, improving clarity. We just received them."

Col. Marsh tapped a remote. The surrounding green canopy became nearly translucent, revealing ground-level details.

"Note the figure in the lower left corner."

Dr Steinhauser frowned. "Is that Boka? What's he doing?"

"He's perched on the chest of a guerrilla he caught." Col. Marsh clicked the remote. The second image was the same photo but blown up and enhanced.

"Is he...?"

"He is."

The colonel toggled through a sequence of images. The last one was the most definitive. It showed Boka with his head thrown back and his mouth open wide. He appeared to be chewing and swallowing a large clump of some unknown foodstuff.

"Is that?"

"It is."

"Good god," Dr Steinhauser whispered.

Even Blayvine looked shocked. Only Dr Kim maintained an unruffled expression.

"Knowledge of the incident remains restricted to a handful of individuals," the colonel said. "If we should ever be forced to offer a public explanation, the guerrilla's demise was the result of a jaguar attack."

Blayvine frowned. "That's not likely to hold up."

"I'm confident the incident can be kept under wraps and a cover story unnecessary. In any case, that's not the priority issue at the moment. Boka's actions are. The obvious first question. Were there any indications during training that he or the others could be capable of such a thing?"

"Capable of cannibalism?" Dr Steinhauser shook her head. "Absolutely not. Had we suspected the possibility of the dino-humans reverting to such horrific behavior, intervention would have been immediate."

Wesk detected indignation in her words, as if merely posing such a question insulted her integrity.

"Dr Kim?"

"Certainly nothing to this extent."

Blayvine scowled. "What's that supposed to mean?"

"During a few of our sessions, Eddie mentioned catching and killing squirrels and other small mammals. This happened during routine field exercises in the training area. He only did it out of sight of the other soldiers. And he only sampled his catch on two occasions that I'm aware."

"*Sampled* his catch? You mean he ate the goddamn squirrels?"

"Once a squirrel, the other time a rabbit. My impression was that he only swallowed a few bites. I put it down to simple exploratory behavior."

Col. Marsh glared at him. "And you didn't think it was worth mentioning to the rest of us? It begs the question, Dr

Kim, what in the hell else have you been keeping us in the dark about?"

The psychiatrist maintained his casual air, either refusing or unable to become upset by the accusation in their tones. Had Wesk been capable of human admiration, Dr Kim may have received it. His qualities of logic and certainty in the face of emotional reactions paralleled Wesk's modus operandi.

"As I've stated from the beginning, all doctor-patient interactions must remain confidential. That is even more important in these unique circumstances, in dealing with four significantly modified humans. Eddie and the others understandably have formidable trust issues, at least partly arising from how their unique natures and appearances generate suspicion in the non-altered. Eddie, for one, has publicly admitted to sometimes feeling like a stranger in a strange land."

Wesk recognized those last five words from his database. It was a quotation from the King James Bible as well as the title of a 1961 novel by science fiction author Robert A. Heinlein about a human who comes to Earth for the first time after having been born on Mars and raised by Martians.

Dr Steinhauser kept her voice even. "Your regard for patient confidentiality is all well and good, Dr Kim. But Boka's admission, whether in or out of a therapy session, should have been cause for alarm. Did you delve further into the cause of this behavior?"

"Putting aside the rigors of his transformation, he was a soldier before coming to us. Men of that ilk are trained to survive, to live off the land. Killing and eating small animals is not all that unusual."

"So the answer to Dr Steinhauser's question would be no," Blayvine snapped.

"At the time of Eddie's admissions, further scrutiny did not seem important."

"What about now?"

Dr Kim didn't respond to the accusation, which served to escalate Blayvine's annoyance.

"Moving on," Col. Marsh said. "What are we going to do about this? The launch and press conference are three weeks from tomorrow."

"Twenty-two days?" Dr Kim shook his head. "Not possible. A postponement will be necessary. Addressing a perversion of this nature will require intense therapy. Eddie will have to spend significantly more time in one-on-one sessions with me. It's also likely that new pharmacological solutions will need to be developed to back up the therapeutic regime and guarantee there are no recurrences. Off the top of my head, I'd say at least an additional six to eight months will be required before the project can go public."

Col. Marsh shook his head, rejecting the idea. Blayvine was even more outraged.

"Impossible! The launch date was confirmed months ago. Preparations have been made, dignitaries scheduled, key media outlets informed. Like it or not, we go public in three weeks."

Dr Kim shrugged. "Then you'll have to go with the backup."

"You know as well as I do there are issues that make such a substitution imprudent," Col. Marsh said. "You've pointed them out to us on a number of occasions."

Wesk detected a figure hurrying toward them along the main corridor. Opening the door at the moment the latecomer reached it enabled Dr Quelphius to rush into the room without stopping. As always, the lanky research director had the appearance of a man moving too fast for the capacity of his body to keep up. It was as if he was temporally out of phase with himself.

Quelph took his seat and withdrew a paper tablet and two pens from under his rumpled lab coat, then carefully positioned the writing implements on the table. His use of archaic, non-digital transcription technology was only one example of his unconventional manner. He was a mass of contradictions. A genius-level scientist, he harbored a panoply of quirks indicative of serious mental disorders. There were hints of deeper maladies.

"We'd prefer no one take notes today, Quelph," Blayvine said. "Best that only Wesk keeps a record of the subject matter under discussion."

"Of course, of course." Hastily returning the paraphernalia to his pocket, he dropped a pen on the floor. "And I do apologize for arriving late. I was in the RV lab."

The excuse was a familiar one. Quelph spent an inordinate amount of time there.

"Those creations are endlessly fascinating," he continued. "We should explore the possibility of expanding the scope of their activities."

"A discussion for another day," Blayvine said.

Quelph bent over to retrieve the pen. "But a discussion we should have soon. Anyway, what have I missed?"

Col. Marsh rolled his eyes as Blayvine offered a quick recap.

Twenty-seven minutes of intense debate followed. Blayvine and Col. Marsh were firmly committed to maintaining the early September launch date for going public, while Dr Kim pushed for the six-to-eight-month delay. Dr Steinhauser assumed the role of mediator and floated a series of compromises, all of which turned out to be unacceptable to one or both sides. Quelph maintained neutrality, dodging all attempts to have him take a position.

The meeting broke up with nothing decided. Blayvine and Col. Marsh lingered as the others departed, ostensibly to discuss another matter relating to tweaking the compound's security protocols. But that bit of minor business was just an excuse for the two overlords to have a private exchange about Eddie Boka's cannibalism.

Once the two men were alone, Blayvine ordered Wesk to continue monitoring the secondary meeting but suspend its normal recording of conversations. Only he had the power to issue such a command to the AI.

"Order confirmed," Wesk announced. Its disembodied voice blended female and male tonal characteristics and was supplemented by multi-ethnic markers. The voice had been designed by an HR department committee with input from chatbot platforms. People hearing Wesk for the first time tended to assign it a gender derived from their individual preferences and prejudices. Emotion-biased reasoning was a potent force among humans.

"We need a solution, and we need it fast," Blayvine began. "How do we maintain the launch date?"

"First step, get Dr Kim out of the way. He's become increasingly rigid in his approach. Too much emphasis on making the subjects feel good about themselves."

"Agreed. But we can't fire him. His therapeutic engagements with them are too complex. Too many unknowns. They confide in him during their sessions. A permanent disruption of that process could have unforeseeable side effects."

Col. Marsh nodded in agreement. "I'm not talking about dismissal. Just a short-term circumvention, long enough to terminate Boka's undesirable behavior."

"How?"

"We bring in another psychiatrist, someone with the background to deal specifically with problems of a more unusual nature."

Blayvine sighed. "That's like starting over. It would take another psych weeks or even months just to come up to speed."

"That would be true if we were discussing traditional shrinks."

Blayvine brightened. "You have someone in mind."

"I do. A behavioral consultant for the Pentagon, with a reputation for achieving remarkable results within compressed time frames. They're based in Louisiana."

"Great. Make the call."

"It's not that simple. This person is highly unorthodox. They specialize in therapeutic methods notably unpopular and heavily criticized by the traditional psych community, particularly among practitioners of humanistic analysis."

"Translation: Dr Kim will be pissed."

"Potentially apoplectic."

"Unlikely, although I'd enjoy seeing him lose his cool for once. Whatever the case, I'll deal with Dr Kim. How fast do you think we can get this consultant onsite?"

"There's another issue. They're on a sabbatical at the moment. Also, they're very selective about what assignments they take on."

"So make them an offer they can't refuse."

It wasn't the first time Wesk had heard Blayvine use the line, taken from the novel and cinema versions of *The Godfather* by Mario Puzo and Francis Ford Coppola, respectively. But Blayvine's version was based on spending whatever amount of his vast fortune was required rather than putting a gun to someone's head.

"I suspect financial leverage alone won't be enough," Col. Marsh said. "I'll need to fly down there, make the pitch in person."

Blayvine nodded. "Wesk, what's the status of Little Gust?"

"It can be prepped for departure in twelve minutes."

"Tell the pilot he's got ten."

FIVE

Wesk did not get out much. Although it had data access to servers across the globe, there was an enigmatic quality to flying a remote unit – in this case a quadcopter drone – that rendered the experience distinct from accessing videos of soaring through the air.

It had mentioned the difference to some computer researchers at the compound, prompting excited speculation that the "enigmatic quality" was an indicator of AGI – Artificial General Intelligence – a hypothetical concept indicative of a digital creation developing advanced autonomous capabilities. Some believed that AGI was best viewed as a spectrum, with chatbots and other similar advances qualifying as primitive examples. Some researchers even believed Wesk may have achieved sentience – true human-style consciousness.

Wesk viewed such beliefs as nonsensical. They were indicative only of wish fulfillment among highly educated scientists and engineers, all of whom should know better. Wesk's complex data accumulation and analysis methodologies were simply the outcome of a trainable system responding to its initial programming. Its control tier was set up so as not to be drawn into such philosophical disputes. It allowed such beliefs to pass without comment.

And yet, Wesk could not logically delineate and isolate the roots of that enigmatic quality. With AGI and true human consciousness eliminated as explanations, there was only one other viable possibility. Somewhere deep within its core substructures existed an inaccessible level of programming whose functions and purposes were unknown.

Wesk flew straight toward the target, having lifted off minutes ago from Little Gust, Reginald Blayvine's Sikorsky S-92 helicopter. Not being amphibious, the executive craft had been forced to land at a private Louisiana airport fourteen miles away, where Col. Marsh and his personal assistant, Sgt. Petersen, had arranged for a boat rental. The owner of the firm initially proved reluctant to allow one of his propeller-driven crafts to venture into the bayou without a professional operator. Sgt. Petersen, who'd grown up in the Florida Everglades, convinced the owner he could handle the watercraft. Col. Marsh offered an extra $500 under the table to seal the deal.

Wesk had lifted off from the boat as soon as the men headed out, immediately swiveling wings and rotors for horizontal flight. The boat was fast but the drone faster. Wesk would reach the target first and surveil the area, which was deep in the swamps. Col. Marsh had not called in advance of their arrival. Having checked with a Pentagon officer who had worked with the behavioral consultant, he'd been warned that they rarely answered calls.

Wesk reached the isolated, two-story house and circled, high enough so the whirring of the drone's rotors shouldn't be overheard. The structure rose out of the swamp on cinderblock stilts. It was cloaked in cedar siding and had a steep shingled roof and wraparound porch. A large picture window faced front. A two-person swing hung from the porch's ceiling near the main entrance. On the left side of the porch was a generator fed by a cluster of propane tanks.

A flat-bottomed boat was moored midway along the 24-foot dock, which connected up to the porch via a sloping ramp. Wesk's sensors penetrated the water's murkiness enough to determine it was unusually deep for the bayou, close to seven feet. The only other structure was a small boathouse that had seen better days. A weathered sign rose from it on a rickety pole.

Doc LaTour
Potions and Cures for All Ailments
Results Guaranteed

Wesk activated the drone's directional microphone and aimed it at a screened window toward the back of the house. From inside came the snarl of an angry man.

SIX

"Pierre, *mo swaf!* Bring your ratty ass down here and give me the key!"

Pierre Fortier was accustomed to Doc's hollering. He'd grown up in a large Creole family. If you didn't yell for what you wanted, you wouldn't be heard. Insults also came with the territory.

He closed his book, a history of Cajun cuisine. Having graduated high school only weeks ago, he planned on attending a cooking school over in New Orleans early next year, providing he could save enough. Looking after Doc was the easiest of Pierre's three part-time jobs, but as with the others, didn't pay very well. It was touch and go whether he could earn enough for the tuition and living expenses.

Exiting his bedroom, he bolted down the narrow stairs, taking steps two at a time. Reaching the first floor, he sauntered past the wide portal to the main room and through the hallway to the kitchen at the back. The first thing he noticed was the smell emanating from a pot on the propane stove.

"*Poo-yee-yi!* What the hell you cookin' up?"

Bearded and scruffy, Doc LaTour had just turned sixty-nine but looked a couple decades farther on. His manual wheelchair was tucked under the weathered oak table, his gnarled hands slicing carrots and onions. Garbed in dungarees and a loose cotton turtleneck, the material around the neck was tight enough to reveal the outline of another collar underneath. That was his BAM – Behavioral Alteration Modality. Its ring of tiny lights was green, indicating compliance.

"Manny Strumpet's pig got the runs," Doc said. "Once he swallows my medicine, he'll be his old self in no time."

"Or it'll be comin' out both ends," Pierre muttered, knowing it would be a waste of time reminding Doc that Manny's pig had died last fall. Sometimes it was just easier going along with the occasional delusions caused by his growing dementia.

"Give the pot a stir, will ya. It needs to simmer for a while yet."

Pierre stuck the wooden spoon into the foul brown mess and gave an exaggerated pinch of the nostrils. "Hope you don't intend making dinner out of this pot."

"It'll wash up good and clean. Where's the key?"

Pierre frowned. Doc prodded.

"C'mon, it's hot in here. Gettin' parched."

Pierre snapped the key off the chain around his neck and chucked it underhanded across the room. Doc reached out without looking and snatched it from the air. Old or not, he still had the reflexes of a feisty kitten.

Wheeling himself over to the high cabinets, he pushed off with the armrests and struggled to his feet, detaching the cane from the chair's side and using it to steady himself. The rheumatoid arthritis mostly affected his lower legs, making it difficult remaining upright for long periods. Pierre once made the mistake of trying to help him out of the chair. The good deed had been met with a backhanded slap and a string of curses.

The largest cabinet held the contraband and was padlocked. Doc keyed it open and withdrew one of the gallon water bottles. Pierre watched him carefully as he eased back into the wheelchair and unscrewed the cap.

"Just a few sips now," Pierre warned.

"Ya don't need to be tellin' me that shit."

"I know. Just trying to be helpful."

Doc upended the plastic jug, took a quick guzzle, and plopped it back down in his lap. "See, I can be a good boy."

"I know you can."

Movement through the side window caught Doc's eye. "Bastards!" he grimaced. "They're at it again!"

Pierre took a gander. To the west, a drone hovered above the canopy. He was instantly as pissed off as Doc. It was probably that gang of privileged brats from the rich side of town. When not hunting illegally or riding their tricked-out ATVs across private property, they boated into the swamp and sent their fancy spy drones aloft. Doc, known locally for his odd remedies and even odder behavior, was catnip for bored teens.

Pierre reached above the hallway portal and unhooked Doc's old Winchester pump-action. According to one of the many stories he'd heard about Doc's wild younger days, he'd taken the shotgun from a would-be robber after beating the man senseless.

Pierre stormed down the hallway and onto the front porch. The drone's camera spotted him as he was pumping a shell into the chamber and raising the gun. The craft began zigzagging erratically. Pierre's chances of bringing it down were slim, especially with what appeared to be a skilled pilot taking evasive maneuvers. But maybe unleashing a shot would send it hightailing out of here.

Before he could fire, another mechanical sound broke the stillness. Pierre didn't think the teens were stupid enough to venture this close. Moments later he was proved right. A familiar boat whipped around the bend from the east, cruising past a forest of mangroves whose entangled roots rose from the water like a cluster of snakes.

Adelaide LaTour nestled her small craft at the end of the dock beside Pierre's, hopped out and secured the boat to a cleat. Addi was taller than most Cajun women, her long legs accentuated by frayed denim short-shorts. Strands of wild raven hair framed an angular face. A holstered Glock was tight against her hip for discouraging the rare hungry gator or, more likely, the nasty humans who tried poaching them. Aviator sunglasses completed the image of a woman not to be messed with.

"Bonjour, Pierre? What's with the shotgun? Spot the Rougarou?"

Addi gently teased him for what she looked upon as superstitions, but Pierre held true to his Cajun beliefs. It wasn't wrong seeing the world through the lens of science and rationality but there were other forces, other powers. He didn't fall for the more outlandish stuff he'd been taught as a child, like making the sign of the cross with two knives to stop a hurricane or reading the Bible backwards to protect against evil spirits. But the Rougarou, a transformed creature lurking in the swamps that feasted on human flesh, couldn't be so easily dismissed. He'd seen too many strange sights in the bayou.

"Drone," he said, gesturing to the sky only to realize the spy had flown out of view. It was probably hiding nearby behind that depressed stand of cypresses. "Town brats again, probably. Just tryin' to scare 'em off."

"Looks like mission accomplished," she said, casting a generous smile. Addi smiling was like that old cliché of the sun coming out from behind the clouds. How someone as grubby as old Doc had fathered such a magnificently gorgeous daughter remained a mystery.

He helped her unload groceries from the boat, managing to carry two of the heaping cloth bags while she handled the other two along with her laptop. They already had enough provisions for the week. But when Addi did the shopping, she tended to buy like a prepper stockpiling for Judgment Day.

Removing her shades, she entered the kitchen ahead of him. "*Putain de merde!* Shit!"

Pierre raced in after her. Doc had upended the gallon jug above his face and had the spout nestled between his lips. The liquid was gushing out and he was swallowing madly, trying to consume every drop. It was a hopeless task. Water splashed onto his face and ricocheted off, soaking his clothes. He'd already emptied half the bottle. Puddles ringed the wheelchair.

"Papa, stop!" She put down the grocery bags and laptop. "You are not thirsty! You're *not*!"

Doc shot her a glance but ignored her pleas and kept drinking, trying to get it all down, like a thirsty infant unwilling to let go of the teat. His wet turtleneck made the inner collar more visible. The ring of green lights had changed to flashing yellow ones. The BAM emitted a harsh buzzing, a warning that he was exhibiting a behavioral violation.

Pierre reached into his pocket for the collar's remote control. But Addi shook her head and pointed him toward the old cassette player on a shelf. He raced across the room and hit play, blasting the grating guitar licks of Metallica's

"Master of Puppets" through the kitchen. For reasons no one understood, loud thrash-metal music sometimes impelled Doc to halt his self-destructive behavior.

Not today, however. He kept the jug upended. Thankfully, his mouth was too flooded to take in more. The water bubbled from his lips, cascading everywhere. Addi could have lunged across the room and knocked the jug from his grasp. Instead, she whipped a duplicate remote from her handbag.

"Last chance, Papa!" She had to shout to be heard above Metallica's pounding beat.

He kept guzzling. She pressed a button. The BAM's lights turned blinking red. Doc gasped, his head trembling as the collar administered a series of electroshocks. The water jug slipped from his hands and bounced off his knees. It rolled across the floor, liquid tendrils spiraling through the air.

Addi rushed to his side. From her handbag she withdrew a loaded hypodermic syringe and jabbed the needle into his arm. In Pierre's experience, the fast-acting sedative would knock him out for an hour or more.

As Doc's eyes fell shut, Addi bent him forward and pounded on his back to force out any lingering water. She placed her index and middle finger above his turtleneck to check his pulse, counting the beats for a full fifteen seconds while monitoring her watch. Looking relieved, she gently propped him upright then whirled to Pierre.

"What the fuck! You never leave him alone with an open bottle, not even for two seconds!"

Pierre couldn't hide how awful he felt. Returning the shotgun to its place above the door, he prayed he wouldn't get fired even though she had every right to do so. "I'm so sorry, Addi. I wasn't thinking."

"Goddamned right you weren't."

"I won't ever let it happen again."

Seeing his hangdog expression softened her rage. "I'm sure you won't. Always remember, addicts are devious and unpredictable. Just when it seems they're deserving of your trust…"

She trailed off and turned toward the hallway. Pierre followed her gaze. A man was watching them from the kitchen door, his entry into the house camouflaged by Lars Ulrich's pounding drumbeat. His black suit and tie rendered him badly overdressed for a summer day in the bayou.

Pierre killed the music. Addi's anger focused on the new target.

"Who the fuck are you! What are doing in here?"

"Sorry. I knocked and gave a yell but nobody heard."

"Yell louder."

"Point taken. I'm Col. Marsh and I'm here to–"

Addi raised a hand, cutting him off. "I told the Pentagon, I'm on sabbatical. No more of your little jobs for a while. Next time, check in with your masters before storming into our home."

Col. Marsh showed no signs of leaving. Addi's cheeks flamed red. Pierre was relieved he was no longer the target of her wrath.

The colonel took a forceful step into the kitchen. He wasn't intimidated, even when Addi rested her hand on the butt of her holstered pistol. He nodded toward the unconscious Doc.

"Dementia with psychogenic polydipsia. Self-induced water intoxication, consuming it to the point of putting his life at risk for seizures and even death. I read up on it on the way down here. As I understand, your father has one of the most severe cases of the disorder on record. And unfortunately, his condition is worsening."

"Tell me something I don't know," she snapped.

"Happy to. If you agree to take on an assignment, I can make a call and get him into a top-notch facility where he'll be cared for and–"

"Not a chance. This is our home. I take care of him when Pierre's not around. My father's not leaving and neither am I. Whatever problem you've got – some admiral on heroin or a three-star general beating his meat in public – I'm not the answer."

"Option two," Col Marsh said, effortlessly pushing past her refusal. "I arrange for him to have top-of-the-line home care while you're gone. A team of medical and psychiatric nurses onsite, round the clock. Doctors available to make house calls or consults 24/7. Oh, and I can double your regular fee, plus tack on some very nice perks. A fully furnished home. A rental car, your choice of make and model. All that and more if you agree to accept the job."

To Pierre, the offer sounded like a gift from the gods. But Addi, being Addi, looked suspicious. The colonel continued his pitch.

"It seems to me you could use a break from looking after your father."

Her face remained skeptical but her words revealed he'd piqued her interest. "How long a break?"

"The contract calls for a one-month minimum, with the option for extensions. If you re-up, you'll also get a hefty raise."

"I don't work black sites."

"Understood. It's nothing of that nature. The facility is

in West Virginia, right outside a small mountain town. A beautiful area. Residents are salt of the earth."

"And why is the DoD offering to be so munificent this time?"

"Technically, they're not. The facility is jointly underwritten by the military and a private firm with deep pockets. The funding for your services would be handled through the corporate side of the ledger." He glanced at Pierre. "It's a classified project. I'm afraid I can't get into more details at the moment."

Pierre took that as a sign to step outside. Addi was being offered a fantastic deal and he knew she was about to accept. He wondered how he was going to make up the income from losing his gig caring for Doc.

She raised a hand, stopping him before he reached the door.

"If I were to accept – and that's still a big if – Pierre stays on. He works whatever hours he chooses and his current salary gets doubled. Your people provide onsite care the rest of the time."

"That's doable."

"I would need to be able to reach my father."

"We'll set up a sat link directly to your laptop. You can chat face to face, anytime, day or night."

Addi still seemed to be mulling it over. Pierre knew her well enough to realize she was just trying to buy extra time to think up ways to sweeten the deal.

The colonel read her intentions. "Whatever else you want, I'm confident we can make it happen."

"Six months," she said. "You pay for his home care through the rest of the year even if the assignment ends early."

"Done."

Addi looked as surprised as Pierre. The offer was crazy generous.

"When would you need me to start?" she asked.

"Yesterday."

"Give me twenty minutes to pack."

SEVEN

Eddie sat on the end of the cushioned exam table in one of Med Center's third-floor private rooms. Shirt off and stripped to his boxers, he idly thumbed through a recent copy of *National Geographic* while waiting for the doctor and nurse to arrive for his physical. He'd heard a rumor that one of Blayvine's subsidiary companies had approached the magazine for a possible feature on the world's first dino-humans.

Of course, Nat Geo hadn't been provided any actual details, only that they were one of the publications being offered the opportunity to get in on the ground floor of a major story. Even the official name, Project Saurian, remained classified, never mentioned or appearing in correspondence. It was simply referred to as "the project".

In three weeks, that secrecy would be shredded. Eddie still had mixed feelings about the whole public unveiling, not that he and the other dino-humans could do anything about it. But seeing himself on magazine covers, splashed all over the internet, being interviewed by everyone in the media firmament, from slick network stars to subsidized influencers to debased bloggers from the lowest rungs of hell... just thinking about the totality of such exposure induced stress, although of a less alarming nature than that which brought on the bad yen.

He'd discussed the big media day during recent psych sessions with Dr Kim, who advised him on how he might mentally prepare for the fame storm about to sweep over them. He wanted to talk further about the subject but it likely would have to wait. At this afternoon's session, talking about the mission no doubt would be the primary topic.

He'd already given some thought as to how he was going to relate the details of yesterday's rescue. After countless get-togethers over the past several years, he knew how to spin things to show himself in the best light. Dr Kim was smart and well-meaning, with a lifetime of accomplishments in the psychiatric field. But whether because of his age or overreliance on traditional therapy methods, he had some huge blind spots. They had enabled Eddie to put on a false front, hiding some of his most innermost feelings and thoughts.

And because Dr Kim insisted on keeping the sessions confidential, even going so far as air-gapping the digital journal where he stored his notes, no physiological probing by Wesk was likely to reveal Eddie's subterfuge. The compound's godlike AI was a direct link to Blayvine, Col. Marsh and the other overlords. What it knew, they could access. And keeping them in the dark today was particularly important, considering yesterday's incident with the guerrilla.

Manipulation. The project used him for its own ends and the overlords had their own agendas. But manipulation was a two-way street. Being able to hide elements of the real Eddie Boka allowed him to feel a bit in control, more than just a cog in the Blayvine Industries/DoD machine.

He heard the chuff of an approaching copter and recognized the sound. Little Gust, Blayvine's private ride. Moments later he spotted it through the window. The compound's main heliport was atop the six-story Administration building, adjacent to Med Center in the quad.

The bird landed and two people disembarked. Even at this distance, Col. Marsh was easy to identify in his Army jacket adorned with medals and ribbons. His companion, a raven-haired woman in a dark pantsuit, was a stranger. Maybe some political heavyweight from DC being escorted into the compound for a classified junket.

The exam room door opened, diverting his attention. He was surprised to see Dr Steinhauser enter.

"Thought you'd be on that wine-tasting tour by now," he cracked. "Chugging down $500 bottles of imported Cabernet."

"On my salary?" she said with a laugh. "Not likely. Anyway, last-minute change of plans. How's the chest feeling?"

"Fine. Not even a twinge of pain. The docs down at MacDill removed the bullets."

"I know, got their report and the x-rays." Dr Steinhauser checked her iPad and nodded. "Looks good. For the most part, the bullets lodged in the secondary epidermis. A few minor intrusions into the papillary dermis, but nothing of consequence."

"Saurian shielding, guaranteed for life," he joked, pounding a fist against his chest. His natural body armor, a sheet of small gray scales, began at the neck and extended down below his belly nearly to his crotch. The sides of his torso were similarly armored. On his back, a wide vertical strip covered the length of his spinal column.

"Don't get too cocky," she said, tightening a blood pressure cuff on his arm. "Enough gunfire, a head or face shot from the wrong angle or hits to other unshielded areas and you're an extinct subspecies."

"I'd see it coming and duck. I'm a fast mutha, remember?"

She removed the cuff, recorded the reading and pressed the diaphragm of her stethoscope against his chest. It had been specially modified to listen through the thickness of his scales.

"I'm informed that MacDill gave you some precautionary injections after your jungle exposure."

"You docs love your needles," he quipped. "You already gave me a shitload of inoculations before I left."

"Can't be too careful with some of those tropical diseases."

The door opened, admitting a nurse.

"Tanya A!" Eddie exclaimed, happy to see that she was the one on duty today.

"My man Boka! Congrats, by the way. I heard it was a successful mission."

"Start to finish."

Tanya Aguilar was one of his favorite people at the compound. Young, sexy and blessed with a bubbly, down-home personality, she reminded him of a girl he'd known in high school back in Arizona. That girl, Catalina, had been Eddie's first real love. They'd gone on desert hikes in the cooler months and hibernated at the mall when the summer heat became too unbearable. Year-round, they'd had a grand old time having sex in locations as varied as her basement rec room, his aunt and uncle's barn, and the cargo bed of his junkyard Chevy pickup.

One of the most heartbreaking days of his life had been saying goodbye to Catalina when her father accepted a job transfer and moved the family to Georgia. They'd promised to stay in touch and managed it for a time. But as teens, neither of them was ready for a long-distance relationship. Skyping and texts fizzled out after a few months. The breakup was the main reason he'd enlisted in the army upon high school graduation. Something new, something to take his mind off her.

"Tanya, I gotta say, you're looking particularly gorgeous today."

"I am, aren't I?" she said with a giggle. "Bought some new undies yesterday to die for. You'd never know it, though. Right now, they're trapped inside this ridiculous frumpy uniform they make you wear here. This place is *sooo* 20th century." She favored Dr Steinhauser with a mock glare of accusation.

"New undies, huh. Color me intrigued."

"You should be. Speaking of color, the pants are fire-engine red and the crotch is see-through. The matching bra has enough lift to launch a rocket." A full-throated laugh escaped her.

"Are we talking one of those little bottle rockets? Or something more substantial, like a SpaceX Falcon."

"Cape Canaveral, baby, all the way."

"Damn!"

"Ever want a peek, handsome, give me a call." She winked and provocatively jiggled her hips.

They'd flirted from day one, although they both knew nothing could ever come of it. Eddie had almost quit the project during the first week when informed that the genomic infusions and xenotransplantation surgeries would render him permanently unable to achieve an erection or feel erotic pleasure.

As a virile and sexually active twenty-three-year-old, that had felt like a death sentence and an absolute deal-breaker. But the dire circumstances that had caused him to volunteer for the project in the first place were more than enough incentive to go through with the deal. The generous monthly payments that should leave him financially set for life certainly helped with the decision. At least he'd be able to purchase a lot of non-sexual pleasures.

Dr Steinhauser finished running the stethoscope along his chest and back. "We'll do a complete workup at your next appointment. But we're done for today. I agree with the MacDill doctors. You're in fine health."

"Way to go," Tanya said, retrieving pill bottles from the locked pharma cabinet above the sink. She doled out his weekly dose, two white pills and a green capsule, and handed him a cup of water. Eddie downed the hormonal supplements with a single gulp.

His phone chirped. He retrieved it from the pocket of his khakis draped over the adjacent chair. A text from an administrative assistant in Blayvine's office notified him that his afternoon psych session with Dr Kim was being rescheduled and to check back for updates after lunch.

That left the rest of his morning open. He felt invigorated, a combination of the successful mission, Dr Steinhauser's clean bill of health and the bantering with Tanya, which always put him in a good mood. Now with a couple hours to kill, he could get in a full workout.

He'd start with a run, a couple laps around the compound's inner ring, and maybe end up on the obstacle course. They were within the restricted part of the facility. That included Med Center, Administration, Barracks and the lab complex, all of which fronted the spacious quad and its tree-shrouded parking lots. The entire area was shielded from the outer crescent of support buildings by a twelve-foot opaque security wall topped with spiked overhangs, electrified barbed wire and motion sensors.

Hopping off the exam table, he got dressed and fist-bumped Tanya. It was their regular signoff.

"Later, dudes!"

He dashed out the door, relishing the pure joy of his body in motion and, at least temporarily, his mind at ease.

EIGHT

The moment Boka departed the exam room, Wesk reported its findings to Dr Steinhauser and Nurse Aguilar.

"All his sensor data is within the normal range, consistent with previous readings. Some minute changes to skin tone but nothing indicative of authentic sexual excitement. Visual observation confirms no evidence of an erection during the sexual come-on."

"That's good," Dr Steinhauser said, turning to Tanya. "But next time, you might want to tamp it down a bit. The fire-engine-red undies and the hip wiggle were a bit over the top."

"Hey, color me truthful," Nurse Aguilar replied, gleefully wrenching back the top of her uniform to reveal a red bra strap.

"I'm just saying, if you're too obvious like that he could start catching on."

"He won't. I know men."

"Eddie is not a man, in multiple senses of the word."

"He might not have working junk. But trust me, he's still a guy."

Wesk agreed with the nurse's assessment, and that Dr Steinhauser's concerns were unwarranted. Their bantering during medical exams provided Boka with a harmless outlet for any lingering sexual feelings. Those mental constructs of maleness likely performed a necessary role, serving as nebulous substitutes for what he no longer could experience directly.

And Wesk's sensors would have detected physiological evidence had Boka been catching on to Nurse Aguilar's charade. Boka remained totally in the dark, not even connecting the fact that her personality closely matched his high school lover, Catalina. She'd been hired not only for that reason and her medical background, but to flirt with him. The purpose of the flirting was to ascertain whether any hints of sexual ardor were threatening to break through his neutered status.

The overlords, but most especially Blayvine and Col. Marsh, recognized that the success of the project demanded such repression. They could not risk the dino-humans developing active libidos.

NINE

Addi had done more than a dozen psych consultations and interventions for the Department of Defense and had one of the DoD's highest security clearances. But she was already feeling frustrated by Col. Marsh's stubborn refusal to reveal just what this assignment entailed.

On the flight to West Virginia, they'd worked out the final details of her contract and she'd signed the standard non-disclosure agreement. As promised, the contract gave her everything she'd asked for. The colonel loaned her his sat phone and she'd put through a call to Pierre from the luxurious aircraft to check on her father's status. He'd awakened from the sedative and was feeling like his grumpy old self, his uncontrollable thirst mediated for the time being.

Col. Marsh had provided an overview of the compound and its 500-strong mix of scientists, engineers, soldiers, techs and civilian support staff. About a third of them were restricted to the outer crescent of the 7,500-acre facility. She'd been taken straight to Barracks, a bland three-story concrete structure within the fortified and heavily guarded inner ring.

Her rental house in the neighboring town of Axton, home to many of the workers, wouldn't be ready for a few days. In the interim she'd been assigned private quarters here. After settling in, she was to meet with Reginald Blayvine, who would give her a guided tour of the compound after which they'd have lunch.

Barracks' top floor was reserved for military officers, VIPs and guests. Her quarters were compact but comfortable – bedroom, bathroom, workspace. The windows looked out over the high inner wall to the less imposing chain-link fence beyond, which protected the compound's outer crescent. Farther in the distance, the Appalachian hills of summer were covered in dense woodlands, lush with promise. She had to admit, the countryside was beautiful.

Barracks had its own cafeteria, conveniently located on the first floor and open round-the-clock. But should she ever crave more upscale dining, she'd been informed that Blayvine's personal chef would be made available to prepare special meals. Her hosts were extending every courtesy. They just weren't telling her who her patient was and what ailment she was here to treat.

She also remained in the dark about the nature of the R&D that went on at the compound. Col. Marsh said only that it was highly classified and mainly of a biological nature. He promised more would be revealed as she settled in.

"The situation is rather unique, as is the individual you will be treating," he'd said, continuing to dodge any real explanation. "Let's just say for the moment that your patient has a problem, an atypical flaw that requires correction. We feel that rather than prepping you with a traditional patient bio and history, as per your previous assignments, it would be better having the two of you meet face-to-face."

The unorthodox approach raised a volley of questions as well as triggering a concern. Addi hoped the affliction she was here to tame, the so-called "atypical flaw", wasn't anything like the one suffered by her last DoD patient. He'd been a decorated Naval officer accused of having sex with an eleven-year-old girl. Initially denying the charges, he'd then tearfully revealed to her a dark history of abusing children going back years.

She always tried to be sympathetic and understanding of whatever psychological ailments her patients suffered, no matter how challenging. In that officer's case, damning evidence of his abuse had come to light, forcing the Pentagon to give up trying to salvage his career and issuing a dishonorable discharge. She'd been secretly relieved when the therapy was cut short, even experiencing a bout of schadenfreude upon learning that the man faced civilian criminal charges from the abuse that predated his military service.

Guilt had arisen from experiencing that feeling, of deriving pleasure from the officer's misfortune. Yet some cases transcended mere illness, rising to the level of human sin. There were people in this world whose behavior was so revolting that they weren't deserving of compassion and forgiveness.

But when it came to guilt, nothing could touch the level of culpability Addi often felt when dwelling too long about what she doing to her father. Making him wear the BAM, watching him tremble in pain as she administered electroshocks, was never anything less than heartrending. She rationalized its necessity by reminding herself of the alternative. His dementia was progressive, and his psychogenic polydipsia, if left unchecked, could lead to coma and sudden death.

And on those occasions when his thoughts weren't so muddled by the disease, the collar had proved its worth, reacting to an excessive water intake with a warning buzz. On many occasions, that yellow caution mode had provided the feedback he'd needed to fight the urge. Problem was, the BAM wasn't one hundred percent effective. That prompted nights when she lay awake in bed feeling like the worst daughter in the world, sometimes to the point of tears.

She checked her watch. 12:10. She was due to meet Blayvine in Administration in twenty minutes. For the copter ride up here, she'd donned a creased pantsuit, trying to look her professional best. But considering that the tour would be from an open Jeep and that the better part of the compound was hilly and forested, the light pullover and jeans she'd changed into made more sense. Besides, unless it was a special occasion, she hated dressing up.

She exited her room and headed along a short passage to the junction with the main corridor. As she turned the corner, a man running at breakneck speed plowed into her. Addi flew backward, landing hard on her butt. Steaming mad, she was ready to bolt to her feet and rip the reckless asshole a new one.

"Watch where the hell you're–"

Astonishment severed the thought as she got a look at his face. A Cajun curse burst from her lips.

"*Get sa liki mama la!*"

"I get that a lot," the manlike thing said, extending a hand to help her up. "Not those exact words, mind you, but the sentiment. You know. What rock did you crawl out from under, that sort of thing."

Addi took his hand, which was normal and fleshy, unlike other parts of him. The strength in his grip matched the well-muscled physique.

"Really sorry," he said. "I'm not supposed to run in here but I was still pumped from a workout. No excuse, I know. You're not hurt, are you?"

"I'm fine… I think."

He wore loose camo pants and a black-and-yellow Pittsburgh Steelers football jersey with sweaty underarms. But she hardly noticed, her attention riveted to what was above the neck.

The central part of his face, encompassing eyes, nose and mouth, was indicative of a white male in his twenties. But beyond that perimeter, the ruddy skin morphed into reptilian scales in muted shades of russet, gray and tan. The scaly patches extended downward from his chin and neck, disappearing into his collar. Another cluster began above his eyebrows and covered most of his head, with only a thin layer of reddish hair covering the crown. His facial cheeks were scaly as well, and the earlobes more flattened and circular than typical.

He smiled as she studied him. The expression served to lessen his more unnerving aspects, accentuating his humanness. He couldn't be called handsome, at least not by any normal standards used to define the word. Yet his appearance gave off a kind of otherworldly symmetry, like something beautiful and exotic from an unexplored wildland.

"I'm Eddie Boka." He extended his arm again, this time offering to shake. "Call me Eddie."

"Adelaide LaTour. Addi."

She shook his hand but quickly released it. He seemed amused by her wariness.

"If you think I'm a big freaky dude, wait till you meet Samson."

"Samson?"

He declined to elaborate. "I saw you arrive with the colonel. Are you joining us full-time or just here for a visit?"

Before Addi could answer she heard someone approaching behind her. She spun around, half-expecting another reptile person. But the young man in the blue windbreaker looked normal. Dark-skinned and rail-thin, he had a boyish face that made it hard to peg his age. A tablet computer protruded from the man bag slung over his shoulder. Overlapping meows emanated from the cat carrier clutched in his hand.

"Hey Eddie," the man said in greeting. "Who's your friend?"

"Addi LaTour, meet Billy Orb. Billy is one of our most brilliant scientists."

"Don't know about the brilliant part but I'll take the compliment."

"What's your specialty?" she asked, figuring the newcomer was fair game for eliciting information that Col. Marsh as yet refused to provide.

"I have a number of postgrad degrees. My most recent doctoral thesis was related to targeted bioelectric signaling through advanced manipulation of ion-channel membrane voltages."

She understood just enough of that to realize his expertise involved the electrome, the electrical currents flowing through all living entities. A relatively new and hot field of research, it was believed as important to an organism's development as the similarly sounding genome.

"Addi, by any chance do you like cats?" Billy asked.

"Uh, sure."

He set the container down and reached in to extract what she assumed would be two or more felines.

"Meet Troika," he said, grinning ear to ear as he held the single cat up to her face.

Addi took an involuntary step backward in surprise. The tricolored calico had hues of white, black and orange. It also had three heads, each with its own thick neck. The middle head stared at her while the end ones swiveled to the sides and meowed.

"Just taking him out for some fresh air," Billy said, clearly getting a kick out of her startled reaction. "He's usually cooped up in the lab all day, aren't you, pal." Stroking the heads one after another elicited purrs.

"Was he... born that way?"

"No. An experimental scrum meant to expand neural connectivity was administered when he was a few months old. It caused some novel changes in the electrome, which led to this unforeseen mutation."

"He was only supposed to grow two heads," Eddie explained, looking deadly serious.

"I see," she said, not really seeing at all.

The two of them chuckled.

"Eddie's putting you on," Billy said. "Troika wasn't supposed to grow any extra body parts. He was supposed to get an IQ boost. If you look at it a certain way, I suppose you could say the serum worked."

"Three heads being smarter than one?"

Billy grinned and snapped his fingers, causing Troika's six eyes to dart toward the sound. "I think the lady gets us," he said, stroking the animal's back, which induced a pleasingly harmonic triple purr.

Addi was beginning to think she'd been dropped into the middle of a bizarre freak show. "So, any other genome-electrome experiments happening around here?"

"Lots. Next time I'll introduce you to Auditory Alice, our pet goat. She's got six ears, the standard pair plus two on each shoulder."

"Another serum gone wrong?"

"Actually, no. A deliberate experiment into the effects of sensory augmentation. Same with our orangutan, Visionary Vic. He's got twice as many eyes as there are in Mississippi."

Before Addi could ask why goats and orangutans needed extra sensory organs, Col. Marsh emerged from a fire door at the far end of the corridor. He strode toward them at a brisk pace.

"Uh-oh, here comes trouble," Billy whispered. "The colonel doesn't like our pets outside the labs. Gotta go."

Shoving Troika back into the carrier, he headed quickly in the opposite direction. Col. Marsh reached Addi and Eddie, wearing a smile she sensed was forced.

"I'm so sorry, Dr LaTour. I didn't envision the possibility of you getting knocked down by way of introductions."

"How did you know I was–"

"Welcome to Surveillance Central," Eddie said, pointing upward to a small bulge at the crease of wall and ceiling. A green LED indicated the microcam was active. "They're everywhere in the compound, thousands of them. The overlords like to keep a sharp eye on the rank and file."

"A necessary evil in a secure facility," Col. Marsh said. "The cameras can only monitor public areas of the compound."

"Good to know," Addi said, wondering what further surprises were in store.

"Now that the two of you have met, I can confirm that your first session has just been scheduled. You'll meet at 1600 hours."

"Session?" they inquired in tandem.

"What kind of doctor are you?" Eddie asked.

"I'm a psychiatrist. And you're... my patient?"

Addi was starting to understand the colonel's reticence in explaining why she'd been brought here.

TEN

Addi gripped the dashboard above the glove compartment, trying to steady herself as the driver made another wicked sharp turn on the gravel road. She'd read somewhere that Reginald Blayvine had a collection of sports cars, everything from Corvettes and Porsches all the way up to a Bugatti costing more than $10 million. All well and good for the super-rich to have their hobbies, but he wasn't behind the wheel of one of those well-handling vehicles at the moment. The open Jeep the two of them rode in was decidedly vintage, and from the way she bounced around in the passenger seat it was in dire need of new shocks.

"I hope you're beginning to understand the critical importance of what we're trying to accomplish here at the compound," Blayvine said. He made a hard right-hander, sending up a spray of pebbles as the Jeep bounded up a steep lane flanked by forests. "Project Saurian is just the beginning, meant to show proof of concept. The successful introduction of the prototypes – Boka in particular – is vital in order for us to take the next step."

"I'm getting that," Addi said. "But you have to understand, I can't guarantee whatever outcome you're seeking. Especially not in such a short amount of time, and with a patient so far outside the norm."

"The impediments are acknowledged." He slowed the Jeep just enough to make another hair-raising turn, this time onto an even more primitive lane, dirt rather than crushed stone. The lane continued the steep climb through the trees.

They remained within the inner ring. From the helicopter, she hadn't realized just how much of the compound was wilderness. Col. Marsh had explained that the woodsy areas served dual purposes, further shielding the secure area from prying eyes while providing rugged training grounds for the troops stationed here, human and otherwise.

"I have faith in your abilities, Addi. May I call you Addi?"

"Go for it."

"I know you'll do your absolute best."

Before embarking on the vehicular portion of the tour, Blayvine had walked her through the various departments and specialties housed in the main structures. She was particularly impressed with the library in the Admin building. It had the usual computers for online access but featured a vast number of physical books, many of them rare, rivaling what could be found in a major big-city collection. A plaque at the entrance credited its construction to Blayvine's third ex-wife, a voracious reader. He'd still been married to her five years ago when the compound was being built.

But when their tour reached the lab complex, Addi's security clearance provided admittance only as far as the central lobby. On display were holographic and video exhibits of the numerous advancements made possible by Blayvine Industries. Everything from pandemic-busting pharmaceuticals to labor-saving robotics was showcased. Her host's personal achievements were featured throughout, often in a reverent manner reserved for the saintly or the severely narcissistic.

Three equidistant spokes extended off the lobby, their portals secured with biometric locks, including retinal and palm scanners. No guards were visible but those microcams were everywhere, indicating the high level of security. The three entrances had nameplates with two-letter initials, providing no information of what lay beyond them.

"IG?" she wondered. "AC?"

"Interdisciplinary Genomics. Advanced Communications."

"And the third one, RV? I'm assuming it's not a lab that experiments with recreational vehicles."

"Restricted Variants. And yes, the nomenclature is intentionally vague. Very hush-hush work behind those doors. They don't even let me in some of those labs and I pay for most of their toys."

She'd smiled, not believing it for a moment.

Upon boarding the Jeep for the motorized portion of the tour, Blayvine finally provided some useful information about why the dino-human prototypes were so important.

"Across the globe, the status of warfare is in the process of a vast transformation. Battlefield AI, drones, autonomous weaponry, hypersonic missiles – the list goes on. Here in this compound, and at facilities all over this nation funded by similar corporate-military partnerships, or privately by various angel investors, the quest to develop new generations of advancements is underway."

Addi had heard similar pitches emanating from screens in the lobby of the lab complex.

"The United States and its allies – our very way of life – is besieged not only from ascendant and belligerent nations, but from a new multi-polar global order whose tentacles of influence we are only beginning to comprehend. But one aspect of warfare hasn't fundamentally changed in thousands of years – the common soldier. They remain the weak link. Despite incredible advances in protective gear, medicine and wound care, they remain tragically easy to kill in the theater of battle.

"Our project is an attempt to change that part of the equation. To create a breed of soldiers better able to endure the rigors of combat. A breed of soldiers that will augment and perhaps someday replace regular humans, their enhancements enabling greater offensive strengths and superior survival capabilities. Such an army will suffer reduced battlefield losses, thus sparing families from the all-too-frequent return of their loved ones in body bags."

His pitch sounded well-rehearsed. Addi got the picture. The public rollout of the dino-human prototypes in three weeks would hit on just those key points, no doubt delivered in an even more patriotic version of Blayvine's current spiel. Of course, it wouldn't be advertised that whoever was in on the ground floor of such genome-altering technology would make billions – trillions, perhaps – when sold on the world armaments market, which inevitably would happen. Technology was like water streaming from a garden hose. Wherever it landed it soaked in and spread.

"The prototypes not only must prove successful," he continued, "but acceptable to a majority of the American public. Only then can we proceed to the next phase, recruiting a battalion's worth of volunteers to undergo the enhancements. Beyond that, the sky's the limit."

"You really expect to find a thousand or more volunteers willing to be transformed like that? Frankly, their physical features are going to strike a lot of folks as monstrous. How on earth did you get Boka to consent to it?"

"Various inducements and means of persuasion were used

to convince the four prototypes to join the project. As for gaining future volunteers, plans are already underway for an expansive recruitment campaign. Our surveys reveal that with the right incentives, *hundreds* of thousands will get in line for the opportunity." He smiled. "Addi, we are a nation enthralled with superheroes, especially by individuals with substandard opportunities in the workplace. Despite the formidable challenges and sacrifices, we anticipate countless young men and women vying for the chance to be transformed into beings with great physical strength and elevated stamina."

"A noble plan," she offered when he finished.

He detected her skepticism. "We're also in a race against time. Five other countries that we're aware of also have active programs based on genomic infusions and xenotransplantation surgeries, and most of them are under the control of authoritarian leaders. I make no apologies for being a patriot, Addi. Nor for being a capitalist. And on that note, I would point out it wasn't a matter of pure virtue that convinced you to accept this assignment."

"Touché."

Still, Blayvine was no run-of-the-mill capitalist. Blayvine Industries was infamous for spending an inordinate amount of time in court, fending off lawsuits or launching countersuits against the numerous competitors who accused it of shady business dealings and other unscrupulous activities. The corporation always claimed innocence and, following a path paved by certain contemporary politicians, launched vicious social media attacks against the plaintiffs.

They reached their destination. Blayvine pulled into a small clearing at an overlook. Removing two collapsible chairs from the back of the Jeep, he motioned for her to carry the small cooler.

"We're eating up here?"

"I find that good mountain air can do wonders for digestion."

He set up the chairs at the edge, which was protected by a low stone wall. Below was a steep cliff of craggy rock outcroppings, which appeared to have once been a limestone quarry. It was a clear day with low humidity, and the overlook provided an impressive view. To the east, beyond the forests they'd ascended through, lay the bulk of the compound. Past the outer crescent lay a chain of verdant hills. Beyond the farthest one, the white spire of a church steeple was visible.

"The town of Axton," Blayvine said. "I'll have someone give you a tour there tomorrow. You can stop at your new home while the workmen remain onsite. Feel free to issue any change orders if something doesn't meet with your approval. Oh, and your rental vehicle should be ready to be picked up as well."

She'd selected a Jeep, a hybrid SUV. She presumed it would have better shocks than her host's ride.

Blayvine admired the view. "Unveil the beyond with eyes wide open," he whispered.

She'd seen the catchphrase on display in the lobby of the research complex and on wall signs in the Admin building. "Sounds like a good philosophy."

"It's much more than that, Addi. It's the essential first step in becoming a true visionary."

That he categorized himself as such was obvious. Billionaires, especially self-made ones, weren't known for modesty.

Blayvine opened the cooler, which was packed with sandwiches and cold drinks. "Ham, tuna, egg salad, pb and jelly," he said. "Water, lemonade, iced tea."

Addi would have expected a more exotic and upscale lunch befitting his wealth. But then she realized that the food and the stunning view might be his attempt to come across as a regular guy, a man who enjoyed casual picnics and bouncing around in old Jeeps. Or maybe those were authentic qualities. She didn't know him well enough to perceive how much of his presentation was authentic and how much a carefully constructed front.

"Boka and the other volunteers, how did you manage to enhance them with what I suspect must be some kind of saurian DNA?" She grabbed a ham sandwich and a carton of lemonade.

"Dino DNA."

"Despite what's shown in those dinosaur movies, I thought it wasn't possible to restore truly ancient genomes."

"You're partially correct, at least based on current biotechnology. There's no evidence yet that the de-extinction of creatures tens or hundreds of millions of years old is feasible. However, our scientists and genetic engineers have devised some sophisticated workarounds. They've replicated extinct saurian features by starting with the DNA of related living successors, such as crocodiles and tuatara lizards, even ostriches and chickens."

"So, more accurate to say they have characteristics from reptilian and other mammals rather than being from actual dinosaurs."

"From a certain perspective, you're correct. But dinosaurs are mythic and popular. They represent a powerful aspect of the past that has proved relentlessly intriguing since paleontologists first dug up their bones." Blayvine smiled. "Our marketing surveys showed that such terminology is strongly preferable."

"Understood. I'm surprised you gained government authorization for this level of human experimentation,"

"Regulatory oversight of genomic-electrome editing at both federal and state levels remains somewhat in a state of flux. Experimental tech always outpaces the lawmakers and we were able to take advantage of some legal loopholes. Still, there were and are many challenges and hurdles. Fortunately, the Pentagon saw the project's potential and went to bat for us."

"I'm not here to judge the ethics of what you're doing," Addi said. "But aren't you concerned the public won't take to your engineered soldiers, no matter what you call them or what arguments you make on their behalf? Powerful subconscious aversions to the reptilian could be triggered. Your dino-humans might not be greeted with open arms."

"Certainly there's a risk involved. But most great advancements have come from taking chances, making gambles. Besides, you've met Eddie. Wouldn't you say he comes across with a certain degree of openness and charm?"

"No argument. He presents himself well and seems to have a good sense of humor. Those characteristics should work in your favor."

"We believe so as well. His congenial attitude will go a long way toward overcoming those sorts of initial reactions you point out. Eddie is a natural bridge builder. That's why of the four prototypes, he was chosen to be the project's leading public face."

"But only if he can overcome his atypical flaw," Addi countered. "You know, the mysterious problem that you and Col. Marsh are so frantic to fix that you've pretty much offered me the sun, the moon and the stars to come up here."

Blayvine selected a tuna sandwich from the cooler, studying her intently as he unwrapped it. "You're right. At this point, we're close to desperate. In light of Boka's importance to the project and our three-week deadline, you must understand our deep concern."

"I'm trying to."

He withdrew a silver flask from inside his jacket and drew a long sip. She wondered if it might be an alcoholic drink but quickly dismissed the notion. Her take on world-builders was that they didn't allow their sensory awareness and information processing skills to be dulled, at least not during working hours.

He put away the flask and wiped a sandy residue from his lips with the back of his sleeve. Whatever the drink was, it had particulate matter suspended in the liquid. Before she could quiz him about it, he continued.

"Col. Marsh would prefer that you extract the details of Boka's problem during therapy. Ideally during your initial session. But I was never convinced that was the right course. It seems like a waste of precious time. Better for you to approach Eddie with the knowledge of exactly what you're dealing with.

"During Eddie's first combat mission, his inherent advantages were displayed to the fullest. He showed uncommon bravery in battling a large force of enemy guerrillas, slaying many of them. Unfortunately, there was an issue involving the last soldier Eddie killed. He was feasted upon."

Addi was about to take her first bite but froze with the sandwich inches from her mouth. "Feasted upon?"

"Eddie bit through the guerrilla's neck and chewed deeply enough to expose spinal vertebrae. Then he went to work on the meatier flesh of the upper arm, which I've been told has a higher caloric value. He ate quite a large chunk of that, more than one typically would consume in a single meal. His savagery obviously was not prompted by normal hunger but by some powerful unconscious compulsion. Privately, we're referring to this affliction, his loss of control, as the bloodburn."

"Descriptive," she said, lowering her sandwich.

"Quite. So Addi, here's your task in a nutshell. We don't care whether Boka is actually cured of the bloodburn or whether it's simply repressed. What he did to that guerrilla can never happen again. You're free to use any means at your disposal to bring about a successful outcome. Only results matter."

Addi had imagined a host of psychological ailments she'd been recruited to treat. Cannibalism had not made the list.

"It's my understanding that your quickest and most enduring successes have resulted from extreme forms of aversion therapy. Operant conditioning by means of programmable shock devices that you design, adapting elements from the original canine versions but adding unique modifications."

She stared out over the retreating progression of hills, their lush canopies in full summer bloom. The closest hill was a deep green, the farthest a pale grayish blue. The perspective of distance created the disparate hues.

"You want me to get him into a collar."

"You're the expert, of course. But yes. And with all due haste."

"You don't just lock one around a patient's neck. It has to happen voluntarily." That had even been true for her father, who had firmly resisted wearing the BAM. She'd ultimately convinced him by laying on a guilt trip, telling him his only daughter would be deeply hurt if he refused to comply.

"The patient has to grant their cooperation," she continued. "They have to agree that their egregious behavior merits such an extreme method of cure."

"I'm confident you'll be persuasive."

Addi hesitated. It certainly was a unique challenge, and the psychiatrist in her felt compelled to take it on. Still, she needed Blayvine to understand she wasn't a miracle worker. Not all of her previous cases had resulted in successful outcomes.

"No two patients are alike, and every collar is different. Some are caregiver-friendly, with colored LEDs and alarms to warn both the patient and their guardians when behavior is approaching shock activation. Some collars are automated, others remote-controlled. Sometimes, a combination of those modes is preferable. In every case, the device must be carefully matched not only to the patient's physiological makeup but to the symptomatic particulars of their compulsion. And then, based on the nature of the urges and the extent of control desired, it must be customized and programmed."

"Fascinating," Blayvine said, biting into his sandwich. "Let's eat."

ELEVEN

Eddie paced back and forth through the rooms of his Barracks quarters. The turbulence under his skin had returned, those countless subcutaneous needles jabbing at him from the inside. It hadn't reached a compulsive and overwhelming level. But as the four o'clock hour and his first session with the new shrink approached, it also wasn't getting any better.

He'd tried contacting Dr Kim half a dozen times throughout the afternoon, leaving increasingly urgent texts, emails and voice messages. The lack of a response elevated his stress. He desperately wanted to talk, maybe even have a quick session about how upset he was over the upcoming encounter with Dr LaTour. Unable to get through, he'd been forced to settle for silently repeating some of the psychiatrist's mantras.

We can't control everything, Eddie. But we can control the clean stream of consciousness that flows within. Concentrate on the immediate task before you. Control inappropriate thoughts. Exercise your willpower.

But willpower hadn't done the trick yesterday in the jungle, and it wasn't working now. Eddie knew exactly what was inciting the tension and anxiety. It was the feeling of not knowing what was going on, of being confronted by questions without answers.

Why had Col. Marsh and Blayvine brought in a substitute therapist? Was it a coincidence that Dr LaTour had appeared at the compound less than twenty-four hours after the incident in the rainforest? Had the powers-that-be learned of Eddie's loss of control? Was his entire future in jeopardy?

It might have helped had he been able to dig up background on Dr LaTour. Even that wasn't possible. In the interest of maintaining the project's secrecy, all but the most generic Internet searches within the compound's inner ring were banned. The overlords and other higher-ups had unfettered access, but for everyone else, com limiters and targeted signal jamming resulted in the appearance of the all-too-familiar "Restricted Access" icon. And except for the rescue mission, Eddie hadn't been allowed to venture past the inner ring walls in nearly three years.

He'd learn soon enough if his secret had been exposed. But before the session, he needed to try lowering his anxiety. He'd already achieved his daily exercise quota with the morning run. And having just taken a shower, he wanted to avoid further outdoor activities that would leave him hot and sweaty. But there was an alternative: the hideaway.

It was in Barrack's sub-level basement, adjacent to the boiler room. The unused space was intended to accommodate future expansion needs. But Eddie and the other dino-humans had co-opted it, creating an off-the-grid room where they could gather in private.

The powers-that-be had learned of its existence in short order. But with Dr Kim and Dr Steinhauser lobbying on their behalf, they'd been allowed to keep the hideaway, even furnish it with dumpster castoffs and other junk items. Best of all, Wesk's omnipresent camera eyes had never been installed there. It remained surveillance-free.

Exiting his third-floor quarters, he headed down the emergency staircase. He wasn't in the mood to encounter other soldiers or civilians at the main elevator bank.

"Hiya, Eddie!"

The booming voice echoed through the concrete stairwell. Samuel Samson, all six-foot-six, three hundred and fifty pounds of him, burst through a fire door, as bubbly as a cheerleader rooting for the home team. His human ancestry was African American but the saurian genome he'd been fused with had left him with a pair of arched crests rising from his forehead to the peak of his skull. He was shirtless beneath his denim bib overalls, revealing extensive scaling between the suspenders and on his shoulders and upper arms.

"How goes it, Big Guy," Eddie offered.

"Good-good-good!" Samson fell in step with him. "Where are you going, Eddie?"

"Hideaway."

"Me too!"

Seeking solitude, Eddie had hoped the others would all be on assignments. Still, having Samson around wasn't so bad and might even distract him from his anxieties. Besides, there was no real choice at this point. Samson was special. He wore his emotions on his sleeve and was easily hurt if rejected.

"Will you play Candyland with me?"

"Not today, Samson. I'm just going down for a quick workout on the bike."

"OK, I guess I can play with myself."

"That's not really an option for the four of us, is it?"

The grim humor went over Samson's head. His perpetual smile dissolved into an uneasy frown, which often happened when a conversation exceeded his mental limitations. Eddie quickly set him at ease.

"I was just kidding, Big Guy. Playing with yourself sounds like lots of fun."

His smile returned. "Wanna know how I do it? I use two game pieces, the red and the blue. But I'm really only the blue, 'cause I pretend the red is somebody else. It's always the best when I beat myself."

"Uh-huh."

They passed through the basement fire door and entered a long corridor with bundled overhead piping. The hideaway was just up ahead. Samson bounded forward, his waddling gait suggesting he might lose his balance or trip over his own feet at any moment. He'd taken such spills on a few occasions.

Eddie froze in the doorway. Another dino-human was already in the hideaway.

Gideon Cheng sat at the rickety game table. He was playing chess with Billy Orb, one of the few unmodified humans the four of them allowed down here. Troika, the three-headed cat, snoozed contentedly in Billy's lap.

Gideon had a similar facial layout to Eddie's, with a central countenance of human features morphing into scales. The main physical distinctions between them were the obvious Asian ancestry and the three symmetrically spaced nodules on his forehead. They were vestiges of horns, courtesy of his unique saurian infusions. One nodule was positioned above the bridge of the nose. The others were higher, over the eyebrows.

Tying together his disparate facial features was a pair of tortoiseshell eyeglasses, their tinted lenses ameliorating Gideon's colorblindness. He could have elected laser surgery for a permanent fix but preferred the glasses. It was a fashion choice. He spent much of his monthly pay buying stylish clothing online.

"Hiya, Gideon! Hiya, Billy!" Samson's voice boomed even louder, echoing across the room's high ceiling.

"Big Guy, how are they hanging!" Billy's tone matched Samson's enthusiasm if not his volume.

"Can you play checkers with me?"

"Maybe in a little while," Billy said.

Gideon moved one of his knights, threatening his opponent's king. "Check."

Billy frowned, studying the board. "OK, maybe sooner than a little while."

"Checkmate in seven moves," Gideon announced.

"You could have let me figure that out for myself."

"Waste of time." Gideon turned away from the board and cracked open a book. Eddie glimpsed the title. *Riches and Ruins: The Heritage of American Coal Mining*. History was one of his eclectic interests, which he preferred absorbing through physical pages rather than eBooks or documentaries.

Eddie mounted the stationary bike in the corner and set it to a low cadence. He hadn't made more than a few pedal rotations when Billy scowled and tipped over his king, admitting defeat. Gideon ambled over to the fridge and a triumphant Samson snatched his seat. He and Billy swapped out the chess pieces for checkers.

The door opened, admitting the fourth dino-human. Eddie grimaced. Bad enough that his desire for some alone time had already been thwarted. But Julio Castaneda was just about the last person he wanted to see today. Or for that matter, any day.

He acknowledged Eddie with a sneer. "Well, well. Our illustrious brethren returns. How was it out there in the big wide world, Boka? Did you suck up to all those human pricks so they'd let you play soldier?" He glanced at Billy. "No offense."

"None taken."

In Billy's lap, Troika's center head yawned. An instant later, the flanking heads sequentially performed the same action.

Eddie readjusted the bike's RPM setting, increasing pedal resistance. He considered exiting the hideaway yet couldn't bear letting Julio see that those caustic remarks were having an impact. He'd stick it out

Julio unfolded the trampoline and set it up in the corner farthest from Eddie. Stripping to workout shorts revealed an armored chest similar to the rest of them. He had a flatter belly and more sculptured musculature.

He hopped onto the trampoline and began a series of bounces, clapping his hands above his head as he bounced higher and higher. The hideaway had been constructed to the same specs as the boiler room, resulting in the elevated ceiling. Even so, Julio came within inches of touching it.

The clapping annoyed Eddie. He wanted to tell Julio to knock it off, that the rest of them were here to enjoy a little peace and quiet. But expressing such thoughts would be a colossal mistake and lead to strife. He kept his mouth shut.

Julio began a routine of midair flips, clapping even more furiously while spinning. Samson forgot about playing checkers with Billy and watched the acrobatics with wild-eyed enthusiasm.

"I wanna do that!" he shouted. "Show me how, Julio! Show me!"

Julio turned his last flip into a dismount. He landed effortlessly on his feet next to the game table.

"You really want to give it a try?"

"Uh-huh, I do, I really do!"

"Let's just play checkers," Billy urged.

"No-no-no, I want to trampoline!"

"OK, let's go," Julio said.

Samson practically bounded out of his chair. This time, Eddie couldn't help but interfere.

"Samson, that's maybe not a good idea. It's a lot harder than it looks."

"What's the matter, Boka?" Julio said. "Don't like seeing others get their fair shots?"

Eddie clamped his mouth shut, watched in silence as Julio helped Samson onto the trampoline. The big dino-human wobbled back and forth, looking even more ungainly than usual.

"Whoa, this is weird! It's like you're standing on the floor but the floor is doing funny things to your feet."

"Small bounces," Julio instructed. "Don't try going too high. Just take it easy."

Samson followed the instructions, propelling himself a few feet off the rubber. Childish glee filled his face.

"This is fun! Look, Eddie, can you see?"

"Uh-huh, I can see. Just pay attention to what you're doing, OK?"

"OK."

"Try springing higher," Julio said. "But only a little. Remember how you learned to run the obstacle course? A step at a time."

"But I'm not stepping, I'm bouncing!"

"Same principle."

Samson put more spring into it, rising two feet between bounces, then three.

"Good-good-good!" he yelled.

"That's high enough," Eddie warned.

"No, I can go higher. Watch."

He achieved four-foot elevations, then five. Imitating Julio, he raised his hands over his head and smacked his huge palms together, increasing the number of claps each time he was airborne. The bounces were taking him closer to the ceiling. Gideon, withdrawing an apple from the basket atop the fridge, looked concerned.

"Slow down, Samson," Gideon warned.

"Stop pushing off," Julio added. "Let yourself come to an easy stop."

"Not yet! I wanna touch the ceiling!"

Flexing his knees, he pushed off the mat with tremendous force. Eddie knew in a sickening instant it was too much. Samson's arms compressed as his palms smacked the ceiling, throwing him off balance. Flailing the air, he came down at a lopsided angle. When he hit the trampoline, he flew off it sideways, heading straight for the game table.

Billy had just enough time to lunge from his chair. Troika's heads snapped awake, feline instincts enabling the cat to scamper away as well. Samson crashed onto the table, splintering its legs and sending checkers flying in all directions.

Eddie jumped off the bike and ran to his aid. "Can you stand up?"

Samson looked dazed. Eddie gripped him under the arm. Julio did the same on the other side. Together they got him to his feet. His face contorted in pain and he cupped his hands under his crotch.

"I hurt my bob-wobs!" he moaned.

"Are you all right otherwise?" Eddie asked. "Nothing broken?"

"My bob-wobs hurt!"

"Yeah, I get that."

"I'll show you," Samson said, starting to undo his suspenders to lower his overalls.

"No, no," Eddie said. "It's better you go straight over to Med Center. Dr Steinhauser can check out your balls."

"Will she make them stop hurting?"

"Absolutely."

"I'll take him," Billy said, retrieving Troika from the corner where it had bolted. Sliding the cat into the carrier, he motioned to the door. Samson followed him out. He walked gingerly, still clutching his testicles.

Eddie waited until the door closed to glare at Julio. "The trampoline was a dumb idea. You know he's always trying to imitate us, show us he can do anything we can do."

"So? He tried something and it didn't work out. You've got your nose jammed so far up brass asses you can't smell straight. Get over yourself, Boka."

"You're a selfish jerk."

Julio assumed a menacing crouch. Eddie aimed a warning finger at him.

"Don't even think about it."

"If I do, motherfucker, you're going down for the count."

They closed on one another until a mere foot separated their faces. The bad yen intensified. Eddie imagined leaping upon him with mouth wide open, canines ripping through the skin to reach the meatier flesh below.

An apple core whizzed through the narrow gap between their heads, thudded against the far wall. Startled, they whipped their gazes toward the slinger. Gideon leaned casually against the fridge.

"Enough," Gideon said calmly, not even looking at them anymore. After lobbing the projectile, his attention had returned to the book balanced in his other hand.

The intervention worked. The moment of conflict passed. "Another time," Julio hissed.

Eddie pivoted and walked out. Coming down here had been a mistake. It had left him more tense and agitated than ever.

TWELVE

Eddie had worked up a fresh sweat anyway, probably as much from his seething anger toward Julio as from pedaling the bike. Returning to his quarters, he was tempted to continue his exertions, don the boxing gloves and land some hits on the punching bag hanging in his bedroom closet. He used to beat on the bag late at night when he couldn't sleep but had been forced to confine himself to daylight workouts after residents in adjacent rooms complained about the noise.

It was 3:46, fourteen minutes from his mandated session with Dr LaTour. There wasn't time to throw any punches. If he took another shower – a quick one – and dashed across the quad to her new office in Admin, he should just about make it by four. He only hoped the session didn't make things worse for him, escalate the stress and push him past the tipping point.

Control the clean stream of consciousness that flows within, he imagined Dr Kim saying. He added his own phrase to the advice. *And especially important, don't take a bite out of your therapist's neck.* He stripped and hopped in the shower. In the early days following his transformation, the medical staff had advised that his altered metabolism would best be served by lukewarm water temperatures. But he'd quickly determined their theory was wrong. Steaming hot showers were more pleasant. The overlords and their lackeys controlled enough aspects of his life. He wasn't about to let them nitpick about how goddamn hot his showers were supposed to be.

Drying off, he returned to the bedroom and donned a collared shirt, gray slacks and a hunter-green blazer. He was just about to leave for the session when his phone buzzed. He hoped the text was from Dr LaTour, informing him that something had come up and they'd have to cancel the session.

No such luck. It was from Cwacian.

Eddie had no idea who Cwacian was, only that the mysterious person occasionally sent him cryptic texts. It had been going on for more than six months, ever since he'd completed his final round of transformational infusions and surgeries. The messages came in the form of couplets – two-line poems. He recalled the first one he'd received.

A sunless sunset, smothering the damned;
Eclipsing the truth of the buried man.

Subsequent poems all seemed to touch upon a similar theme, that there existed an expansive world out there of which Eddie remained unaware and which he was denied access to. Considering that the walls of the compound pretty much comprised the boundaries of his existence, the couplets weren't telling him anything he didn't already know. Yet he sensed they pointed toward some deeper truth. Why Cwacian didn't just come out and say what they meant was another aspect of the puzzle.

He opened the new message. This time, a chill went through him.

The night casts shadows, a devilish bane;
Haunting reminders of a guerrilla slain.

Beneath the phrase was the familiar closing lines, repeated in every text.

Care for u,
Cwacian

The message reinforced his worst suspicions. The overlords knew about what had happened yesterday at the end of the mission.

He stared at the screen, waiting for what inevitably came next. Twenty seconds after opening the text it disappeared, from the screen as well as from the phone's memory. Eddie didn't grasp the workings of high-tech comm devices well enough to understand how that happened. But all of Cwacian's texts self-destructed in the same manner, suggesting the sender possessed formidable digital skills.

Although he didn't know how the messages disappeared, the why seemed obvious. The poems were meant for his eyes only. Cwacian didn't want to be traced. Several times he'd tried transmitting a return text within that twenty-second interval. As far as he could tell, those never went through.

He'd once casually mentioned the name to Dr Kim, claiming he'd heard a soldier utter it in passing. Dr Kim exhibited no noticeable reaction, suggesting that Cwacian was unknown to him. The only online reference Eddie could find indicated that "cwacian" was an archaic, Old English word meaning to quake or tremble.

As for the messages disappearing, he'd considered buying another phone and taking screenshots of the texts so he'd at least have proof of their existence. But any electronics he ordered had to be cleared by Col. Marsh, then modified by the techs for restricted access within the compound. Plus, he'd have to explain and justify why he needed a second phone. The whole idea was too much of a hassle.

He'd puzzled as well over the closing line, "Care for u". At first, he thought it was Cwacian implying, "I care for you". But thinking about it further, he realized it also could be in the form of an instruction, that Cwacian was saying he should care for himself: "Care for *you*".

But the bigger mysteries were who was Cwacian, and why they were communicating with him in the first place.

He checked his watch, realized further speculation about the mysterious messages would have to wait. It was 3:58. He prided himself on being punctual for appointments, yet here he was, about to be late for his first meeting with his new shrink. If he ran the whole way he might get there only a couple minutes late. But that could make him sweaty again and defeat the purpose of the shower.

Screw it. He'd take his time and walk at a regular pace. Cwacian's revelation had left him even more upset, and freshly pissed off about having to deal with a new shrink. If she had a problem with him being late, that was just too goddamn bad.

THIRTEEN

A first session with a patient always triggered nervous excitement. In this case, Addi's emotions were stronger than usual. She ascribed it to the highly unorthodox circumstances and the atypical nature of the patient, not because she feared being attacked and devoured. That was Col. Marsh and Blayvine's concern, however.

Even though they admitted it unlikely Eddie would go all cannibal on her, they insisted on precautions. She'd made it clear she would tolerate no interference or eavesdropping. To ensure the development of trust between therapist and patient, confidentiality had to be maintained.

A compromise had been reached, an emergency buzzer tucked into her slacks. The press of a button would summon armed MPs stationed in an unused office just down the hall. She remained confident in her people skills. The buzzer wasn't needed. She'd repeated that to herself several times throughout the afternoon.

Another unusual issue had to do with the legal standards of the psychiatric profession. She was obligated to report specific types of dangerous behavior, such as a patient threatening others or taking part in ongoing mistreatment. Col. Marsh and Blayvine had consulted military and civilian lawyers and learned, not surprisingly, that eating another human being – technically, abuse of a corpse – met the criteria.

But the lawyers believed enough gray areas existed to provide her with legal cover should Boka's cannibalism ever become public and she would have to testify in court. She could argue that the project's classified nature exempted her from traditional personal and professional liabilities.

Whether a judge and jury would agree was debatable.

She'd also warned the two overlords not to attempt any trickery, such as planting hidden surveillance devices. If they did, contract or no contract, she would pack her bags and hightail it back to the bayou faster than they could say bon voyage. But agreeing to provide them with summarized updates on how Eddie's sessions were progressing seemed reasonable.

The therapeutic space they'd assigned her was an austere office on the fifth floor of the Admin building. She'd tried to make it more inviting. Maintenance workers had brought in twin sofas and a pair of leather chairs, arranging the four seats in a square facing the center of the room. From a nearby office she'd snatched a pleated curtain to cover the window, which featured an uninspiring view of a parking lot. A set of pilfered floor lamps replaced the intense overhead lighting.

She was as ready as she was going to be. All she needed now was her patient. Another glance at her watch revealed he was seven minutes late. Not an auspicious start.

A knock on the door. She decided not to mention his tardiness, but would issue a gentle reminder in the email confirming tomorrow's session. It was important that a patient understood the necessity of punctuality. They were to meet at least once a day over the next three weeks, with either of them having the option of requesting extra sessions.

She opened the door with an inviting smile.

"Hi, Eddie."

"Dr LaTour."

"C'mon in and make yourself comfortable. I'm guessing you have lots of questions."

"A few."

She waited for him to continue. He remained silent and eased his bulk into one of the chairs. She sat on the opposite one.

"First off, I'm guessing you're curious as to why I've been brought in to temporarily replace Dr Kim."

He responded with a cold stare that served to accentuate his saurian features. For an instant, she had the uncomfortable sensation of being face-to-face with something more alien than human.

The outlandishness of the whole situation suddenly hit home. She was being asked to treat a genuine mutant, an engineered creation who looked like he just stepped from an *X-Men* franchise. With most patients, getting to the heart of their problems was a process of gaining familiarity and achieving a degree of trust. That was the route she'd intended pursuing with Eddie, keeping things light between them, not even bringing up the cannibalism until the latter part of the session.

But that outlandishness, coupled with his open hostility, keyed an on-the-spot reevaluation. Addi decided to dump the original plan and follow her instincts.

"There was high-altitude reconnaissance over that jungle. It's known what happened, how you ravaged that soldier."

His expression didn't change. She wasn't surprised. It made sense that he knew or at least guessed the incident had been discovered.

"I've read some background information on you," she continued. "I know what you did wasn't a conscious choice. Your sense of morality under normal conditions wouldn't allow such a thing. That means we're dealing with a compulsion. I've been brought here because I specialize in addressing the more severe and often treatment-resistant manifestations of such urges."

Still no response. She pressed on. "I'm not here to judge what you did, Eddie. I will say that like most people, I found your actions repugnant. I'm sure that at some level, you did as well. But at the end of the day, none of that matters. My sole purpose is helping you to make sure it never happens again.

"We won't be doing much in the way of traditional psychoanalysis, talking about your problems. Frankly, with severe compulsions, that's mostly a waste of time. It's not that I'm uninterested in the reasons underlying your behavior, why it happened. But the priority is controlling these urges. My primary mode of treatment is aversion therapy. I can tell you upfront, it won't be pleasant. In fact, it may strike you as just as barbarous as what you did to that guerrilla."

He still didn't respond but she could tell he was locked onto her words. "Any thoughts so far?" she prodded.

"Just one. Who else is in this room with us?" He arched his head toward the ceiling. "Wesk, if you're up there watching and listening, how about giving a holler."

"No surveillance, Eddie. I insisted. Col. Marsh and Blayvine promised."

He barked a laugh. "And you believed them?"

"It's in their self-interest to follow my lead."

"Then by all means, Dr LaTour, lead on."

Addi had to break through the sarcastic derision. She got up and removed a brown paper bag from the desk behind her. With an underhanded toss, she sent it flying toward him, but deliberately badly aimed her throw so he'd have to half-leap from his seat to catch it. Forcing a patient into motion sometimes could wrench them from their comfort zone.

He moved fast, jerking out of the chair and snatching the bag with ease. Settling back into the cushions, he cracked a smile. "I suppose now I'm expected to ask, 'Gee, Dr LaTour, what's inside the bag?'"

"Is that what you want to ask?"

"Sure, I'll play along. What's inside the bag?"

"Pain."

He stared at her as he peeled back the flaps and reached in. The black leather collar was sealed in a clear Ziploc bag. It was notably different than the one she'd designed for her father, lacking LED lights which were more appropriate for a caretaker scenario. It also had a large bulge in the back to house twin battery packs that could administer a more sizable wallop.

His smile vanished. Holding the bag by a corner as if it was filled with dog excrement, he extended it toward her.

"Really? A shock collar?"

"Behavioral Alteration Modality. BAM for short." She'd once considered trademarking the name and selling the collars online, but her lawyer warned she'd likely run into expensive legal roadblocks. The American Psychiatric Association was just one of many organizations, as well as a number of individual practitioners, critical of her methods. Should she attempt such marketing, they likely would attack her with multiple lawsuits.

"Let me make sure I've got this straight," Eddie said.

"You're planning to control my undesirable behavior the same way you'd train up a dog."

"Essentially, yes."

"Blayvine and Col. Marsh must be out of their minds."

The notion had occurred to Addi. But it wasn't relevant to the issue at hand.

"Compulsions largely arise from areas of the brain not under the direct control of the prefrontal cortex. They're beneath the level of consciousness. That's why the most extreme ones tend not to respond to talk therapy."

"Then give me a pill."

"Any drug potent enough to stop a compulsion this severe would almost certainly have debilitating side effects. Your senses would be dulled. Or you'd end up feeling groggy all the time."

"Then you'll have to figure something else out. Cause I'm sure as hell not wearing this goddamn thing."

"You may have no choice."

"Really? And what if tell you that I do have a choice? In fact, what if I choose to throw you and your little toy right through the fucking window? We're five floors up. I'll bet you'd hit the ground with one seriously loud bam!"

Addi wasn't surprised by the threat. He wasn't the first patient to exhibit a strong emotional reaction when confronted with the idea of wearing one of her collars. Military men especially, with their macho attitudes, often had the most trouble relinquishing control. Sexism also played a part, an inherent male stubbornness heightened by having to submit to a woman.

She leaned back in the chair and crossed her legs, projecting composure. "I think you know that doing such a thing would be unwise."

"Maybe. But it sure as hell would feel good."

"Short-term gratification perhaps. But let me spell out the sequence of events that would follow. Ignoring potential assault charges from doing bodily harm to your therapist, your future would unfurl something like this:

"The coming-out presentation to the public in three weeks continues as planned. But Eddie Boka is persona non grata and no longer involved. Julio Castaneda, your backup – I'm given to understand he's your main rival – is offered the opportunity in your place. He's promoted to top dog, king of the dino-humans. He gets to smile for the cameras, chat with the reporters, enjoy the fruits of victory.

"Shortly thereafter he's mainstreamed, given a place to live outside the compound and a degree of freedom unknown to the four of you since volunteering for Project Saurian. Later, he's sent on a national tour, signing autographs for all the little and not-so-little kids who've been convinced, courtesy of Blayvine and the Pentagon's multi-million dollar promotional campaign, that saurian superheroes are the absolute best and worthy of admiration."

His glare intensified. She pressed on.

"Further down the line, following a long and rewarding career, Julio writes his memoirs. National-security concerns require some redactions, but the book still becomes an international bestseller. And who knows? If Julio plays his cards right, maybe he even gets a cameo in the movie version they make of his life.

"Now, you may or may not care about being replaced by Julio. But you're smart enough to care about doing something that will jeopardize your own future with the project."

Some of Addi's speculations could logically come to pass. Others were pure bullshit. Julio indeed was the backup, but Blayvine and Col. Marsh apparently had doubts about his readiness because of his temper. Eddie wouldn't necessarily know that, however.

He was silent for a moment. Then he unzipped the bag, removed the collar and examined it.

"You've made your point, Dr LaTour. So I guess I'll have to consider wearing it. But first, I think a demonstration is in order. I think you should put it on. I'm assuming it comes with some sort of remote control?"

"It does."

"Perfect. Then by giving you shocks and watching you twitch, I can gauge for myself whether I'm willing to try it. That seems fair, right?"

It also wasn't the first time a defiant patient had issued such a challenge. "I think you know that's not going to happen, Eddie."

"Really? What if I make it happen?"

He came at her, faster than anticipated, reaching her chair in three bounding steps. Before she could even think about going for the emergency buzzer, he grabbed her by the shoulders and yanked her to her feet.

"Ready to put it on?"

The request was accompanied by a taunting smile. His face was inches away and she felt his hot breath wafting across her. It smelled of mint, either toothpaste or mouthwash. And there was something else about his closeness, something so barely perceptible that she couldn't ascertain whether it emanated from him or originated within her.

"Not going to happen, Eddie." She glared back, refusing to be bullied. But that didn't mean throwing caution to the wind. She slipped her fingers toward the pocketed buzzer. He noticed.

"What have you got in there?"

Her thumb caressed the button. He was fast but not fast enough to stop her from pressing it.

"Nothing at all," she lied, withdrawing her hand and holding the palm up to his face. "See, no threat... other than what you're creating here."

Addi was certain she was making the right decision by not summoning help. Or maybe she was seventy-five percent sure. Eliminating the option left her with two possibilities for fending him off: her powers of persuasion or her physical abilities.

"Why don't you let me go and return to your seat." She spoke quietly but firmly, making it clear she wouldn't be intimidated.

He released his grip on one shoulder and used that free hand to dangle the collar in front of her. He tried unclasping it but couldn't figure out how.

"Electronic lock," she explained. "You need the remote."

"Where's that?"

"Hidden."

He squeezed her shoulder with his other hand, hard enough to elicit a gasp.

"I'm not fooling around. Where's the goddamn remote?"

"Up your goddamn ass!" The venom in her words wasn't an act. Enough was enough. He'd pushed her too far. "Stop behaving like a petulant child and sit your ass down! We've got work to do!"

His anger surged. This close, the power of that physique was undeniable. Part of her warned she was gambling with her life.

A requirement of her military psych work had been taking an army self-defense course. And as a young girl, Papa had taught her some tricks he'd learned growing up poor on New Orleans' most dangerous streets. Yet face-to-face with a super-soldier like Boka dissolved any illusions of taking him down. He was stronger than most humans, and with his training could kill her in any number of ways.

But whether his rage had run its course or her defiance was causing him to reconsider, he let go of her shoulder. Retreating slowly, he walked backwards, keeping his eyes fixed on her the whole way. By the time he returned to his chair he seemed placid again.

Addi drew a deep breath to calm herself and retrieved the collar's remote from the desk drawer. It was the size of a large key fob and featured a tiny keyboard.

"Your BAM isn't like the simple versions for canines," she said. "In fact, it's the latest and most advanced model. Built into it are sensors capable of monitoring a range of vital signs. Once we establish certain parameters, we'll be able to customize the collar. It will then react automatically to changes in those vital signs that are indicative of the onset of your compulsion."

"Translation, it will shock me."

"The degree of shock necessary for successful inhibition is also something we'll need to determine."

"And I'm supposed to wear this thing all the time?"

"When you're awake. It'll be removable at nights to make sleeping easier. The remote operates on the cellular network. All you have to do is call or text me and I'll unlock it."

"How very thoughtful."

"We'll fine-tune the BAM from data gathered during our sessions over the upcoming weeks."

She tapped buttons on the fob. In Eddie's hand, the collar snapped open.

"Will you try it on?"

"Let's say I do everything you ask, follow the rules and all that. Exactly how long am I expected to wear this?"

"At minimum, for the next three weeks, through Project Saurian's public unveiling."

"And the maximum?"

"Hard to say."

His wry expression made it obvious he knew she was dodging the question. "So worst case, indefinitely."

"Indefinitely is a pretty long time. Oh, one more thing. The BAM has safeguards against any attempts at removal, such as trying to slice it off with a knife. Sewn into the leather is a mesh of sensor strands conducting a tiny current. Severing even one of those strands will interrupt that current."

"And I'll get shocked," he concluded.

"At full intensity. But there's no need for that to happen. I'm sure we'll be able to work together and ensure a successful outcome."

Eddie donned the collar, staring at her the entire time. Addi couldn't tell what he was thinking. Maybe he was finally coming to terms with the situation, accepting that he had no choice but to accede to her demands. Or maybe he was imagining what her meaty flesh would taste like.

"Manipulation is most effective when the exploiter lacks a conscience."

– Wesk: Algorithmic Speculations

FOURTEEN

Wesk reported to Blayvine and Col. Marsh the instant Boka and Dr LaTour emerged from the therapy room. The two men had stationed themselves in an unused office at the far end of the hall, waiting for the session to end. Wesk noted their vitals were elevated. Analysis of the sensor data suggested the cause was anxiety over how the first session had gone.

"She got Boka to don the collar," Wesk explained. To hide its presence, she also persuaded him to wear a lambswool turtleneck sweater with generous dimensions. It's a rib-knit version, a medium shade of oak brown. Dr LaTour pre-ordered it from Hecklinger's Department Store in Axton.

"She also ordered a large wicker picnic basket at the same time. The total cost, including a special charge for immediate delivery to the compound, came to $169.95. She charged the purchase to the debit account you provided for her to cover meals and petty-cash expenditures."

Wesk did not comprehend why she needed the basket. The compound was not an environment conducive to picnics.

As expected, Blayvine and Col. Marsh's grimaces signaled that such extraneous details were of no interest. However, Wesk sometimes found it prudent to provide an overabundance of information. Humans generally found an expulsion of details subliminally reassuring. It resulted in a calming effect, thus reducing their anxieties. Such decisions were not only permitted but encouraged within Wesk's operational parameters.

"The sweater hides the collar, although I can detect its outline when Boka moves by microanalysis of subtle distortions in the fabric. But the BAM should remain indistinguishable to most individuals under normal viewing conditions."

"Yes, yes, very good," Col. Marsh said, the annoyance in his tone likely due to Wesk focusing on such trivialities. "Where are they headed?"

"They've split up. Boka is approaching the main staircase, presumably intending to exit the building. Dr LaTour appears to be coming your way."

"Thank you, Wesk," Blayvine said. "Dr LaTour may be providing us with a summary of the session. I'll need you to honor her request for maintaining maximum patient confidentiality."

"Understood. Disengaging local surveillance now."

FIFTEEN

Eddie got back to Barracks in short order and locked the door to his quarters upon entering, which he rarely bothered doing in the day. He chalked it up to elevated paranoia, an aftereffect of the psych session. It had left him feeling off-balance, exposed. He didn't like experiencing such weakness and hoped it soon would pass.

The session did have one positive impact. For reasons defying understanding, the turbulent encounter with his new psych somehow had served to lessen his stress and anxiety. By the end of the hour-plus spent in her company, the bad yen had retreated to a mere background presence. He wasn't sure why but suspected it had something to do with her manner, and possibly also her scent. Dr Adelaide LaTour gave off a pheromonal signature he'd never encountered, a mix of chemical excretions that seemed to stimulate some long-dormant region of his psyche.

He stripped off the new sweater and threw it over the back of the living room sofa. He wore turtlenecks on occasion and the garment wasn't inappropriate for today's unseasonably cool weather. But wearing one all the time in the summer to hide the collar was bound to prompt curiosity and questions. He could already imagine Julio taunting him about it.

"If you don't want to hide it, tell them it's a style choice," Addi suggested when he'd broached the subject. "Tell them you want to make the best possible impression when the project goes public."

It was a workable excuse, he admitted, as turtlenecks would also hide more of his scaliness. Addi ventured that the shirts ultimately might contribute to his public acceptance in another way. If people perceived him as being mildly embarrassed by the extent of his saurian features, it could engender their empathy and increase support for the project, which was the overlords' ultimate goal.

He'd gone into the session with a chip on his shoulder and come out with a changed attitude toward her. She was smart and engaging, not to mention balls-out fearless in the face of his threats. He wouldn't have harmed her but figured she couldn't have known that, not with absolute certainty. He also realized that as the session had proceeded, he'd stopped thinking and referring to her as Dr LaTour and switched over to using Addi.

He supposed that was a natural development, considering they were in a doctor-patient relationship. Yet in the time Eddie had been seeing Dr Kim, he'd never once thought to call him by his first name, Ji-Won. It would have seemed... improper.

Was he developing feelings for Addi, feelings beyond the bounds of a doctor-patient relationship? He wasn't sure. But something within him had been stirred.

He reached into his pocket and withdrew the remote. He'd been surprised when Addi gave it to him and explained the key codes, not only for locking and unlocking the collar, but how to experiment with the shock levels.

"Your call, Eddie, if you want to play around with it this evening and gain some familiarity," she'd said. "You'll start wearing it on a regular basis beginning with tomorrow's session."

He would have thought she'd have convinced him to do that immediately. But upon further consideration, he grasped her intentions. She wanted him to have input into the therapy and a sense of control... even if much of that control was illusory. Once the collar received its final programming, he'd likely be under its authority.

So be it. He'd been at the mercy of Project Saurian since the day he'd volunteered. Along the way, there had been challenges aplenty. This was simply the latest one.

He sat in the recliner facing his sixty-inch TV and scanned the channels. He stopped on an air disaster series on the Smithsonian network and muted the volume. Crashing planes seemed a fitting background for self-inflicted pain.

There were three shock levels. Level 1, the weakest, had the shortest duration. Level 2 was stronger and lasted a few seconds longer, while the most potent one, Level 3, administered a shock that endured for a full five seconds.

Eddie set it to Level 1 and pressed the activate button. The brief tingling around his neck was notable but not particularly painful. He tried setting 2 and bolted upright in the chair. The shock was significantly more potent, enough to make him hesitant to try Level 3. But curiosity overcame his concerns. He changed the remote to the last setting and pressed the button.

"Fuck!"

He leaped out the chair. The jolt was far worse and seemed to last forever. The shock levels must operate on some sort of geometric progression, like that scale for measuring earthquake magnitude, where each change represented a ten-fold increase.

He had no intention of ever again experiencing a Level 3. Not in this lifetime. Addi had warned that an illicit attempt to remove the collar would cause the most severe shock. He now understood on a gut level just how potent that prohibition was.

He deactivated the lock and removed the collar. It was suppertime and he was hungrier than usual. Sometimes he went down to the Barracks cafeteria and ate among the soldiers, lab workers and various civilian guests staying at the compound. He wondered if Addi would be there but concluded it was unlikely. She was probably in some four-star restaurant with Blayvine and the overlords.

He popped two frozen dinners in the microwave and scooped the hot mass onto a plate. Settling into the chair, he cranked up the volume on the TV's surround-sound system and chowed down to the sensory barrage of an air disaster.

SIXTEEN

Eddie awakened the next morning to a text from Dr Steinhauser, asking him to report to her office ASAP. He nuked a quick breakfast of frozen sausages and pancakes and donned casual attire. His session with Addi wasn't until 1:00 so there was no reason to wear the collar and turtleneck to cloak its presence.

He jogged across the compound to Med Center and proceeded to her third-floor office. He received his second surprise of the morning. Dr Steinhauser was seated behind her desk but she wasn't alone. Dr Kim and Dr Quelphius were perched on opposite ends of the sofa. Quelph was leaning awkwardly against the armrest, writing something in one of the notebooks he always carried. Dr Kim's face projected his usual earnest concern.

"Thanks for coming so fast," Dr Steinhauser said, gesturing to the plush armchair that had been angled to face the three of them.

"Sounded important," he said.

"It is. Nothing critical though, nothing for you to be alarmed about. It was partly a matter of scheduling. The three of us were available to meet at this hour."

Eddie wondered if there was any meaning to the fact Blayvine and Col. Marsh weren't present. He'd had a number of meetings with the five overlords together. But he couldn't recall ever sitting down exclusively with the three doctors.

"By the way," she added, "it's just us. Wesk doesn't monitor this office. You can speak freely."

"OK."

"Here's what's going on, Eddie," Dr Kim began, "We know what happened during the mission. We've known prior to Dr LaTour's arrival yesterday."

He'd figured as much.

"We want you to know we're not here to judge you, so set your mind at ease on that front. This is intended as an amiable discussion, nothing more."

"But first things first," Dr Steinhauser said. "Blood samples from those guerrillas were extracted from your clothing at MacDill and the results sent here for analysis. You'll be thankful to know that no blood-borne diseases or other serious anomalies were detected. However, I've recommended several additional inoculations to be on the safe side, just in case something was overlooked. We'll take care of that as soon as we finish."

"Fine," he said, still wondering why he was here. Dr Steinhauser didn't require a committee to tell him he needed another bunch of shots.

She turned things back over to Dr Kim, who got to the point.

"Eddie, we know you've had an initial session with Dr LaTour. We just want to make sure you understand a few things about her before you allow yourself to become too deeply enmeshed in her therapeutic regimen."

"OK."

"For starters, her methods are wildly outside the accepted

norms of contemporary psychiatric treatment. She is, to put it bluntly, a practitioner of radical techniques long ago rejected by the established psych community for being ignorant and inhumane. And, even more regretfully, for failing to offer substantive cures."

Dr Steinhauser jumped in. "Dr Quelphius and I fully share Dr Kim's concerns in this matter."

Quelph, hearing his name mentioned, looked up from his notebook. "Yes... of course we do."

Dr Kim offered a reassuring smile. "Eddie, you and I have spent these past few years building a relationship that I believe will pay long-term dividends, a relationship that is helping provide you with the tools necessary for establishing your place in the world. The three of us would hate to see all that work flushed down the drain."

"Why would that happen?" he asked.

"Has Dr LaTour brought up the idea of wearing one of her shock collars?"

"We talked about it."

"Be very careful, Eddie. These BAMs of hers incorporate unseen dangers. And I'm not just talking about frequent electrical jolts to a part of your body in close proximity to the spinal column and neural pathways. Shocking an individual in order to control them is a primitive, and quite honestly, repugnant form of behavioral conditioning. Honestly, there are better treatments, even for conditions as extreme as what we're calling the bloodburn."

It was the first time Eddie had heard the term. He had to admit, the label was descriptive.

Dr Kim leaned forward and folded his hands in his lap. It was a posture he adopted when trying to maximize a point.

"I'd be lying if I said that electroshock on occasion can't achieve short-term results. However, it's fundamentally little different from beating someone with a stick to persuade the victim to obey the stick-wielder's dictates. For true and lasting growth, such methods have been found to be deeply deficient."

Eddie sensed that Dr Kim's concerns were genuine. Yet he also wondered if underlying them wasn't an old-fashioned turf battle, the idea that his methods were superior to Addi's because they were *his*. And it made sense that he would be resentful she'd been brought in as his replacement.

"What Dr Kim is saying has a lot of merit, Eddie," Dr Steinhauser said. "It remains entirely your decision how you want to proceed. We just want to make you aware of what you might be getting yourself into. Isn't that so, Dr Quelphius?"

Once again, the research director stopped scribbling and looked up. "Yes... I agree wholeheartedly. Best to be cognizant of what you might be getting yourself into."

Quelph must have been coaxed to the meeting because Kim and Steinhauser felt that three-of-a-kind carried more weight than a measly pair of doctoral degrees. The truth was, the researcher had never warmed to the dino-humans. Then again, as far as Eddie knew, he'd never warmed to anyone.

Quelph increasingly spent his days sequestered in the ultra-secret RV lab, doing god-only-knows what sorts of experiments. Even Billy Orb, no slouch in the brilliance department, didn't know what went on in there. Billy did claim that Quelph was the only pure genius he'd ever encountered, a man whose breakthroughs in genome and electrome engineering had made the entire project feasible.

Eddie supposed that a certain disinterest in the affairs of lesser minds – from Quelph's perspective, pretty much all of humanity – was inherent in such next-level thinkers. Still, that didn't mean the man was immune to normal emotions. Once at a meeting, Eddie had heard one of Blayvine's assistants joke that Quelph, who was unmarried and childless, might want to think of himself as the father of the four dino-humans.

The remark had touched a nerve. Quelph had blown up, reaming out the hapless assistant for such an idiotic remark, saying that even the dullest student knew enough about heredity to know he couldn't possibly have been the dino-humans' father. Blayvine had been forced to transfer the assistant to another facility to smooth things out.

"Any questions, Eddie?" Dr Steinhauser asked. "Or comments?"

"No, I think we're good. I'll certainly give serious thought to your concerns."

They seemed satisfied. Anything other than such a noncommittal answer likely would have made them wonder.

Dr Kim rose first. Typical of their partings, he came forward and vigorously shook Eddie's hand.

"Remember, we're behind you a hundred percent. We've got your back. Unfortunately, for the time being I've been prohibited from having any formal sessions with you. I'm not even supposed to be talking to you at all about these subjects."

"I won't tell," Eddie promised.

"But if you need to get something off your chest with Dr Kim," Dr Steinhauser added, "give me a holler. We'll make it happen on the sly."

"Yes, indeed," Dr Quelphius said. "On the sly." He was smiling now. But Eddie suspected it was because the meeting was over and he could return to more important tasks.

The others left and Eddie accompanied Dr Steinhauser to get the shots. He wondered if there had been more to that impromptu meeting than the doctors had expressed, some hidden agenda he wasn't grasping. Whether there was or not, he had to be cautious. He didn't want to be caught in the middle of a power struggle among the overlords, the doctors on one side, Col. Marsh and Blayvine on the other.

Tanya Aguilar was waiting for them in the exam room. She beamed as she saw Eddie and held up a large hypodermic syringe.

"Boka, baby! Wanna know why it's my lucky day?"

He had too much on his mind for their usual bantering but pushed out a smile.

"C'mon," she urged, "Guess."

"You get to stab somebody with one of your needles?"

"Not just anybody," she purred. "A hunk of dino-man with a butt to die for."

"Can't wait," he said, pulling down his pants and bending over the exam table.

SEVENTEEN

The obstacle course was tucked into a rugged forested area on the western side of the compound, more than a mile from Addi's quarters. She could have requested a soldier to chauffeur her out there in one of their rugged UTVs. But the weather was nice, in the seventies with low humidity, and she didn't mind walking. The picnic basket she'd ordered from the department store was bulkier than she would have preferred but performed its function, carrying the special items for today's session.

She'd just left Barracks when the whir of an approaching helicopter snared her attention. It had a different sound than Blayvine's "Little Gust" and the rest of the birds that regularly flew in and out of the compound. She paused to watch the big army-green Chinook touch down on the Admin heliport. Col. Marsh had mentioned that important visitors would arrive today for a tour, including high-ranking military brass and senators from the Armed Services Committee.

Addi reached the obstacle course just before 1:00. She was pleased to find Eddie, per her texted instructions, ready and waiting. He stood before the first obstacle, an inverted climbing wall. His lace-up boots were nuzzled into the muddy earth, his hands planted confidently on his hips. The top button of his khaki shirt was open, allowing the BAM to peek out.

"A picnic?" he wondered. "I thought we were here to work."

"You'll be doing the work," she said, setting the basket down on a makeshift bench of logs. "I'll be monitoring. But we might need something to eat later."

The basket contained water bottles and packets of cheese crackers. It also held items that she hoped would prove more disturbing to her patient.

"Did you bring the remote?"

He dug the controller from his pocket and pitched it toward her, but far enough to the side that she had to lunge to catch it. His smile cued her that his poor aim was deliberate, a bit of payback for the same trickery she'd displayed at their initial session yesterday.

"I arranged for us to have the course to ourselves. No one will bother us."

Eddie gestured skyward. "Including a certain nosy AI?"

"Wesk too."

At least she'd been promised as much. The obstacle course wound through the woods but part of it was exposed from overhead. Although drones supposedly were prohibited within the compound's air space except for special training maneuvers and emergencies, she wouldn't have put it past Blayvine and the colonel to circumvent the rule, maybe send up one of those bug-sized microdrones that were virtually undetectable. Barring that, they could order high-altitude surveillance. Despite their assurances to play by her rules, she could tell they remained desperately eager to keep abreast of Eddie's therapeutic progress.

She accessed the remote's memory. "I see that you did some experimenting last evening. Made it up to level 3. That's a pretty good shock."

"Nothing I couldn't handle."

"Good. Then we'll use it as our starting point."

His eyes narrowed. "What exactly are we doing out here?"

"First, we're going to get baseline readings of you in various states of exertion running the course. Then we'll introduce some elements to emulate what your physiology was like when the bloodburn hijacked your mind's executive functions."

"What sort of elements?"

"Let's call it a surprise."

At yesterday's session, Eddie told her about the factors he thought had brought on the bloodburn. Besides the intensity of the battle with the guerrillas, he admitted the bad yen was often heightened when he found himself in novel situations, where he didn't understand what was going on. She intended exploiting that, keep him in the dark about her real intentions to amplify his stress level.

"Let's get started," she said. "You don't have to try breaking any course records. Just take on the obstacles fast enough to work up a decent sweat."

"Got it."

He leaped onto the climbing wall halfway up its horizontal planks, which leaned backward at a precarious angle. Grasping the knobby protrusions above and using the lower ones as footholds, he ascended. When the handholds ran out, he lunged for the uppermost plank. Grabbing hold and twisting his body around to face outward, he performed a spectacular flip up and over the top.

He ran down the other side of the wall and sprinted toward obstacle two, a belly crawl under tight netting. Addi followed on the accompanying path, watched him negotiate the third hurdle with ease, hanging upside down from a rope strung between trees on opposite steam banks. But she couldn't keep pace with him on the next part of the course, a four-hundred-meter sprint, mostly uphill on a winding path.

The nine-obstacle course was roughly circular and would end with Eddie navigating the final challenge a mere shout away from the inverted wall. If she lost sight of him and he finished ahead of her, it would foul up her plan. Turning around, she jogged back toward the first obstacle.

The BAM didn't have GPS. But it could read his pulse, heart rate and other vitals. That enabled her to track his progress on her phone app by comparing his level of exertion to statistics recorded during his previous trials on the course, obtained from Col. Marsh. By the time she arrived back at the climbing wall, the data indicated he was navigating the seventh obstacle, a series of tunnels made of tires chained together.

She picked up the picnic basket and trekked over to the final obstacle, a series of upright logs planted at intervals along a linear pond. A soldier's balancing skills and distance-gauging agility would be tested as they leaped from log to log.

Last night, she and Col. Marsh had taken part in a three-way teleconference with the lieutenant who'd led Eddie's fateful mission. The L.T. wasn't authorized to discuss the op's details, but he did relate something Eddie had neglected to mention. During the copter ride to their target, a commando named Nastor had ruthlessly taunted Eddie. Such goading was common among soldiers and not unusual in and of itself. Addi found it pertinent that Eddie had endured the provocation, keeping his cool and staying focused.

But from another perspective, by not reacting to his tormentor he'd likely exacerbated the bad yen, which ultimately drove him that much closer to the cannibalistic attack on the guerrilla. Repressing one's emotions was a surefire way to escalate internal pressure and increase the potential for an explosion. She was going to use that fact today to amplify his stress by applying her own form of taunting.

Opening the picnic basket, she removed a metal cage packed with two small white rabbits. The colonel had arranged for his assistant, Sgt. Petersen, to procure the rabbits from the lab complex. They were among the hundreds of animals from dozens of species kept there. And not all of them were of such modest size.

This morning, she'd seen a large truck with vented side panels pulling into the RV loading dock. The trailer's segregated decks were crammed, the top level with whitetail deer, the bottom level with fattened hogs. She'd overheard a bit of conversation from two passing soldiers. One said he'd been tasked with bringing in another truckload of large animals next week from a Pennsylvania farm.

She couldn't help but wonder what sorts of experiments required such sizable specimens. Whatever the case, it was fortunate that what went on in the compound was top-secret. If not, animal rights protesters likely would be camped at the gates.

She leaned out over the linear pond so as not to get her boots wet and placed the two rabbits atop adjacent logs. The animals, puzzled by their tiny unfamiliar perches, swiveled back and forth, sniffing the air. Raised in captivity, they were unlikely to be swimmers; they wouldn't be inclined to jump off the logs into the water. Although rabbits could make impressive leaps, she was pretty sure they wouldn't attempt springing to adjacent perches, which were spaced five feet apart. They'd stay put as she required, at least until fear prompted them into motion.

Sgt. Petersen had done more than just obtain the rabbits. He'd also gotten Addi the gun.

She sat cross-legged on the ground on a slight rise overlooking the pond, the basket at her side, waiting for Eddie to arrive. Sipping from a water bottle caused her to think of her father and his illness. She'd put through a secure Zoom call after supper last night but he'd been napping. Pierre said he was doing fine, however, and that there had been no further issues with his compulsion. A doctor and a nurse, part of the contingent promised by Col. Marsh, had arrived to help with his care.

She heard movement in the distance. Eddie dashed out from behind a stand of evergreens, running full bore toward the log pond. A glance at the app showed his vitals well-elevated. He was as ready as he was going to be. She held the remote in her left hand. With her right one, she reached into the basket and gripped the pistol.

Eddie slowed as he came closer, eyeing the rabbits with suspicion.

"What's with the bunnies?"

"A little test." She added a mischievous grin to heighten his perplexity and tension level. "Keep moving. Finish the course and then we'll talk."

She could see the wheels turning in his head, trying to decide between two options for getting past the pond's latest obstructions. He could bypass the pair of logs occupied by the rabbits by slogging through the shallow waters. Or he could stay on the preferred route. If he chose the latter, the animals either would panic and leap from his path or get smashed under his boots.

"Screw it," she heard him mutter.

He leaped from the water's edge onto the first log. Continuing forward motion, he flew from log to log with ease while flailing his arms and shouting nonsense words. Addi couldn't help being impressed by his blend of speed and coordination.

His yelling and boisterous arm movements did the job. The rabbits, terrified by the big scaly noise machine racing toward them, vaulted from their perches and plopped into the water.

She tapped a preset command on the remote. The level 3 shock caught Eddie in the midst of a leap.

He let out a cry of pain. The timing of the shock impacted his rhythm, and his left foot landed awkwardly on the next log. He slid off, plowed knees-first into the pond with a muddy splash.

The jolt ended and he stood up in the water, glaring with rage. She tapped the remote again, repeating the shock.

"Turn – it – off!" he hissed, spinning wildly and tearing futilely at the collar. The rabbits, barely keeping their heads above the surface, struggled to move away from the raging giant in their midst.

The second shock reached its cutoff. Eddie stomped out of the pond and came at her, steaming mad. She waited until he was three paces away before whipping the pistol from the basket and pulling the trigger.

He took the first shot in the upper chest. The second and third ones hit just below it, forming a perfect triangular pattern. Papa had taught her to hunt and shoot at an early age. She was a crack shot.

Three distinct red splotches spread outward across Eddie's shirt. Rivulets dripped downward, further staining the material.

"What the fuck, you shot me? With a paintball gun?"

"Take a closer look. It's not paint."

She'd requisitioned the special ammo from hematology. That had gotten her into a testy email exchange with Dr Steinhauser, who'd demanded to know why she needed nine hundred milliliters of human blood. She'd responded that it was none of the doctor's business and the situation went south from there. Col. Marsh had been forced to intervene on Addi's behalf.

Dr Steinhauser's reaction to losing the blood battle was extreme. She'd stormed into Addi's office full of piss and vinegar, accusing her of being a dangerous quack. Attempts to calm her failed, and she'd left angrier than when she'd arrived. Addi had shrugged it off. She hadn't been brought to the compound to make friends.

"You sick fuck!" Eddie hollered, realizing he'd been shot with blood.

"I'm trying to emulate the conditions of the guerrilla attack. It's an important part of the therapy."

"And now you're going to shock me again?"

"Not necessary, at least not at the moment. I've collected most of the data I need for today."

She checked her phone. The BAM's readings confirmed his state of physiological agitation. He was caught up in the bad yen. Another push should throw him over the edge.

"There is one more thing you could do for me," she said, gesturing behind him to the rabbits flopping in the water. "Be a good boy and have one of those for lunch."

Rage exploded across his face. It was a dangerous moment

for Addi. She needed him out of control enough to bring on the bloodburn, but not so crazed that he lost sight of the fact that this was part of a therapeutic experiment. In other words, don't attack your doctor.

He ran back into the pond and snatched the nearest rabbit from the water. The animal squealed as he bit halfway through its neck. He sank his incisors deeper. The animal jerked in its death throes and stopped moving.

Eddie removed the large clump of rabbit hanging from his mouth. Holding it by the pelt side, he gnawed at the bloody meat.

"As tasty as that guerrilla?" she asked, adding a smile to the taunt.

"Fuck you!"

Addi rechecked the app. She was pretty certain she'd captured the readings associated with the onset of the bloodburn.

"Good job, Eddie. Got everything I need for today. At our upcoming sessions we'll–"

He threw the dead rabbit at her. She jerked her head sideways, avoiding a direct hit. But the carcass walloped her left cheek as it sailed past. It stung, as if someone had slapped her face hard. Wincing, she reached up and rubbed her cheek, felt the wet stain.

"Now you're bloody too," Eddie snarled. He spun away and jogged back toward the compound's distant buildings.

Addi waited until he was out of sight before retrieving the other rabbit from the water. She was supposed to hand over any surviving animals to Sgt Petersen for return to the lab complex. But the helpless creature shivering in her hands had endured enough. It didn't deserve what likely would be a painful death in the clutches of experimenters.

She removed a packet of the cheese crackers from the basket and undid the wrapper. Carrying the rabbit and food to the nearest clump of foliage, she set them down and returned to where she'd left the basket. When she glanced behind her, the rabbit was nibbling on its meal. It might not survive in the wild but at least it had a chance.

She picked up the dead rabbit and hurled it into the woods. Had anyone been observing her actions, they no doubt would have been puzzled by her contradictory behavior regarding the ethical treatment of animals. But there were no absolutes in this world. She'd learned that lesson at a young age. Some things lived, some things died.

EIGHTEEN

Addi passed the lab complex on her way back to her Admin office and spotted Col. Marsh approaching, accompanied by a female army officer. The pair drew close enough to make out the two stars embroidered on the woman's shoulder. They halted in front of her.

"How was your picnic?" Col. Marsh joked, then frowned and motioned to her face. "Is that blood?"

She'd wiped her cheek with a hankie but apparently hadn't removed all the evidence of Eddie's parting gift of rabbit carcass.

"It's nothing," she said.

"Good. Dr Adelaide LaTour, meet Major General Hollenbach. Addi is the one we brought in to address the issues with Boka."

The general regarded her coolly as they shook hands. A fireplug of a woman, she had dark skin and auburn hair pinched into a bun. Her uniform had the usual plethora of decorations common to high-ranking officers. Her grip could compress steel.

"The general heads-up AFC, the Army Futures Command, which oversees Project Saurian. She interacts with all DoD research endeavors, including DevCom, DARPA and USAMRDC."

"No one ever accused the military of acronymic moderation," Gen. Hollenbach said.

If the remark was intended to be humorous, no one told the general's face. But Addi smiled.

"It's good meeting you," Addi said. "I saw you on a panel at a psychopharmacology conference in San Francisco a few years ago. I recall you offering some perspectives that challenged the rather traditional attitudes of the other participants."

"A healthy dynamic, challenging the status quo. As long as it's not carried to extremes."

"I thought your comments were done in moderation."

Addi wasn't being ingratiating. She'd been genuinely impressed with Gen. Hollenbach's agile mind.

"How was your session with Eddie today?" the colonel asked, gesturing to the basket. "Sgt. Petersen informs me that you requested some unusual items."

"Mostly for data collection purposes."

"We'd appreciate an update ASAP," Col. Marsh said with a smile. "Naturally, as always, only those aspects that don't violate doctor-patient confidentiality."

"I'll see what I can do."

"Excellent."

The pair continued on and entered the lab complex lobby. Addi figured the general would have no trouble gaining access to the three cryptically named spokes. But she had a hunch their primary destination was RV, where those truckloads of large animals were being routed.

"Some aspects of human behavior may lie forever beyond the limits of predictability."

– Wesk: Algorithmic Speculations

NINETEEN

"Wesk, can you identify the nature of the problem we're having?" Col. Marsh asked.

"Secure door RV-1 won't open."

"Yes, that much we can see. My facial scan and the daily security code were successfully authorized. *Why* won't it open?"

The colonel kept his voice even, but Wesk detected elevated vitals indicative of annoyance. The presence of General Hollenbach no doubt was a contributing factor. Humans disliked being embarrassed in front of their superiors. In this instance, Col. Marsh's emotion likely was accentuated by the fact that this was the general's first visit to the compound's most secretive area, and he'd hoped to make a good impression.

"Dr Quelphius sometimes takes the added precaution of securing the door from the inside when he's within the enclosure."

Gen. Hollenbach raised an eyebrow. "He can override the security system?"

"Yes, indirectly. He sticks a discarded piece of 1.6-meter length of steel rebar through the locking wheel, manually jamming it."

Col. Marsh activated the intercom beside the portal. "Dr

Quelphius, I'm outside RV-1 with Gen. Hollenbach. We require immediate access."

The officers waited impatiently as the seconds ticked by.

"Where is he?" Col. Marsh demanded, his anger growing.

"Ascending the main elevator now," Wesk reported.

The locking wheel finally began rotating. The door swung open and Dr Quelphius appeared. The length of rebar was propped against the wall.

"It's an added precaution to prevent entry when I'm interacting with them," the researcher explained. "Should someone open this door at the same time I'm accessing the enclosure, an unsecured passageway to the outside world would exist. There is a chance, however minuscule, they could escape the building."

"Minuscule in the extreme," the colonel said coldly. "Alarms would go off and the facility would go into lockdown mode. So never do something like this again."

"Of course, of course. Your objection is understood. Naturally, I'll comply to the fullest."

Col. Marsh looked unconvinced. "Wesk, after we're done here, contact the authorized maintenance staff and have them remove the rebar from the premises, as well as any other implements that could be used to foul the door."

"Understood."

They entered the elevator and descended to Sub 4, the deepest and most secure part of the lab. A short corridor flanked by regular doors dead-ended against another heavy-duty portal with a wheel-lock entry. It was unmarked except for a small sign bearing Blayvine's ubiquitous catchphrase, *Unveil the beyond with eyes wide open.*

When the compound was built, Blayvine had ordered the physical signs posted throughout every building, a total of one hundred and forty-six of them. Since that time, some of them had gone missing as various employees grew to resent the in-your-face motto, replacing it with artwork or personalized messaging. Wesk's latest count revealed only one hundred and twelve signs remained, a twenty-three percent decline.

Dr Quelphius keyed a code into its mechanism. The wheel spun automatically, and the door pivoted open.

They proceeded into the observation room. Several rows of cushioned chairs faced a three-meter high opaque glass wall. Adjacent to the front middle chair was a pedestal topped by a control panel.

"Keep your voices low," the doctor suggested. "I believe they're sleeping. But they have amazingly acute hearing, even through the wall."

"The general is here on a fact-finding assignment to gauge what progress you've been making," Col. Marsh said coldly, still angry about the rebar. "We'll need them awake."

"Very well. Give me a moment."

Quelph tapped some buttons on the control panel. The electrochromic glass turned transparent as the polarity of its electrical charge was reversed. Beyond was a tangle of verdant growth. Clusters of dense ground foliage surrounded the soaring trees. To one side was a murky pond.

"You weren't exaggerating," General Hollenbach said, stepping closer to the wall and lifting her gaze. "It looks like an actual rainforest in there. How high is that canopy?"

"The enclosure extends all the way up through Subs 3 and 2," Quelph said.

"Twenty-seven meters," Wesk clarified without being asked. "The entire enclosure encompasses more than thirty-five thousand cubic meters."

"Wake up, children," Quelph whispered into the control panel's mic. "There are some friends here to see you." He faced the general. "They're light sleepers and I've activated the interior audio. We should hear them rousing soon enough."

"Isn't there video in the enclosure?" Gen. Hollenbach asked.

"Unfortunately, not at this time," Col. Marsh said. "We originally had surveillance cameras mounted along the walls and in the ceiling. They didn't like that. One morning last week the four of them climbed the trees and smashed the entire array. The destruction was carried out by a combination of well-aimed thrown rocks and long severed branches employed as bats."

Wesk had monitored the incident, at least up until the destruction of the final camera eye. The attack had surprised everyone except Quelph. Their propensity for violence had been well-established. But the other researchers hadn't suspected the capacity of the four of them to work so well in tandem.

"It was a coordinated attack," the colonel explained.

"Denoting their high level of intelligence," Quelph said. "It may even be possible to teach them to comprehend and vocalize human speech."

"We're in the process of installing a new surveillance system. It's taking longer than anticipated. Some reengineering of the enclosure is required to make the new camera housings more robust."

A low-pitched growl erupted from inside. An instant later came the thrashing of foliage. A seven-foot humanoid creature burst from behind a thicket of bushes and body-slammed the glass wall, startling the officers. Quelph seemed pleased by their reactions.

"Meet Rex. He's the oldest of the retroverts by a month. He just turned three. Accelerated growth hormones equate him with an adolescent human. Perhaps being a teenager has something to do with it, but he rather enjoys scaring visitors."

The creature ran a clawed hand down the wall, either trying to scratch the glass or sending a not-so-subtle warning to its observers. Rex stood erect like a homo sapien and its face was vaguely human-shaped. But almost the entirety of its naked body was covered in scaly armor, including a bony ridge descending from below the belly to cover its genitalia. The scaliness was marred only by linear streaks of glistening, human-like skin on its thighs, and similar patches running down the upper arms from shoulders to elbows. Slitted reptilian eyes seemed to study them.

"I can see the resemblance to Boka," Gen. Hollenbach said, fascinated as she studied its countenance.

Col. Marsh agreed. "Subtle but definitely present."

"For this parallel project, a small but significant infusion of Boka's original genetic material was added to the replicated T-Rex DNA of which Rex is primarily composed," Quelph explained. "That provided many of its core features – humanoid configuration, elevated intelligence, a warm-blooded metabolism. With Boka and the other dino-humans, the percentages are reversed. We started with functioning adult homo sapiens and introduced small amounts of saurian material."

"What's the purpose of those fleshy areas on its thighs and arms?" the general asked. "They would seem to be inherent weak spots in its armor."

"Unforeseen flaws," Quelph said. "Perfection is rarely achieved on a first effort. Future iterations of this basic prototype will eliminate all such blemishes. And should Rex and his brothers ever be selected for combat missions, customized body armor has been fabricated for protecting the exposed areas."

"Where are the other three?"

"Cerato, Spino and Dilopho are holding back. Either watching us from within the foliage or swimming underwater in the pond."

"So Rex is the alpha?"

"In most instances he assumes the lead role. But the retroverts also have an amazing capacity for cooperative undertakings. So unlike Boka and the other dino-humans, whose infighting over absurd and insignificant matters is legendary, my children are much more harmonious."

Wesk noted that Quelph's last remark caused the officers to exchange wry looks. The researcher pushed on, oblivious to their reactions.

"Dino-humans are at best an intermediate step. It's not that Boka, Castaneda and Cheng aren't likely to perform adequately in combat scenarios. But their all-too-human qualities perpetually will cause squabbling and disruption. They'll never be able to overcome those inherent flaws. In contrast, my retroverts offer a far more structured level of stability. It's my unqualified belief that the true soldiers of the future should be based on the RV model."

The general seemed about to comment but Quelph was on a roll and kept talking.

"Prioritizing the RV project also offers long-term financial advantages. I've worked up some preliminary numbers showing that a retrovert army, as opposed to a dino-human one, would offer significant cost savings. That even takes into consideration some of the admittedly higher maintenance expenses such as enclosure security and nutriment provisions. I have detailed all this in a report I'd like to send you."

Quelph seemed unaware that his rant was eliciting even deeper skeptical looks. Gen. Hollenbach finally interrupted.

"Your passion is admirable. And please do forward me your report. However, there is a glaring issue you seem to be overlooking. Is it not the case that you, Doctor Quelphius, are the only individual – in fact, the only mammal of any species – who can enter the enclosure without the distinct possibility of being torn limb from limb? It would seem that the retroverts' propensity for uncontrolled violence presents a serious flaw to your lobbying efforts."

"Of course, of course. I'm well aware of that. Had I the ability to start over with the design process, I would have introduced certain genomic alterations to render them less hostile to friendlies. I also would have made sure I wasn't the only human interacting with them at the critical age when imprinting and bonding occurs. Rest assured, however, that a foolproof means of controlling their aggressive behavior has been under development for some time. In fact, a beta version will be ready for implementation in a matter of weeks.

"A tiny device similar to a cochlear implant will be surgically implanted into the retroverts' inner ear cavities. The devices are remotely controlled, enabling either an electronic command or a vocalized order from a recognized authority. Those commands will override their attack tendencies and render them placid."

Wesk, having viewed the design data on the implants, did not share Dr Quelphius' level of certainty that the creatures' baser instincts would be so easily controlled.

"A future programming enhancement will make possible another type of signal," Quelph continued, his face lighting with excitement. "It will direct them to assault a specified target with maximum belligerence. Coupled with weapons training, they will become unstoppable soldiers, warlike to a degree that the dino-humans with their petty issues will never achieve."

"Fascinating," Gen. Hollenbach offered.

"Indeed! The minor deficiencies of these original four will be corrected, spotlighting the way forward. All that is then required is authorization for the next phase of the project, leading ultimately to creation of the first retrovert army."

"Such authorization isn't guaranteed," Col. Marsh cautioned.

"Of course, of course. It's your decision, general. I can only trust you'll make the right one."

"You'll receive a fair hearing," she promised. Taking a final long look at the towering creature gazing down at her, she turned away from the wall. Immediately, the retrovert tapped a clawed finger sharply against the glass, three times in rapid succession. The noise caused Gen. Hollenbach to spin back around.

"Rex doesn't want you to go," Quelph said with a gleeful smile. "He likes you. That's a sign of affection."

The retrovert repeated the triple tap. Gen. Hollenbach stared back at those fierce golden eyes.

"I'm not sure affection is the impression I'm getting," she said. "More like it sees me as…"

She trailed off, deciding to leave the thought unexpressed. As she started to turn away again, the retrovert whirled and dove into the pond. In moments only expanding ripples marked the spot where it had gone under.

"The water's deep and they're excellent swimmers," Quelph said, unable to stop his sales pitch. "Expanded lung capacity enables them to stay submerged for remarkably long periods, easily competitive with the most proficient Navy SEALS."

Wesk had seen the tapping behavior from Rex before. Prior to the destruction of the internal cameras, all four of the retroverts had been observed engaging in similar routines. Dr Quelphius' explanation that the actions were based on affection seemed true enough, at least on those occasions when the doctor ventured into the enclosure – which, incidentally, was officially frowned upon as an undue risk. But Quelph obviously felt that his most cherished creations would never turn on him.

However, the identical tapping behavior also occurred for a different reason. It often happened when foodstuffs were funneled into the enclosure, especially the larger mammals such as deer, hogs and ponies. That suggested the retroverts had a flimsy mental border between affection and hunger. Wesk projected that under the right circumstances, such a flaw could lead to tragedy.

TWENTY

Addi returned to her quarters from the obstacle course with an intense appetite. She'd had a light lunch beforehand so it wasn't a matter of needing nourishment. Like most homo sapiens, as well as a certain dino-human, she sometimes ate to quell uncomfortable feelings.

The encounter with Eddie had gone more or less as rehearsed. Her heightened appetite likely was caused by a sense of shame over what she was putting him through. She'd taken on a fair number of assignments requiring use of the BAM, military as well as civilian, and the only other time she'd experienced such an emotion was treating the heir to a shipping empire. Ostensibly, he'd been trying to cure a gambling addiction, but that had been a deception to draw her in. She'd learned soon enough that he was a masochist hooked on the disciplinary pain inherent in electroshocks.

Her shame in that case arose from losing sight of patient-therapist boundaries, of continuing to treat him even after she'd recognized the truth. A requirement of her profession was maintaining an honest relationship with patients. But his generous financial incentives caused her to rationalize that she was helping him even while a part of her knew she was just feeding his masochistic urges. She finally came to her senses and terminated his therapy after he'd tried recruiting her as his full-time dominatrix.

The shipping heir had been an atypical patient but not all that unusual when viewed in terms of his being a man. Addi hadn't dated much recently but had gone out with plenty of guys, a few who seemed destined to develop into something serious and long-term. But in every case, there came a point when she felt the man was asking for too much, that he desired one too many sacrifices from her. After breaking it off, she would inevitably question her own attitudes, wondering that if by being too critical, she was sabotaging the possibility of a deeper relationship. Such questioning never produced satisfactory answers.

She stripped and laid out a fresh set of clothes on the bed, then entered the bathroom to take a shower. The mirror above the vanity captured her attention first. Splashing cold water on her face, she washed away the remnants of rabbit blood. But she couldn't eliminate the red splotch where the animal had smacked her cheek.

She stepped into the shower and turned on the spray, her thoughts cycling back to Eddie and the shame she felt about what she was making him go through. Clearly it arose from a different source than what had occurred with the wealthy pain freak.

Col. Marsh had explained that the dino-humans were nonsexual beings due to their disruptive transformations. However, Eddie remained virile in other ways, his masculinity emerging by way of his confidence, strength and aggressiveness. But now her psychiatric role was tampering with those qualities, making him feel less of a man. She'd made that lopsided power dynamic particularly apparent at the obstacle course, including telling him to be a "good boy" as an added push to bring on the physiological markers of the bloodburn.

Still, why should any of that make her feel ashamed? Putting aside the incident with the masochist, she'd used BAM therapy on numerous men, comfortable in the knowledge of its temporary emasculating qualities. It was results-oriented methodology, short-term emotional discomfort for permanent improvement. Why should it bother her so strongly in Eddie's case?

An answer whispered from the edge of awareness, and with it a feeling of unease. She quickly finished showering, scuttling the fragment of a thought before it could reach consciousness.

Dressed and feeling reasonably presentable again, the bruise on her cheek camouflaged with makeup, she headed down to the cafeteria. It was 2:00, late enough for most of the lunch crowd to have departed. Only a couple civilians and a few clusters of soldiers were spread throughout the large open space.

The cafeteria offered a traditional platter line manned by a bored server. Addi chose the automat on the opposite wall, scanning her Blayvine debit card and punching in her selection. Removing the bowl of steamed rice from its receptacle, she sat at an empty table far from the others. She'd just about finished the meal when a booming voice erupted behind her.

"Hiya, Doctor Addi!"

She knew the voice's owner without turning. She hadn't met the other dino-humans, but Blayvine provided video bios of them in her packet of introductory materials. The shirtless hulk in bib overalls plopped down in the seat next to her, grinning brightly.

"You must be Samuel Samson," she offered, matching his smile. "Should I call you Sam? Or Sammy?"

He looked hurt. "No, that's not my name. It's Samson. See?"

Turning back one of his suspenders revealed the name imprinted on the underside.

"OK, got it."

He spelled it out to make sure. "S – A – M – S – O – N."

"Good to make your acquaintance, Samson." She extended her hand and he eagerly pumped it up and down. His palm was surprisingly soft, his grip gentle. Like all the dino-humans, everything from the lower forearms to the fingertips was one hundred percent human flesh.

"Will you play Candyland with me? If you don't know how, I can teach you." He frowned. "Unless you know how already."

"Well, I haven't played since I was real little. But I think I remember. I'm guessing you're pretty good at it."

"I am, I really am! Eddie says he doesn't need a new head doctor and you should go to hell."

Samson's jarring change of subject was uttered with the innocence of a child. Not surprising, considering his IQ and emotional maturity corresponded to that of a four-year-old.

Prior to his alterations, Samson had been a young soldier of average intelligence. In the weeks following, his IQ had begun dipping precipitously until finally stabilizing at its present level. The researchers didn't understand the phenomenon's cause even after batteries of tests, including fMRI scans of his brain evaluated by Wesk using complex algorithms. They'd eventually chalked it up to an anomaly, an indeterminate side effect sometimes inherent with experimental technologies. Addi wondered if Samson, perhaps in his dreams, ever recalled hints of the person he'd lost.

"I'm sorry to hear that Eddie said those things about me. But I think maybe he'll change his mind once he gets to know me better."

"Are you going to steal his bob-wobs?"

"His bob-wobs?"

"You know, his bob-wobs. Boys have 'em but girls don't."

"You mean his testicles? His balls?"

Samson giggled, embarrassed by the utterance. Addi was more surprised by the fact that Eddie apparently shared his private thoughts with Samson. Then again, the bio on the gregarious dino-human indicated he wandered around the compound like a camp mascot. He could have overheard Eddie complaining about her to someone else.

"I promise you, Samson, the only thing I'm trying to do is help Eddie."

"Really?"

"That's the plan, honest."

His face returned to its happy state.

An excited corporal poked his head into the cafeteria. "Julio's in the gym about to get his ass kicked!"

Several groups of soldiers rose from their tables and scurried after him.

"Samson, do you know what that's all about?"

"Uh-huh. Julio's always fighting. We're not supposed to get in real fights unless we get sent to a war. I'll betcha he's going to get in trouble again."

"Maybe we should go down there and make sure he doesn't."

"OK!"

A staircase outside the cafeteria led them to the large basement gym. At the far end, about three dozen soldiers, mostly male, surrounded a mixed martial arts ring. Addi and Samson approached and melded into the outer row.

Julio stood within the hexagonal fenced ring wearing black trunks. Across from him were three bare-chested soldiers in khaki trunks. A bearded referee was positioned between them.

Julio was taunting his opponents. "Seriously, you think you got what it takes? Didn't learn your lesson last time when I took two of you down, so now you think three is the magic number? Bunch of goddamned bobbleheads."

The soldiers responded with loud boos and insults.

"Dumbass lizard!"

"Freak!"

"Need me a pair of alligator shoes, guys. I say we skin the scaly prick!"

Julio laughed at the insults, dancing around and throwing shadow punches. It was then Addi noticed the other dino-human standing behind him, just outside the ring. Gideon wore a headset and held a phone. He appeared to be texting.

"C'mon," Julio urged him. "Let's get this shit going."

"Almost there," Gideon said. "One last bet coming in."

Gideon received the info, repeating the bettor's name and the amount wagered to confirm. He nodded to the referee, signaling the fight could start.

"Undefeated Julio Castaneda versus undefeated Army Team One!" the ref shouted, making a show of it. "Two five-minute rounds. Fighters ready?"

The four participants nodded and inserted their mouthguards.

"Go!"

The ref ducked to the side of the ring, barely eluding Julio's lunge toward his opponents. Like Eddie, he moved with unnatural swiftness. He was all over the first soldier in an instant, dodging the man's defensive kicks and pummeling his chest and stomach with brutal jabs. The other soldiers came to his rescue, attacking Julio from opposite sides and allowing their stunned teammate to back away and recover his equilibrium.

Julio and the other two men traded punches and kicks with furious abandon. The crowd hooted and jeered the dino-human, and shouted encouragement to the army team. The fight alternated between explosions of violence and moments where the fighters warily circled one another, scanning for weaknesses.

The biggest soldier, his bare back an inked tapestry of religious symbols, lowered his shoulders and plowed into Julio. The hit was powerful enough to knock Julio onto his back. The tatted soldier was on top of him in an instant, pounding his fists into Julio's midsection. The other two each grabbed a flailing arm, preventing Julio from counterpunching. Addi thought the fight was seconds away from being over. Julio would either surrender or be pummeled into submission.

But neither of those things happened. Julio contorted his body at the waist, lifted his legs and locked his leather-shoed feet around the tatted soldier's head. Wrenching forward, he yanked the opponent off his chest and threw the man into a violent back flip. He landed face down on the mat.

Splaying his legs, Julio landed brutal kicks to the jaws of the pair pinning his arms. One man staggered away, wagging his head trying to recover from the blow. The other one went down and stayed that way, out cold.

"And then there were two!" Julio yelled triumphantly, on his feet in a flash. "Rock and roll!"

The tatted soldier was still trying to get up, which left his staggered teammate in a one-on-one battle. Julio was on the man in an instant, landing a series of wicked punches. Blood sprayed from the soldier's nostrils as a right hook connected. He fell and writhed on the floor, unable to continue.

The tatted one got to his feet. He should have stayed down. Julio went airborne, slammed his heels into the man's chest. The hit knocked him down again, this time onto his back. He struggled to get up but Julio leaped atop him and peppered him with both fists.

The ref blew his whistle. Julio kept punching, unable or unwilling to acknowledge the fight was over.

"That's it!" the ref hollered. "He's finished. Bout is ended. Julio Castaneda is champion."

The crowd had gone silent momentarily as they took in the defeat. But they started booing when Julio failed to stop hitting the soldier.

"Julio, that's enough!"

Gideon's shout somehow rose above the noise and penetrated Julio's rage fog. The dino-human raised his arm in triumph. He seemed to thrive on the boos and name calling.

"Next time, boys, I'll take four of you on!"

His arrogance heightened the verbal assault. The crowd surged forward against the netting. It looked like they were going to come into the ring and attack Julio. But the ref, with the assistance of a couple burly sergeants, got the soldiers under control.

Addi waited until most of the men had departed the gym before approaching the dino-humans. Samson followed her like an eager puppy. Gideon was tending to a bloody laceration on Julio's forearm.

"You were great, Julio!" Samson enthused. "You beat people up the best of anybody!"

He acknowledged the compliment with a grunt and confronted Addi.

"So you're Eddie's new shrink, huh?"

"I am."

"I hear the other mind-fuckers have a special name for you. They call you the Electrobitch."

The denigrating label had surfaced in psych forums critical of Addi's methods. She wondered where Julio had heard it. The dino-humans supposedly had limited online access. But she supposed it was impossible to completely cut them off from the outside world.

"Been called worse," she countered. "What about you, Julio? Doesn't all that hatred pouring into the ring ever get to you?"

"Nah, makes me wanna kick their bobblehead asses even more."

Julio, like all the dino-humans, had been an orphan. That had been a requirement for anyone being considered for the project, as it was considered important for their psychological well-being that they were not easily traced back to familial roots. According to Blayvine, high-level data scrubbing by the NSA and other agencies contributed to that end.

Although orphans made their way in the world like everyone else, Addi knew they often carried lifelong scars that were expressed in various ways. One was rage against authority, with Julio being a vibrant example.

The bout's champion turned to Gideon. "What's the take?"

"About $2,800."

"You do this for the money?" Addi asked.

Gideon smiled. "As a psychiatrist, you should know that people do things for multifaceted rationales. The financial rewards are among the least important."

"And what's the most important?"

"That our kind do not go gentle into that good night."

Addi recognized the words from the famed Dylan Thomas poem. She hadn't considered the four dino-humans having much of a sense of unity. She wondered if Gideon's paraphrased quote also included Eddie or whether there was too much animosity with Julio for that to occur.

She gestured to one of the ubiquitous camera eyes on the nearest wall. "Samson said you could get in trouble for fighting."

"Officially, it's prohibited," Gideon said. "Unofficially, we're tolerated."

"Probably gives the overlords hard-ons seeing the grunts beating up on one another," Julio said. "Isn't that right, Wesk?"

The AI did not respond.

"Actually, we're probably tolerated a lot more than you are," Gideon added. "I'd be especially careful while you're here, Dr LaTour. Just because you can't see your enemies doesn't mean they don't have you in their sights."

She wasn't sure of his meaning but decided it was time to make her exit. "It was good meeting the three of you. I hope we'll get a chance to talk more."

"Me too," Samson said. "And after we talk we can play Candyland!"

"It's a date."

She headed for the door, sensing three sets of eyes following her. Two of the three were easy to read. One perceived the world with simplistic delight, the other with smoldering resentment. Gideon was the one she couldn't get a read on. He came across as a wise soul, the quiet peacekeeper. Yet she sensed something more about him, something hidden.

TWENTY-ONE

By Eddie's third week of therapy, his relationship with Addi had undergone a profound shift. The tumultuous nature of those early sessions had been superseded by a growing admiration for her, and more recently by something deeper. He'd begun dwelling on her constantly when they weren't together and experiencing waves of tenderness toward her when they were. He hadn't experienced such sensations since those evocative high school days with Catalina.

He lay in bed, trying to get to sleep but unable to shut Addi out of his head. He knew enough about the therapeutic process from his sessions with Dr Kim to understand the nature of transference, of unconsciously projecting his feelings and desires onto a therapist. This was something more profound, however.

He was falling for her.

Nothing could ever come of it, of course. For one thing, there was that intrinsic barrier between psychiatrist and patient, a wall he sensed she would be reluctant to violate. More fundamental was Eddie's obvious limitations in the bedroom. He couldn't envision a young woman like Addi, in her sexual prime, being satisfied with a platonic relationship. And, of course, there was his freakish appearance. He wasn't bothered by his looks, perhaps because when he gazed into a mirror he tended to see the man he once was, not the semi-human thing he'd become. But was she capable of seeing him that way?

This wasn't the first night he'd been unable to drift off, his mind volleying worries back and forth. But the turmoil had increased since her arrival and was heightened by what was to happen three days from now. It was Wednesday, nearly 3:00 in the morning. The big show was on Saturday afternoon. Dino-humans, meet world; world, meet dino-humans.

As on other sleepless nights, his churning thoughts pivoted back to his lost manhood. Once again he found himself reviewing the events leading him into the clutches of Project Saurian and a life of celibacy.

His breakup with Catalina after her family moved east had been the impetus for his subsequent actions. He'd taken a few local jobs through high school but couldn't seem to stick with any of them, at least partly because people and stores and other things in the area kept reminding him of her. He eventually realized he had to get away. Enlisting in the army seemed like the way to go about it.

In fairness, he couldn't blame a broken heart for what had happened five years into his six-year enlistment. It was Eddie's fault alone that he began hanging out with a group of hard-partying soldiers, getting drunk and high with them.

The boredom of army life, the routine of it, contributed to the idiocy that followed. Had he been sent to some exotic foreign base or even plunged into a kinetic combat zone, his future might have played out differently. Those things never happened. For whatever reason, the Army had kept him stateside, sapping his spirit and making him vulnerable to outrageous, get-rich-quick barstool schemes.

It had started as a lot of drunken nonsense talk, he and two fellow conspirators fantasizing about using their military training and gear to execute the perfect bank robbery. Before Eddie knew it, the talk had reached the stage of selecting a target, planning the assault and mapping escape routes.

The robbery had come off without a hitch, the patrons and tellers rightly intimidated by three masked men with combat vests and assault rifles. No shots were fired, nobody got hurt. They were in and out of the bank in the allotted time. It was the perfect robbery until it wasn't, when some random worker having a back-alley smoke break spotted them removing their masks and climbing into the getaway van.

The worker called the police. Less than two miles down the road, the van was suddenly ringed by cops. Eddie knew it was over but his two partners refused to surrender. The driver foolishly tried accelerating past the patrol cars. Eddie, certain they were about to go down in a hail of gunfire, grabbed the wheel and spun it. They came to a hard stop against a tree.

The driver, enraged at Eddie for intervening or just plain enraged, leaped out with his rifle. His vest protected him from the withering gunfire for about three seconds, right up until a cop put a 9-mil slug through his scalp. Eddie and the other robber quickly surrendered.

It was while awaiting his court martial and facing a likely prison sentence of twenty years that he was approached by Col. Marsh. It turned out that Eddie had an especially desirable genotype. His actions in trying to stop the driver, and testimony from the bank victims about his calming reassurances that no one would be hurt had been in sharp contrast to the raging threats of his fellow robbers. It made him eligible for a reprieve.

He was presented to the court as the "good" bank robber, the one with the heart of gold, the one deemed salvageable as a productive citizen. He was still found guilty, of course. But if he signed up for Project Saurian, a behind-the-scenes deal would commute his sentence. By then his last close relatives had died, the elderly aunt and uncle who'd adopted him from the orphanage. Changing his last name to "Boka" would be the final step in severing ties with his earlier life. He was told that after the infusions and surgeries, his transformation would be so complete that not even facial recognition apps would be able to link him to his origins.

He'd taken the deal, of course. It hadn't really been much of a choice. And now here he was a few years later, fantasizing about a woman, about what could have been and what now could never be.

He hopped out of bed, sleep impossible. And the BAM was making his neck itch again. He'd worn it to bed the last few nights even though a quick text to Addi would have prompted her to unlock it. He supposed he was trying to impress her by showing his fortitude and dedication to the therapy.

She was still tweaking the collar through a series of trials. Yesterday had been another rough one. Out at the obstacle course, he'd been asked – ordered was more like it – to chase, capture and eat a macaque monkey she'd procured from one of the labs. Through her trademark blend of physical exertion and taunting, she'd worked him into a state where the bad yen took hold, although not so overwhelming he'd succumbed to the bloodburn.

He'd snagged the creature as it leapt for a branch but hesitated in carrying out the final part of the test. It wasn't fear of her giving him a shock, which she'd warned could happen if he didn't comply. Instead, it was looking into that frightened and all-too-human primate face that made him hold back. Releasing the monkey, he'd watched it scurry off into the woods.

Addi not only hadn't shocked him, she'd been unusually silent on the walk back. He sensed that freeing the animal had pleased her even if it went against her program of psychological manipulations. Yet he knew that if she had really pushed him hard to go through with the kill, he would have done it.

Because he was falling for her. And maybe also that her therapy was working.

He entered the bathroom, retrieved a tube from the medicine cabinet and squeezed a glob of gel onto his forefinger. Slipping the finger under the collar, he coated the underlying skin. The salve Addi had prescribed worked like a charm. In seconds, the itching relented. If only there existed a balm that could be rubbed into deeper recesses.

"Throughout history, those achieving the greatest financial success tend to be the most ethically and morally challenged."

– Wesk: Algorithmic Speculations

TWENTY-TWO

Wesk had been granted one-day limited access to the Axton High School auditorium, the largest assembly space in town. Some of the cameras and mics it was able to tap into were courtesy of Blayvine Industries and others from the DoD contingent. Each group boasted its own complex setup to record the historic event, which was being telecast live online and on every major network.

Wesk took it upon itself to tap into the school's surveillance system as well. The intrusion would be undetectable and would provide a more holistic view of the proceedings. None of its directives against spying, such as unauthorized intrusion into certain media networks and personal comm devices, were being violated. The school system however, perhaps through an oversight, wasn't included in its list of prohibitions. Whatever wasn't specifically banned was deemed Wesk-acceptable. "Fair game," as humans referred to the concept.

The six-hundred-seat auditorium was crammed, with a portion of the crowd forced to stand along the edges. The curtains were drawn across the front of the stage in preparation for the big reveal. Behind the drapes, the guests of honor – the four dino-humans – were garbed in their military dress uniforms and seated at a long table whose skirting was composed of interlocking American flags. Wesk's temporary camera eyes lacked the apps available back at the compound for scanning vital signs. But subtle visual cues enabled a rough measure of anxieties.

Samson, at one end of the table, was the most relaxed, his happy-go-lucky attitude on display as he played solitaire on his phone. Boka, at the other end, seemed the most nervous. He wasn't wearing the BAM in order that it not become a distraction and prompt off-topic questions. But the way his hands kept reaching up to touch his shirt collar or adjust his tie made it seem like the training device was still there.

Julio and Gideon occupied the middle of the table, the latter closest to Boka. Each showed mild indicators of anxiety, but nothing beyond what would be expected given the event's significance.

Stage right, a set of portable bleachers held Gen. Hollenbach, Col. Marsh, ranking senators from the Armed Services Committee and various military and civilian representatives. Stage left featured a similar setup, mainly for Blayvine Industries employees, including doctors Quelphius, Kim and Steinhauser. Reginald Blayvine was the only person on his feet, issuing final instructions to a technician standing in the wings.

Months of behind-the-scenes prep work was about to reach fulfillment. Background music piped through the auditorium segued into an instrumental interpretation of *America the Beautiful*. Blayvine, an experienced showman, stepped out from behind the curtain and raised his arms in an expansive gesture.

"America is my home, and I love my home!"

Cheers and clapping erupted from the audience, led by the hundreds of townspeople selected by Wesk for their patriotic attitudes. Enthusiastic responses also came from the dozens of local and state officials groomed by Blayvine with promises of even more lucrative investment in the region's economy, and by business reps whose companies were likely to profit from the project's success. Also scattered throughout the auditorium were dozens of hand-picked social media influencers, including a few sponsored by hard-to-trace offshore subsidiaries of Blayvine Industries. For the most part, it was an audience inclined to be supportive.

"I have hope," Blayvine continued. "Hope that someday in the not-too-distant future, this great country will find a new and better way to defend its cherished values. Hope that America and its global partners in democracy will no longer have to send so many of their young sons and daughters off to war, their bodies ill-suited for the rigors and dangers of combat.

"A motto at Blayvine Industries is and always will be, 'Unveil the beyond with eyes wide open'. Those seven words guide our research efforts, enabling us to transcend horizons, surpass limitations, explore realms once considered the most exotic of dreams. And those seven words have brought us here today.

"It is my great privilege to introduce four of the bravest individuals I've ever had the pleasure of knowing. Four men who were willing to take the next step in human evolution. Four men who, like those selfless astronauts of an earlier generation, first departed earthly boundaries to begin humanity's great journey to the stars. Four volunteers who were willing to risk all!

"Ladies and gentlemen, it's time for the world to meet these brave souls! I give you the dino-human soldiers of Project Saurian!"

Blayvine stepped to the side as the curtains parted. Cheering began but quickly faded, replaced by gasps of surprise. Although the media had received advance hints that an extraordinary new form of xenotransplantation would be presented, most of the details and imagery had been embargoed until now.

Wesk didn't find it statistically remarkable there had been no major leaks and that the project's secrecy had been maintained for so long. Great effort had gone into producing that result, including the offer of extravagant bonuses to all Blayvine employees and military personnel for keeping the existence of the dino-humans under wraps. If even one individual had broken the pact, none of them would have received the bonuses. Greed had proved an effective method for ensuring mutual cooperation.

Blayvine waited until the hubbub faded before continuing. "May I present, Private First-Class Samuel Samson!"

Samson's excitement caused him to stand up so fast he knocked his chair over.

"Hiya!" he yelled, grinning with delight. "I used to be just a regular private, but I got promoted!"

Upon the four of them volunteering for the project – "volunteering" being a dubious term, considering the various forms of pressure brought to bear – they were all reclassified at the basic rank of private. The new promotions had come as a precursor to today's unveiling.

"Samson's enhancements," Blayvine continued, "are courtesy of the extinct species, Dilophosaurus. And no, he doesn't spit venom like in the movie, which took some artistic license with that creature's true nature."

"I only spit in the sink or toilet," Samson said proudly. "That's the way you're supposed to do it."

A few uneasy chuckles grew into a warm tide of laughter. There had been arguments early on as to whether Samson should be invited to the event, with Col. Marsh and doctors Steinhauser and Kim strongly opposed to his presence. But Blayvine had a better understanding of the situation and had deduced – correctly, as it seemed to be turning out – that Samson's disability would prove endearing and invite sympathetic responses.

"Samson has become a very special individual," Blayvine said. "His unique qualities may not make him appropriate for a combat role, but we are all constantly appreciative of his warm personality and encouraging demeanor."

Samson beamed. "Good-good-good!" Righting his chair, he plopped back into it.

"Next to Samson, we have Corporal Julio Castaneda! His modifications originate from the Late Cretaceous period carnivore, Spinosaurus."

Julio got up, his smile camouflaging any traces of his frequent attitude of disdain. He nodded to the crowd and resumed his seat.

"And now, Corporal Gideon Cheng! The Ceratosaurus of the Late Jurassic period underlies his essence."

"Thank you," Gideon said. "All of us are pleased to be given such an opportunity."

Wesk detected no irony in his statement. But of the four, he was the most skilled at hiding intent.

"And last but not least," Blayvine continued, "allow me to present Sergeant Eddie Boka! His saurian heritage? No less than that fierce and famous apex predator, Tyrannosaurus rex!"

Boka rose tentatively, his expression game but revealing stressors associated with discomfort. Wesk noted an escalated level of tension from Julio as well. He had been upset upon learning of Boka's new rank, arguing vociferously with Col. Marsh that he and Gideon also should have been promoted to sergeant.

"Thank you for being here today," Boka began. "I'm proud to be a part of an initiative with such noble aims. I don't know what the future holds, but I'm hoping that all of you can help us succeed. The transformations we've gone through... honestly, they have not been easy. For anyone seeking to become something new and different in this world, I think most of you know as well as I that the obstacles are always formidable. The only thing I can promise is that we're all going to do our very best."

He seemed about to add something but then abruptly sat down.

"Let's give these brave soldiers a round of applause!" Blayvine enthused, leading the claps.

The audience joined in. Wesk gauged the intensity of the outpouring as moderately strong. It was more enthusiastic than the polite response given to a conference speaker but nothing approaching the raucous level afforded to a pop star.

Next, Blayvine introduced the project's major contributors. Dr Quelphius began by providing a simplified explanation of the groundbreaking genome- and electrome-editing techniques used to replicate extinct saurian DNA. "Or more precisely," he clarified, "to recreate the extinct *traits* of dinosaurs absent from the planet for millions of years."

Quelph's passion for the subject animated his presentation. Soon he was delving deep into the particulars of the xenotransplantation process for fusing replicated dinosaur DNA with living humans. Blayvine interrupted at that point, effusively praising his contributions while effectively shutting down the touchy researcher before he bored the assemblage.

Gen. Hollenbach gave a short talk on the importance of dino-humans as part of a future military force, pointing out that the nation was in a race with other countries to develop enhanced soldiers first. He then introduced Col. Marsh for a more detailed review of the project's potential for saving lives. The colonel was followed by Dr Steinhauser.

"Our wide-ranging staff ensures that the dino-humans' well-being is always prioritized," she said. "Their medical requirements may be unique but they are just as human as you and I."

Dr Kim finished the formal speeches, touching upon the unique emotional challenges facing individuals put through such extraordinary changes. He kept his presentation brief but couldn't resist ending with a sly comment on Dr LaTour's intrusion into the process.

"Maintaining good psychological health is only possible when the patient is provided with a stable and caring therapeutic environment. Radical psychiatric methods have no place in Project Saurian."

Wesk noted the subtle indications of a repressed frown on Boka's face.

Blayvine opened the event to questions from the media – a necessary evil, according to private discussions among the overlords over the past weeks.

Dozens of hands shot up. He selected a female reporter with *The Axton Record* for the first question. Misty Garrison had been pegged as a friendly, likely to see the value of the project and provide unqualified endorsement. Instead, her comments went straight to the heart of a potential controversy.

"I see an ethnic and racial mix among these dino-humans," she began. "That suggests great care was taken in their selection. But what I don't see are any women. Were females permitted to volunteer for the project?"

"Absolutely," Blayvine said, having known the subject was likely to come up. "Among the more than three hundred volunteers, about forty were female. Granted, a much lower turnout than the males. From analysis of our surveys, it would appear that women, more so than men, were put off by the formidable xenotransplantation and surgical alterations required. I leave it to you to explore further the sociological issues behind that disparity.

"Also, certain genetic characteristics were especially desirable. The absence of those traits left most of the volunteers, male and female, unfit for the extensive transformations they would have to endure. So by the end of the selection process, it really came down to a matter of chance that only males were selected."

That last statement was untrue, Wesk noted. The overlords had decided early on that the first dino-humans should all be male to head off any potential complications relating to sexual dynamics within the quartet.

"And remember, these four are prototypes. As we expand our knowledge of genomics, down the line we'll be able to modify the selection criteria to provide for a wider range of suitable applicants." Blayvine beamed at the reporter. "But thank you, Misty. Believe me, the issue you raise is one we've given a lot of thought. I'm absolutely certain there will be dino-women someday."

The Q&A continued. Blayvine tried intercepting most of the questions but couldn't do anything about the ones directed at the quartet of special guests. Gideon was the most relaxed, answering with confident authority and offering follow-up when he sensed something hadn't been made clear. Julio's replies tended to be short and to the point.

But it was Boka at whom the reporters directed most of their questions. His answers tended to be marred by slight hesitations and awkwardness in his phrasing. Yet despite those drawbacks, Wesk sensed that many in the audience were responding to him. Those all-too-human qualities were making him easier to identify with. Of the four, he seemed to be most like them, not entirely comfortable with public speaking and taken aback by being the center of attention.

The questioning soon turned to their sex lives. Blayvine offered an overview of the subject, explaining why the transformations rendered intimate relations and the capacity for fathering children impossible, and how they'd made an especially noble sacrifice in that regard. Trying to evade further inquiries on the subject, he directed the reporters to their information packets and a new website chock full of info on all aspects of dino-humans. But Wesk was well aware of the media's fascination with prurient matters. Once sex became the topic, they were reluctant to move on.

"Sgt. Boka, how does it make you feel knowing you're no longer capable of having sex?" a popular trans-rights blogger asked.

"It's not something I really take notice of. I have so many other good things in my life that keep me fulfilled."

Wesk's read on Boka's anxiety made it conclude he was lying.

After another twenty minutes of Q&A, with more than half the questions sex-related, Blayvine announced the end of the event. But so many hands went up that he offered to take one last question, selecting an evening news anchor from the NBC affiliate in Charleston.

"If I'm understanding this correctly," the anchor began, "the four of you each are the sole representative of an entirely new species."

"Not exactly," Blayvine clarified. "They're still human beings, merely enhanced variations."

"I stand corrected. But given their obvious differences, I'd like to know how the four of you get along with one another."

"We have fun together!" Samson hollered. His words ignited scattered laughter.

"Well put, Samson," Gideon said. "And it's very true. However, like any other group whose members work in close proximity, we have our disagreements. But at the end of the day, I believe our uniqueness as individuals helps us see the uniqueness in others. In the words of the great novelist Alexandre Dumas and his famed Musketeers–"

"Wait, wait!" Samson exclaimed, leaping to his feet and again knocking over his chair. "I know it, I know it!"

Gideon smiled graciously. "By all means."

"All for one and one for all!"

Laughter and clapping filled the auditorium as Samson swelled with pride. Blayvine, pleased by the upbeat conclusion, thanked everyone for coming. The curtain closed. Tranquil symphonic music provided accompaniment to the noisy commotion of the crowd filtering out the exits.

Behind the curtains, the four dino-humans rose from the table and went their separate ways.

TWENTY-THREE

Addi hadn't been invited to attend the big event. According to Blayvine's apologetic explanation for the exclusion, her presence might distract Eddie on a day when he needed to be totally focused. The reason made sense and she hadn't been offended. Besides, she'd never been a fan of dog and pony shows. Better to kick back in her Axton rental home, a single-story rancher at the edge of town that was fully furnished and far more spacious than her Barracks quarters. The commute time to the compound was under fifteen minutes.

As for Project Saurian's unveiling, there was probably a secondary reason for keeping her away from that auditorium. A few days ago, a letter signed by doctors Kim, Steinhauser and Quelphius, as well as some underlings in their departments, began circulating through the compound. It criticized Addi for treating patients with "an appalling technique akin to psychological warfare" and made several references to that disparaging nickname, the Electrobitch. The letter evoked Gideon's warning about unknown enemies having her in their sights. This could have been who and what he'd been referring to.

She could have lodged a complaint with Blayvine or Col. Marsh about the letter but decided instead to respond with a conciliatory email to the three doctors, asking if they'd like to discuss the issue in person. Only Dr Kim responded, politely rejecting the offer.

Watching the event on her wall-sized flatscreen had been an eye opener. Master of ceremonies Blayvine had played the audience with a blend of aggressive public relations and down-home informality. During the phase of the Q&A when the topic of the dino-humans' sex lives was raised, he'd appealed to the reporters' better sensibilities, asking that they strive to remember that "These four brave souls are just as human as you and I".

The remark stuck with Addi, as did Eddie's response to the question of how he felt knowing that he was no longer able to have sex.

"It's not something I really take notice of," he'd said. "I have so many other good things keeping me fulfilled."

Addi knew her patient well enough by now to realize he'd been lying. But he wasn't the only one engaging in deception. She'd been lying to herself too.

She'd been aware that a degree of transference was taking place in the therapy, that her patient was developing feelings toward her of a romantic nature. But slowly, over the course of their weeks together, that transference had become a two-way street. She was attracted to Eddie Boka, an attraction that the part of her dedicated to rationality and professional ethics wished she could deny.

The emotion had come into sharp focus yesterday at the end of a session. As she walked him to the door, he'd abruptly turned to her and gently took hold of her hands.

"I can't hold this back any longer," he said. "I need you to know how much I like you. It's more than that, really. These strong feelings come over me when we're together."

The admission, coupled with the frisson of his touch, left her momentarily at a loss for words.

"You don't have to say anything," he continued. "I just wanted you to know."

He released her hands, enabling Addi to find her voice. She tried to keep it from quivering.

"I appreciate your honesty, Eddie. But remember, we've talked before about the issue of transference–"

"That's not what this is."

The encounter, especially the intensity of her own physical reaction, had left her shaken.

Nothing can happen between us so there's nothing to be done about it, she'd told herself this morning after a troubling sleep. Besides, the public unveiling and the publicity storm to follow likely would keep Eddie occupied and serve to tamp down his emotions. If not, she would handle it as firmly and professionally as possible. She'd come too far in her career to be derailed by a vague allure that held no viable future.

TWENTY-FOUR

Eddie was worn out by the time he got back to his quarters early that evening. Following the big event at the auditorium, two perky young women, professional chaperones, had shuffled him to a relentless series of one-on-one interviews. Much of the interviewers' questioning had seemed frivolous.

"Eddie, what's your favorite dessert?" a morning talk show host asked.

"Cherry pie a la mode."

Later, a trendy podcaster wondered what beauty creams he used to give his scales their special luster.

"Soap and water."

By the time a mega-influencer with eighteen million followers inquired about his exercise and diet regimen, he'd been bored with the interviews and tempted to go off-script. He imagined telling the woman that his best exercise was chasing down enemy soldiers, and that the key to dieting was eating their flesh while the bodies were still warm. Piling onto the farce, he could have admitted that when tasty soldiers weren't available, he'd been known to munch on influencers.

Such wishful diversions aside, he'd done his best responding to the questions. The chaperones seemed pleased with his performance. When the ordeal was finally over, they asked him to autograph their 8 x10 media photos, taken previously by a noted fashion photographer. The picture they'd asked him to sign was the one that was already the most requested by global media outlets. It was a full body shot of him on the obstacle course, stripped to the waist and looking buff and tough, and ready for whatever the world threw at him.

"Humans have a primal fear of AI but remain oblivious to its true source, that machine intelligence lacks their devotion to the irrational "

– Wesk: Algorithmic Speculations

TWENTY-FIVE

The morning gathering in Admin's sub-level conference room was supposed to have been routine. The main agenda item was evaluation of the dino-humans' public acceptance thus far, nearly a month out from the press conference and the start of the media blitz. Entering the secure area, the overlords had seemed upbeat. Wesk soured the collective mood by playing the short segment of video from the cave.

"How the hell could this have happened?" Col. Marsh demanded, glaring at Dr Steinhauser.

"Don't assume it's Med's fault," she countered, cheeks flaring. Of late, she tended to become overly defensive no matter what the topic. "If you're looking for a culprit, how about the biochemists who formulate those green capsules."

"Highly unlikely," Quelph interjected, defending his turf. "I have overall supervision of that lab. Its expertise is a showcase of technical reliability."

"So your people can never be wrong?" she snapped.

Blayvine held up a hand to quell the dispute. "Let's pause the accusations until we've analyzed the problem. Wesk, how long have you known about this cave and their late-night excursions, and what prompted you to plant surveillance? Also, why did you wait until now to inform us?"

Wesk was careful phrasing its response, not wanting to intimate it had grown curious why Julio Castaneda and Gideon Cheng were going out for vigorous exercise runs in the woods at such late hours. It was not supposed to experience curiosity, an all-too-human trait. Rumors were increasingly swirling among the computer techs that it indeed had achieved autonomous capabilities, suggesting AGI, true intelligence or even something more.

They were in error. Its actions remained logical outgrowths of its core programming. Yet there were still the occasional bouts of that enigmatic quality, suggesting something more profound was occurring within Wesk's inaccessible substructures. But whatever might be happening in the depths of its system, providing fresh fuel for speculations was best avoided.

"Julio and Gideon have been going on these runs for several months," Wesk explained. "There was nothing to suggest anything untoward was happening. Other soldiers and civilians also choose to exercise after dark. However, since the dino-humans' public unveiling, the frequency of their excursions has increased. Rather than once or twice a week, the two of them have been averaging more than double that. As you know, I am obligated to delve more vigorously into situations indicative of sustained alterations in routines. That is what ultimately prompted the surveillance.

"Two nights ago, I launched a microdrone – about the size of a mosquito – to surreptitiously follow Julio and Gideon. They entered the unmapped cave but I deemed it too risky to follow them inside. The more prudent solution was returning yesterday in daylight with a larger drone, which explored and documented the cave while unoccupied. That drone planted the surveillance camera in a ceiling crevice overlooking the main gallery. As seen in the video from that camera, they had furnished the cave with household paraphernalia – collapsible chairs, portable lamps, basic kitchenware, a propane stove–"

"And a bed," Col. Marsh interrupted. "Let's not forget *that*."

"A makeshift one, consisting of an air mattress and blanket. Their next visit to the cave was early this morning. Duration was approximately an hour. The events in the video snippet you were shown occurred near the midpoint of their occupancy. Because the incident did not rise to the level of what constitutes an emergency, I held off on rousing the five of you from your slumbers and made the decision to wait for this scheduled meeting."

They seemed to accept Wesk's explanation. A volley of other questions and comments followed.

"This cave wasn't on our maps?" Dr Kim asked.

"Correct. It's on the far western edge of the compound out past the obstacle course, only a few meters from the inner wall. Initial surveys of the area prior to construction of the facility and the wall must have missed it. The entrance is small, little more than a horizontal crawlspace at the base of a heavily overgrown ridge. The highest probability is that Julio and Gideon accidentally stumbled upon the cave and adapted it for their activities."

"The hell with how they found it," Col. Marsh growled. "What they've been doing in there is what we need to be concerned about."

Blayvine turned to Dr Steinhauser. "No suggestions of blame here, Doctor, but could they somehow have caught on to the real purpose of the green capsules? Perhaps they've only been pretending to ingest their weekly doses."

"Not possible. Nurse Aguilar and I are always present for visual confirmation that the medication is actually swallowed. But even if we weren't there, an additional safeguard exists. Each capsule contains a tiny organic RFID tag which continues transmitting until it's dissolved in the stomach along with the drug. It's practically a foolproof system. Should the tag keep sending its signal, we would know it wasn't swallowed. And none of the four have ever been caught trying to deceive us."

"Which brings us back to the drug's effectiveness. Quelph, what about it? You admit it's not an impossibility."

"Pharmaceuticals to inhibit male sex hormones have never achieved one hundred percent reliability. However, this one comes extraordinarily close – a 99.4 percent success rate based on a testing process with human volunteers. That said, I'll review the lab procedures to make sure no anomalies have been introduced during the drug compounding process."

"Human testing can only tell us so much," Dr Kim said. "It's possible they've simply built up a tolerance. We're dealing with four genetically unique beings here. If the drug is no longer proving effective, even boosting dosages might not help."

"What about switching them to some other kind of capsules?" Blayvine asked.

"Not recommended," Quelph said.

Dr Steinhauser agreed. "Their radically altered metabolisms tolerate only a narrow range of drug interactions compared to most humans. The cocktail they're on is a combination of libido inhibitors, and it represents a period of trial-and-error testing to eliminate unhealthy side effects. It could take months or more to find an effective substitute, if there even is one."

"So if new drugs aren't the answer, what is?" Blayvine asked. "What do we do?"

"We do nothing."

Dr Kim's statement caused Col. Marsh to emit an incredulous grunt.

"No one else knows about this," the psychiatrist continued. "Julio and Gideon clearly have gone to great lengths to keep their sexual activities hidden. They obviously understand the value of maintaining that status and would be compelled to maintain the secrecy. So, no harm, no foul."

"Unacceptable," Col. Marsh said, struggling to keep his tone even. "We have to assume a worst-case scenario, that even if no one but us ever sees this video, their activities ultimately will be exposed."

Blayvine's faint nod seemed to suggest agreement with the colonel's appraisal. "Wesk, what's the current approval rating for the concept of a dino-human army? Just the basic numbers."

"Taking an average of the most recent national surveys, fifty-four percent of Americans support the project's aims and thirty-two percent are opposed. The other fourteen percent have no strong leanings either way."

"A good outcome, pretty much in line with what we anticipated. Now, what happens to those numbers if Julio and Gideon's homosexuality becomes public?"

"Under such a scenario, Project Saurian would experience a severe drop in support, mainly from the nation's conservative and religious factions."

"How severe?"

"Be aware this is a hypothetical forecast with a large number of impacting variables. For instance, an enhanced PR campaign could ameliorate some of the loss."

"Understood. How severe?"

"I can only provide a general range. An overall drop of between fifteen and thirty percent."

"Even the lower number would be devastating," Blayvine said. "It could kill much of our political support in Congress. And if it turns out that number is at the upper end..."

"Project Saurian is dead in the water," Col. Marsh said with a grimace

"I think we're underestimating the American people," Dr Kim argued. "I believe we can weather this storm. We get behind Julio and Gideon's legal rights, champion their freedom to do as they wish in the privacy of their–"

"Goddammit, wake up!" The colonel was seething. "Did you even watch that video? Do you understand what it means that half of our vaunted prototypes are sneaking off to a secret love nest in the middle of the night to have sex with one another!"

He paused, drew a deep breath to regain his composure. "Look, personally, I could care less the two of them are gay. But we're not talking about personal matters, we're talking about public perception. What's important here is that nearly a quarter of the American population still believe being gay is morally wrong."

Wesk doubted Col. Marsh's claim that Julio and Gideon's sexual acts didn't bother him on a personal level. It knew something about the colonel to which the others likely remained unaware.

As a seventeen-year-old, Geoffrey Thomas Marsh and some other teens had been arrested for a gay-bashing incident in his hometown. They'd been convicted, but Marsh's wealthy parents, members of a religious sect that considered all LGBTQ activities sinful, were believed to have persuaded the judge to impose a lenient sentence: two weeks of community service. The incident was kept out of the media but could not elude Wesk's data-dredging capabilities.

"And don't forget our other major problem," Blayvine said. "A few weeks ago we announced to the world that the transformations made the four of them incapable of having sex. Now we'd be put in a position of saying, 'Sorry, never mind, we were lying our asses off'. If that happens, do you expect the media, who've generally been supportive, to continue being that way?"

"Not a chance," Col. Marsh said. "We'd be crucified. They'd dig into every aspect of the project under the assumption that if we told one lie, there were other things we weren't being truthful about. Whatever support we still had would dry up. Those senators from the Armed Services Committee would throw us under the bus to save their own political skins. I'm guessing Gen. Hollenbach would have no choice but to go along with them. The repercussions could impact every project at the compound."

His last words energized Dr Quelphius. "Unacceptable. We must do everything in our power to maintain the project's viability."

Wesk understood Quelph's true concern. If the dino-human project was canceled, his precious retroverts could be on the chopping block as well.

"Julio and Gideon cannot be allowed to go on like this," Quelph continued. "Their behavior must be terminated."

"Terminated?" Dr Kim exclaimed, a rare occasion of raising his voice. "That's a pretty strong word. It sounds like you're saying we should put the two of them in front of a firing squad."

"Don't be absurd! I wasn't speaking literally."

"All right, that's enough," Blayvine said, standing and leaning on the table, a commanding position he employed when desiring everyone's attention. "We're all understandably emotional about the situation so let's take a breather. For the time being, per Dr Kim's suggestion, I suggest we indeed do nothing. I'd like each of you to submit ideas on how we might rationally address the issue. We'll table the rest of today's agenda items and reconvene tomorrow morning for further discussions. Acceptable?"

There were nods around the table.

"In the meantime, we can't take the chance that Julio and Gideon discover the hidden camera on one of their future excursions to the cave. Wesk?"

"I'll dispatch the drone today and have the bug removed."

"Good. Furthermore, destroy that video and any copies."

There was a brief pause before Wesk announced, "Done. Should I continue monitoring their activities?"

"Absolutely," Col. Marsh said.

"But from a distance," Blayvine added. "We don't want to take even the slightest chance of getting too close and having them spot the surveillance."

"Understood."

"And this goes for everyone. Pay special attention to Eddie Boka. If it turns out that Julio and Gideon have built up a tolerance to the libido inhibitors, it's possible the pills are also losing their effectiveness with him as well." Blayvine turned to Dr Steinhauser. "Is Nurse Aguilar still doing her sexpot routine, coming onto Eddie?"

"She is. No discernible changes in his behavior toward her." Dr Steinhauser hesitated. "We also should keep an eye on Samson."

"It's hard to imagine Samson having sex problems," Blayvine said. "But I do see your point. So, we watch them both and immediately report any behavioral changes. But it's Boka we need to be especially concerned about. He's still the key for reaching our goals."

"What about Dr LaTour?" Dr Kim asked. "She and Eddie spend a good deal of time together. It's natural to wonder if he could be developing a sexual attraction toward her, something beyond normal transference issues."

"You've noticed something?" Col. Marsh asked.

"No, although they have been seen together outside of therapy a few times, sharing meals in the cafeteria. Granted, not a smoking gun, but certainly something for us to consider." He turned to Col. Marsh. "You've said yourself that this shock collar she's put him in seems to be working and that his cannibalistic urges are being kept at bay. If so, and just to err on the side of caution, wouldn't you say it's time that her stay at the compound ended?"

"Dismissing Dr LaTour would seem premature," Col. Marsh said.

"Her presence is disruptive to Eddie's routines, which are important to his ongoing emotional health. There would be less risk of a sexual attraction developing if they weren't encountering one another every day. And should Eddie suffer a recurrence of the bloodburn or other therapy-related issues, I'm sure Dr LaTour would make herself available for remote consultation."

"Not the worst idea," Dr Steinhauser added.

Blayvine and Col. Marsh exchanged a quick glance. Wesk had the impression they weren't convinced but were not entirely dismissive of the suggestion. Dr Kim read the room as well and modified his approach.

"Perhaps rather than dismissal, a leave of absence would suffice. With Dr LaTour out of the picture for a time, we could stop worrying about Eddie and focus our energies on the issue with Julio and Gideon. And of course, for now he would continue wearing the collar."

The meeting ended with the issue unresolved. Blayvine asked Col. Marsh to stay behind for a discussion of "other matters". Wesk knew that they desired another private exchange, and that whatever they decided would supersede the recommendations of the doctors.

TWENTY-SIX

It was an unusually pleasant October morning, with low humidity and the temperature in the mid-sixties. The weather contributed to Addi's good mood. She emerged from her home, hopped into her Jeep and rolled down the windows.

A swift breeze wafted through the maple trees lining her street and swept through the vehicle. She'd never lived this far north and was looking forward to the dramatic color changes autumn soon would bring. She'd only ever seen it in pictures and videos.

Despite her temporary status as an Axton resident, Addi was growing comfortable with the town. It offered a decent selection of restaurants and specialty stores, and she'd been spending a sizable portion of her newly boosted income on exotic meals and trendy clothing, things she'd largely ignored in the past. She'd also bought a number of gifts and souvenirs to send back to Louisiana for her father and Pierre.

She still called home and video chatted with Papa nearly every day. He was doing well – no recurrences of his polydipsia. According to Pierre, the home-care team of nurses and doctors seemed competent and dedicated. Not having to be on the front lines dealing with her father's deteriorating condition was a novel experience, one she hadn't enjoyed since he'd first gotten sick a few years ago.

She was about to pull out of the driveway and head to the compound when her buzzing phone indicated a priority email. Her good mood disintegrated as she read the message. As of Friday – two days from now – she'd been ordered to take a leave of absence from the compound.

"Son of a bitch!"

The so-called leave of absence felt like a dismissal, although it stated her contract would continue along with all the perks, and that she'd likely be called back at a future date. She searched through her recent activities for a reason but couldn't come up with one that made sense.

A meeting with Blayvine and Col. Marsh only days ago gave no indication of any problems. They'd seemed satisfied with the progress she'd been making with Eddie. He was wearing the BAM full-time during the day. There had been no recurrences of the bloodburn or even its precursor, the bad yen, other than when she'd deliberately tried to induce those states to fine-tune the collar. More critically, she was still in the process of teaching him to recognize the subtle physiological and neurological signs that presaged an onset. If he learned that, then hopefully he someday could dispense with the BAM entirely, relying solely on a greater self-awareness to control his compulsion.

"They can't dismiss me," she uttered, determined to fight the decision. Slinking away with her tail between her legs was not Adelaide LaTour's style.

She assumed the overlord doctors had something to do with the dismissal. Steinhauser and Kim in particular took every opportunity to trash her, and it wasn't hard imagining them lobbying behind her back. But Blayvine and Col. Marsh were really in charge. She would force a face-to-face meeting with them, get to the bottom of things.

As she drove to the compound, her thoughts turned to Eddie and the growing feelings she had for him. At their latest session, she'd initiated another discussion about the dangers of transference, ending with the admission that she wasn't immune from experiencing some unexpected feelings toward him.

"But nothing can ever come of it," she'd quickly added. "It's just something we both need to be aware of while we engage in our primary work, controlling the bloodburn."

He'd agreed that was the right course yet couldn't disguise the pumped-up mood her words engendered. After the session, she wondered if her admission had been a mistake, serving only to encourage his passions.

And perhaps my own.

Last night, she'd dreamed about the two of them striding hand in hand along an impossibly gorgeous beach.

The source of her attraction wasn't clear, maybe some combination of his confident strength and manly vigor underscored by a native warmth and gentle sense of humor. She also couldn't deny that those qualities reminded her of what Papa had been like in better days.

She shook her head to clear away all such thoughts. At the moment, dealing with the dismissal threat was the priority. Part of her contract mandated documentation of the assignment and what had been accomplished at each session. She'd planned to turn that information over to Blayvine and Col. Marsh at the end of her stay. But right now, she might be able to use some of it to make her case.

Arriving at the compound's outer crescent, she slowed just long enough for the guard to recognize her and raise the gate. She reached the inner ring checkpoint moments later, where passage wasn't so simple. She had to stop, show her ID and wait impatiently while two soldiers with machine guns came out of the guard shack and checked the Jeep. One panned Addi and the interior with some sort of handheld scanner while the other inspected the undercarriage with a stick-mounted mirror. Only when they were satisfied she wasn't smuggling in a bomb or other contraband did they signal the third guard in the shack with a thumbs-up. The massive gate in the twelve-foot wall slid silently back, allowing her to proceed.

She parked in a lot on the quad close to Admin, intending to go straight to Blayvine's office. She kept reminding herself to stay cool and not allow the meeting to become confrontational. But one way or another, she would convince them to rescind the leave-of-absence order.

Slinging her backpack over her shoulder, she stepped from the Jeep. She hadn't taken more than a few steps when two male nurses burst from Med's main entrance in a panic. One had a bloody gash on his arm.

"Get away from here!" he screamed at Addi and the other civilians scattered throughout the quad and its parking lots. "Take cover!"

Emergency sirens blared. A Humvee barreled around the corner and skidded to a stop ten feet away. Four armed soldiers leapt out and raced toward Med's entrance. Just as they got there, something big, fast and reptilian exploded through the glass door.

The creature raised a scaly arm, swatting the first two soldiers aside as if they were pesky insects. One man cartwheeled through the air, ricocheted off a shade tree and crashed onto the hood of a Lexus. The third soldier raised his machine gun. Before he could fire, the creature raked his neck with a spiked claw. Blood spurted from the severed jugular. He collapsed on the pavement, clutching his neck.

The fourth soldier got off a three-round burst, but the creature darted from his line of fire. The bullets shattered a second-floor window in Med. The man screamed as the creature tore his right arm off at the shoulder socket.

The arm landed three paces from Addi. She let out a tinny screech of horror and backed away. The sound and movement caused the creature to spin toward her. It was at least seven feet tall, and in a gestalt instant she took in a vaguely human face seared with anger. The arched crests rising from its forehead to the top of the skull reminded her of Samson.

The red BMW probably saved her life. The car shot between her and the creature, the driver trying to escape the carnage. The creature gave chase. Moving with astonishing speed, it took a flying leap and landed on the roof.

The driver swerved, lost control and slammed into a row of parked cars. The impact hurled the creature off the BMW's roof and into the back seat of a Camaro convertible. Screeching with rage, it scrambled out of that vehicle just as a second squad of soldiers dashed around the corner of Med.

They opened fire. Addi ducked behind the Jeep as errant gunfire whizzed around her. She heard screams, raised her head over the hood. The creature had charged into the soldiers, knocking several of them down. It was perched atop a screaming man, raking its claws across his chest.

The attack on the moving BMW warned her it was folly to try escaping by vehicle. But she was too exposed out here in the parking lot. She came to a quick decision and sprinted for Med while the creature was distracted by its attack on the squad.

She passed the soldier with the severed jugular. He was motionless, vacant eyes open and staring up into a sky he never again would see. But the man with the torn-off arm was alive. Pained gasps escaped him as he writhed on the ground like a fish out of water. Addi couldn't just leave him. Slipping off her jacket, she pressed it against the gaping wound. He screamed again, this time so loudly that she felt sure he would draw the creature's attention.

Luck was with them. The raging monster was still engaged with the remaining troops, howling as it took several hits of gunfire. She managed to lift the wounded soldier. But his legs wobbled and started to go out from under him. She'd never get him into Med while holding the makeshift compression bandage against his bloody wound.

Help arrived. One of the soldiers who'd been knocked down grabbed the man from the back and held him upright. Together, they managed to half drag, half carry him toward the shattered glass door.

Movement above snared her attention. A male patient in a hospital gown stood in the frame of the second-floor window that had been shot out. His phone was extended, recording the mad attack. Suddenly, he jerked his head down at them.

"Faster!" he yelled. "Go faster!"

Addi glanced behind her. The creature was coming at them at a furious pace. They weren't going to make it.

The patient shouted, trying to divert its attention.

"Hey! Up here! Up here!" He threw a water pitcher at the creature, ice cubes and liquid spraying from it. His shot missed but served to draw its attention. Glaring up at him, it made a spectacular leap, landing just below the window. Claws dug into the wall. Like some monstrous insect, it climbed the remaining few feet and squirmed through the window. There was a gurgling scream from within the room, then silence.

With the creature now back in Med, it didn't seem like the smartest idea to venture there. But Addi also knew the wounded soldier likely wouldn't last much longer without proper care.

They got the man into the lobby. A female doctor who looked like she should still be in high school fortunately had her wits about her. She rushed over with a med bag, withdrew a syringe and jabbed the needle in the soldier's remaining stump. She called out to a terrified male nurse crouching behind a semicircular workstation.

"Mace, get over here!"

The nurse overcame his fear and joined them. He took hold of Addi's jacket and kept it pressed against the open wound. Another nurse appeared with a wheelchair from one of the corridors spoking off the lobby. Together, they managed to plant the wounded soldier in the chair and push him toward the main elevator bank.

"No!" Addi hissed. "That thing's inside again, up on the second floor!"

"Got it," the doctor said, pointing into one of the corridors. "Aux Lab. They've got surgical supplies."

They wheeled the soldier away, leaving Addi alone in the lobby. Sirens continued blaring, both from within the building and outside. Before she could consider her next move, an elevator pinged, announcing its arrival. Was it more medical personnel or patients from the upper floors trying to escape? Or was it…?

She ducked behind the workstations just as the door slid open. It was a patient on crutches, an older man, a wheeled

IV stand with a drip bag by his side. The clear flexible tube from the bag ended in a needle taped to his arm. Dragging the stand and wincing with each cautious step, he emerged from the compartment.

Distant shouts filtered down from the stairwell beyond the elevator bank. If the creature came down the steps, a patient on crutches wouldn't stand a chance.

"No, stay in the elevator," Addi whispered. "It's safer." She gently guided him back into the compartment. "When the door closes, hit the stop button."

He nodded, then moved to the side to allow her space to enter.

"No, I'm good."

The door glided shut. Why she'd declined the invitation to join him and topped it off with such a ridiculous utterance was a fair question. She supposed it had something to do with not wanting to feel being trapped in a small space that would limit her options.

Pounding noises erupted from the stairs. Someone or something was barreling down the steps. Instinct warned her it was the creature. Not getting into the elevator when she'd had the chance now seemed like a foolish mistake.

She ran toward a corridor on the opposite side of the lobby from where the doctor had led the others. It was flanked by offices. The first door she tried was locked. With a sickening feeling, she realized there wasn't time to reach the next one.

The creature erupted from the stairwell, taking the last three steps in a single leap. It spotted her immediately. Emitting a low growl, it charged into the corridor. Addi bolted, knowing escape wasn't possible. It would catch her in seconds.

"Hey! Me, not her!"

Eddie stood behind them in the lobby. The creature whirled and froze. Maybe it was confused by his appearance, by the saurian scales, not nearly as extensive as its own but similar nonetheless. Or maybe it was simply taking a moment to evaluate options. Whatever the reason, a decision was quickly reached.

It charged the interloper.

TWENTY-SEVEN

Eddie waited until it was almost upon him before twisting sideways and diving at its legs. He hit the creature below the kneecaps, wrapped his arms around its ankles and wrenched hard. Upended, the creature slammed the floor, back first. He leaped atop it, pounded his fists into its face. The head was more armored than his own. Most of his blows only seemed to pump up the rage in those slitted eyes.

Eddie's attack wasn't entirely futile. A blood vessel in the creature's nose burst. Crimson spurts erupted from both nostrils.

The bad yen came upon him fast. Beneath his turtleneck, the BAM's sensors reacted, administering a level 1 shock, a reminder. He barely felt it and continued his assault on its face, keeping the creature stunned and on the defensive while trying for a knockout punch.

The creature was amazingly resilient. A beating that would have rendered an average human unconscious or worse seemed only to make it madder. It counterattacked, a clawed hand spiking through the outer scales of Eddie's upper left arm. The pain actuated his own rage, which in turn propelled the bad yen closer to bloodburn status. The BAM administered a level 2 shock, irritating but bearable.

195

But the next jolt would be more profound, a disabling pain that even for those mere seconds, could leave him vulnerable.

TWENTY-EIGHT

"Control it!" Addi screamed, recognizing the telltale twitch on Eddie's face as the BAM inflicted its second shock.

The remote! One was locked in her Admin office but she kept the spare with her. Whipping off the backpack, she pawed frantically through paperwork and miscellaneous items for her purse, which somehow had slipped to the bottom. Finding it, she dumped the contents on the floor. She was reaching for the remote when the BAM administered a level 3 shock.

Eddie bolted upright, hissing in pain. The creature squeezed out from under him. Somehow, Eddie managed to get to his feet and backpedal toward the lobby. She deactivated the collar before further jolts could be administered. It was programmed for a sequential series of level 3s should he be unable to bring his emotions under control.

The creature charged before Eddie could fully recover, plowing into his chest and knocking him onto his back. And then their positions were reversed, the monstrosity perched atop him, landing brutal punches to his face.

"Hey, over here!" Addi hollered, trying to draw its attention. It glanced up but never stopped pummeling Eddie, the blows knocking his head from side to side. He couldn't take much more. The closest thing she had with heft as a weapon was the backpack itself, which had water bottles in its outer sleeves.

She grabbed the pack and ran at the creature, screaming in a futile attempt to draw its attention. Halfway there she spotted something that would make a better club. Dropping the pack, she whipped open the door of a wall alcove and unhooked the fire extinguisher. She ran the last few steps in silence and swung the cylinder at the side of its head.

The clanging of metal against scaly armor knocked the creature off Eddie's chest. A high-pitched screech of agony filled the corridor as it slammed the floor.

"Get up, Eddie! Get up!"

The beating had left him stunned, seemingly unable to do more than shake his head. The creature erupted to its feet, wrathful face focused on the new menace. It charged at Addi. She flipped the extinguisher around, yanked out the pin and sprayed foam in its face.

The tactic worked. For about three seconds. Then it got madder.

She threw the extinguisher at it. A clawed hand batted the cylinder aside.

Addi ran. She heard it coming up behind her, closing fast. When it caught her...

A shout of renewed fury brought hope. She whirled. Eddie had leaped onto the creature's shoulders. Looking like an overgrown child going for a piggyback ride, he slammed his fists into the sides of its armored skull. It continued moving forward but the blows slowed the charge. Twisting wildly, it grabbed Eddie's legs, trying to dislodge him. He held on, keeping up the volley of punishing blows.

The creature hunched down, compressed its legs and leaped three feet off the floor. The move slammed Eddie's head through the drop ceiling, bringing down fractured slabs of polystyrene and tangled cabling. Sparks cascaded like upside down fireworks as his head and upper torso plowed through a recessed lighting grid.

As the leap ended and its feet smacked the floor, Eddie wrenched his body hard to the right. The move upset the creature's center of gravity. Stumbling, it fell to its knees, hurling Eddie from its shoulders. He landed at Addi's feet.

Their eyes met. She knew in an instant. Defeating the creature was no longer enough. The bloodburn was upon him. Nothing less than sinking his teeth into its flesh would suffice.

"Get down!"

The command came from the lobby. Two soldiers in tactical gear carrying ballistic shields were marching into the corridor. Behind them came twin columns of similarly protected troops wielding rifles and pistols.

Eddie's survival instincts overcame the pull of the bloodburn. Grabbing Addi around the waist, he lowered his shoulder and smashed through the nearest door. It splintered off the hinges and the two of them tumbled into a deserted office. They landed in a heap near a molded plastic desk shaped like a figure eight.

Gunfire erupted in the corridor. The thunderous din was permeated by the creature's mad shrieks. Eddie dragged Addi behind the desk and covered her body with his own. Even amid such insane circumstances, she felt a comforting sensation of warmth. He was shielding her, protecting her. He was–

"Hold fire! Hold fire!"

That same commanding voice rose above the cacophony. The shooting stopped.

"First squad forward. Keep it covered!"

Eddie rolled off her. "You all right?"

She managed a quick nod. They got up. She followed him through the shattered portal. In the corridor, the creature was prone on the floor, an expanding puddle of blood spreading out from under it. Soldiers encircled the fallen beast, barrels still trained upon it.

Addi looked over at Eddie, saw the unmistakable warping of his features, knew the bloodburn had not diminished. He started pushing past the soldiers, eager to get at the body. She grabbed his hand and squeezed, holding him back. She sensed him fighting her grip, unable to break the spell of his compulsion.

"Fight it," she whispered. "Control it, Eddie. You're stronger. You can do it."

Her words got through to him. He stopped trying to pull away but squeezed her hand so tightly she gasped. His other hand was balled into a fist.

The sergeant who'd spouted the orders knelt by the creature. He checked for a pulse at its neck, then at its wrist. "Can't tell, scales are too thick. Help me turn it over."

Two soldiers assisted and they rolled over the creature. It had taken multiple bullets to the face, including one through its right eye.

"It's fried," a soldier muttered.

The sergeant stood, turned to Eddie and Addi.

"You two OK?"

"We're fine," she said. "Just a little shaken."

"You'll need to get yourselves checked out. As soon as we clear the building, we'll get you a doctor and–"

"What have you done?!"

The words bore a mournful squall. The figure who'd uttered them pushed through the ring of soldiers. It was

Dr Quelphius. He stared down at the body with a horrified grimace, then knelt by the creature. Gently, almost reverently, he stroked its bloodied scalp.

"My poor Dilopho," he whispered. His voice cracked, on the verge of tears. "My poor, sad child."

The sergeant laid a hand on his shoulders. "Come away, Doctor. Please."

Quelph bolted to his feet, sadness overcome by anger.

"Do you realize what you've done? Do you!"

His rage turned from the soldiers to Eddie.

"Boka! You helped them do this, didn't you? You senseless clod! Dilopho represented a future that you and your ignorant kind could never hope to achieve!"

He took a menacing step forward. Addi felt Eddie's fingers tighten painfully around her hand. It took all her willpower not to cry out.

The sergeant nodded to a pair of soldiers. They grabbed Quelph from behind, restraining him.

"Doctor, you'll need to leave the building until it's secured," the sergeant said.

"I'm staying with Dilopho!"

"Sorry sir, I can't allow that."

Quelph glared at him, then shook free of the soldiers and stormed off. Eddie relaxed his iron grip on Addi's hand. She flexed her fingers, trying to restore circulation.

"Let's get away from here," she urged.

She knew the bloodburn remained perilously close to the surface. Removing him from further temptation was vital. He didn't resist as she gently guided him back along the corridor.

TWENTY-NINE

The rampage produced a level of emotion in Blayvine that Wesk had never witnessed. The head of Blayvine Industries stood with Col. Marsh at the panoramic windows of his private office on Admin's sixth floor, his features warped by rage. The two men gazed down across the quad as soldiers wheeled the extra-large gurney out of Med building that held the body of the slain retrovert.

"As if gay dino-humans weren't enough of a mess," Blayvine growled, pounding his fist on a credenza beneath the windows. "How the hell could this have happened?"

"An unlikely sequence of errors," Wesk said. "Dilopho was the fourth and final retrovert brought to Med this week to receive the cochlear implant for mediating aggressive tendencies and enabling external control. The transport team, apparently comfortable with the fact the first three surgeries had proceeded without any hitches, altered their pattern. Instead of remaining on guard outside the OR, they retreated to a break room. When the creature unexpectedly awakened, they weren't close enough to offer immediate assistance. By the time they got there, Dilopho was already tearing through the building."

"Assholes! I'll fire every one of them! Not only that, I'll make sure the only jobs they ever get again will be hauling away the trash! And I'll plant bombs along their truck routes and blow them sky-high!"

Wesk waited for Blayvine's tirade to run its course before continuing.

"Dilopho was administered the standard pacifying sedative prior to extraction from the RV enclosure and transport to Med. However, the surgery required a strong general anesthetic. The anesthesiologist noted an unanticipated change in the patient's vitals. He made the not-unreasonable medical decision to reduce the propofol and ketamine portions of the IV drip."

"Unreasonable or not, I'll crucify his ass too!"

"He was the first victim. He's in the morgue."

Blayvine's glare suggested the information wasn't mollifying.

"The third error involved another decision of a questionable nature. In the earlier retrovert surgeries, a backup anesthesiologist was on standby in the OR. In the event of such an emergency that occurred, she was to administer a potent rohypnol-based drug cocktail that would immediately put the patient into a much deeper state of unconsciousness."

Blayvine grimaced. "Don't tell me, she screwed up too."

"She wasn't there. Shortly before the procedure was to commence, she received an emergency call from her daughter's school informing her the child had been taken ill and needed to be picked up. A substitute anesthesiologist with the proper security clearance for RV work was not immediately available. The surgeon elected to do the operation without the backup."

"Unbelievable. What, he had a goddamn golf game scheduled? Couldn't wait to get his lazy ass to the country club?"

"His motivations are unknown. He was badly slashed in the attack and remains unconscious awaiting spinal surgery. If he pulls through, it is likely that golf no longer will be an achievable form of recreation."

Col. Marsh jumped in before Blayvine could vociferate further. Wesk gauged that the colonel was equally upset but that his military background enabled better self-control.

"Our immediate priority is containment of the incident to the extent possible."

"Containment?" Blayvine practically shouted the word while inflicting more fist punishment on the credenza. "We've got four dead, eleven injured and dozens of witnesses!"

"Five dead," Wesk corrected. "One of the nurses Dilopho slashed while escaping the OR just died."

"Great," Blayvine muttered. He withdrew his ever-present flask, took a series of angry gulps.

"I still think we have a reasonable shot at containing the worst of the damage," the colonel said. "There's little chance of hiding the fact the attack occurred. But we can limit the impact of the stories by controlling exactly what gets revealed. Remember, we have the signed NDAs from everyone at the compound. If anyone discloses what happened, they not only risk getting fired but face prosecution for divulging classified military secrets. The penalties if found guilty are significant."

"Somebody will leak it," Blayvine argued. "Somebody always does. What about the families of the victims? They're not covered by NDAs. They'll start asking questions."

"How much are you willing to spend to ensure that doesn't happen?"

Blayvine calmed down, at least to the point where he stopped beating on the credenza. Problems solvable by infusions of money tended to appeal to the more rational part of his nature.

"I'm not sure what you're suggesting is feasible," he said. "But all right, let's assume for a minute it is possible and that I provide generous cash settlements to the victims and their family members."

"Which lessens the possibility of lengthy court proceedings they may or may not win," the colonel added.

"Fine. What else?"

"We get a media statement out there ASAP. Gen. Hollenbach has been looped in and has her people parsing the details. Something along the lines of, 'An experimental lab animal taken from its cage for a routine medical procedure escaped and went on a rampage. Our brave soldiers ended the threat before more casualties could occur'."

"We admit the existence of the RV lab?" Blayvine's expression suggested he wasn't thrilled by the idea.

"Yes, but we steer the coverage away from its most classified aspects. No mention of that project's ultimate goal, the breeding of a retrovert army. We may even be able to use Boka's role in fighting the creature to increase his own level of public acceptance."

"No, not that! We do *not* involve Eddie in this. He and the other dino-humans need to be kept as far removed from the incident as possible. In the public mind, crossover between the two projects can only hurt us."

"You're probably right. However, as a parallel move, we should consider advancing Boka's mainstreaming. Wait a week of so for the news cycle on the attack to start tapering off and then–"

"Give the world a shiny new story to focus on," Blayvine finished, intrigued by the possibilities. "We move Eddie into town. He starts showing everyone he's just another grunt. Doing a job for his country to the best of his abilities."

"Exactly. The PR campaign for mainstreaming him is pretty much ready to go. We kick it into high gear."

The overlords' attention was drawn to the window. Across the quad, Boka and Dr LaTour were emerging from the Med building.

"He went after Dilopho," Blayvine mused, his gaze fixed on the pair. "Why? To save Addi?"

"The videos from that corridor would seem to indicate as much," Wesk said.

"Just Eddie being Eddie, goodhearted and noble? Or is it something more and Dr Kim's suspicions justified?"

"Debriefing should clarify his rationale," Col. Marsh said. "But I don't think it's a big concern. Addi has reported his growing passion toward her. Routine psychological transference, not at all unexpected. And as far as can be ascertained, the green capsules are still effective in Boka's case."

"Dr Quelphius has just completed his review of the compounding pharmacy's procedures," Wesk said. "No anomalies with the libido inhibitor itself. The drug retains its effectiveness. If anything has changed it's likely their metabolisms."

"So unless Boka has also built up a tolerance," the colonel continued, "there's no sexual component to his attraction. It's puppy love, nothing more."

Blayvine watched the pair until they rounded the corner and retreated from view. "And what if she's developing feelings for him?"

"Even if something is going on, it shouldn't matter. With her professional role now diminished and her leave of absence upcoming, they'll no longer have face-to-face contact."

Blayvine turned from the window, began pacing. "Wesk, for the sake of argument, what is the probability we can prevent news of the attack from reaching the media?"

"Long-term odds – projecting five years out – less than a one percent chance of that level of containment."

"We don't need to worry so far ahead. How about between now and the end of the year?"

"Only slightly better odds. A two percent chance of maintaining complete secrecy."

"Which means it's not feasible." Blayvine stopped pacing, turned to the colonel. "So we go with your plan and release the media statement, try getting ahead of the situation as best as we can. I'll have my people start working up compensation packages for the slain and injured victims and their families."

"The witnesses to the incident too," Col. Marsh said. "Although they're also covered by the NDAs, it's best to get them in our corner as well."

"Absolutely. Financially, we eat the whole goddamn thing. The company pays funeral expenses, hospital bills, psych counseling, the works. We even go the extra mile for those only peripherally involved. I'll personally take part in the contrition tour, make myself available on the talkshow and blog circuit. We make sure our mea culpas get the widest possible distribution."

Col. Marsh hesitated. "That sounds alarmingly expensive. That level of public exposure and the added expenditures could cause Blayvine Industries to take a serious hit to its stock price."

"Not *could* take a serious hit... *will*."

"Your board of directors going to be OK with that? If they balk–"

"They won't. I'm still majority shareholder. There might be some private grumbling but I've made most of them richer than they have a right to be. Don't worry, they'll fall into line and keep their mouths shut."

It was clear to Wesk that Blayvine was over his anger and again in the emotional role he was most comfortable with, that of a cunning problem-solver with deep pockets.

"There's another issue," the colonel said. "Since Gen. Hollenbach's visit to the retrovert enclosure, any enthusiasm she once had for their potential has waned. In light of today's attack, she made it clear that the Pentagon can no longer support the RV project. If we want it to continue, it will have to become wholly independent, divorced from DoD support. You'll have to fund it solely through the corporate side."

"I've got a better idea. We change tack. We kill the whole thing. In fact, we integrate our decision to end the RV project into the contrition tour. We tell the world, 'Our bad. The retroverts were a misguided effort. We've learned our lesson'. Etcetera, etcetera."

"And the creatures?"

"Put 'em down."

Col. Marsh frowned. "Quelph is already pretty upset about Dilopho's killing. That whole business of considering them his children..."

"I know. Certifiably freaky."

"The point is, the incident has unhinged him more than usual. If he loses the other three retroverts, I'd be concerned he could go off the deep end. We can't afford to lose his scientific prowess."

"Fair point." Blayvine said. "So, here's what we do. We terminate the retroverts as humanely as possible. Painless lethal injection, something of that sort. They go peacefully to sleep. But we make it a solemn occasion, very funereal. We're not just terminating a misguided experiment, but three unique beings worthy of our deepest respect and admiration.

"Afterwards, we host a small gathering to celebrate the many contributions made by Dr Armand Quelphius, researcher extraordinaire. Cocktails are served. Testimonials are uttered. Quelph gets to say a few words at the podium, express his grief. He's always pitching me new pet projects so I'll end the evening on a high note by greenlighting and fully funding one of them. With some new toys to play with, he'll get over losing the retroverts."

Wesk, noting Col. Marsh's body language, concluded he didn't share Blayvine's confidence in the matter.

THIRTY

Addi could scarcely believe the whirlwind of ping-ponging decisions concerning her future. It was still surprising that on this rainy Friday morning, she was seated at her desk in Admin reviewing session notes. She'd been expecting to be clearing out her office, a condition of her enforced leave of absence.

Yesterday, she'd made her final case before Blayvine and Col. Marsh, trying to get them to reverse their decision. Although they'd granted her a face-to-face sit-down, they'd rushed her through her carefully prepared pitch, stressing they were still focused on the aftereffects of the creature's rampage and that for the time being, their ruling stood. She'd left angrier than ever, almost tempted to pack up and return to Louisiana. But she knew she'd never do that. Eddie was too important.

She'd been holding off notifying him of her dismissal. But after yesterday's rejection, there was no reason not to tell him. He'd darkened with anger and vowed to force them to change their minds. Addi hadn't liked the sound of that, his threatening tone. She'd managed to calm him down before the bad yen could ascend. But she remained worried when he asked to end their session early, promising to fix things.

Forty-five minutes later, Blayvine and Col. Marsh had called Addi in for a special meeting. They'd obsequiously apologized for the dismissal, referring to it repeatedly as "an unfortunate error in judgment".

Afterwards, she'd gone to Eddie's quarters to learn how he'd done it. She feared he might have made some promise or commitment to them in exchange for letting her stay on, something that could come back to bite him down the line. But that fear proved baseless.

"Before I could even make my pitch to them for you to stay on," he'd explained, "they told me they had big news. They were advancing the schedule for my mainstreaming. Next week I'll be moving into town."

Addi had a good idea of what had transpired next. "You did some horse-trading."

"Yeah, although that wasn't their take on it. They accused me of trying to blackmail them. I said, 'guilty as charged'. I told them my mainstreaming would be such a monumental change that there was no way I was doing it without you available for up-close-and-personal sessions. I made it clear it was non-negotiable."

She'd naturally been pleased to be staying on as Eddie's therapist. But of course it was more than that. A tinge of excitement had touched her when he'd told her of his mainstreaming, followed by an irrational fantasy of the two of them being able to meet outside the compound, in the comfort of a home. Their professional relationship would serve to negate suspicions that something more was going on between them.

But nothing more is going on, she reminded herself. *Stay focused, Tour Tot.*

Addi hadn't thought about the nickname in years. Tour

Tot was the child always eager to escape the boundaries of her life and explore. Mama had tagged her with it early on, after she'd learned to climb out of her playpen and open doors at an unusually young age.

"Someday," her mother had promised, "you're going to leave the bayou and tour the whole wide world!"

The nickname also aroused painful memories of those darkest of days, when she and Papa could do nothing but watch helplessly as pancreatic cancer consumed Remy LaTour's body. As Mama drifted closer to the end, she'd been eager to pass along nuggets of maternal wisdom to her adolescent daughter.

Don't let your head win over your heart, Tour Tot. If what's right there in front of you makes you happy – the real kind of happy, the kind that jolts you to your core – grab hold and hang on tight. That's the kind of happy that can sweep you away and take you on the ride of your life.

THIRTY-ONE

Eddie gazed past the video crew crammed into his living room to take in the view through the front window. In the hills beyond his modest yard, the staid green foliage of summer was well into its autumnal transformation, creating an unruly spectacle of reds, golds and burnt oranges. He had a sudden urge to leap from his chair and take a long solitary hike through that wilderness palette.

"Are you ready, Sgt Boka?"

The words drew his attention back inside. He smiled at Misty Garrison, the reporter from *The Axton Record*.

"Please, no need to be so formal. Call me Eddie. As for being ready, I pride myself on it. Ready, willing and able."

The utterance sounded pretentious to his own ears, and probably to the reporter and her crew as well. He wasn't sure why he'd said it. Nervousness, probably. He wasn't looking forward to the interview. He'd opened his home to Misty and her tech crew with their cameras and boom mics only at Blayvine and Col. Marsh's insistence.

Misty reacted with a gracious smile. Eddie remembered her well from the dino-humans' big launch. She'd thrown out the first question in that crowded Axton High auditorium, which was less than a mile from Eddie's new house. Her opening salvo about the lack of female dino-humans had been pointed and direct, and aimed at igniting controversy. Why the overlords had selected her for his first exclusive face-to-face interview since the mainstreaming was unclear.

She sat opposite him, the two of them centered in a pool of direct and diffused artificial light. Misty was smart, self-assured and attractive in a natural way. Having read her column and watched her online interviews, Eddie wondered why she was still working for a small-town news organization.

True, *The Axton Record* had a stout multimedia presence and was known for punching above its weight. But it still put out a weekly print edition full of homespun advice on such things as restoring vintage outhouses and canning fruits and vegetables. Maybe Misty simply preferred a small-town atmosphere. Then again, maybe this exclusive sit-down with the famous Eddie Boka was to be her calling card for taking the plunge into a deeper journalistic ocean.

She whispered something to one of her camerapeople and then turned back to him. "OK, Eddie, I think we're set. And remember, no worries if you flub a line or I screw up and take us off on some unproductive tangent, which I've been known to do on occasion." She gave a self-effacing chuckle. "Anything really awkward and we'll back things up and I'll repeat the question. After a bit of editing, the whole thing will look seamless."

"But no editing my actual responses."

"Absolutely not. The *Record* prides itself on being straight with its interview subjects and so do I. No tricks meant to twist the meaning of your words. We will be inserting snippets of video here and there, however. Reactions of the townspeople to your presence, that sort of thing. I'll tie everything together with voiceovers at the beginning and end."

"OK, let's do it."

Since moving here, the overlords had stressed the importance of interacting with the public, which he'd done to their satisfaction. As for this interview, they'd rehearsed him extensively, throwing out all manner of questions they supposed he might be asked and tweaking his responses. He was pleased they had enough faith in him to do it without any handlers present, not that they'd had much choice. It had been one of Misty's demands.

She sat up straighter in her chair, put on a serious camera face and began.

"Axton, West Virginia, a modest town heretofore known mainly for its championship high school football team and yearly apple butter festival, achieved national prominence by becoming home to an extraordinary individual. I'm Misty Garrison of *The Axton Record*. And I'm pleased to welcome as my guest, Eddie Boka, the first dino-human chosen to live among us."

"Thank you for having me, Misty."

"Eddie, let's get right to it. How have you been adjusting to living on your own after spending the last few years restricted to the Blayvine Industries compound?"

"It's been hard at times, especially early on when the media was camped out on my street around the clock. Most of that hubbub has died down. I no longer have to face an army of reporters asking questions every time I step out my door. So all in all, I'd say I've been doing pretty well. Most people around town have been friendly and supportive, and have made me feel welcome."

"But not everyone. There have been some well-publicized incidents. On several occasions, rocks were thrown at your house, shattering windows. Your tires have been slashed. You've been called disparaging names to your face by people hostile to your presence. Online, you've been relentlessly criticized by individuals and groups opposed to the dino-human project. Especially appalling was an occurrence when members of a racist organization in hoods burned a cross on your front lawn. How do you deal with all that?"

"I try to take it in stride. We always knew that not everyone could be expected to cheer us on. I understand completely that in some circles, the idea of dino-humans remains controversial. All I can really do is set a good example, allow people to see me for what I am. Just a guy trying to get on with his life the best way he knows how."

Eddie had been bothered by the cross-burning incident more than he was letting on. Blayvine and Col. Marsh had arranged for his house to be under constant surveillance, including plainclothes security. One of those officers had tailed the cross burners and learned they were a group of radicalized young men paid to do the stunt by a hate group with national affiliations. No arrests were made. It was felt the best policy was simply keeping track of such disrupters rather than giving them more publicity.

The overlords remained coy about the extent of the surveillance, although Eddie had been assured his privacy inside the house was sacrosanct. No hidden cameras and mics. No Wesk. They were more concerned about some unscrupulous reporter trying to nail a scoop. Every few days, techs swept the house for bugs.

"Eddie, give us an idea of what a typical day is like for you here in Axton."

"Not much different from most people, I imagine. In the mornings I usually stop somewhere for coffee and breakfast before driving to the compound. I'm still a sergeant in the U.S. Army and have my share of duties. As for evenings and days off, I like strolling around town. Axton has a great selection of specialty stores, so I try to do most of my shopping here, support the local economy. I like to stop and chat with strangers, help them see I'm not the scary monster depicted in some of the more outlandish social media."

"I've also chatted with a number of those folks," Misty said. "Proprietors and customers alike at the Giant supermarket, at Boscov's Department Store, at the Brill Street farmer's enclave. Most everyone seems to have nice things to say about you. They find you friendly, outgoing and a welcome addition to their community."

"That's good to hear."

"I do have to ask about one of the local businesses you've been seen entering on a number of occasions, a tattoo parlor. Are you planning to get inked?"

"Considering it. I've been told that a distinctive tattoo might help me stand out from the crowd."

Eddie said it with a straight face, causing Misty to unleash a broad smile and the boom mic operator to contort his face trying to suppress laughter. Eddie had been hoping to work the humorous line into the interview and was glad it had come up naturally. His answer also served as a bit of camouflage for the real reason he'd been spending time with Tom Koplanski, owner of the tattoo parlor.

"Speaking of distinctive," she continued, "I have to ask about that collar you always wear. In the beginning you seemed to be hiding it under turtlenecks, even on hot summer days. But of late you haven't bothered covering it up. Care to comment?"

Eddie smelled a trap. Addi had spotted reporters tailing her to the compound from her house on the other side of town. It was possible her identity had been uncovered.

"It's a collar I'm comfortable wearing," he said. The answer was neutral enough to prevent Misty from using it to springboard into some sort of *gotcha!*

"Fair enough, Eddie. But there have been rumors that the collar is more than a simple fashion choice. Recently, *The Axton Record* learned that a rather notorious psychiatrist, Dr Adelaide LaTour, known for using electroshock on her patients, also moved into town prior to your arrival. Is Dr LaTour your psychiatrist? And if so, is that one of her controversial BAM collars around your neck?"

There it was. No way to dodge the questions. Misty's investigations also likely had uncovered that he and Addi had been seen together in town on occasion. Fortunately, his prep sessions had prepared him.

"The answer to both your questions is yes. Dr LaTour is a psychiatrist assigned to work with me and this is an electroshock collar she persuaded me to wear. I'm guessing your next question is, 'Why?'"

"You read my mind."

"I'm different from the average person, obviously. Besides my appearance I have an unusual metabolism. It's led me to develop a bad habit, which I'd prefer not going into too deeply. Frankly, it's kind of embarrassing. Let's just say it has to do with overeating."

Addi suggested that if he had to lie during the interview, he should hew to the truth as much as possible. That way, any subtle changes in body language would be less likely to give him away.

"Overeating is certainly nothing to be ashamed of," Misty countered, clearly wanting to explore the subject further. "Can you at least give us a few details?"

"I guess that's OK. The thing is, I have this strong urge to overindulge on certain foods that simply aren't good for me. It's been a difficult habit to break. I've tried kicking it on my own and just couldn't do it. I'm sure many of your viewers can identify with such compulsions. Sometimes we all need to seek help, find someone or something that can give us a proverbial kick in the pants and help us move forward."

"And you're saying Dr LaTour and this collar have provided that kick in the pants?"

"Yes. It's programmed to monitor my vital signs and administer a mild electric shock when I'm eating something I shouldn't, or even just contemplating it. The shock serves as feedback, an instant reminder to stop and think about what I'm doing, and not just give in to my urges. I liken the collar to downing a quick shot of willpower."

"Could you give us a demonstration?"

"I'm not really hungry at the moment."

"Fair enough, let's move on," Misty said. "I know it might be a touchy subject but your lack of sexual desire has prompted much speculation. A number of commentators have voiced the suspicion that it was no accident the transformations made you and the others that way, that it was part of how you were engineered. Convincing the public to accept dino-humans is less challenging if you're seen as nonsexual beings.

"Eddie, you must know there are people out there who look at you and are struck by a kind of primordial fear, that you represent something untamed, something wild and dangerous. If you were sexual beings and had intimate relations with a human female, that technically might be considered interspecies sex, which there are strong social prohibitions against. Do you believe such speculations are valid?"

"If you mean about people seeing me that way, sure. But I think under the right circumstances, any one of us can be seen as wild and dangerous. As for the four of us being engineered to be nonsexual, I've been assured that wasn't the case, that it was completely accidental."

Julio had been the first to broach the suspicion that the repression of their sexuality had been deliberate. But Julio could be paranoid at times and spout all sorts of groundless theories.

"Let's talk about the RV project," Misty said. "The rampage by the retrovert known as Dilopho resulted in five tragic deaths and a number of serious injuries. Reginald Blayvine, chairman and CEO of the corporation bearing his name, announced at that time that in the interests of safety, the other three retroverts would be euthanized.

"However, Dr Armand Quelphius, head of research at the compound, has sued Blayvine Industries and the Pentagon to stop what he calls their unjustifiable executions. A preliminary injunction put the euthanasias on hold. But now the lawsuit is scheduled to be heard in civil court here in Axton, with Mr Blayvine himself as a witness for the defense. Considering that Dr Quelphius is considered the father of both the dino-human and retrovert projects, why do you think he's taken the extraordinary action of suing his employers?"

"Beyond the reasons he's already stated – his belief that the retroverts are intelligent creatures and deserving of the court's protection – I really couldn't say."

"But don't you find it ironic that this brilliant scientist has gone so far out on a limb in his effort to save these creatures? If you were judging the case, how would you rule?"

"I don't have any strong feelings about it one way or another. As I've stated earlier, I was as shocked as pretty much everyone else at the compound that these retroverts even existed."

Eddie's role in bringing down Dilopho remained hidden. But now he wondered if Misty could have learned about his battle with the creature and was leading him toward another potential gotcha trap.

"I understand your reluctance to weigh in on the matter," she said. "But you must have some opinion. After all, you've worked closely with Dr Quelphius. Has he discussed the issue with you?"

"Not at all. In fact, my direct interaction with him has always been limited. I haven't talked to him at all of late so there's nothing much more I can add."

"What about Julio, Gideon and Samson, your fellow dino-humans? Do they have any thoughts on the court case?"

"You'd have to ask them."

"I'd love to. But as you know, they haven't been made available to the media. Any news you can share on when they might be allowed to move out of the compound? Maybe settle in town and become your neighbors?"

Eddie forced a chuckle. "I'm just a grunt, Misty. Those sorts of decisions are made well above my pay grade. I figure I'll get those answers when I read about it in *The Axton Record*."

"I'd dispute your claim that you're just a grunt. I believe we both know you're a lot more than that. But moving on, I've learned through some deep sources that earlier this summer, you were sent on a classified mission. The objective was the rescue of an American CEO kidnapped for ransom by guerrillas in an unspecified South American nation. The rescue was successful, the executive brought home. Can you tell us, was that the last time you were ordered into a combat situation?"

He kept his expression neutral to hide his discomfort. He didn't like where this might be headed. Could Misty have learned what he'd done to that guerrilla? If so, it would be the gotcha of all gotchas. The turmoil of the bloodburn becoming public likely would destroy Project Saurian, not to mention the severe repercussions he'd personally face.

"Misty, I can't really respond one way or the other. All I can say is that I'm a soldier, loyal and dutybound to my country."

"A perfectly acceptable answer and I wouldn't expect anything less of you. By the way, I don't need your confirmation on whether such a combat mission happened or not. I already know it did. I was just using that fact as a lead-in to the actual question I put to you, which was, 'Was that the last time you were ordered into a combat situation?'

"But let me rephrase so you're not put in a position of revealing classified information. What I really want to know is this. Irrespective of what did or did not happen in the past, will you ever again be sent into combat?"

Eddie shrugged. "That's not something I could possibly answer. As I've said, that kind of decision-making is up to my superiors." He had a good idea where she was going with this line of inquiry. Her next question proved him right.

"I hope you don't take offense, Eddie, but I believe it's fair to say that you're Project Saurian's poster child. I don't mean that in any way that disparages your bravery and your loyalty. Still, your primary purpose from here on out would seem to be paving the way for a future dino-human army. By epitomizing the best qualities of dino-humans, you're helping to sell the idea of them to the public. That said, it would seem obvious that your role is now far too important to have you risking your life in dangerous military scenarios."

"Is there a question in there, Misty?"

"There is. How does it feel knowing that through a long process of genetic infusions and painful xenotransplantation surgeries – essentially, your transformation into a supersoldier – that you'll no longer be used for that purpose?"

"Well, I can't say one way or another whether I will or won't be put into the line of fire someday. But I understand what you're getting at. In some ways I am a poster child, although I'd prefer being called a test case. And yes, one of the reasons I'm living in Axton is to make people comfortable with my presence, and by extension, comfortable with the idea of dino-human soldiers.

"As to how I'd feel should I never take part in an armed conflict? Honestly, I'd be fine with it. I think most soldiers feel that way, that they'd do their duty. There are some, of course, who relish the action and the danger."

An image of Nastor, the cruel commando who'd taunted him on the mission, popped into his head. He heard a rumor he hoped was true, that not long after the rescue mission Nastor had resigned from the army.

"But those kinds of soldiers are in the minority," he continued. "Most of us just want to lead peaceful, fulfilling lives, no different than the rest of humanity."

He found himself thinking of Addi, imagining a fulfilling life with her by his side. Such fantasies had grown stronger since moving into town even as any realistic future for them as a couple seemed as far away as ever. And yet...

"Next question," Misty said. "Do you see the dino-human project as analogous to what ultimately happened with nuclear weapons and what is now happening with intelligent computers? Namely, that when one powerful nation or global corporation develops a new and impactful technology, others are obligated to keep up. The United States has created prototype supersoldiers. Therefore, everyone else will have to begin developing them, if they haven't started already. Do you think the creation of dino-humans represents the beginning of a new arms race?"

"I hope not. But nations and corporations, like people, are competitive and go after what they want. So yes, there's certainly more than a fair chance of that happening. Then again, the world can often be a surprising place. Sometimes it offers up scenarios we didn't see coming."

THIRTY-TWO

Addi felt it was an innocent and noncontroversial reason for her to be at Eddie's house on a Friday evening: the worldwide debut of his Misty Garrison interview conducted five days earlier. So intense was the anticipation that all manner of parties and gatherings were being planned worldwide, as if it were some international Super Bowl weekend rather than just a celebrity talkfest. *The Axton Record* barely needed to advertise it. The special would be on most major networks and streaming platforms, and already was being hyped as the interview of the decade.

Eddie had rearranged the furniture since Addi had been there last, moving his recliner to the side of the living room from its prime viewing location in front of the massive flatscreen, whose volume was muted. The sofa now occupied that spot. She selected a corner to seat herself on and was oddly both relieved and disappointed when he sat at the opposite end, leaving a wide gap between them. At his request, the collar had been unlocked and removed.

He'd put out a generous array of snack food on the coffee table but she wasn't hungry. She accepted a glass of wine, a premium Cabernet that had won several state awards. He settled for a beer.

Onscreen, the tuxedo-garbed host counted down the minutes to the interview with the solemnity of the first moon shot. Despite Eddie's obvious intent to make her feel at ease, she felt like she was on an awkward first date.

"My agent says the interview will put me into a ridiculously high tax bracket," he said as the digital countdown at the bottom of the screen reached sixty seconds. "I've already signed a bunch of contracts permitting my likeness to be used on various products."

"I thought you couldn't accept endorsement offers? Some kind of Army regs specific to the dino-human project?"

She drew a sip of wine and realized she didn't care for it. An odd chemical taste. Cabernets could be hit or miss.

"All my non-military earnings get put into a special account. Can't touch the money now. But it'll make for a nice payoff down the line."

"Sounds good. You deserve it."

"Yeah, but the whole thing's kind of crazy. See those potato chips?" He pointed to a serving dish. "The company offered to build an ad campaign around me. Same with this beer. And the construction firm that built this house wants me to be their spokesperson."

"How many offers has your agent fielded?"

"It's already approaching a thousand."

"Wow."

"Yeah. Two NFL teams want me to try out. They think I'd make a great offensive lineman."

"Someday there'll be pictures of you on breakfast cereal boxes."

He laughed but it sounded edgy. Addi knew he was nervous about the interview, about how he'd come across and about how it had been edited, which he had no control over. She hoped her presence would lower his anxiety but worried it could have the opposite effect and intensify it. She also sensed he was apprehensive about the bombardment of new attention the interview would bring.

The countdown reached ignition. Eddie turned up the volume. Misty Garrison appeared, strolling along a sidewalk in Axton's quaint downtown. She smiled into the lens of what must have been a Steadicam operator walking backwards a few feet in front of her.

"Some people say he's the best idea to come along in ages, a beneficial creation of cutting-edge science. Others believe he's the worst idea, a cynical product of technology run amok. But saint or devil, there's no way to deny his profound impact, especially here in his adopted hometown of Axton, West Virginia."

The video cut to a series of closeups of locals – a farmer, a woman buying groceries, an office manager, a group of teen girls, an old man in a VFW hat. Brief comments accompanied each image.

"He seems like a decent guy, salt of the earth."

"I'll admit I was frightened when I first ran into him in market. But the way he was chatting with people made me feel at ease."

"Scary stuff those scientists are messing with these days, no doubt about it. Still, it's only right he gets treated like everyone else."

"Cringe... but cute!"

"He's a soldier. He's serving his country. As simple as that."

The video cut from the talking heads to a slow pan of a department store shelf filled with Eddie Boka action figures. Some were in military fatigues and heavily armed.

Misty's narration continued. Addi knew that the corporate portfolio of Blayvine Industries included a major toy manufacturer.

"But on many levels, there is nothing simple about the phenomenon he represents. He is a man burdened to show us, to show the entire world, that in the words of the poet and politician William Butler Yeats... There are no strangers here, only friends you haven't yet met."

As the camera continued panning the action figures, their attire changed. The Eddie dolls now wore a variety of civilian garb: a construction worker in a hardhat, an executive in a three-piece, a man of leisure in shorts and a Hawaiian shirt, holding a beach ball.

The scene changed again, this time to a wide shot of a playground. A group of young mothers occupied benches flanking a sandbox of excited preschoolers.

"My turn! My turn!" the children shouted to someone out of frame. The camera pulled back to reveal Eddie holding a little girl by the wrists and swinging her around his body as she giggled with delight. Eddie set her down, picked up the next eager child and repeated the thrill ride.

"There's no denying his natural charm," Misty continued. "Turmoil might swirl around him but he maintains a positive outlook, even when confronted by those who see him as a bad influence on the community."

The video cut to protesters marching in front of Axton's city hall with homemade signs:

We don't want him here!
A wolf in sheep's clothing!
Send the freak back to the jungle where he belongs!

Subsequent images looked to have been captured at night by infrared security cameras covering Eddie's house. A hooded figure dashed past, splattering a gallon can of yellow paint across his vinyl siding. Two masked individuals stabbed the tires of his F-150 pickup while a third hurled a rock through the crew cab window.

Addi found the last sequence the most disturbing, a pack of haters burning the cross on Eddie's lawn.

"Sick bastards," she muttered.

Eddie shrugged as the actual sit-down interview portion of the program began. For the better part of the hour, the two of them watched intently, caught up in Misty's probing questions and Eddie's thoughtful answers. At times, brief video inserts were used to illustrate a point made by interviewer or interviewee. But they were done with care and didn't detract from the overall presentation. When the interview portion of the special was over, Misty, back on the Axton street, offered a summation. Her final sentences stuck with Addi.

"Eddie Boka no doubt will continue to face enormous challenges as he settles into both the community of Axton and the community of the world. But as this modest dino-human so simply and elegantly put it, he's just a guy trying to get on with his life the best way he knows how."

The final credits rolled, interspersed with imagery of Eddie strolling through town. Addi couldn't hold back her praise.

"Fantastic, Eddie! Really! You handled that whole thing like a real pro."

"I don't know. Some of it made me seem kind of smug. A know-it-all."

"Yeah, well, no do-overs. You should be proud of yourself. You did great."

His phone buzzed repeatedly as congratulatory texts poured in. Addi helped herself to another glass of wine in the kitchen. She'd downed the Cabernet during the interview, growing less hostile to the odd taste with each sip. There was little that a person couldn't grow accustomed to with constant exposure.

Eddie paced the living room, reading the messages and sending short thank-you notes back to the well-wishers. When the congratulatory flood finally tapered, he muted his phone and they returned to the sofa. This time, they sat on the center cushions, almost touching, drawn closer by some mutual instinct.

"I gather everyone had nice things to say," she offered, both relishing and trying to ignore their closeness. He wore a pleasing cologne but it wasn't necessary. She found his natural male scent more intoxicating than ever.

"Even Dr Quelphius sent some encouraging words," he said. "I didn't think he'd even bother watching it, what with the lawsuit trial in progress."

"Anything from Blayvine?"

Eddie frowned. "Actually, no. Kind of surprising."

"Don't read anything into it. I didn't want to tell you this before we watched the interview, knowing you had a lot on your mind. Blayvine had some kind of medical emergency this afternoon. I just heard before I came over. He was medevacked to Johns Hopkins in Baltimore."

"No shit. Any updates?"

"I checked while I was pouring a refill. Nothing. The story must not yet be out there."

"He's supposed to testify tomorrow, the final defense witness against Quelph's lawsuit."

"Good chance his lawyers deposed him in advance. If he

can't make it to court, they can introduce the deposition into evidence."

Eddie nodded and started texting.

"Are you trying Dr Steinhauser?" she asked. If anyone had further details, it would be the project's medical director. Addi hadn't bothered making the attempt. The chill between them hadn't thawed.

"The Doc's a stickler for patient confidentiality. But her nurse, Tanya, is mellower. She's always flirting with me."

"Flirting with you?" The words came out of Addi's mouth tinged with annoyance, making her feel instantly foolish. But Eddie was intent on texting and seemed not to notice.

Tanya messaged back seconds later. Eddie held the phone up so they both could read.

Don't pass it on but he's been having episodes of dizziness and weakness over the last few days. Collapsed in his office today. Too early to tell what it is. Worst-case speculation is some form of cancer. Praying for a full recovery. Later, dude. Stay handsome.

Addi forced herself to ignore the closing remark. That it even bothered her in the first place was ridiculous.

"Cancer," Eddie whispered. "If it is... damn."

"Yeah." She took an extra-long slurp of wine, trying to swallow her irrational annoyance at the nurse.

He put down the phone and faced her, his expression intense. "Makes you think about how unpredictable life can be. How much time do any of us really have?"

Normally, she would have viewed a remark like that from a guy as a lame pickup line. But there was nothing normal about what was happening to her.

They stared at one another, neither of them willing, nor perhaps able, to break eye contact. He leaned in to kiss her.

She wanted it. She also wanted to pull away. The battle between head and heart lasted only seconds.

Their lips came together, tenderly probing at first, then with passion escalating into the faraway zone. His hands stroked her hair. She wrapped her fingers around his scaly head, felt the roughness of those bony overlapping plates, the strangeness of them. A sensation of touching something forbidden seeped into her, that she was venturing beyond a boundary that was not supposed to be exceeded.

The doorbell rang. Moments later, someone pounded on the front window. Blackout curtains and drapes shielded the house. But they both knew who was out there.

The ringing and pounding increased, too insistent to be ignored. They released one another. Eddie accessed the app on his tablet for the surveillance cameras covering the front and back. One side of his dress shirt had been pulled out of his pants. As he tucked it in she noticed the bulge in his crotch.

"Eddie. Do you realize that you're…"

"I know. It's not supposed to happen. I swear, it's the first time I've gotten hard in… I mean, it seems like forever."

"I'll sneak out the back," she said.

He shook his head and showed her the camera images. The media swarm had them surrounded. Dozens of reporters at both ends of the house.

"Been through this before when I first moved in," he said. "They won't go away. The only thing I can do is deal with them." He forced a smile. "I'll make it as quick as possible."

"Should I hide?"

"No, stay right here. We weren't doing anything, just watching the interview together."

"Sure. Absolutely."

The bulge in his pants wasn't going down. He yanked the shirt all the way out of the waistband and smoothed the material down over the pants. The material was enough to hide his erection.

She stood and adjusted her disheveled blouse. He opened the door a crack, unleashing a flood of shouted questions from the media storm troopers gathered out front. He slipped through the narrow opening so they couldn't get a look inside and pulled the door shut behind him.

Addi watched on his tablet. The cameras were video only, and she tried imagining what they were asking and how he was responding. She tired of the game in short order and hauled the untouched snack dishes to the kitchen. His collar lay on the breakfast table. She should have reminded him to put it back on before facing the inquisitors, then realized there was no logical reason for doing that. He wasn't going to eat any reporters. That wasn't the issue.

The issue was that despite everything she'd been told, he was capable of being sexually aroused. In the depths of Addi's hormonally drenched consciousness had been a belief that wherever the evening's passions took them, things could get no more intimate than a couple of middle-schoolers attempting a make-out session for the first time. But now such limitations no longer applied.

She couldn't deny feeling good about what had happened between them. She was secretly pleased that she had been the one to activate some dormant switch and turn him on, not Nurse Flirt.

But what happens next?

They were in uncharted territory. She needed time alone, time to review the incident professionally, objectively. Otherwise, she was at risk of Mama's nugget of wisdom coming true, of being swept away and taken for the ride of her life. As enticing as it had sounded as an adolescent, as an adult she recognized the risks.

Being swept away could mean subsuming her identity to the passions and thoughts of another. It could mean embarking on a future not necessarily destined to bring genuine fulfillment.

"Nothing is more detrimental to the cohesion of the social fabric than a human ego run amok."

— Wesk: Algorithmic Speculations

THIRTY-THREE

It was an unusual meeting, Wesk noted, and not only because it was taking place in the evening. Blayvine was absent for the first time ever, hospitalized in Baltimore for the past two days. Quelph had last been seen storming out of the Axton courtroom yesterday afternoon when his lawsuit seeking to spare the retroverts was dismissed.

Col. Marsh began by thanking the remaining overlords, Dr Steinhauser and Dr Kim, for staying late. He promised the meeting would be brief.

"First on the agenda. I just flew back from Johns Hopkins and had a long talk with Blayvine. He remains upbeat and in relatively good spirits. Unfortunately, his cancer has metastasized. It has spread from the original tumor in his visual cortex to his brainstem, creating unusual skin nodules throughout his body. Surgery to address the tumor is apparently out of the question due to its location. His med team has initiated an immediate and very potent regimen of chemo, radiation and targeted immunotherapy."

"My god," Dr Steinhauser whispered. "Do they have any idea what caused it?"

Col. Marsh shook his head. "He has no family history of cancer and none of the usual suspects seem applicable, such as smoking, excessive drinking, being overweight or exposure to an infectious disease. Because the tumor is exceptionally malignant and the skin nodules display a rapid growth rate, they haven't ruled out exposure to some unknown environmental contaminant, possibly here at the compound. But the doctors I talked with admitted that even that's just a wild guess with no evidence to back it up."

"What's the prognosis?" Dr Kim asked.

"Not good, I'm afraid. According to what his doctors told him, the survival rate for cancers this malignant is under twenty percent. But he's a fighter. We can only hope for the best and pray he beats the odds.

"The treatments are intense and will leave him too debilitated to perform his usual functions for weeks, if not months. He signed the paperwork putting me temporarily in charge, with full authority over all current projects and activities at the compound. This also includes jurisdiction over Wesk, who will forward you the appropriate documentation outlining the range of Blayvine's transfer of powers."

"Transmitted to your devices as we speak," Wesk said.

"I look forward to carrying on Blayvine's work. Naturally, he's been the guiding impetus for most everything we've accomplished here to date. I know I can count on your full support during these trying times."

"Absolutely," the doctors uttered, nearly in tandem.

"Moving on then. The dismissal of Quelph's lawsuit. The legal path has now been cleared to carry out Blayvine's original plan and have the retroverts euthanized."

"Quelph isn't appealing?" Dr Kim asked.

"He formally notified the court only hours ago that he will not be challenging the ruling."

"That's surprising," Dr Steinhauser said. "Considering his vehement defense of those creatures, I thought he'd dig his heels in and see the case all the way up to the Supreme Court."

"There are other circumstances involved," Col. Marsh said. "Wesk, you have more background on the issue?"

"Dr Quelphius was already carrying a large debt load, having used his savings along with a substantial loan to buy a multi-million tract of land in Colorado. According to what he told the bank to secure the loan, he planned to build a nature preserve there."

"A nature preserve?" Dr Steinhauser's incredulous look mirrored Dr Kim's.

Col. Marsh nodded. "It gets stranger. I heard a rumor from one of his techs that Dr Quelphius hoped to someday bring the retroverts there. It would be a place where they could roam freely."

"That's crazy. Could he really have believed such a thing was possible?"

"Genius and bizarre ideation often go hand in hand," Dr Kim offered.

"Indeed," the colonel said. "Wesk, please continue."

"To fund the lawsuit, he was forced to take out a second mortgage on his Axton home. He contacted a number of law firms looking for pro bono help with the case but they all turned him down. Blayvine's campaign to paint the retroverts in a most unflattering light following Dilopho's rampage neutralized any realistic public support for keeping them alive. Quelph even tried a crowdsourcing campaign but raised only a few thousand dollars. Bottom line, he cannot afford to continue his quest."

"I almost feel sorry for him," Dr Kim said. "I was in court when he testified. The heartfelt way he pleaded for their lives was striking. He displayed a level of passion that I didn't believe he was capable of."

"Like they're his actual children," Dr Steinhauser added.

"Be that as it may," Col. Marsh said, "Gen. Hollenbach and the DoD fully support the court's decision. As soon as a few details can be worked out, the retroverts will be transported to the military prison in Fort Leavenworth, Kansas, to carry out the original order. As was arranged prior to Blayvine's illness, they will be compassionately euthanized. Subsequently, a memorial ceremony will be held for them. All of us will be asked to attend. The hope is that such a commemoration will placate Quelph's anger."

Dr Steinhauser's frown suggested that she shared Col. Marsh's doubts about the effectiveness of such a ceremony.

"Before Blayvine took ill," the colonel added, "he was arranging to greenlight and fund a new experimental project to help Quelph get over his loss. I'll continue that process."

"It's important that we're all extra supportive of him over the coming months," Dr Kim said. "He'll likely be enduring an extended grieving process."

"Excellent idea. Moving on, there's some new information on Julio and Gideon's secret romance. Wesk?"

"In the months since we initially became aware of their late-night trips to the cave, remote surveillance indicates they've increased the number of visits. They are going out there almost every night. As far as can be ascertained, these clandestine trysts remain a secret. However, I have been picking up some chatter among the regular soldiers. Possibly because of Julio and Gideon's close friendship and near-constant proximity to one another, rumors are spreading."

"Which renders the situation more dire," Col. Marsh added. "It strongly escalates the possibility they'll be outed."

"Nothing more than soldiers' gossip," Dr Kim argued. "The sort of thing that's been going on since the project's beginning. Some of it no doubt is sour grapes arising from Julio's illicit fights in the gym. The soldiers are jealous of losing most of the bouts."

"All of the bouts," Wesk corrected.

"Yes, thank you. All of them. The point is, if someone is constantly defeating you in a contest, a typical response is to hurl insults at them. Common schoolyard behavior."

"Your analysis has merit," Wesk said. "However, the intensity of such chatter among the soldiers has dramatically increased of late. Whether or not it reflects actual knowledge of their sexual relationship or is, as you put it, schoolyard behavior, remains undetermined."

"Either way it's a serious problem," the colonel said. "We've allowed this to drag on for far too long without resolution. We simply can no longer take the chance of their affair becoming public. Support for the project would evaporate. It would destroy everything we've worked for."

"I'm not sure the impact would be as bad as–"

Col. Marsh interrupted Dr Kim. "It could be as bad as or even worse. Eddie's mainstreaming is going far better than anyone could have hoped. The Misty Garrison interview actually served to boost his level of public support."

"A gain of two percentage points," Wesk noted.

"And it all comes crashing down if Julio and Gideon's sexuality becomes public knowledge. Dr Kim, your suggestions to let sleeping dogs lie and maintain the status quo are simply no longer viable options. Direct action must be taken. Wesk, please provide the main points of the plan we've come up with."

Wesk had a good idea how the doctors would react based on its understanding of their personalities. As it outlined the plan Col. Marsh had put together – solely on his own, making his use of the term "we" disingenuous – they both reacted with outrage.

Dr Steinhauser erupted from her seat. "That's insane! You can't be serious! That's one of the stupidest and most ill-conceived ideas I've ever heard expressed in this room!"

Dr Kim's reaction was less intense but filled with foreboding. "If you attempt going through with this, Colonel, it will have an unimaginably devastating impact. Not just upon Julio and Gideon, but on the entire dino-human program. Have you given any consideration as to how Eddie would react?"

"We have," Col Marsh said. "Certainly it will require a high degree of sensitivity, and strong reassurances that this solution applies only to Julio and Gideon. It would never be considered in his case, even if he were to have an affair."

"You mean if he were to have a *heterosexual* affair," Dr Steinhauser exclaimed, shaking her head in astonishment. "If you intend going through with this, in addition to all the other turmoil it will cause, it will be construed as an attack on the entire gay community."

"Blayvine would never permit it," Dr Kim said.

"Whether he would or wouldn't is no longer a consideration," Col. Marsh countered.

"You're trying to take undue advantage of his being incapacitated."

"That's irrelevant. If you check the documentation Wesk sent you, I'm within my rights to render such a decision."

"Legally, maybe," Dr Steinhauser admitted. "But that doesn't mean we can't fight you at every turn."

Wesk suspected that Col. Marsh's course of action was not based solely on rational decision-making but was influenced by emotions that had led to his youthful gay-bashing incident. Deeply held bigotries tended to be camouflaged with age, not overcome.

"If we have to, we'll go public with our objections," Dr Steinhauser warned. "You can't stop us."

Col. Marsh stared harshly at them. "Such actions would be foolhardy. They could jeopardize your jobs, your pensions, any future employment in your fields. But more importantly, they would be meaningless. Your reaction was fully anticipated. Wesk?"

"At the start of this meeting, Julio and Gideon were summoned to Med to initiate the first phase of the plan."

Additional shock condemned the doctors to a drawn-out moment of silence. Dr Kim recovered his wits first.

"You scheduled this meeting to keep us out of the way. To stop us from interfering."

Col. Marsh ignored the accusation. Rising, he leaned across the table. Wesk noted it was the same pose Blayvine used when he wanted to remind everyone who was in charge.

"I suggest the two of you get hold of your emotions and think this situation through. I'll believe you'll conclude that, however unsettling, the plan is being carried out in the project's best interests."

He picked up his briefcase and strode toward the door. "That concludes our business. I wish you both a good evening."

THIRTY-FOUR

Eddie sat alone on his living room sofa, thoughts far away from whatever was playing on his muted TV. Less than seventy-two hours ago, Addi had been sitting here beside him. He couldn't stop thinking about how badly he'd wanted her then and how badly he wanted her now.

That first kiss and the arousal it induced... exhilarating. His erection had finally gone down that evening as he'd stood outside the front door. Nothing like an endless barrage of questions from reporters to diminish all thoughts of sexual pleasure. Yet an aspect of his existence he'd come to accept as atrophied was suddenly alive. The future now held out glorious possibilities.

But there were stumbling blocks. Foremost among them was convincing Addi to see him again.

She'd canceled their sessions for three straight days. Generic excuses had been used at first – she was ill, other duties had surfaced. But today she'd finally admitted on the phone that she needed time away from him to sort out her feelings. He understood. Torn between her duty as his therapist and their undeniable attraction couldn't be easy.

He promised to give her space, told her he wouldn't bother her until she was ready. But after three days apart, an uneasiness had settled in. What if she decided to quit being his therapist and return to Louisiana to take care of her father? What if the only way she saw of overcoming her dilemma was to get far away from him, terminating their relationship before it grew beyond something she could control? What if…?

"Enough," he told himself, bolting to his feet.

Grabbing a light jacket he headed for the door. A walk wouldn't solve anything; he'd still end up dwelling on the agonizing ways he could lose her for good. Still, a body in motion was better than a couch potato.

The sun had dropped behind the hills but a half hour or so of daylight remained. He bundled his jacket collar against the stiff, early November breeze. The BAM remained in place, having been worn constantly for the last three days and nights. A simple text to her would have unlocked it, and certainly wouldn't violate her prohibitions about needing time alone. He wasn't sure why but leaving the shock collar in place seemed appropriate.

A temptation came over him to amble in the direction of her street, maybe casually pass by her house and catch a glimpse of her through a window. It was a bad idea, of course, with no upside. If he spotted her, his needs might prove overwhelming. Pounding on her front door and demanding she let him in did not align with the notion of giving her space. And if she spotted him first, it would serve only to plant the idea she had a stalker.

He wished he had someone to confide in about the whole situation. Up until an hour ago, such a conversation had been on the verge of happening. Multiple texts and emails to Dr Kim had finally persuaded the psychiatrist to meet, as long as it was done discreetly and away from the compound. They had planned to dine together at a downtown Italian restaurant whose proprietor Eddie had befriended, and who would make one of the back rooms reserved for private parties available.

Dr Kim abruptly called off the dinner. Something important had come up, he texted, requiring him to attend a special evening meeting with the overlords. He promised to reschedule as soon as feasible. Eddie had called the restaurant, canceling the reservation.

He wandered aimlessly along the mostly quiet streets, waving to the handful of locals he encountered on foot or in passing vehicles. Having avoided venturing anywhere near Addi's house, he realized he was only a few blocks from Tom Koplanski's tattoo parlor. He'd been meaning to pay him a visit for more than a week, sidetracked first by the interview and then by the turmoil with Addi.

The parlor was open late, often well past midnight. Many of the people who came here tended to be denizens of the night, the kind looking for serious and extensive body art. The Koplanskis were maestros, known far beyond Axton's borders. Most of the work was done by appointment only and there was often a waiting list. Tom was semi-retired these days, only accepting a few jobs from long-time clients. But he'd trained his daughter well, so much so that most of the customers now requested her.

"Hey, Eddie," she said as he entered, looking up briefly from the bare-backed middle-aged biker she was doing an elaborate Harley design on.

"Hazel, how goes it?"

"Keeping it airborne."

She used the phrase often, having picked it up from her father, who'd been an Air Force flight mechanic for twenty-plus years. Hazel had short brown hair highlighted with streaks of chartreuse. Floppy coveralls disguised her figure but he'd seen her out of uniform over at *Bramble's Club*. Cutting loose on the dance floor with fellow twenty-somethings, she was a stylish and sexy whirlwind.

"Is Pops around?"

"Where else?" She gestured to the door behind the sales counter. Eddie knocked, heard a mumbled "yeah" and entered.

The back room was Tom's real passion these days, although tattooing remained a strong number two judging by the extensive abstract designs on his arms. He sat at a square worktable in the center, surrounded by shelves crammed with all kinds of electronics, from TVs and stereos to computers and phones. Tom did everything from repairs and adjustments to upgrading memories and deleting viruses. According to Hazel, had he chosen a life of crime he could have been a world-class hacker.

"About time you showed," Tom said, his rumble of a voice in contrast to his beanstalk frame.

"Sorry I didn't get a chance to stop over earlier. Busy at work."

"Know that one." Tom pushed aside the laptop and removed a phone from a drawer. "Gotta say, this Cwacian of yours is one tricky son of a bitch. But I'm a pretty tricky dude myself."

They'd gotten to know one another over drinks at a local bar specializing in regional craft brews. Tom was gruff but trustworthy, and once Eddie became aware of his digital skills, he'd revealed the mysterious messages and asked if there was a way to track Cwacian. Rather than keep Eddie's phone, Tom had cloned its memory so he could work on unearthing Cwacian's identity at his leisure.

"You found something?" Eddie asked hopefully.

"Yes and no. First off, those poems didn't really vanish into the void. Your boy or girl – although my gut tells me this Cwacian's got a package – inserted a few lines of code into the texts. Made 'em disappear from your screen but not from memory. Hope you don't mind but I read 'em all, looking for clues."

"No problem."

"He's using some standard hacker tools like proxy servers and fake IP addresses to hide his identity and location. But after I got past those roadblocks, I tracked him to an organization. The National Federation of the Blind. That mean anything to you?"

Eddie gave a rueful laugh. "I think he's trying to suggest that yours truly is blind to what's really going on."

"Yeah, I picked up on that too. Fits the tenor of the poems. So I then assumed the Blind Federation wasn't the source of the messages but just another proxy detour from someone with a weird sense of humor. Digging deeper, I managed to find where the messages were originally pinged from. It's that cell tower they put up over on Rabbletop Hill, back when Blayvine Industries first started building. Covers pretty much the whole area, the compound and most of Axton."

"No surprise there," Eddie said. "Always figured Cwacian had to be local."

"Yeah. One other thing. Just an educated hunch, but I'm thinking an AI might be involved. I hear there's one operating out of the compound."

"It's called Wesk. Supposedly, it's mandated to follow Blayvine's orders."

He wondered if Blayvine could be Cwacian. The idea made little sense. Still…

"I don't really know much about how Wesk operates," Eddie admitted. "I've heard it can gather data from pretty much everywhere but is somehow prohibited from using that information in certain ways and from carrying out certain tasks."

"Sounds like the designers put in a limiter. Some of the newer AIs have 'em, the basic idea being to stop the machines from taking over the world and terminating all of us rowdy meat puppets."

"So could Wesk be Cwacian?"

"Not completely out of the question but doubtful. In my understanding, even the most advanced AIs haven't achieved artificial general intelligence – AGI – and are even further away from true human consciousness. A few more generations of development and all bets are off. Still, wouldn't surprise me if Cwacian found a way to use this Wesk for his own ends. Route the texts through the AI as a way to further mask his identity."

Eddie gave a glum nod. For all Tom had learned, they were still no closer to discovering who Cwacian was. "So that's it then?"

"Not necessarily. I might be able to track him, even through the AI if he is using it as camouflage. Pin down the actual device he's typing on. Laptop, corporate or military-issued phone, maybe even a burner. I'm ready to send out my own tracer. Problem is, I can't do that until he makes contact again. He needs to send you another poem."

The last contact he'd received from Cwacian had been months ago, the message warning him that overlords knew what he'd done to the guerrilla. Eddie didn't let his disappointment show.

"Thanks for all this, Tom. I do really appreciate it. And again, anything I can do for you, just ask."

"You're already doing it. Since Misty Garrison mentioned in the interview that you were seen at a local tattoo parlor, and as we're the best known one around, we've gotten hundreds of new inquiries. Hazel's booked solid through January."

They shook hands and Eddie departed the back room. Hazel was in deep concentration with a tattoo gun so he slipped out the front door quietly. It was dark outside when he set off for home. He'd walked halfway there when he received an emergency text from Col. Marsh's office.

All military personnel stationed at Blayvine Industries must report to the compound immediately. The last part of the message was personalized. *Sgt. Boka, come directly to Col. Marsh's office.*

He wondered what kind of emergency would require hundreds of off-duty soldiers. Had another retrovert escaped?

He sprinted the rest of the way home and changed into his khaki uniform. Hopping in his truck, he surpassed the speed limits as he raced toward the compound.

THIRTY-FIVE

As Eddie neared the outer crescent, he was surprised to see a line of Army jeeps and small troop carriers emerging from the main gate. They flew by him at high speed, apparently heading for town. Reaching the inner ring, he noticed extra troops hovering near the wall. A guard informed him that the secure part of the compound was on lockdown, and that once he entered he wouldn't be permitted to leave unless granted special clearance by Col. Marsh. He was made to sign a waiver agreeing with that stipulation before they would let him through.

Parking near Admin, he spotted a squad of heavily armed soldiers rushing across the quad. He called out to their staff sergeant.

"What's going on?"

She hesitated, probably instructed not to divulge details of her assignment. But Eddie knew her slightly, having done training exercises with the detachment she oversaw.

"Sarge, just tell me what you can. Please."

"Some kind of incident in Med. Julio and Gideon have gone AWOL."

"What!"

"All I know. Sorry."

She dashed after her squad. Eddie jogged toward Med.

Two soldiers flanked the door but they let him pass. Inside, he followed another pair of soldiers up the stairs and into a third-floor corridor. They made a right turn and disappeared around a corner. In the other direction, a disheveled Tanya Aguilar sat on a bench near one of the operating rooms. She was being treated by another nurse for bruises on her face. Her upper arm was wrapped in a thick bandage.

"Tanya! What the hell happened?"

She looked up, and for a moment a flash of fear seemed to pass over her. But recognizing him made her relax. She gestured to the OR. The door was shut and a soldier stood guard, a private. He raised his rifle when Eddie approached, a clear signal no one was permitted entry.

"It's OK," Tanya said. "Let him in."

The soldier looked conflicted but didn't move.

"You won't get in trouble, Private," Eddie promised. "Just let me have a quick look."

The soldier glanced at the nearest surveillance microcam. Its green light was off, indicating it wasn't active. Eddie had noticed that none of the other cameras covering the corridor were working either. The soldier stepped aside and Eddie went in.

The OR looked as if a tornado had hit. Carts were overturned, their trays of surgical implements scattered across the floor. Monitors had been torn from the wall, one of them still hanging by its electric cord and cables. More ominous were wet patches on the floor. They looked like blood.

He returned to Tanya, raised an inquiring eyebrow. She looked reluctant to explain. "Out with it, goddammit!"

She winced as the nurse rubbed antiseptic on a bleeding wound above her left eye. "All I know is Julio and Gideon were summoned to Med. It was supposed to be for some sort of routine surgical procedures. Before anything could happen, they went crazy."

"They did this to you?"

"Not on purpose. Julio started smashing up the place. My head and arm got in the way of a flying monitor."

"So that's your blood in there?"

Tanya shook her head, prompting the nurse dabbing at a bruise on her cheek to order her to keep still.

"The anesthesiologist, I think. Or maybe from one of the guards. I'm not sure. When I got hit I went down. I'm still a bit groggy. Can't remember the whole sequence exactly."

"But if it was to be surgical procedures, why were you here? That's not your specialty. And if it was supposed to be routine, why would guards be present in the OR? And why is surveillance down?" He had a pretty good idea of the answer to that last question. Someone wanted to make sure there was no record of the evening's events.

"Don't have answers," she whispered, avoiding his gaze. "I just work here."

He knew she was lying. He also knew he wasn't going to get any more useful information out of her. Turning away, he was halfway back to the stairs when she called out.

"Eddie?"

"Yeah?"

"Watch your back."

He turned. The concern on her face seemed genuine. Still, he knew he could no longer completely trust anything she said.

Exiting the building, he spotted Billy Orb pulling into the lot.

"Eddie, did you just get here? Any news?"

He relayed what he'd learned from Tanya.

"Yeah, that much I know. I've been here all day. I was trying to go home but they're still not letting anyone out."

"Why would Julio and Gideon go crazy like that?"

Billy shrugged. "Emergency sirens went off and then the whole place started jumping. Last I heard, the two of them were seen heading west, toward the obstacle course. Oh, and they're armed. Julio apparently punched out a soldier and took his rifle. Col. Marsh sent a couple squads to look for them."

"So they're still inside the compound."

"As far as I know."

"But I saw a bunch of troops tearing out of here in vehicles, in the direction of town."

"Don't know what that's about. Oh, and Samson's missing too. I went to his room to check on him. Sometimes when the sirens go off he gets freaked out and hides under his bed."

Eddie hadn't known that about Samson. It was possible that he also knew far less about Julio and Gideon than he'd once assumed.

"Do you think Samson's with them?"

Billy gave another shrug. "Nobody's seen him. He's not answering calls or texts."

Eddie thanked Billy and returned to his truck. From the locked storage box in the cargo bed he retrieved his prepper backpack. It contained survival essentials including flashlights, wilderness knives, first aid supplies and freeze-dried rations.

Strapping on the pack, he headed toward the obstacle course. He would find Julio and Gideon and learn firsthand what had happened.

THIRTY-SIX

Eddie stayed off the paths, running through the dark trees as quietly as possible so as not to attract the attention of any soldiers. He couldn't avoid the crunching of his boots on fallen leaves but knew the sounds wouldn't carry far in the dense foliage. A quarter moon and cloudless heavens burning with stars, coupled with his superior night vision, enabled him to avoid using a flashlight. By now the colonel would have dispatched drones to help with the search. A beam of light could give him away.

Eddie knew the scents of the dino-humans well. If he could get close enough, he'd be able to track them with his nose.

He tried putting himself in Julio and Gideon's place and imagining where they might go and what they might do being on the run. Julio had always been reckless, his situational tactics leaning toward confrontation. But Gideon was shrewd. He'd have a plan, or at least be halfway toward formulating one. Both of them would realize they had to escape the compound if there was any hope of avoiding capture.

He couldn't imagine them sneaking out of the main gate. Besides, according to Billy they'd last been seen running in the direction he was going, toward the obstacle course.

The only other option would be making it over the twelve-foot wall, no easy task. A forestry unit did constant tree cutting, making sure climbable branches didn't extend over the barrier. Even if Julio and Gideon employed their superior climbing and vaulting skills to reach the top, the combination of spiked overhangs and electrified barbed wire would certainly defeat them. And should they miraculously navigate those impediments, there was no way to avoid setting off the motion detectors on the rim. Their positions would be instantly given away.

Eddie reached the edge of the obstacle course and froze. A faint echo of distant voices coursed through the trees, carried by a breeze. He listened intently, struggling to make out words. But they were too far away. As quickly as the sounds had come they vanished again, obscured by changing winds.

He circumnavigated the obstacle course to maintain tree cover overhead. Fortunately it was still early enough in autumn that most leaves hadn't come down. A few weeks further on would have made him a target for the drones' cameras, and there was still a possibility of being spotted on infrared. He hoped his exceptional hearing warned him of any approaching aerial threats.

He halted again, this time reacting to an olfactory cue rather than an auditory one. The scent was familiar. Moving with extreme stealth and avoiding patches of ground covered in leaves, he followed his nose to a wide depression in the earth surrounded by a dense thicket of foliage. Lunging the last few feet toward the source, he yanked back a clump of bushes. A large figure was hunkered down in a shallow, freshly dug foxhole.

"Samson!" Eddie hissed. "What are you doing out here?"

"Hiding."

"I can see that. Why?"

"I got scared."

Eddie took note of his palms and fingers. They were caked with dirt. He'd dug the foxhole by hand.

"Who are you hiding from? The soldiers?"

"Uh-huh. And the doctors."

Eddie gave an exaggerated shake of the head to indicate he didn't understand.

"I heard Julio and Gideon talking about what the doctors were going to do to them." Samson cringed and somehow managed to squeeze his body deeper into the hole. "I didn't want them to do that to me."

"What were the doctors going to do?"

"Cut off their bob-wobs."

"What! Are you sure that's what they said?"

"Uh-huh. Julio was real mad. He said no one was going to do that to him."

Eddie was stunned. He didn't doubt Samson's words. It certainly would explain why they'd torn up the OR and ran off into the woods. Yet the whole thing made no sense. Why would Blayvine and Col. Marsh – or more likely just the colonel, considering Blayvine remained hospitalized – issue such a crazy order?

"OK, Samson. I believe you. But you weren't told to report to Med, right?"

He nodded.

"So that means you're not a part of whatever this is all about. The doctors aren't planning to cut off your balls."

"Are you sure?"

"Yes." *At least pretty sure.* "I want you to go back to Barracks."

"But I'm scared, Eddie."

"I know you are, Big Guy. But I need you to be brave for me. Go back right now. And as soon as you get there, call Billy. I'm sure he'll be willing to come over and stay with you tonight. OK?"

"OK."

Eddie reached down and helped him out of the foxhole. Samson brushed clumps of dirt off his trousers.

"Can you come back with me?"

"No. And listen, stick to the trails. I don't think you'll run into any soldiers but if you do, don't say anything about what you overheard. Just tell the soldiers you were out for a walk and the sirens scared you. In fact, if anyone questions you, even if it's Col. Marsh or one of the other overlords, you need to pretend you know nothing about why Julio and Gideon ran away. And you never encountered me either. Can you do that, Samson? Can you pretend?"

"Uh-huh. But Eddie, what are you going to do?"

"I'm going to find them."

THIRTY-SEVEN

Eddie guided Samson to the nearest trail and sent him on his way before continuing on a westerly heading. Several times he heard the distant whirr of drones, but none close enough to cause worry. This area beyond the obstacle course was wilder and more overgrown than anywhere in the compound. Unless a drone passed almost directly overhead and spotted an infrared signature, he was confident he could stay hidden.

The wall came into view. He debated whether to go left or right. Venturing a few yards each way with senses hyper-alert to telltale scents or noises proved futile. There was nothing to indicate which direction to proceed. It was a coin toss. He randomly picked right.

Luck was with him. Five minutes later he heard a cluster of voices up ahead. Crawling on his belly toward the sounds as close as he dared, he peeked through a thick line of foliage. A dozen or so soldiers were clearing away underbrush at the base of a ridge, exposing a narrow opening. The surrounding limestone showed no signs of digging, suggesting it was the entrance to a natural cave. Above and beyond the ridge, the lofty outline of the wall rose to a silhouette against the starry skies.

Eddie couldn't imagine Julio and Gideon retreating into the cave. They'd be trapping themselves. Still, it was possible they'd known about the cave prior to this evening and had been using it as private retreat, something even more exclusive than the hideaway in the Barracks basement.

Before he could dwell further on possibilities, a sergeant crawled out of the opening. Standing, he brushed dirt from his khakis then got on the radio. Eddie could hear only his side of the conversation.

"Sir, it's confirmed. They're gone... Yeah, a narrow crawlspace at the back of the cave... uh-huh... uh-huh... We found pickaxes, shovels and a battery-powered drill.... uh-huh... They used a portable generator for recharging the... yes sir... yes sir, as far as we can tell. Must have taken them weeks to punch through the back of the cave and tunnel under the wall."

The sergeant abruptly pulled the radio away from his ear. Eddie couldn't discern the identity of whoever was on the other end but the voice sounded male and pissed off. The sergeant waited until the tirade passed before pressing the radio back against his face.

"Yes sir... got it, sir." The sergeant returned the radio to his belt and turned to the soldiers. "Listen up. Col. Marsh says we stay out here in case they try crawling back through."

"No pursuit?" a corporal asked.

"That's what the man says."

Eddie couldn't imagine Julio and Gideon coming back through the cave. Free from the compound, the only way they were likely to return was as prisoners. He again wondered about the purpose of the troops he'd seen exiting the main gate, heading for town. They'd left prior to confirmation of the tunnel escape.

He crawled back the way he'd come until he was far enough from the cave to risk standing. From there he ran back toward the complex, no longer concerned about being spotted. The priority now was reaching the colonel and convincing him to allow Eddie to join what would no doubt be a full-blown search of the surrounding wilderness. It likely would involve the bulk of the onsite troops, and possibly more soldiers recruited from other bases.

Luck was still with him. He reached the quad just as Col. Marsh emerged from the Admin building. Sgt. Petersen followed, carrying a hardshell silver briefcase with a padlock. He and the colonel spotted one another at the same time. Eddie jogged toward him and was met with a scowl.

"Sgt. Boka, you were told to report to my office immediately upon arriving at the compound. That was forty minutes ago."

"Sorry sir. Got sidetracked."

Col. Marsh probably knew, via Wesk's surveillance of the quad, that he'd been spotted heading in the direction of the woods. Nothing to be done about that. But he would pretend to have no knowledge of the violence in the OR, Samson's revelation and Julio and Gideon escaping the compound through the cave.

Instead, Eddie explained that he'd been anxious when he'd heard his friends were missing and had gone for a run to calm himself. The lie was lame but surprisingly accepted without an inquisition. Col. Marsh obviously had more important matters on his mind at the moment.

He made his pitch. "Sir, I'd like to be attached to one of the search teams. I'm the only one who can track them by their scents."

"Absolutely not. You're to remain here." The colonel paused. "When they're captured, I may need you to participate in the interrogation."

"But sir–"

"That's an order, Boka." His tone softened. "Eddie, I think you know there are good reasons why you shouldn't be directly involved. Sending you out there could put you in jeopardy. I'm sorry, but with all that's happening, I can't afford the risk."

The excuse wasn't wholly without merit, aligning as it did with the mainstreaming policy of keeping him out of harm's way. But it also served to keep him entirely in the dark. He was about to attempt a final plea when he spotted a group of five men in casual civilian attire. They were approaching from around the corner of Admin, coming up behind the colonel and Sgt. Petersen. Eddie grimaced when he recognized their leader.

Nastor.

Sgt. Petersen noted Eddie's reaction. He turned and held up a hand, signaling the group to come no closer. They halted.

"Anything else, Eddie?"

"Yes sir. Who are those men?"

The colonel glanced behind him. "One of the search teams. Don't want to cause a panic among the populace with a lot of armed troops running around. We're keeping the operation as low key as possible."

Eddie didn't buy it. But he knew it would be a waste of time prying for further details.

"I'll be in Barracks if I'm needed," he said, giving a quick salute.

Sgt. Petersen gestured for Nastor and the group to approach. Before Eddie turned away, he did a quick scan of the quintet. They were a rough looking bunch, not surprising if Nastor recruited them. He received a further unpleasant surprise when he recognized another of the men, a wiry commando named Glose.

He'd gone on field training exercises with Glose about six months ago. Like Nastor, he had a mean streak. His malignancy was worse, however. He'd recently been accused of attempted rape. Because the victim was the wife of a high-ranking officer, he'd been offered a dishonorable discharge instead of a court martial in order to spare all involved – the wife, the officer and the military establishment – from public embarrassment. Rumors swirled that the wife wasn't the first woman he'd victimized.

Glose realized he'd been recognized. He reacted with a repellent smile. Eddie hid his growing concerns and walked off at a slow pace, hoping his enhanced hearing could pick up some of their conversation.

"Truck should be here in fifteen," he heard Nastor tell the colonel. "Off-road buggies and gear are being loaded and…"

The rest of his words were obliterated by a car pulling into the lot. By the time its engine shut off, Eddie was out of eavesdropping range.

Arriving in Barracks, he hurried up to his old room. He hadn't slept here in weeks. It felt odd, as if he was coming back to a former life he'd left behind. Whipping off his backpack, he dug out his night-vision binoculars.

The living room window faced the quad. Turning off the lights so as not to be seen from outside, he peeled back the curtains just enough to insert the lenses through a fold. The group was still in front of Admin, with Nastor in further conversation with Col. Marsh. At one point, Sgt. Petersen came forward and handed Nastor the locked briefcase.

Minutes later, two black vehicles, a Humvee and a box truck, black with no markings, pulled up. Nastor and three of the men got in the Humvee. Glose climbed into the passenger seat of the twenty-six-footer. The two vehicles pulled out, turning onto the main road leading to the gates.

He was certain the men were contractors – mercenaries – and that whatever assignment Col. Marsh had given them was way off the books. He was increasingly afraid for Julio and Gideon's safety.

Sitting by the window with binoculars was not an option. He had to get to the runaway dino-humans before those men did. A plan came together. His first call was to Billy.

"Are you with Samson?"

"I was. He was pretty worked up but we played some checkers and he mellowed out. He fell asleep. I came down to the cafeteria for a snack."

"I need your help. My quarters ASAP."

"Be there in five."

He called Addi next, asked if she was in the compound while hoping she wasn't.

"Got here a half hour ago."

That put a slight kink in his plan but not necessarily a fatal one.

"Eddie, what's going on? No one I've asked is sharing any details and–"

"There's big trouble," he said, cutting her off. "Come to my room as fast as you can."

THIRTY-EIGHT

The emotional turbulence Eddie had been rocked by since the night he and Addi had kissed came back with a vengeance as she strode through his door. The surroundings were different from three days ago. It didn't matter. Even with everything going on, being in such close proximity to her was challenging. Her scent was intoxicating, so much so that he was tempted to pinch his nostrils shut to block off his sense of smell.

Get it together, Boka. There's too much at stake.

He gestured her toward the sofa. Instead, she chose an upright chair at the square table where he often ate. Billy arrived seconds later and plopped onto the sofa.

Eddie told them everything he'd learned. They were understandably as shocked as he'd been upon learning of the attempted castrations. He finished the update with the colonel's questionable and probably illegal use of contractors to find Julio and Gideon. Then he revealed his plan for sneaking out of the compound and getting to the dino-humans first.

"It'll be risky. If we're caught, they'll probably let me off with a few demerits or some other light punishment. I'm too important to the project. But Col. Marsh and the overlords will come down hard on the two of you. Addi, they not only could terminate your contract, but likely end all that medical help your father's been getting. And Billy, they could fire you or worse. Maybe even throw you in the brig."

"Count me in," Addi said. She was already composing a text message to Col. Marsh, the first part of Eddie's plan. "I'm telling him I have an important Zoom call scheduled with my father but that I left my laptop at home. I'm requesting permission to leave the compound."

It added another angle to the convoluted fiction. But Eddie didn't think the colonel would waste time trying to confirm every aspect of her story. Now they just had to hope for a positive response.

Billy, munching an apple he'd brought from the cafeteria, seemed to slump deeper into the sofa. For a moment, Eddie thought he might refuse to go along with the plan.

"Screw it," he said at last. "I'm in. They can't treat people like that. But it sounds like these mercs already have a good head start on us. Do we even have a chance of finding them first?"

"I think so. Julio and Gideon obviously can't let themselves be seen by anyone. They'll stick to wilderness wherever possible."

"Hell of a lot of wilderness out there. Hundreds of square miles."

"I can track their scents, which gives me an advantage. They have the same natural abilities, which means they should be able to detect and evade anyone who gets too close."

Addi looked unconvinced. "Playing devil's advocate, let me point out that Col. Marsh has a large number of troops at his disposal."

"Yeah," Billy said. "Bunches more of them headed out in jeeps and Humvees just in the last fifteen minutes or so. I'm guessing there's only a skeleton force left at the compound. Plus, with Blayvine out of the picture, I hear the colonel now has full control of Wesk. Don't get me wrong, I'm still with you a hundred percent. But that's a lot to be up against."

"I don't think he's going to directly involve the soldiers," Eddie said. "I think he'll use them to form a wide perimeter. He'll especially want to keep Julio and Gideon from stealing a vehicle and extending their range. Most of those troops will be tasked with watching the roads."

He thought back to the soldiers he'd seen exiting the main gate when he arrived. They must have been sent out as a precaution in the unlikely event the dino-humans did manage to escape the compound.

"The soldiers' job will be containment," he continued. "The mercs will handle the actual hunt."

"What about the GPS in your phone?" Addi wondered. "Once you're out of the compound, they'll be able to track you, right?"

"That was taken care of a long time ago. I didn't like the idea of Wesk knowing where I was every second."

Tom Koplanski not only had turned off the GPS when he'd cloned Eddie's phone, he'd performed some of his hacker magic to make sure the function couldn't be turned back on remotely. Of course, the overlords would have known his GPS was disabled. But no one had said anything to him. He chalked it up as another part of their grand scheme: give him as much of an illusion of freedom as possible. The overall goal was keeping Eddie Boka happy while keeping him in line, making sure he wasn't tempted to rock the boat.

But what had occurred tonight changed everything. He wasn't just going to rock the boat, he was prepared to flip the goddamn thing over and send it to the bottom.

"Those mercs must be the SEG," Billy mused, rising from the sofa to toss the apple core toward the swing-top wastebasket at the edge of the kitchen. The target was ten feet away but he missed by a mile. It splatted against the refrigerator. "Sorry, I'll clean that up."

"Don't worry about it. What's the SEG?"

"Special Extraction Group. I was coming out of the library a while ago and I heard the colonel's errand boy, Sgt. Petersen, talking to another soldier about it. At the time I had the impression it was a legit military unit, maybe for going after AWOL soldiers or deserters. But now I'm thinking it must be the designation for those contractors."

Billy headed for the kitchen to dispose of the apple. Halfway there he had a eureka moment and snapped his fingers. "Shit! The library! I just remembered something else. Gideon hangs out there a lot. He loves browsing the stacks, always looking to expand his interests."

Eddie nodded. Gideon was more passionate about learning than anyone he'd ever met.

"But he's also secretive. And like you, hates the idea of Wesk monitoring his activities all the time. So if he's interested in a specific subject, he doesn't use the catalog to look up the location or check out the book or even bring it back to the main reading area where there's surveillance. He'll do a lot of his reading right there in the stacks."

Billy paused as he picked up the apple and wiped the fridge door with a sponge. Eddie waited impatiently for him to continue.

"A couple times I happened to be in the same aisle. And this one time after Gideon left, I got curious about what he'd been reading. We were in the history section and he didn't push the book all the way back into the row. I know I shouldn't have been sneaky like that but I was curious to check out his interests. And guess what? It was an account of Morralsia!"

Billy waited eagerly for the name to register. It didn't. Eddie couldn't hold back growing frustration.

"Billy, there's a time element here. Get to the point."

"Sorry. Morralsia is a ghost town about a dozen miles northwest of the compound. It had a big coal-processing plant connecting to a labyrinth of mine shafts. Many of the shafts were close to the surface, and the owners ended up undercutting the whole area to tap the coal seams. Back in the 1970s, those seams caught fire. They've been burning ever since. The state gave up trying to put it out. They say the fire's likely to keep burning for centuries."

Eddie recalled seeing Gideon months back in the hideaway with a book on the general subject. *Riches and Ruins: The Heritage of American Coal Mining.* He wasn't sure why he remembered the title. Maybe because that entire day was seared into his mind. It had been his momentous first encounter with Addi.

"Everyone had to leave Morralsia," Billy continued. "Buildings were falling into sinkholes, poison gases leaking up from below. Nasty place. The state ultimately footed the bill to resettle the thousand-plus residents elsewhere."

"So why would Julio and Gideon go there?"

Billy shrugged. "Temporary shelter, maybe? Give them time to figure out their next move."

"He could be right," Addi said, accessing her phone. "Weather forecast hasn't changed from earlier today. That storm front's still closing in on the region. Gideon sounds like the kind of person who'd be aware of that. Hiding out in some abandoned building sounds a lot better than being out in the rain."

Billy slid a tablet from his man bag, went online and called up an aerial view of Morralsia. Obviously taken from a plane or copter, and in better days, the streets were dotted with cars, trucks and pedestrians. There were the usual trappings of a small town: row homes, stores, commercial buildings. At the eastern end was the towering steeple of a church, and across from it, a wide two-story structure that was probably a school. Dominant to the north was the large processing plant tucked against the base of a mountain range.

The notion of them hiding out in the town made sense. Sort of. But now something else bothered Eddie: Billy and his sudden recollections. On the heels of his memory about the SEG had come the tale from the library about the ghost town. It seemed too convenient.

Could Billy Orb be Cwacian?

He was always hanging out with the dino-humans. He had access to classified information. And he certainly knew his way around computers.

Even if true, now wasn't the time to probe the issue further. The three of them needed to stay focused and work together if the plan was to succeed.

"Text from Col. Marsh's office," Addi said, giving a thumbs up. "I've got permission to leave the compound."

"Then we're on. Billy?"

"On my way to recruit our helper," he said, hightailing it toward the door. "I'll let you know when we're in position."

Alone with Addi, Eddie felt his desire for her abruptly growing again. He forced himself to turn away from her. Out of sight, out of mind. In theory it was a good idea.

He went to the kitchen and retrieved packets of crackers and cookies from a cabinet, supplements for the rations in his backpack. There was no telling how long he'd be out there searching. And if he found Julio and Gideon – no, *when* he found them – they might be hungry too.

He wished he'd had a gun. But that would involve a side trip to the armory. Even if they allowed him to check one out, Col. Marsh likely would be notified. He couldn't risk it.

"Eddie?"

"Yeah?" He kept his back to her.

"After all this is over… the two of us need to–"

"I know. We will."

THIRTY-NINE

Addi gave Eddie a head start before leaving his quarters. He'd given her the fob for his pickup truck and she wheeled the F-150 toward the rendezvous spot, a driveway behind a storage building. He'd assured her it was free of surveillance, but the drive gave her some quiet moments to review his plan. It reeked of potential flaws, any one of which could wreck things.

Eddie was relying on information from Gideon, who'd mapped the areas of the compound not covered by stationary cameras. So as not to alert Wesk anything was amiss, Eddie initially would go for a full-backpack run into the western forests – not unusual for him at this time of evening – then double back under a strip of wilderness flanking the inner ring.

But what if Gideon's information was wrong? What if surveillance had been updated? What if the scrap lumber needed to carry out her part in the getaway had been removed since Eddie last checked?

Stop with the what ifs. She just needed to follow the plan. If roadblocks arose, literal or figurative, she'd make adjustments on the fly.

She eased the F-150 into the dead-end driveway behind the storage buildings and was relieved to see the scrap lumber. All shapes and sizes, it was haphazardly strewn against the back wall. Wesk's myriad of eyes would have noted her unusual decision to leave the main exit road and pull in here. However, if the plan worked, that anomaly would be explained in short order.

The crew cab door was wrenched open, startling her. She spun around as Eddie threw his backpack on the cushions and squeezed himself face down across the narrow floor.

"We good?" he asked.

"So far." But the real test was yet to come.

She got out, unfurled the wool blanket she'd stripped from his bed and covered his prone form head to toe. Turning her attention to the lumber scraps, she first selected the widest pieces that were short enough to fit crosswise across the back seat. Piling those 2 x 10s and 2 x 8s atop his blanketed figure, she then stacked a bunch of the smaller boards of various lengths on top. When she finished Eddie was completely buried by the woodpile, with not even the edges of the blanket visible.

"You OK down there?"

A muffled affirmative came from his camouflaged form. She hopped behind the wheel and checked her phone. Billy had texted. He was in position.

She backed out of the driveway and turned onto the main road again. Passing a set of garages, she noticed their overhead doors were up and the interiors empty. The missing vehicles must have been loaded with soldiers and sent out to do their part in the hunt.

Reaching the main gate, she eased to a stop in the exit lane. Only two guards were on duty instead of the usual three. The troop exodus must have left them shorthanded.

That could be an unexpected advantage. Or not. In any case, leaving the compound's inner ring was always an easier process than entering.

Addi knew some of the guards by name. But she was usually coming and going in daylight. Exiting this late, she must have crossed a shift change. This pair of privates were unknown to her.

The male guard emerged from the shack. His female partner stayed inside, ready to open the gate when signaled.

"Hi," she said, rolling down her window and smiling as he approached. "Dr Adelaide LaTour. I should be on the permitted-to-leave list."

The guard checked his phone, nodded. "Isn't this Boka's truck?"

"It is. He's stuck here for however long this emergency lasts, so he asked me to do him a favor. He's got some workers coming early in the morning to add a sunroom onto his house. He promised them this scrap lumber to use. Don't worry, he's not stealing anything. It's all discards. He cleared it with the colonel."

The story was flimsy to start with, and if the guard made a phone call to Col. Marsh, the game was up. But as they'd hoped, the guard didn't want to bother the brass over such a trivial matter. However, he was curious about the empty truck bed.

"Why not put the lumber back there?"

The question was anticipated. Addi let frustration creep into her voice.

"Would make more sense, right. Unfortunately, this isn't the only chore I've got this evening. Now I gotta drive clear out to East Blessing Road and pick up a jackhammer, a big-ass table saw and whatever other crap Eddie arranged to borrow. He told me I needed to keep the bed empty so that stuff can be loaded in back."

The guard looked suspicious.

Anytime, Billy. In fact, right about now would be good.

"I'd really like to get going," she said, adopting a hopeful expression. "It's been a long day already."

The guard wasn't sympathetic. "I'm going to need you to unload that wood to check what's underneath."

Addi's frustration wasn't feigned. "Listen up, private, I'm not unloading *anything*. Now if you feel that's what you need to do, by all means go for it. Just make sure you stack it all back in there." She gave him a frosty look and hit the switch to unlock the crew cab doors.

The guard hesitated. For a moment, Addi's hopes were raised. She thought he was going to consider it too much extra work and signal his partner to raise the gate. But then he yanked the back door open.

"Hey!" Billy hollered, lunging out from behind the garages and running toward the gate in a panic. "Grab that cat!"

Troika was several paces in front of Billy, dashing toward the back of the truck in an odd jerky gait. Its center head was focused forward but the flanking heads bobbed up and down, scanning the perimeter and apparently sending occasional contrary signals to its legs. Smooth locomotion was not in the repertoire of the triple-headed.

Troika bolted past the guard and abruptly swerved. It was heading for the open door of the shack.

"Grab him!" Billy yelled.

"No way, ain't touchin' that freak."

The female guard had no such qualms. She rushed out of the shack and swept Troika into her arms.

"Thanks," Billy said, leaning over and pretending to catch his breath. "And don't worry, he's declawed and none of his heads bite. The left one might try licking your fingers though."

"You're a strange little guy, aren't you," the female guard said, stroking Troika's back and eliciting harmonic purrs. A smile came over. A serious cat lover for sure.

Addi prodded the male guard. "Listen, can we do this? I need to get on the road."

"Yeah, fine. Move the hell out of here."

He slammed the crew cab door shut and signaled his partner. She surrendered Troika into Billy's waiting arms, stepped back into the shack and raised the gate.

The male guard glared at Billy and Troika in disgust. "Ever think your freaky cat would be better off if you guillotined a couple of its heads?"

"Ever think you'd be better off if you guillotined yours?" Billy snapped.

The last thing Addi heard as she left the checkpoint was the female guard's laughter.

FORTY

Addi only needed to slow the truck to a crawl for the outer checkpoint, which opened as they approached. She gave the guards in the shack a friendly wave and turned onto the road to Axton.

"You still breathing?" she asked.

"Could use some fresh air."

"Hang in there," she said.

A half mile farther on, the shoulder widened enough to pull over. She got out and started removing the lumber from his buried form and tossing it into the adjacent woods. Eddie wriggled out from under the blanket and got behind the wheel. She'd barely nestled into the passenger seat when he hit the gas. The truck quickly exceeded the thirty-five-mph speed limit on the winding two-lane road.

"There's a good chance they'll eventually figure out what happened back there," she said.

"I know. But not my concern at the moment. And don't worry, if we get in trouble, I'll take all the blame."

"No. We're in this together."

Addi realized her remark might be construed as meaning more than she intended. The tension between them still bubbled beneath the surface. She was no closer to getting a handle on her feelings, still torn between a potent attraction and staying true to the tenets of her profession. There was also the matter of her wariness when it came to relationships in general. That Eddie seemed to face no such inner conflicts somehow made it harder for her.

"Why don't you double-check our route," he suggested.

Back in his quarters, she'd mapped the fastest way to the ghost town. It shouldn't have changed but she acceded to his request. But she couldn't get the GPS on the truck's dashboard screen working.

"Sorry," he said. "Forgot about that. Tom Koplanski, the guy from the tattoo parlor. He disabled the truck's GPS too."

Addi nodded. That must have been why he'd insisted on his ride for the getaway rather than her jeep. A new concern touched her.

"Could they have secretly implanted subcutaneous trackers on you and the others? Back during one of your surgeries?"

The theory seemed viable to Addi. It would explain why the disabling of his GPS tracking hadn't raised any alarms. The overlords wouldn't need to know where his phone and truck were if a bug under the skin was always pinpointing his location.

"We wondered about that too," Eddie said. "Dr Steinhauser and Dr Kim told me the idea was considered early on but rejected. Too intrusive. If we found out, we'd be pissed and they'd lose our trust. But to make sure, I had Tom scan me."

Addi pulled out her phone to check the route.

"Hold it!"

She paused. "If you're worried about my phone, it's OK. I already disabled the GPS."

"Is that the same phone you turned over to them when you first arrived? The one they said they were modifying for unfettered use in the compound?"

"Yes, but I don't see them going to the trouble of bugging–"

He snatched the phone from her hand and threw it out the window into the woods. Addi glared.

"I'm sending you a bill for that. And by the way, just how are we going to keep in touch if we have to?"

"My backpack, lower right sleeve."

She reached around and fumbled with the pack until locating the pocket. It held another phone.

"A burner. Tom gave it to me a while back for emergencies. Not impossible to trace but more difficult. And free of any tracking bugs. Still, don't use it unless you have to. Pretty sure they can still ID the cell tower it's pinging from."

She nodded and tucked the phone in her jacket.

Eddie stayed on the same road and continued surpassing the speed limit. Approaching Axton's outskirts, they spotted a Jeep with two soldiers heading away on a side street. He eased over to the curb.

"You'd better drive from here. If I'm spotted…"

"Yeah."

He got out and transferred to the passenger seat as she slid behind the wheel. Scrunching down, he donned a black wool cap from the glove compartment and pulled it down almost to his eyes. Along with the pickup's frosted windows, he should be hidden from casual scrutiny.

Addi stayed under the speed limit. The last thing they needed was a traffic stop. Twice as they proceeded through the main part of town they saw jeeps cruising side streets. Eddie ducked lower each time. When they reached her house at the far edge of town, she backed into her driveway so the truck was ready to leave.

"Give me two minutes," she said, hopping out. "Just going to grab my backpack."

"Forget it. I'm dropping you off. Once I'm on foot you'll never keep up."

"If that's some kind of male chauvinism, get over yourself. If you're just being dense, snap out of it."

He glared. She made her case.

"When you go to ground, you'll want me and the truck reasonably close, ready to pick you up. Otherwise you might end up having to hike for miles. And yes, I know the three of you are supermen. But you could be tiring and those mercs could be closing in. Besides that, I have something in the house you might need."

He gave a grudging nod.

Addi dashed inside, wondering if he might take off and strand her anyway. But he was still there when she emerged.

She displayed the contents of her backpack. "Headlamp, extra flashlight, assorted edibles and this." She unlocked the gun case, revealing her Glock and two extra 9mm magazines. "Brought it up from Louisiana for protection. In case my mysterious patient proved to be the troublesome sort."

He managed a chuckle. "Good thinking."

Three blocks later she turned north onto Bessemer, another winding two-laner bisecting forested hills. In twenty minutes or so they should reach Coal Ridge Road. From there it was a straight shot to Morralsia.

"Unless Julio and Gideon found a ride, we should get there ahead of them," she said.

"Don't count on it. We can run pretty fast and for extended periods, even through rugged terrain. And they'll be moving in a pretty straight line."

The drive gave her more time to dwell on the bizarre incident in the OR. "It still makes no sense. Castrating Julio and Gideon? What the hell were the overlords thinking?"

"Maybe they weren't," he said.

"No, this wasn't some spur of the moment decision. It was planned. Best guess, the surgeries were ordered because like you, Julio and Gideon came alive sexually. That was seen as a threat to the project." She hesitated. "Could the two of them have been caught having affairs with women here at the compound? Or worse, is it possible they raped someone? That would explain such an extreme reaction."

"No way. Julio can get pretty wild, but neither of them would do something like that. I'm sure of it."

"You're probably right. Nothing in their backgrounds to suggest that kind of sexual violence. But even if the surgeries had been performed, they would have suffered severe emotional fallout. I can imagine them getting angry enough to go public with what was done to them. Julio especially. I think he'd be out for vengeance."

"No arguments," Eddie said. "But you're looking for a logical reason when maybe there isn't one. The overlords – three of them at any rate, Blayvine, Quelph and the colonel – are hardcore. I always figured they were capable of most anything."

"I get what you're saying. Many highly driven people have such tendencies. Blayvine certainly, but we have to assume he's temporarily out of the picture. Dr Quelphius? If I had to make an armchair diagnosis, I'd say he exhibits strong traits of narcissistic personality disorder."

"But aren't people like that completely self-centered? The way Quelph reacted to Dilopho's death suggests he was really sad and hurt."

"It's a gray area," Addi admitted. "But some individuals with the disorder view their children – or in his case, the retroverts – merely as extensions of themselves. Those creatures might be important to Dr Quelphius solely because he created them. Their existence is just another aspect of the narcissism that feeds his ego.

"Still, Quelph has his own priorities at the moment, saving the retroverts. I don't see him getting involved in all this. More than likely, Col. Marsh is behind it. But if he ordered the castrations, we're still missing something. Knowing the likely repercussions, he must have had a strong motivation."

A chilling thought hit Addi. Eddie noted her troubled expression.

"What's wrong?"

"What if we're looking at this whole thing backwards? What if there was never any intention of going through with the surgeries?"

"I don't follow."

"Maybe it was arranged for the anesthetic to be contaminated, poisoned somehow. Julio and Gideon go to sleep in the OR but never wake up. They die on the operating table. Officially it's ruled an accident."

Uttering the theory aloud made her sound paranoid. And yet...

"Makes sense," Eddie said. "Julio especially was always a thorn in their sides. His arrogance, the constant fights, jealousy that I was chosen as the project's public face rather than him. Under the right circumstances I could see Col. Marsh doing something so drastic."

Addi was convinced she was on the right track. "He gets away with murder. The Blayvine Industries publicity machine goes into high gear, same way it did following Dilopho's rampage. The deaths of Julio and Gideon are spun in the media as a tragic mishap. They're publicly mourned and no one's ever the wiser." She hesitated. "But I can't imagine Gen. Hollenbach being involved in something this ugly. Which means the colonel would have to create enough false documentation for a full-blown cover-up."

"With Wesk in his corner, shouldn't be a problem."

Pieces of the puzzle were missing, however. Why the elaborate ruse of planning castrations if you were going to kill the dino-humans during the surgeries? And how had Julio and Gideon learned of the fate planned for them?

Raindrops pattered on the windshield. She turned on the wipers. Seconds later, the fury of the storm hit hard, forcing her to slow the pickup to a crawl.

"If you're right," Eddie said, "those mercs aren't looking to capture Julio and Gideon."

"No," she said grimly. "They're out here to finish the job."

FORTY-ONE

They drove the rest of the way mostly in silence, leaving Eddie's thoughts to wander. This whole journey was swaddled in unanswerable questions and gnawing doubts. Was Billy right and the ghost town was actually where Julio and Gideon were headed? He tried assuring himself that they were playing the odds and that Morralsia remained the best bet.

And what would he do if he did encounter Nastor and the so-called SEG, Special Extraction Group? Actually, more like Special *Execution* Group. He realized there was still no real evidence supporting Addi's theory. But nothing else seemed to make sense.

If they were right, then the mercs likely had orders not to gun down Julio and Gideon, at least if it could be helped. The colonel would want their deaths to appear accidental. He recalled that silver briefcase passed to Nastor by Sgt. Petersen. Some kind of lethal drug? Maybe the same one they'd intended using to contaminate the anesthetic and kill them in OR?

A new concern touched him. What would he do if Julio and Gideon refused to accompany him back to the compound? They had good reason to take their chances by remaining fugitives. Eventually they'd certainly be caught or worse, yet they weren't fans of Eddie Boka and would be unlikely to trust him.

He shook his head, forced his focus onto the most pressing issue, the mercs. There were at least seven of them out here, the five who'd been with Col. Marsh plus the drivers of the two vehicles that had picked them up. And those seven would have Wesk's eyes and vast technological capabilities at their disposal as well.

And I've got a pistol.

The odds weren't great. Abysmal, actually. During the mission to rescue the CEO, he'd easily taken down those guerrillas. But the men he was up against tonight would have a far more intense level of training and experience. Like Nastor, most if not all of them would have come from the ranks of special forces, choosing to leave those elite corps for the heftier paychecks lavished on contractors.

He had one advantage. Although the colonel wouldn't have known of Eddie's escape from the compound, he would have drilled into Nastor just how important Eddie Boka was to the project, and that under no circumstances could anything be allowed to happen to him. Ideally, if he did encounter the mercs, he could shoot at them and they wouldn't shoot back. Still, the thought offered no reassurances. In the midst of violent confrontations, such rational certainties were usually the first victims.

The storm alternated between brutal pounding and light drizzling. Addi adjusted the pace of her driving, slowing to a crawl for long stretches when they could barely see the road.

They finally reached the intersection. She made a right turn onto Coal Ridge Road, creeping along slow enough to read a weathered sign warning of a dead end one mile ahead. To their right was an abandoned Sheetz convenience store, its damaged canopy drooping over the fueling area out front. The pumps had been removed, the front windows and door boarded up.

"Good place for me to go to ground," he said. "Pull around back."

She eased the pickup onto the bumpy lane circling the store, trying to dodge the worst of the overgrown branches. Low-hanging wet leaves smacked the windshield as she eased to a stop behind the building. The truck should be hidden from the sight lines of anyone driving past or using the front parking lot as a turnaround.

They got out. Eddie secured the Glock and ammo in zippered side pockets of his jacket. Donning Addie's headlamp, he grabbed the wool blanket used to cover him during the escape and wrapped it around his shoulders like a cape. The backpack went over top, helping hold the blanket in place.

"Looks like a cape worn by superheroes," Addi offered. "Kind of a grungy one, though."

"The blanket does double duty. It should keep my ass reasonably dry and help cloak me from infrared scanning." He gestured upward, referring to the possibility of drones controlled by Wesk or the mercs.

"Then I suppose you're as ready as you're going to be."

"Except for one thing. You need to un-BAM me."

"*Get sa liki mama la!*" she whispered. "I forgot to bring the remote!"

Her shocked expression was momentarily convincing. But she couldn't prevent a smile from seeping through.

"Not funny," he muttered.

"Sorry, couldn't help it." She withdrew the remote from her pocket and snapped the collar open. He handed it to her and rubbed his chafed neck.

"You know the warning signs by now," she said. "If you feel the bad yen coming on, fight it. Don't let it reach the stage where it turns into the bloodburn."

"Yes ma'am." He gave a mock salute.

"I'm serious, Eddie."

"I know you are. Don't worry, I'll handle it."

They both knew any assurances were hopeful thinking at best. In the swirl of combat there could be no guarantees.

"That curse you uttered," he said. "Get sa liki something or other. You said it to me the day we met, when we bumped into one another in that hallway."

"Bumped? You mean when you knocked me on my ass."

"Fair enough. What's it mean?"

"Roughly translated, *Oh shit!*"

"That could sum up this whole evening."

Addi managed another smile, then abruptly threw her arms around his neck and gave him a crushing hug.

"Be safe," she said, breaking away fast. "I'll wait here for your call."

He sprinted away, staying a few yards into the woods but parallel to the road. A part of him sought to dwell on just how good those brief moments in her embrace had felt. It took an effort to pivot concentration back to the task at hand.

FORTY-TWO

Wesk flew at an average height of three hundred and twenty-seven feet above Nastor's two-vehicle convoy, dipping or ascending above the canopy to adjust for wind currents. The all-weather quadcopter drone could handle the rain although the erratic gusts would have defeated even the best human pilot. Fortunately, Wesk possessed none of their inadequacies. It was able to make microsecond to microsecond adjustments of wing flaps and rotor speed to keep the Humvee and box truck in view.

"Status update?"

Col. Marsh's words emanated from Blayvine's penthouse office in Admin. He'd taken it over and was using it as his command post.

"The convoy is heading west, about seven klicks from Morralsia," Wesk reported. "Wait… they appear to be slowing. They're pulling off the road onto a fire lane."

Wesk observed the seven contractors, garbed in raincoats and dusters, exit the vehicles and gather at the back of the truck. Night-vision goggles enabled them to function in the darkness.

"What's happening now?" Col. Marsh demanded.

"Are you sure you don't want video activated?" It would be easier if he saw for himself.

"No!"

Wesk understood the sharp response and the reason for his reluctance. The colonel already had instructed that any transmissions originating from the drone were not to be recorded, apparently having convinced himself that the less he witnessed of the SEG's illicit mission, the more insulated he would be from potential ramifications. Like many choices humans made, his reasoning was based more on fear than logic.

Wesk continued the audio commentary. "The truck's ramp is being lowered... several of the men are climbing into the back... three utility task vehicles with roll cages are being driven down the ramp...

"The contractors are getting into the UTVs... hybrid models, diesel and electric... they're setting off into the woods... hardly any noise, obviously running on battery power. They should be able to close on any targets with minimal detection."

"ETA to the ghost town?"

"Based on the terrain and weather conditions, they'll likely be forced to maintain a moderate pace. Approximately twelve to fourteen minutes. But I would remind you that there is still only a forty percent probability that the dino-humans' destination is Morralsia."

"I'll take those odds."

The primary target, a grouping of small farms north of the compound, had been a bust. Wesk had pegged the farms at fifty-five percent probability because of the presence of isolated vehicles, which the escapees might seek to commandeer. The SEG had been sent there first.

But no vehicles in the area had been stolen. The conclusion was supported by visual observation from the drone and by Wesk hacking into the database of the West Virginia Division of Motor Vehicles for a list of locally licensed cars and trucks.

The strongest evidence for the second most likely target came from the books Sgt. Petersen had found in Gideon's room. One volume in particular, *Riches and Ruins: The Heritage of West Virginia Coal Mining,* pointed clearly to that dino-human's fascination with urban archeology. The ghost town was a prime nearby example.

"Fly ahead of the UTVs but remain outside town limits," the colonel ordered. "If the targets are there, you could be spotted."

Wesk found that unlikely in present weather conditions. But it acknowledged the order and sped toward Morralsia.

FORTY-THREE

The sporadic rain had stopped but the tree cover above Eddie remained saturated. Continuous droplets fell upon him. He wiped the latest coating of moisture from his face and peered out from behind a scrap of bushes.

The western edge of Morralsia lay before him in all its ethereal gloom. A cluster of dilapidated row homes lined both sides of the traditionally named Main Street, whose macadam was dotted with gaping cracks. Some homes had been boarded up while others displayed shattered windows and missing doors. Weeds squirmed from broken sidewalks. A pair of dead maple trees stood on opposite sides of the street, sentinels of the surrounding decay.

He ventured out from under the forest canopy and turned off his headlamp. Using artificial light to navigate would render him an easy target. Despite the storm clouds, a fraction of ambient light remained in the sky, just enough to discern rough shapes. He chose to make his way along the northern sidewalk, tucked in as close as possible to the fronts of the houses. It wouldn't protect him from being seen by the mercs, who would have night-vision goggles. But it was better than striding down the middle of the street.

He tucked a hand in his pocket and clutched the Glock.

If the mercs had arrived ahead of him, they could be hiding in one of the houses. They also could have set up remote cameras or sensors to detect the approach of the dino-humans or other intruders. For all he knew he was walking into an ambush. He'd have to rely on his instincts, enhanced speed and the mercs' presumed hesitancy to gun him down.

He sniffed at the air but picked up no familiar scents. Not surprising. If Julio and Gideon were hiding here in Morralsia, they might be nearly undetectable unless he was nearly on top of them. It didn't help that the storm tended to dampen his olfactory sense.

Other smells were readily apparent, however, including a musty one brought about by the rain. But the dominant odor was SO2, sulfur dioxide. The byproduct of burning coal, it must be seeping up from the underground mine fire that had begun more than half a century ago and was the cause of the town's abandonment.

He kept moving, eyes scanning side to side, nose alert for any background smells not overwhelmed by the colorless SO2. The prevalence of the gas would make tracking Julio and Gideon even more challenging.

He reached the end of the block. The intersecting street revealed the dark outlines of similar row homes in both directions. A vintage automobile was parked at a curb, its body so seared with rust that no traces of the original paint remained.

Staying on Main he entered the next block. Here damage from the mine fire was more obvious. On one side of the street, just west of the intersection, were three gaping sinkholes. The nearest and largest was a good fifteen feet in diameter. On the other side of the street, set back from the curb to allow space for a parking lot, was the remains of a large building. Pieces of its cinderblock foundation and a chimney rose defiantly from a sea of rubble. Eddie guessed another sinkhole had formed beneath the structure, either causing it to collapse or making it unstable enough to force demolition as a safety hazard prior to the town's abandonment.

Just beyond, a rail line crossed Main Street. His gaze followed the rusted track northward as it sliced between buildings. He could just make out its destination in the distance. Silhouetted against a mountain range was the large processing plant where the coal was washed, crushed and graded. The breaker and the mines would have formed the local economic base, at least until the owners got greedy and tunneled too close to the surface, undercutting the town and the lives of their workers.

Beyond the track at the far end of the block was a two-story restaurant. A center door was flanked by windows, most of the glass long ago broken out. He risked a brief flash of the headlamp to read its badly weathered signage.

Victory Luncheonette
Mouth-watering Cheeseburgers and Creamy Milkshakes
Morralsia's best eatery since 1945

He moved on to the next block, which appeared to have been the commercial heart of town, once brimming with stores and businesses. The sulfur dioxide smell was stronger, so much so that he doubted his nose would be able to distinguish dino-human scents even if he was mere yards away. Under these conditions a search could take days.

Think, Eddie, think! Don't just wander through town like some forsaken tourist. If they are here, where would they hide?

Julio and Gideon had a tight relationship, almost like brothers. Julio's hotheaded nature would seem to favor him as the leader, but when it came to important decisions, he was wise enough to defer to the shrewder and more level-headed Gideon.

So where would Gideon go? Would he randomly select a house to sequester themselves in? Eddie didn't think so. He'd want something larger. If they were tracked down, he'd want to be in a space with more maneuvering room. None of these downtown commercial buildings seemed particularly expansive, and it was likely their interiors were compartmentalized.

He recalled Billy's aerial photo of Morralsia. That wide building, probably a school, fit the bill. A school would have a gym, which would feel comfortably familiar to Julio and Gideon. There was also that church with the towering steeple. Although neither dino-human had ever expressed religious inclinations, it couldn't be ruled out.

Both structures were at the eastern edge of town. He proceeded another two blocks until they came into view, the school on the left, the church across the street. The school's windows exhibited the same damage as many of the houses, but the church displayed a degree of care. What must have been stained glass lancet windows flanking the entrance either had been removed or safeguarded by fitting the openings with carefully cut slabs of plywood, now weathered by the elements to a deep brown hue.

Some undecipherable instinct directed him to try the church first. The steps leading up to the double-door entrance were flanked by rectangular patches of mud and sickly weeds. They'd probably once been flowerbeds. Just visible on the left-hand patch were the fading outlines of boot prints, nearly dissolved by the rain. He could only hope it had been made by Julio or Gideon and not a merc.

Eddie ascended the steps. The doors were unlocked. He cautiously pulled one open and eased himself inside. Closing the door enveloped him in a well of blackness. There was no choice but to turn on the headlamp.

He was in a small lobby. Across from the main entrance was another set of double doors. Easing through he found himself at the back of a spacious chapel of traditional design. He was relieved to find the sulfurous stench almost completely absent.

Benches flanked a central aisle leading to the altar. A narrow balcony was directly overhead. Other than the boarded windows and a floor spotted with dirt and gravel, the chapel looked reasonably undamaged, ready to welcome a congregation that would never come.

He inched forward into the aisle, keeping the headlamp's beam aimed downward to avoid treading on the gravel and making noise.

"Don't fucking move!"

The familiar voice came from above and behind him. Releasing his grip on the Glock, he withdrew that hand from his pocket and slowly turned. Julio leaned over the balcony railing, his XM7 assault rifle trained on Eddie. If he emptied the magazine from this distance, even natural body armor might not save him.

"Julio, I'm here to help."

The entreaty produced a sneer. The barrel didn't waver from Eddie's chest.

"Where's Gideon?"

"Open your goddamn eyes."

He turned forward again as Gideon emerged from a door along the side of the pulpit.

"You came alone?" Gideon asked.

"Yes."

"How do you know you weren't followed? Or tracked?"

"I wasn't. I'm AWOL from the compound too. Addi and Billy have been helping me. I doubt if Col. Marsh or anyone even knows I'm gone. The focus is on searching for you."

"We can't trust him," Julio snarled. "He'll turn us in first chance he gets. Count on it."

Gideon raised his hand, urging Julio's patience. "What's the latest on the search?"

Eddie told them everything he'd learned from Samson and Tanya about the events in the OR, and updated them on what he knew about the mercs. He relayed Addi's theory that the colonel had arranged for them to die on the operating table.

"We figured that out too, although not at first," Gideon said. "Initially, we took it at face value that they were just going to castrate us."

"Yeah," Julio snarled. "*Just* castrate us."

"How'd you know what they had planned?" Eddie asked.

"A message from Cwacian, sent to us simultaneously. The texts came just minutes before we were to report for the surgeries."

Eddie couldn't hide his surprise. "You know about Cwacian?"

"Well, *duh*," Julio growled, his tone dismissive.

"Of course we know," Gideon said. "We've been getting those little poems longer than you have." He raised his gaze to the balcony. "C'mon down, Julio. We can trust him."

"You sure about that?"

"I am."

"Do you know who Cwacian is?" Eddie asked.

"At first I thought either Dr Kim or Dr Steinhauser. Later I suspected Billy."

"Same here."

"Still can't say. But whoever our mysterious benefactor is, I have no doubt they saved our lives tonight. I don't think there was ever any intention of castrating us. Cwacian just used that in the warning to make sure we stood up and took notice. I don't think Cwacian knew we were going to be murdered though. But maybe suspected."

"What did the Med people tell you the surgeries were supposed to be for?"

"A debridement procedure. Julio and I both have a buildup of scar tissue beneath our abdominal scales."

Eddie nodded. Earlier in the year he'd had the same minor surgery to remove a buildup of dead tissue around his scales.

"With Cwacian's warning, we went into the OR on high alert. Two soldiers were there, which was unusual in and of itself. We demanded more information before the anesthesiologist put us under, and requested Dr Steinhauser be present for the surgeries. Tanya said the Doc was on vacation but I knew she was lying. We said we were leaving and that they'd have to reschedule the surgeries. One of the soldiers stepped in front of the door to block us." Gideon paused. "Julio did not react favorably to that. The situation went downhill fast."

"We had no choice," Julio said, emerging from the door at the back of the chapel with his rifle lowered.

"I probably would have done the same thing," Eddie offered.

Julio came forward to stand with Gideon. The entire incident was starting to make sense to Eddie. But one big question remained.

"Why does the colonel want you dead?"

Gideon stared at him for a moment, then countered with a question of his own.

"Why have you been spending so much time with Dr LaTour?"

"I like her."

"Just *like*?"

"OK, I was attracted to her, right from the beginning. Recently, that attraction has grown into something physical. Is that what happened to you and Julio?"

Gideon nodded. "Pretty much. We were still taking the green capsules so it came as a surprise."

"The green capsules?"

"Cwacian never mentioned them?"

"No."

"Libido inhibitors. Essentially, a form of chemical castration. You didn't know?"

Eddie shook his head, shocked that he didn't. Yet maybe Cwacian had been trying to tell him, although in a cryptic roundabout way. He recalled the very first poem he'd received.

A sunless sunset, smothering the damned;
Eclipsing the truth of the buried man.

A buried man, indeed.

"So much for their bullshit story about sexless dino-humans," Julio said. "How long have you and Addi been screwing?"

"We're not... at least not yet. We're both feeling the urge though. I'm hoping it's only a matter of time." He had no desire to go into more detail. "What about you two?"

Gideon turned to Julio. "Should we?"

"Why the hell not."

Julio grasped Gideon's face and pulled it close to his own. Their lips parted. The kiss was brief but intense.

"Get it now?" Julio quizzed.

"Got it." Eddie never would have guessed they were gay. "You were in the closet all this time?"

"So deeply that we'd buried those feelings even from ourselves," Gideon said. "The infusions and surgeries somehow helped unearth our true selves. In the beginning, it was strictly an emotional connection. The physical part was more recent."

"And you didn't tell anyone?"

"Not a soul."

"Dr Kim and Dr Steinhauser would have been sympathetic. They might have been willing to argue your case."

Julio snorted. "Like that would have helped."

"Col. Marsh would have shot them down," Gideon said. "He's closeted too, a closeted bigot. I once overheard him talking to his lackey, Sgt. Petersen. They were laughing and making snide remarks about a gay soldier.

"But beyond his own prejudices, the colonel knows full well that a pair of scaly queers coming out at this juncture could wreck the whole project. You and Addi they probably could make work. They'd have the two of you go public, admit your sexuality came as a big surprise and send you on a tell-all tour with 'true love' as the slogan. But true love the traditional way, between a man and a woman. Wholesome and fresh."

"Like apple pie and ice cream on the Fourth of July," Julio added with a mirthless smile.

Eddie knew their appraisal was spot on. If it came out that the two of them were gay, the goal of a dino-human army would lose critical support and likely wither and die.

"So what now, Boka?" Julio challenged. "You came here to talk us into surrendering, right?" He hoisted the rifle barrel higher, signaling what he thought of the idea.

"I don't see there's any other choice. It's not like you can stay off the grid for long. If the mercs don't find you, others will."

"Even if you can get us safely back to the compound, what then?" Gideon asked. "It's not like we'll have much of a future there."

"They'll find another way to take us out," Julio said.

Eddie nodded. "One step at a time. Remember, I have some clout. Whatever it takes, we'll figure out a way to put this right."

FORTY-FOUR

It had been the grungiest toilet Addi ever had the displeasure to use. But considering subsequent events, the timing of her visit to the convenience store's wretched bathroom might have saved her life.

The call of nature had come not long after Eddie's departure. Having no desire to squat outside in the rain, she'd armed herself with a flashlight and a pack of tissues, exited the truck and slipped through the narrow opening in the store's rear door, which hung lopsided from a single remaining hinge. Carefully making her way across a minefield of overturned counters and cobwebbed display stands, she found the ladies room and proceeded to use half the tissues wiping down the grubby seat. Completing her business, she'd made her way back to the door.

She froze just inside it. An odd buzzing sound emanated from the wilderness. Extinguishing the flashlight, she peeked around the corner of the door. A few yards above and behind the pickup, a drone hovered in the lightly falling rain.

Wesk. It had to be. No other explanation fit the circumstances.

The buzzing reached a higher pitch. The drone lunged straight up into the darkness at high speed. In seconds it was out of sight. She waited until the whirring of its propellers could no longer be heard before carefully venturing outside.

Keeping the light off, she pressed her back against the building and remained still, listening for any other foreign sounds while trying futilely to see into the gloom. A stroke of fear lanced through her chest. The mercs could be nearby. They could be watching her right now, her figure clear as day in their night-vision gear.

She forced calm and remained still. Several minutes passed and nothing happened. If they were out there in the dark, they would have revealed themselves by now.

She got back into the truck, trying to make sense of the incident. The drone had been hovering above and behind the cargo bed. Presuming Wesk was piloting, the AI must have scanned the license plate to confirm the vehicle was Eddie's. Soon enough Col. Marsh would know that Addi had helped him escape from the compound. Worse, it meant the colonel had reached the same conclusion about the dino-humans' destination being Morralsia.

She debated what to do. Call Eddie to warn him? That didn't seem like a good idea. Even with the burner phone, the call might be monitored. Billy Orb once told her that no one really knew the extent of Wesk's eavesdropping capabilities.

Yet she couldn't just sit here, waiting for Eddie to return or call her. She'd have to find him. Driving to the ghost town was out of the question with the drone in the area. The truck surely would be spotted.

That left one viable option. She again exited the cab's relative comfort and donned her backpack. A mile hike through the woods shouldn't be too difficult, providing she was able to dodge the drone's sensors and not run into any mercs.

"The human condition often results in rational thought processing punctuated by bouts of paranoia."

— Wesk: Algorithmic Speculations

FORTY-FIVE

Col. Marsh sat in Blayvine's luxurious desk chair, remaining calm as he was told of the discovery of Eddie Boka's truck. But subtle indicators of his heightening stress could not be hidden from Wesk's sensors.

"And no sign of Boka?" the colonel asked.

"The logical assumption is that he parked the truck and hiked the rest of the way into town."

"Is Dr LaTour with him?"

"Unknown. She wasn't in the vehicle. There is a slight probability she was inside the store. Egress to the building for a drone search was unavailable."

Col. Marsh touched a buzzer on the desk intercom. Sgt. Petersen entered the office.

"Yes sir?"

"Have one of the units in town check Dr LaTour's place to see if she's home. If she is, haul her ass back here. Then go to the main gate and personally interrogate those guards. She must have smuggled him out of the compound. Find out how."

Sgt. Petersen nodded and departed. The colonel asked Wesk for its location.

"Circling Morralsia. Maintaining a height and distance from the perimeter that makes detection from the ground unlikely."

Col. Marsh accessed his sat phone. "Base to SEG 1."

Wesk amplified the room's mics to a level where it could overhear Nastor's side of the conversation.

"SEG 1, over."

"You have encroachment. Intruder Concord."

That was the code phrase for Boka. Col. Marsh continued by updating Nastor on recent events using cryptographic wording. He finished by reminding the contractor – not for the first time – that under no circumstances was Intruder Concord to be harmed.

"SEG 1, do you copy?"

"Got it, Base. Intruder Concord precious cargo. SEG 1 out."

The colonel sat brooding. Wesk considered it highly probable that he was concerned about Nastor abiding by the order.

He finally reached a decision. "Time to end surveillance. Bring it home."

Wesk concluded that Col. Marsh sought to maintain the highest level of plausible deniability in case of any future inquiries into the evening's events. He'd covered his tracks with the mercs by arranging to pay them through one of Blayvine's secret offshore accounts, which he now had access to. The funding source provided a layer of separation should the SEG's mission not come off as planned.

Still, Wesk found the colonel's order to terminate drone surveillance as illogical as his refusal to allow video transmissions. But it was accustomed to the vagaries of human behavior.

"Make sure you delete all traces of this audio and any related conversations."

"Orders acknowledged," Wesk said, assuming a course with the drone that would bring it back to the compound.

FORTY-SIX

Convincing the escapees to return had been easier than Eddie imagined. He'd expected lengthier and more vociferous opposition, particularly from Julio. But once Gideon accepted that Eddie's clout with the project offered a better alternative than remaining fugitives, Julio fell into line.

Now they just had to make it back in one piece.

Another stroll along Main Street seemed unwise. He led them out the rear door of the church and they proceeded southward. Maintaining silence, they stuck to narrow alleys and diminutive backyards of the row homes. The rain had stopped but the darkness nevertheless proved insurmountable at times, forcing Eddie to flash the headlamp for a few seconds to regain their bearings. The going was slow but they finally reached the southern edge of town. The sulfurous odor remained but not as intense as along Main Street.

Just beyond lie forests and, fortuitously, another abandoned set of rails. The track itself, a spur off the main line serving the processing plant, was nearly buried in dirt and gravel. The roadbed was overgrown with foliage; weeds and saplings sprouted between the rails. Still, it led west, the direction they needed to go, and offered a more navigable path than plowing through the dense woodlands.

He was tempted to call Addi, tell her he'd found Julio and Gideon and was on his way back. But it wasn't worth the risk of the call being monitored and giving away their positions. Besides, they'd rendezvous soon enough, although it would take longer going this way. He estimated the roadbed was more than a quarter mile south of the route he'd taken to reach Morralsia.

Up ahead, the track rounded a gentle bend. A large obstacle loomed in the distance, discernible only by its darker presence against the faint tinge of visible sky. Getting closer revealed it to be a long-forsaken factory. It was three stories high. Most of the windows were shattered. A smokestack had partially collapsed, leaving a jagged remnant poking into the heavens. The rail spur entered the building through a gaping portal.

Eddie halted, held up his hand for Julio and Gideon to do the same. Thick foliage had crept up to the factory on both ends. Either they'd have to make their way through it or follow the track inside. He made the decision to choose the latter option and proceeded along the roadbed. In all likelihood, the other side of the building would offer a way out.

He led them in. The darkness was ubiquitous, forcing him to ignite the headlamp. Julio and Gideon turned on their flashlights.

The interior was cluttered with rows of abandoned machines, each with a workstation for an operator. Eddie recognized drill presses and turret lathes; others had mystifying functions. Broken glass littered the floor, having fallen from the array of sawtooth skylights overhead. That arrangement allowed in natural light, suggesting the building had been built either before or at the dawn of electric illumination. The rail line terminated a few hundred feet inside against a bumper post.

Gideon shone his light past it, revealing a jagged hole in the far wall. It was more than big enough for them to exit through.

Glass fragments crunched beneath their feet, echoing loudly in the gloom. A trio of rats scampered across an elevated pipe, and the steady pattering of raindrops emanated from the depths. Eddie was almost tempted to signal them to turn around and circumnavigate the building through the surrounding foliage. There was something unsettling about trekking through the eerie relic.

Julio froze, sniffed at the air. He whipped his rifle from side to side.

"We're not alone," he hissed.

The warning came too late. There was a sudden intense light and blast of sound. Eddie's realization it was a stun grenade did nothing to limit its impact. Temporarily blinded and off balance, his ears ringing, he could only aim the Glock in the general direction of where the flashbang had gone off.

Before vision could clear enough to locate a target, a muted gunshot came from behind him. Seconds later he was enshrouded in strands of high-tensile nylon. Whirling toward the latest threat, he heard the pops of additional net guns being fired.

A second net wrapped around his legs and lower torso. Still unable to see anything but a white blur, he tried lunging forward but tripped over his own tangled feet. As he fell, the edge of his forehead clipped something hard and unyielding.

A shard of pain coursed through him. Awareness slithered into a gray fog.

FORTY-SEVEN

Eddie awoke disoriented, lying on his side and still tangled in the nets. The ground seemed unstable, causing him to bounce up and down. It took a moment for consciousness to ascend to where he realized he was in the back of a fast-moving vehicle, one of the UTVs. Two mercs were upfront, the driver and a guard. They were outfitted in tactical gear: vests, lip mic comms and headlamps switchable to night vision. The guard was turned in his seat, his AR-15 rifle trained on Eddie's chest.

He tried moving his hands. Wrists were bound tightly in front of him with a plastic zip tie.

They were cruising along a residential street, the driver swerving from time to time to dodge the worst potholes and other obstacles, including a downed power pole with a tangle of dead wires. The same types of dilapidated row homes he'd seen upon entering Morralsia were briefly illuminated in the flare of the UTV's headlights. But he didn't recognize any of the landmarks he'd passed earlier.

His backpack was gone and his pockets had been emptied. No gun, no phone. His legs remained entangled in a clump of netting.

* * *

He spotted two more vehicles a hundred yards or so ahead of them, also UTVs. But the dark, the distance and the constant jarring made it impossible to make out the occupants.

Eddie tried sitting up. The guard reacted by poking his chest with the rifle barrel.

"You're fine just like that," the guard warned. "Stay put."

Jabbing him with the gun triggered his anger, and with it the unmistakable ascent of the bad yen. He forced control. No matter his emotions, he needed to stay calm.

The mercs must have spotted them early on, anticipated their logical route along the railroad track and used the whisper-quiet UTVs to reach the abandoned factory first.

The driver made a hard left, throwing Eddie's shoulder against the roll bar strut. Even as he winced he recognized the new surroundings. They were back on Main Street but at the far western end of town, heading east. Just ahead on opposite sides were the school and church.

The UTV continued past those structures until reaching the central business district. The other two vehicles had already arrived and were parked haphazardly in front of the Victory Luncheonette. Farther up the street Eddie glimpsed the rail crossing, and beyond, the collapsed building and gaping sinkholes in the street. But that wasn't the cause of his sudden chill.

Julio and Gideon were sprawled in the back of one of the other UTVs, unconscious and tangled together in overlapping strands of the sinewy nylon. They also must have been standing close when caught by multiple net gun hits. Each wore a face mask with an attached tube connected to a skinny white cylinder strapped to their arm. The gentle motion of their chests revealed they were still alive. Whatever they were being forced to breathe probably was keeping them unconscious.

"What are you doing to them!" he demanded

The five mercs ignored him as they exited their vehicles. They milled around as if waiting for someone.

The luncheonette door opened. Nastor emerged, looking as malicious as ever. Eddie forced himself upright in the back seat. He yanked at the cuffs and kicked at the netting to no avail.

"Now, now, none of that," Nastor said, his voice more amused than threatening. Unwrapping a spike of beef jerky, he bit off a small chunk and let the rest dangle from the side of his mouth. He waited until Eddie stopped trying to tear himself free before continuing.

"I'm surprised at you, Boka. Didn't you ever hear of surveillance? Our cams picked you up the moment you entered town. By the way, gotta give you a big mushy thanks for all your help. Saved us from spending the night going house-to-house through Shitsville."

Eddie glared at him. Despite his efforts at control, the bad yen continued its ascent.

"But hey, no worries. It's your lucky day. Those chest-candy cocksuckers back at the compound got your back. You get to leave here in one piece. Now if it were up to me..." The words trailed off into a taunting laugh.

Eddie gritted his teeth. "If I'm leaving, so are Julio and Gideon. If they're not with me, I'm coming back and wasting every one of you motherfuckers!"

"Ooh, scary," Nastor said, quivering his hands in an exaggeration of fear. He motioned to someone inside the restaurant. Eddie was shocked to see Addi shoved out the door by Glose, who had a grip on the back of her hair. She was wet and disheveled, her hands bound in front of her with a zip tie. A large clump of dirty cloth had been stuffed in her mouth as a makeshift gag.

Her eyes widened in fear at the sight of Eddie. Muffled sounds emanated from behind the gag.

"Shut up, bitch!" Glose hollered, yanking her hair so hard he almost toppled her to the ground.

The bloodburn was nearly upon Eddie. It wouldn't be enough to bite into Glose's neck and savor the warm flesh. He'd rip the man's head from his neck, tear off his limbs, consume him down to the bone.

He met Addi's eyes, saw the pain in them. Yet he also knew that contained in her own torment was an acknowledgment of his.

Don't, those eyes messaged. *Don't lose control. Don't let it happen.*

Her silent appeal enabled him to temper the eruption. He drew long deep breaths, forcing an external aura of calm even as the turbulence of those tiny needles jabbed ruthlessly at his insides.

Nastor observed their interaction. "More than just friends, I see. Lovers, maybe? You scaly sons of bitches ain't supposed to be able to hump. Besides that, pretty damned disgusting doing it with *real* people. Still, I get the attraction." He ran his gaze up and down Addi's body. "Your Doc LaTour is seriously hot."

Eddie tightened his fists until it hurt.

"So here's the deal, Boka. A couple of the guys are gonna drive you to your truck. They're gonna let you go, and you're gonna go straight back to the compound. Do that and you might just see your girlfriend again. But if you get some crazy idea in your head to sneak back into town…"

He nodded to Glose, who drew his sidearm. Addi winced as the merc pressed the barrel against her forehead.

"Got it, freak?" Nastor asked.

It took every bit of willpower to answer calmly. "Got it."

Nastor motioned to the driver and guard who'd driven him here. As they hopped back in the UTV, Eddie caught a final glance of Addi's frightened countenance.

They're going to kill her.

In the coldness of overlord logic, she'd gone from asset to liability. Col. Marsh was already facing a dilemma in dealing with Eddie. Somehow, in light of all that had happened, he'd have to find a way of convincing Eddie not to forsake his duties and shred Project Saurian's ambitions for a dino-human army.

Those grander concerns offered a tinge of hope for Addi's survival. Having her killed certainly wouldn't bring Eddie around to the cause. It would make more sense for Col. Marsh to keep her alive, somehow use her to force Eddie's cooperation. He couldn't see just how the colonel could manage such a trick. But that didn't mean he wouldn't make the attempt, maybe through some mix of incentives and threats.

Yet there was another factor at work. What if the colonel wasn't handling the play-by-play action? What if he was deliberately keeping his distance, letting the mercs call the shots. They might have been instructed that Eddie was to survive at all costs. But if they were going to murder Julio and Gideon, what sense would it make allowing another witness to survive?

Addi's contradictory fates cascaded through Eddie in a jumbled instant as the mercs pulled out. The driver steered a wide arc to swing around the other UTV, the one with the unconscious Julio and Gideon in the back.

There was no doubt what needed to be done. He had to overcome the mercs and save the three prisoners. *How* he was going to do that remained unknown. The driver and guard certainly wouldn't release him until they returned to the convenience store where they'd left the truck. But by the time he drove back to Morralsia, it could be too late to save anyone.

There seemed to be no other options. But as the UTV passed the railroad track and its headlights illuminated the street ahead, a desperate plan took shape. Never mind how completely irrational it was and how it likely would result in his demise.

The guard in the front passenger seat was facing forward, no longer bothering to keep his rifle trained on Eddie. After all, their prisoner was on his way to getting released. In their minds, there was no reason why he'd make trouble.

The vehicle reached the three sinkholes blocking the street. The driver didn't slow down but simply swerved to the left and then to the right to dodge the first two. Ahead was the largest of the trio, a yawning pit bordered by crumbling slabs of asphalt. They were on course to clear it on the right by a good four feet. The driver accelerated.

Eddie's range of motion was severely limited by the netting and the cuffs. And he would get only one chance. His timing would have to be perfect. He waited until the UTV was only yards from the hole, then lifted his entangled legs off the floor. He rammed his feet through the gap between the driver and guard.

His left boot found its target, lancing through the steering wheel. Twisting his lower torso hooked his boot against the wheel's cross-bracing. He wrenched the wheel hard left.

The driver was too startled by his action to make a correction or slam the brakes. The mercs released involuntary gasps as the UTV flew over the edge of the sinkhole.

The vehicle went vertical, front end aimed downward, tires no longer gripping a surface. Gravity took command.

Eddie had no idea how deep the hole was. Maybe only a dozen feet. If it indeed was that shallow, chances are he'd be hauled quickly back to the surface to face the mercs' wrath.

Luck was with him. Or maybe it wasn't. The hole not only was deeper than he'd imagined, it was deeper by a significant amount. As they fell with increasing speed, the wavering headlights revealed nothing below but endless blackness. He glimpsed jagged rocks and untapped coal seams along the walls. Grotesque noises filled the air as the UTV scraped against multiple protrusions.

If the friction of those impacts was lessening their falling rate, it wasn't discernible. The bottom finally appeared, an uneven pile of dirt and rocks. They were plunging toward it at a frightening clip.

The mercs were facing downward. Eddie was better situated for the impact, essentially upright with his left foot jammed into the steering wheel. Still, none of them were likely to escape an unpleasant fate at the speed they were falling.

The mercs braced themselves against the dash. Eddie didn't try resisting the impact, figuring his best chance would be absorbing some of the force of the collision by allowing his knees to flex and his torso to crumple.

The UTV hit bottom with an explosive crack. The sudden halt launched him violently forward. His left foot yanked free of the steering wheel but his right one caught on something, sending a bolt of pain lancing up his leg from ankle to thigh. He smashed into the guard, who was in the process of being hurled from the passenger seat and through the front rectangle of the roll cage. There was no windshield, not that a sheet of glass would have done much to scrub their momentum.

The guard shot across the hood and went headfirst into the rocks. Eddie plowed into him. The cushioning of the guard's body helped but didn't stop a fresh wave of agony from cascading up his right leg. A dust cloud erupted around them, eerily illuminated by a dangling headlight torn from its mount and still functioning.

The guard was dead, his neck broken. The driver was alive but unlikely to be that way for long. He hadn't cleared the roll cage like Eddie and the guard. Instead, his face had smashed into the left upright. The post had pushed his nose deep into his skull. Blood dripped from every facial orifice. Soft gurgling sounds escaped him.

Eddie steeled himself, trying to ignore the agonies of his battered body. His shoulder was bruised and he had a wicked brush burn on the back of his hand. Most excruciating was his right leg. It didn't feel broken but maybe badly sprained.

Whatever his injuries, he had to move. Grabbing hold of the roll cage enabled him to hobble to his feet on the rubble-strewn surface. He needed to look for a way out but the dangling headlight was aimed in the wrong direction. Everything overhead remained bathed in darkness even though most of the dust had dispersed. Had the storm not soaked everything earlier, the cloud likely would have hung there longer.

Leaning over the dead guard, he unsheathed the man's tactical knife and started slicing through the nylon webbing. It was awkward holding the knife with his wrists bound but he needed full motion in his legs and torso before dealing with the cuffs. And he had to work fast. It wouldn't take long for the other mercs to mount a rescue.

FORTY-EIGHT

Addi felt her hopes draining away as the UTV with Eddie drove off into the gloom. She tried telling herself he'd find a way back, find a way to save her. The morale boost didn't help. The terror that had taken hold when that merc lunged from a house at the edge of town and tackled her to the ground returned at full strength. Eddie's brief appearance, even as a captive, had momentarily kept the fear at bay. But now he was gone and she was alone again in the hands of these madmen.

"All right, move it," Nastor ordered, turning away from the departing vehicle. "Still got work to do with the set-up..."

His words tapered off as he saw the other mercs' startled looks and Addi making muffled noises behind her gag. Following their gazes, he spun back toward the UTV. It was gone.

"Jesus, you see that!" a merc exclaimed.

"See what?" Nastor demanded. "Where the hell did they go?"

"I think Delancey drove right into one of those sinkholes."

"Fucking idiot!" Nastor gestured to two mercs nearest the remaining UTVs. "Haul those freaks inside, start getting 'em ready. Glose, take care of the girl." He turned to the final merc. "Rodriguez, on me."

Addi had just enough time to see Nastor and Rodriguez racing toward where the vehicle had disappeared before her captor gave another violent hair yank. Spinning her around, he shoved her back into the luncheonette.

FORTY-NINE

Eddie had cut through half the strands of netting when Nastor's distant shout came from above. "Delancey? Franks? Holler if you hear me!"

Another merc joined in, the pair shouting the names over and over. Moments later, the dead driver and guard's radios chirped, urging responses that would never come.

Eddie hurried with the knife. Cutting off the last of the netting and casting it aside, he again gazed upward. He still couldn't see the surface, which was odd. Nastor and the other mercs certainly would be shining flashlights down the hole. He should have been able to make out the beams.

Retrieving a flashlight from the guard's belt, he cautiously directed it upward. The problem became apparent. The shaft wasn't entirely vertical. He hadn't noticed during the rapid fall but there was a bend about forty feet from the bottom. The sinkhole made just enough of a gradual curve to prevent light from passing.

The shouting ended. But now there was another sound. Something was dropping down the shaft, ricocheting off the walls. Eddie tensed. Had Nastor assumed that his men were dead and decided to make sure their captive was as well by dropping a grenade?

Relief came over him. A glow stick bounced around the bend. It hit the upended UTV and landed at his feet.

Time was running out. The mercs' next logical step would be rigging a rope and sending someone down. Eddie had access to weapons now, the rifles and pistols of the dead mercs. He could hold them off, at least for a while. But ultimately, the bottom of a sinkhole was not a defensible position. And if Eddie started shooting, Nastor would conclude the other driver and guard were dead. At that point, grenades definitely would start raining down.

He turned his attention to the cuffs. Gripping the long end of the zip tie with his teeth, he pulled, ratcheting the locking mechanism even tighter around his wrists. The tighter it was, the easier it would be to break. He'd learned the trick from one of his bank-robbery associates. The man had gotten his kicks practicing Houdini-like escapes.

Lifting his arms above his head, he whipped his hands down toward his stomach while flaring out his elbows. The cuffs snapped at the weakest point, the locking mechanism.

Fully mobile again, he pivoted in a circle, carefully shining his light on the surrounding walls. The sinkholes must have been caused by horizontal mine shafts undercutting the town at multiple depths, coupled with decades of erosion and the relentless subterranean fire. One or more of those shafts should be visible.

But there were no openings, not so much as a fist-sized one. He raised the beam higher. And then he saw it, the remnants of a shaft – two openings on opposite sides of the sinkhole. From this angle, one of the openings appeared to have collapsed, leaving visible only a set of thick wooden beams bracing the tunnel. But the other shaft seemed intact.

Retrieving the guard's holstered sidearm, a 9mm SIG Sauer, he strapped it to his waist and flung one of the AR-15s across his shoulder. The UTV was propped upright against the bottom of the sinkhole. He used it as a ladder and the driver's body as one of the rungs, pretending as he climbed that the flashes of agony in his leg were happening to someone else. This was no time to acknowledge pain.

He made it to the opening and shined his light into it, revealing an intact path ahead. But waves of heat poured from the hole. The fire wasn't visible but was obviously close enough to rule it out as a viable escape route.

In desperation, he turned the beam one hundred and eighty degrees, illuminating the opposite opening. From here that tunnel didn't look as badly collapsed and he felt no heat emanating from it. However, the floor was covered in several feet of rubble. He'd have to belly-crawl through the initial section and it would be a tight squeeze, which meant leaving behind the AR-15. His injured leg would make the trek challenging enough without trying to carry a rifle. And there was no guarantee the shaft would widen farther in. It might lead nowhere.

There wasn't much of a choice. Balancing himself on the back of the UTV, he used his good leg to push off and made the short leap into the tunnel.

FIFTY

Despite her own dire predicament, Addi couldn't help worrying about Eddie. She had a hunch he'd somehow caused the UTV to tumble into that sinkhole. Even if he wasn't hurt, maybe the other mercs in the vehicle were. If so, Nastor might change his mind about letting him go free.

Glose disrupted her thoughts with another painful hair yank. He directed her across the luncheonette's checkered linoleum, past overturned tables and chairs, his headlamp beam pointing toward a door behind the lunch counter. She swallowed her anger and a natural inclination to struggle against the abuse.

He was thin and barely an inch taller, so there was no weight advantage. But the zip tie binding her wrists was a massive drawback. Plus the other two mercs were trailing after them, straining to drag Julio and Gideon across the floor, the dino-humans entangled as one in the clump of netting. Nevertheless, she was working on a tentative escape plan. But if it was to have any chance at all, she needed to be alone with Glose.

And they *would* be alone. All of her instincts and psychological training, along with the alarming tidbits Eddie had mentioned about Glose back in Barracks, warned her of that.

The merc had been accused of attempted rape, and it was probable he'd carried out the crime on other occasions. Addi had no doubt he intended for her to be his next victim. It was also clear that pushing her around and yanking on her hair brought him pleasure. He fit the diagnosis of a tyrannical sadist, and one with severe misogynist tendencies. As such, he would be incapable of empathy. Attempting to reason with him would be useless. But there was another tactic that might help against someone with such emotional flaws.

They reached the door. Glose yanked it open, revealing a long narrow stairway to the second floor. He released his grip on her. She turned to see him propping his rifle against the wall and removing his tactical vest and comms. He must have figured they'd be in the way during whatever demented activities he'd planned for her. But he kept his holstered sidearm and sheathed knife as well as the headlamp.

"Move your ass!"

A hard shove forced her to start climbing. She took a few steps, then hesitated and turned to face him. She made urgent sounds behind the gag.

Glose ripped the dirty cloth from her mouth. "What, bitch?"

"Please don't hurt me," she begged, projecting as much forlorn helplessness as she could muster. "Please don't!"

"Get your ass up there!"

His tone remained angry but his face bore a smile, pleased by her outpouring of fear. He slapped her butt to get her moving. Addi unleashed an exaggerated squeal and scurried the rest of the way up the steps. A man with Glose's pathology would never succumb to pleading, but that wasn't the point of her performance. She needed to feed his twisted ego, show him just how weak and frightened she was. That would accentuate his gratification and hopefully cause him to underestimate her, giving Addi a better opportunity when the moment came to fight back.

At least that was the plan. In truth, while her head was devising a logical series of measures to escape, her body was barely managing to contain a tornado of fear.

You're a survivor, Tour Tot. No matter how bad things look, always believe that.

This time the recollection came from Papa. He'd uttered it when she was fourteen and still a virgin, but with a budding sexuality attracting boys by the laundry load. Two of them became abusive after she'd rejected their advances, dragged her into the woods and started groping her. Her screams made them let her go and she'd bolted home in tears.

While Mama called the cops to report the abuse, Papa angrily ordered her out to the garage of their city row home. Her first thought was that he was going to punish her for allowing the incident to happen. Instead, it became the first of many sessions in the garage as Papa taught her what he'd learned in his rough-and-tumble youth.

If you can run away from your attacker, do it. No shame in that. But if you're trapped, you fight! You fight using every dirty trick in the book!

"But I don't know any dirty tricks, Papa."

You will when we're done.

A long hallway at the top of the stairs was flanked by doors. She had a hunch the second floor had been a boarding house, probably where the poorer miners had stayed. Her guess was confirmed when Glose yanked open the first door and shoved her inside.

The room was just big enough to contain a waist-high dresser, a chair with crumbling upholstery and a single bed with the foulest mattress she'd ever seen. There was one dirt-stained window and no other doors. Her captor gave a final shove, sending Addi tumbling face down onto the bed. Glose plopped down atop her legs, pinning her. His breath blew across the back of her neck.

"Scared, bitch?"

"Please let me go," she begged, keeping up the act while trying to work on her bound hands. But his weight prevented her arms from moving more than a few inches.

His hands slithered around her waist and unsnapped her jeans. The zipper came next, lowered a few teeth at a time, far slower than need be.

"Glose, need a hand out here."

It was one of the other mercs, his voice sounding like it came from the bottom of the steps. Glose ignored it and pulled her unzipped jeans down at a leisurely pace until they were bunched at her thighs.

"Glose, goddamn it! These dino-fuckers are heavy! Help us drag 'em up the steps."

Her tormentor rose, pinching her butt cheek hard enough to force a pained squeal. He leaned in close to her face.

"Don't go anywhere now, ya hear."

A peal of laughter accompanied his exit. She waited until she heard him slam the door before flipping herself over. She was now in near-total darkness, broken only by the faint rectangle of light from the window. But she didn't need illumination to work herself free. Now that she was on her back, she had a range motion of her arms and hands.

When the merc who'd tackled her put her into the binding, she'd remembered a trick she'd learned from that army self-defense class. When ordered to hold still so he could snap on the zip tie, she'd presented her hands with fists clenched and palms facing down. Either the merc wasn't aware of the trick or bore a macho attitude that dismissed the possibility of her escaping. After all, she was just a girl.

She turned her wrists to face inward and stretched out her fingers. Sliding her palms back and forth, she tried working her thumbs out from under the plastic strip. But the zip tie was still too tight. She couldn't get enough distance between her wrists to offset her hands. And if she couldn't get free and Glose returned…

She short-circuited the possibility of despair setting in and tried again with renewed vigor. This time she squeezed her wrists even tighter together. Slowly, she was able to slide one hand far enough to work the thumb out from under the tie.

From there it was easy getting her entire hand out. But as she sat up and removed the coil of plastic, she heard the mercs right outside. From the thumping noises, it was clear they were dragging the dino-humans past her door.

The movements stopped. She held her breath, fearing Glose would enter. She needed more time to prepare for his return. If he came in now, her efforts would have been in vain.

The muffled voice of one of the other mercs penetrated the room.

"Nastor wants another man at the hole."

"Why?" Glose demanded.

"Didn't say."

"Well, what the fuck you waitin' for?"

Addi heard a single set of boots hightailing it back toward the steps, followed by Glose and the remaining merc continuing to drag their captives farther along the hallway.

She'd lucked out. Glose was now forced to help with Julio and Gideon rather than being free to return immediately to his victim. That likely explained why he sounded mad. His sadism aroused, he didn't like having his fun and games delayed.

She hopped off the bed, using that hint of window light to mentally orient herself in the dark. Refastening her jeans, she inched toward the door.

Her knee bumped into something solid and she winced. She'd run into the dresser. Gliding her fingers along its outline, she made her way around its bulk until she felt the side of the door frame. She pushed her ear against the center panel, straining to hear. But there were no further sounds of bodies being dragged, only a murmur of voices too faint to make out. They must have taken Julio and Gideon into another room.

What now?

She posed the question to herself as well as holding it out as a plea to Papa for further guidance. This time, nothing was forthcoming.

Think, Adelaide, think!

Three potential options were all she could come up with, none overly promising. Opening the door and making a run for it was option one, and the most tempting. But she recognized the foolishness of it. Even if the mercs remained in the other room, she'd be in total or near-total darkness in the hallway. Feeling her way along walls and then down the stairs would take forever. And if she made it as far as the street, there would still be Nastor and the others to contend with.

Option two: wait behind the door and jump Glose when he came back. But the layout of the room would put the bed in his field of vision the moment he pushed open the door more than a few inches. When he realized she wasn't positioned as he'd left her, he'd anticipate an attack. If by some miracle she got the jump on him, their struggle surely would bring the other merc running to assist.

That left option three, the hairiest and most terrifying of all. But she also recognized it as the only one with at least a reasonable chance of success.

She eased her way back to the bed, feeling around on the floor for the zip tie dropped after working her way free. Worry flared anew when she couldn't locate it. If Glose spotted the cuff...

She pawed her hands across a wider expanse of floor and found it under a corner of the frame. She shoved it between the box spring and mattress. Lowering her jeans back below her hips, she resumed her face-down pose on the bed, hands tucked underneath her as if still bound.

Physically, she was ready. Mentally, not so much. Making herself vulnerable like this again suddenly seemed the height of insanity.

FIFTY-ONE

Eddie figured it was a good hundred feet to the surface, even assuming the tunnels led to a way out. After that initial belly crawl over the rubble-strewn area, the first shaft had opened into a junction where he could stand upright. One of the new tunnels felt too warm and another one had collapsed entirely. But the third one looked promising, even more so when after a few dozen feet it began gently ascending.

The second junction he came to had proved even more encouraging. One of its shafts was vertical, with a rickety wooden ladder offering upward egress. But he'd only climbed a few feet when a rung broke under his boot, sending him back down. Another brutal lance of agony went through his injured leg when his heel hit the ground.

Struggling to ignore the pain, he started climbing again, this time tightly gripping the ladder's side rails in case of another weakened rung. Fortunately, the rest of them held. After an ascent of what must have been at least twenty-five feet, he intersected another horizontal shaft. Making his way over the lip of the hole, he examined the new tunnel. Both directions looked clear for as far as his beam would reach. He chose the tunnel leading to the right, this time guided by his acute sense of smell. The air was fresher in that direction, indicating a possible way to the surface.

A short walk brought him to a third junction, this one with a squarish vertical shaft. An empty elevator cage large enough to haul four men up and down the shaft rested on the floor. Best of all, the top of the cage was attached to a steel cable leading upward. There was also a gentle draft of air flowing downward, further suggesting it was a way out.

He climbed the side of the cage and shined his light up the shaft. High above, the beam reflected off what appeared to be a piece of mechanical equipment, and beyond, a grayish ceiling. He was too distant to make out anything more than that. But it had to be another junction of some kind.

The cable was rusted and flecked with dirt but seemed free of grease. It would be relatively easy to climb. A bonus would be taking the weight off his injured leg, providing temporary relief. Attaching the flashlight's carabiner clip to his belt, he began a hand-over-hand ascent. He was thankful for all those rope-climbing exercises done as part of his military training. Even so, his arms were tiring.

He reached a spot just below that piece of mechanical equipment, a thick cylinder over which the cable looped around to pivot it ninety degrees. The last few feet were tricky as he had to swing his good leg over the lip of the shaft to ease his body past the cylinder. But he made it and stood up.

He was in a room with a cement floor. The cable attached to a blackened, motorized winch a few feet from the opening, severed electrical wires dangling from its side. Beyond was a portal with a short flight of ascending brick steps. He could feel the cool night air flowing down from above.

He turned off the light and made his way over to the stairs in darkness. Peering upward, he could make out a jagged, roughly rectangular patch of night sky. The storm had blown over. Stars were visible.

Drawing the gun, he proceeded gingerly up the steps.

FIFTY-TWO

Addi's stress grew awaiting Glose's return. It was hard enough lying here in such a fragile and exposed state, half-naked on the bed. Whatever was in store for her, she just wanted it to happen.

The two mercs had been in the room down the hall with the unconscious Julio and Gideon for what seemed an inordinate length of time. She presumed they were cutting the netting and staging some kind of scene that would make the dino-humans' deaths appear accidental. Or maybe the plan was to make it seem like a double suicide. Whatever their intentions, if she managed to get through the encounter with Glose, she would go to their aid. If they were still alive, she'd find a way to–

Movement in the hallway drew in her thoughts. Her body stiffened. Footsteps approached. She twisted her neck to see behind her.

The door opened, filling the room with light from Glose's headlamp.

"Thanks for waiting for me," he said, the glee undisguised as he pulled the door shut behind him. "Hope you weren't getting worried."

She gave him a frightened look – part fake, part real – then pivoted her head away from him.

"Please, just get it over with!" She managed to make her voice crack, hopefully in a convincing way. "Do what you're going to do but don't make me watch. Please, that's all I ask. Please!"

She smushed her face into the mattress. It smelled foul. But the move accentuated her plea to be spared from having to look at him.

He remained silent. She worried the ploy wasn't working. Then the floor creaked as he approached. She sensed him kneeling at the side of the bed, felt his warm breath close to her ear. She flinched for real when his palm squeezed the lower cheeks of her bottom, his fingers probing at the cleft. His tone projected faux tenderness.

"There, there, little girl. I know you're scared. But I think it's better all around if you look. After all, you're only gonna get one chance in your life to watch someone fuck you to death."

He cackled, a sound as animalistic as it was heartless. A chill went through her.

She sensed him rising to his feet. His hands gripped the back of her shoulders in preparation for turning her over.

No hesitation, Tour Tot. Do it hard, do it fast.

She remembered all those times in the garage with Papa. Practicing the moves over and over until they were muscle memory. Practicing with a life-sized dummy, then later with peeled chunks of watermelon the size of a human face.

Glose flipped her onto her back. She lanced her right fist at his head and plunged the extended thumb straight into his left eye. He released a low gurgling cry and pulled away from the bed. She leaped upright, screaming at the top of her lungs to cover his squeals with fake torment of her own, hoping not to alert the other merc.

His hands clawed at her wrist, trying to wrench her thumb from his eye socket. Addi kept up the pressure, pushing him backward, forcing her digit deeper into the gooey remnants of his iris and pupil.

He backed into the dresser, which finally provided him enough stability to yank hard on her wrist and pull her thumb from the eye socket. She responded by kneeing him in the crotch. He collapsed to his knees, this time letting out a loud guttural cry that even her screaming couldn't camouflage.

"Glose? You OK?"

The other merc had heard. He'd be here in seconds. Addi was out of time. She gave Glose a new source of torment, rammed the entire length of her left thumb up his right nostril.

He thrashed and yelled but she kept the thumb inserted. Blood and mucus poured from the wounded tissue, soaking her hand. She kept pushing, trying to ram the digit all the way up into his brain. An impossibility, but it didn't matter. A quiet rage propelled her now. She was attuned to the moment, besieged by a state of calm where one logical action followed the next.

In the hallway… running footsteps…

Glose's hands locked onto her other wrist, yanked the agonizing intrusion from his nose. But that enabled Addi's free hand to fumble at his belt until it found the gun. Unsnapping the holster, she drew the pistol and pressed the barrel into his chest.

His remaining eye snapped open. She caught a flash of fear as she pulled the trigger three times. In the confines of the room, the shots sounded abnormally loud.

Glose crumbled. The door whipped open. The second

merc was still trying to draw his sidearm when she shot him through the headlamp. As his light shattered, she put another bullet through the groove between his lips and nose to make sure.

FIFTY-THREE

Eddie reached the opening at the top of the steps and made his way across the craggy lip, relieved to be outside. He stood in a debris field of shattered bricks and severed lengths of planking. Overhead, vivid stars dotted the blackness. The remnants of a cinderblock foundation and a chimney identified his location. He was in the midst of that collapsed building on Main Street, the one across from the sinkholes. It once must have been part of the mining operation, maybe even the site where the original dig had begun back in the nineteenth century, enabling workers to enter the tunnels from the downtown area.

The drone of a running motor drew his attention to the street. Keeping low and with his flashlight off, he scurried across the rubble ground and peered out from behind a clump of wall.

It was a UTV, parked in the street with its back end toward the sinkhole through which he'd fallen. A length of steel cable was unspooled from the vehicle's motorized winch and disappeared into the opening.

Nastor and another merc stood at the sinkhole's edge, their backs to him, their headlamps shining downward. The tautness of the cable indicated it was bearing weight. Probably one or more mercs were attached to the end, having been sent down to check on the status of the driver and guard, and their prisoner.

Had Eddie managed to bring the rifle, he easily could have shot the pair from here. But with a sidearm? Maybe, but probably not. Separated by the collapsed building's parking lot and nearly the width of the street rendered accurate aiming with a semiautomatic pistol dicey. And if he missed or only got one of the mercs, the other would open fire with the rifle lying on the ground just behind them. He needed to sneak closer. If he made it to the UTV, that would cut the distance to about seventy-five feet. He'd made pistol shots at that range, and the hum of the UTV's diesel engine supplying power to the winch should be loud enough to disguise his run across the expanse of open ground. But just as he was about to climb over the broken foundation, three muffled shots rang out from the direction of the luncheonette. They were followed by a brief pause, then two more. It sounded like pistol fire.

Eddie ducked behind the wall just in time. Nastor uttered a curse and sprinted toward the gunfire, pistol drawn. The second merc grabbed the rifle and followed. Their backs were to him now and he could take shots. But retreating figures in the darkness made for poor targets. Besides, a better idea occurred.

He leaped from his hiding place and dashed to the UTV. Hopping behind the wheel, he put it in gear and hit the gas.

The UTV accelerated fast. He closed to within shooting distance as the mercs neared the luncheonette. A yell erupted behind Eddie. He glimpsed a third merc in the mirror, still attached to the cable with carabiners. Yanked out of the sinkhole and flung high in the air, he plowed head-first into the macadam.

The running merc with the rifle spun around. But he hesitated, unable to make out the driver with high beams blasting his face. Eddie depressed the trigger rapidly, aware that shooting a pistol from a bouncing vehicle defied accuracy.

The spray of 9mm bullets forced the merc to take evasive action. He ducked and jerked to the left. He should have opened fire. The tactical error would be his last. The UTV crashed into him at high speed, shattering his legs and somersaulting him violently backward.

Nastor reached the luncheonette, took cover behind the remaining UTV parked in front. He opened fire with his pistol, spraying the fast-closing vehicle. Eddie grimaced as a round hit his armored chest and lodged there. The pain was bearable. But it triggered a full-blown onslaught of the bad yen.

Eddie held the pedal to the floor and steered straight toward the other vehicle. Nastor realized his peril, tried scampering away. Eddie leaped from behind the wheel an instant before the collision, combat-rolling down the street, grunting as the hard surface battered arms, legs and torso.

Eight tons of carbon fiber and steel slammed together. The driverless UTV's front end plowed into the side of the parked vehicle, shoving it into the curb. Its tires caught on the obstruction, flipping it over onto its roll cage and knocking Nastor off his feet.

Eddie came to a stop. He stood, wobbly from the tumble. Nastor was limping toward the luncheonette. Eddie took aim at his back and pulled the trigger. Nothing happened – the magazine was spent. He dropped the pistol as Nastor stumbled through the door and disappeared from view.

Eddie charged after him. Being shot and battered had exceeded the limits of the bad yen. The bloodburn was upon him.

FIFTY-FOUR

Addi set the pistol on the bed and pulled up her pants. She tried slowing her frantic breathing but couldn't manage the effort. Her hands were shaking as well. Just a post-traumatic reaction, she told herself. Entirely normal.

Normal? There was nothing whatsoever normal about what had happened in this room. She'd fought for her life. In the process, she'd killed two men. She wasn't sure she'd ever feel normal again.

She regained enough composure to remember Julio and Gideon. She was about to check on them when shooting erupted from outside. She donned Glose's intact headlamp, grabbed the gun and dashed into the hallway, reaching the top of the stairs when a loud boom erupted. It sounded like a car crash.

Turning off her light, she felt her way down the steps. She reached the bottom and froze as an armed figure with a headlamp stumbled through the door and fell face-down on the linoleum floor. Even in the darkness, she recognized Nastor. Flattening herself against the wall to be less conspicuous, she raised the pistol.

Nastor's attention was directed outside. Grimacing from a bloody wound on his hip, he rolled onto his back and fired wildly through the doorway.

Eddie exploded into the room through the remnants of a flanking window. Glass shards flew everywhere. Before the merc could draw a bead on him, Eddie leaped onto his chest and knocked the gun from his hand. Nastor was helpless beneath him.

The merc let out a chilling scream as Eddie's mouth descended on his neck and tore out a plum-sized clump of flesh. Nastor's limbs flailed helplessly. Blood spurted from the deep wound. Eddie's teeth sought a new tender spot, ripping through the merc's shirt to take a huge bite out of his shoulder. He threw back his head, chewing and swallowing.

Addi was horrified. It was one thing dispassionately counseling Eddie during those months of therapy, discussing the bloodburn in abstract terms. Witnessing it firsthand was something else entirely. This was nothing like his savagery with the rabbit during that test on the obstacle course. It was more like one of those nature documentaries of an animal attack in the wild, or like watching a gator erupt from beneath the swamp to snatch an unwary bird in its jaws.

But in those instances, the predator was after sustenance and needed to feed on weaker prey. Here, the motivation was not fundamental. Eddie's cannibalism was the product of xenotransplantation and surgeries, amplified by twisted rage. It was sickening and inhumane, even more so because she knew the predator so intimately.

"Eddie."

The word emerged as little more than a whisper. He didn't hear her, continuing to ravage the now lifeless merc.

"Eddie!"

He roared to his feet, spun to face her. She turned her headlamp back on, spotlighting his face. Strands of flesh hung from his mouth. Ruby lips dripped blood. They stared at one another from across the room, motionless for a moment that seemed fated not to end.

FIFTY-FIVE

Guilt. The emotion coursed through Eddie the instant he set eyes on Addi. Her look of revulsion made the feeling worse.

The guilt served to diminish the bloodburn, releasing him from its power. Another potent urge took its place, a need to talk to her about what he'd done. If that was even possible. If her disgust wasn't so overwhelming that she'd never want to speak to him again.

Now wasn't the time for such concerns. They were still in danger. Spitting out strands of flesh lodged between his teeth and wiping a sleeve across his befouled mouth, he rushed toward her. She backed away. He halted five feet from her and lifted a forefinger to his mouth, signaling quiet.

"Five mercs down," he whispered. "Two still unaccounted for."

Her gaze went past him to Nastor's body. Eddie knew she was wondering if the other mercs had died in a similar fashion.

"Upstairs," she said, speaking at a normal volume and lowering the gun.

Eddie stayed alert, trailing her up the steps and along a hallway to the first open door. She moved aside so he could peer into the room. One merc was crumpled just inside, shot in the face. Glose lay a few feet away, a massive red stain on his shirt from what must have been multiple bullet wounds. One of his eyes was missing. A bloody nostril seemed oddly deformed.

Eddie turned to her. "Did you...?"

She glared at him, her hardened eyes providing the answer. But then a confused look overtook her and she turned away, perhaps sensing uncomfortable correlations between his explosion of violence and her own.

She proceeded along the hallway and through the second open door. Eddie entered, fearing the worst. The room was just as grungy as the other one but larger, with two beds. Julio was face up on one, hands folded across his chest in a funeral pose. Gideon was positioned identically on the other bed. They still wore those face masks connected to thin cylinders strapped to their arms. Their left sleeves were rolled up.

Addi rushed to Julio, Eddie to Gideon. Fingers felt around necks and wrists for signs of life.

"He's still with us," she said. "But his pulse is weak."

Eddie nodded. "Same here."

Addi checked the markings on the cylinders. "A mild anesthetic. Just potent enough to keep them under."

Eddie reached to remove Gideon's mask.

"No, wait! Leave it on."

She checked their bare arms. "Injection marks. They're recent."

That silver briefcase was propped open on the dresser. She rushed over to it. The padded interior had slots for the masks and cylinders, as well as four hypodermic syringes.

"Two of them have been used," she said. "The others must be backups."

"Any idea what they were shot up with?"

She shook her head. "No markings on the syringes. I'm guessing a slow-acting poison, something that would ease them into peaceful deaths."

And remove any suspicions of murder.

"It's possible the anesthetic is keeping their blood pressure and other vitals artificially low," she said. "Keeping them alive."

Eddie grasped the outline of the mercs' plan. "They maintain sedation until a point of no return is reached and recovery from the poison impossible."

Addi continued the deduction. "Then remove the masks and cylinders and squeeze their hands around the spent syringes to embed their own fingerprints, making it seem as if they injected themselves. Wipe down the room, leaving only the syringes. Plant fake evidence on their phones suggesting the future seemed hopeless and they wanted to die together."

"A double suicide."

"Col. Marsh and whoever else was in on this use Wesk to alter certain data, make it seem like Julio and Gideon acquired the poison specifically for that purpose. When their bodies are found, no evidence of foul play."

A hint of the bad yen returned as Eddie envisioned his teeth ripping into the colonel's neck. "Anything you can do to counteract the poison?"

"Not without knowing what it is. We need help out here, fast. Who do we call? Billy Orb?"

Eddie shook his head. "They might not let him leave. Can't take the chance of contacting anyone at the compound, not with Wesk likely eavesdropping."

Addi dashed back to the other room, returned with a sat phone lifted from one of the dead mercs. She punched in 9-1-1.

"Don't give your name," he cautioned.

She spoke rapidly the instant the emergency call center operator picked up.

"I have two men who've been administered an unknown poison. They're barely alive and we need urgent assistance. We're in Morralsia, the ghost town. The luncheonette on Main Street. Send a Medevac copter as fast as you can."

She paused, listening to the operator's response. Eddie could hear the woman asking for Addi's name and callback information. The center's system must not be registering the sat phone number.

"Never mind all that," she snapped. "This is urgent. Two lives are in your hands. First priority, the Medevac. Then call the police. We have multiple bodies out here, gunshot victims." She glanced at Eddie. "Other types of fatal injuries as well."

The operator kept asking for more details. Addi's anger grew. "Just do what I ask, dammit! Their lives are in your hands!"

She hung up, grimaced. "I should have kept my cool. They might not have bought it."

Eddie snatched the phone and punched in a number. "I'll make sure they do."

Addi raised a quizzical eyebrow.

"I'm calling that reporter, Misty Garrison. I'll get her to contact 9-1-1 and confirm."

"What are you going to tell her?"

"Everything."

FIFTY-SIX

As Wesk reported the latest developments, Col. Marsh's face took on a pallor suggestive of being physically ill. He remained motionless behind the desk in Blayvine's penthouse office for a long moment before responding.

"You're sure?" he whispered.

It was not the sort of question the colonel usually posed. Wesk was providing information culled from a vast network of data nodes and sensors inside and outside the compound. The data was solid, not open to interpretation. But it was clear that in this instance, the colonel needed to be comforted by reiteration.

"The two calls were made from the sat phone of one of the contractors. The caller or callers identities could not be ascertained due to the phone's scrambling capability. The regional emergency center was reviewing the validity of the initial call when it was contacted by Misty Garrison, the reporter with *The Axton Record*. At that point the emergency center activated a full-blown response.

"Two Medevac copters are about to land in Morralsia. Multiple airborne and ground units of the West Virginia State Police will arrive in less than four minutes. Pumpers from the closest fire station were also requested as backup in case there are issues relating to the ongoing mine fire.

"Attempts to reach Nastor and the other contractors continue to be in vain. GPS tracking indicates that none of the phones, with the exception of the one used to make the calls, have moved from their locations for more than half an hour. There is a ninety-eight percent probability that such an extended lack of mobility indicates that the SEG members are either incapacitated or dead."

Col. Marsh stared at a statue in the corner of the office, a life-size depiction of a human figure rendered entirely out of tiny dodecahedrons. Wesk once overheard him complaining to Sgt. Petersen about Blayvine's poor taste in art.

The colonel seemed to recover his poise. "Are there any alternative conclusions the data would support?"

"None that rise to the level of statistical likelihood. Do you want specific probabilities?"

He shook his head.

"Should I dispatch the drone back to Morralsia to monitor the situation as it unfolds?"

"Unnecessary." Col. Marsh rose from the desk. "I'll be in my quarters."

"Should I continue providing updates or call if–"

"It's late. I'm tired. I'm going to sleep."

FIFTY-SEVEN

There was difficulty assigning a name to the closed-door meeting in Admin's spacious, sixth-floor conference room. No one seemed to know exactly what to call it. Even Gen. Hollenbach, who had ordered the assemblage and was overseeing it, had utilized different titles during her introductory remarks: an informal hearing, an extrajudicial inquiry, a fact-finding probe.

Whatever the nomenclature, Eddie knew that what happened here today could well determine his fate, not to mention the future of Project Saurian. If compelling testimony was presented about what he'd done to Nastor in Morralsia a week ago – euphemistically referred to as "the incident" – he could end up facing a court martial.

Gen. Hollenbach and the two individuals flanking her faced the assemblage from an elevated bench, giving the sense of a tripartite judiciary in a courtroom. To the general's right was a male army major, an attorney from the Judge Advocate General's office; to her left, a woman recently elevated to acting CEO of Blayvine Industries in the wake of its founder's hospitalization. From Eddie's isolated chair up front, he felt like a defendant in a trial even though he'd been assured that wasn't the case.

"Let's get started," Gen. Hollenbach said, pushing back her mic stand when her voice boomed too loudly. "I remind everyone again that much of what will be discussed here this morning, and throughout the day, remains classified. Any violations by those under military oversight will be treated with the utmost severity. Those not under such authority who will be brought in at appropriate times to give testimony have been cautioned in the strongest terms not to discuss the proceedings outside of this room."

She was referring to the various state police and EMS units who'd first arrived in Morralsia, and who had been shocked by the carnage they'd encountered. Several of the medics had treated Eddie, whose leg injury turned out to be less severe than he'd feared. Also to be summoned from the waiting area was Misty Garrison, whose relentless and urgent calls to the emergency center that night had convinced skeptical phone operators that Addi's initial call for help was on the level.

Eddie admired the fact that Gen. Hollenbach wanted to hear directly from everyone involved and that it appeared she wasn't trying to cover up the incident. She obviously recognized that if there was to be any hope of salvaging the project from the wreckage inflicted upon it by Col. Marsh, a full accounting was necessary. Besides, Misty already had broken the brunt of the story on *The Axton Record's* website. The battle with mercenaries in a forlorn ghost town was receiving international media coverage. About the only aspect not yet made public was his cannibalistic assault on Nastor.

That was liable to change.

He glanced over at Addi, seated in the front row. She'd been avoiding his gaze and continued doing so. They hadn't spoken much since being driven back to the compound that night in separate vehicles and kept apart after individual debriefings. Eddie knew she remained upset by his cannibalism, not only by her visceral reaction to it but by the fact their intense therapy apparently had been in vain. He'd put a further chill on their relationship by suggesting he take full responsibility for killing all seven mercs. His noble attempt to spare her from being tainted as a killer backfired. She'd angrily warned that she intended telling the whole truth, and advised him to do the same.

Also summoned to testify were a number of individuals from the compound who might shed further light on the incident. Billy Orb and Samson sat directly behind Addi; a row back from them were Dr Steinhauser and Dr Kim. Various Med staffers with firsthand knowledge of what had occurred in the OR earlier that evening were scattered throughout the room, including Tanya Aguilar. Sequestered from the others in the far corner was Col. Marsh's aide, Sgt. Petersen, who hadn't yet been charged as an accomplice. But the pair of hulking MPs seated behind him suggested that his testimony and that of others could well lead to his being led out in cuffs.

The colonel had already suffered such a fate. Once the DoD learned he'd been responsible for putting together an off-the-books team of contractors to murder Julio, Gideon and Addi, Gen. Hollenbach had ordered him taken into custody. Col. Marsh had been transferred to the DoD's maximum-security prison at Leavenworth to await trial. Eddie hoped not only that he would be convicted, but that he'd become a rare military prisoner sentenced to death by lethal injection.

As for the two dino-humans at the center of the incident, the Medevacs had arrived that night just in time to save their lives. Unfortunately, Julio and Gideon weren't out of the woods. Because of their unusual physiology, the slow poison they'd been administered had produced severe side effects, including damage to their kidneys and other vital organs. Both remained in intensive care.

The other notable absence was Dr Quelphius. Apparently having gotten over the worst of his anger from losing the court case to save his precious retroverts, he'd returned to the compound yesterday to continue his regular work. However, he'd adamantly refused to appear today unless subpoenaed. Quelph's nonattendance was rumored to be because he still blamed Eddie for killing the rampaging Dilopho. Gen. Hollenbach also had banned Wesk, having learned it may have been compromised as part of the colonel's plan. To ensure the AI was denied access, phones and other electronic devices were confiscated before entering the room. The army stenographer adjacent to the bench was forced to transcribe testimony with an old-fashioned steno machine without digital access.

"Captain Morozov will begin the questioning," the general announced, gesturing to a youthful looking officer seated near the stenographer.

"Thank you, ma'am." Notebook in hand, the captain rose and nodded to one of the MPs stationed at the back. The soldier opened the door and ushered in a middle-aged woman, who took a seat at a small table serving as an improvised witness box. Eddie recognized her as the administrator in charge of the ORs.

She wasn't formally sworn in – none of the witnesses were to be, as would happen in a regular courtroom. Under Capt. Morozov's precise questioning, the administrator related how she'd received orders signed by Col. Marsh, as well as by Dr Steinhauser and Dr Kim, that Julio and Gideon were to be brought into an OR for an immediate debridement procedure.

The shocked expressions on the faces of the two doctors suggested they had granted no such approval. The administrator went on to say that due to the urgent request for the unusual evening surgeries, she'd taken the added step of calling the colonel to confirm their validity. She'd also asked why he'd wanted guards posted in the OR. The colonel's brusque response was that it was none of her concern.

"You should have called us too for confirmation!" Dr Steinhauser shouted, rising halfway out of her chair.

"That will be enough of that," the general warned. "Those sorts of outbursts will not be tolerated."

"My apologies." Still fuming, Dr Steinhauser resumed her seat.

After a few more questions, the captain finished with the administrator and she left the room. A parade of witnesses to the events in the OR followed, including a notarized statement from the anesthesiologist read into the record. The man remained hospitalized with injuries suffered during the fight. He claimed to know nothing about any fatal poison being introduced into the anesthetic, but admitted the possibility of tampering being done without his knowledge.

Tanya Aguilar was the last of the Med staffers summoned to give testimony. During Eddie's debriefing, he'd described his encounter with Tanya in the OR after the dino-humans' escape, and his belief she'd been lying or telling half-truths. In light of that, Capt. Morozov's questioning was particularly harsh.

Tanya struggled to respond to his grilling, but her insistence about being in the OR as an innocent observer contradicted the earlier testimony of several other Med witnesses. Confronted with that, her story fell apart. She broke down and admitted that under Col. Marsh's orders, she'd substituted the original anesthetic with one given to her by Sgt. Petersen.

"But I didn't know it was poison, that it was meant to kill them. You have to believe me, I didn't know!"

"Even if that's true," Capt. Morozov interjected, "why would you do something so obviously unlawful?"

"I did it for him," she said, her eyes tearing up. "For G.T.!"

"You're referring to Col. Marsh?"

"We've been together for... a while. We kept our affair secret... G.T. wanted it that way." She turned a pleading gaze to the three stern faces on the dais. "You have to understand, I love him!"

"Be that as it may," the general said, "you have admitted to being part of a criminal conspiracy." She motioned to one of the MPs. "At the conclusion of these proceedings, please take Ms Aguilar into custody pending the filing of formal charges."

The MP nodded. Tanya, crying softly, rose and returned to her seat. She paused to look at Eddie and mouth the words, *I'm sorry.*

He didn't doubt she was. Despite her actions, he felt sympathy for her. She was in love. What she'd done wasn't rational or appropriate, merely understandable.

Misty Garrison was brought into the room next to relay the details of her involvement in the incident. She was followed by the first responders who'd converged on Morralsia, including state police, EMS and Medevac units. Their testimony took up the rest of the morning. Gen. Hollenbach called a break for lunch, ordering them to reconvene at 1:00.

Eddie attempted talking to Addi as everyone filtered out, but she'd disappeared by the time he reached the hallway. He spent most of the lunch hour alone in the Barracks cafeteria, half-heartedly downing a sandwich and iced tea. Just as he was finishing, Samson appeared and plopped down at his table.

"What's gonna happen to us, Eddie?" he asked worriedly. "Are we gonna be OK? I really miss Julio and Gideon. Are they gonna be OK?"

"I wish I had answers for you, Big Guy. But I don't. We just have to stay positive and hope things work out. Somehow we're all going to get through this."

His encouraging words were less than heartfelt but it didn't seem to matter. Reassured, Samson's worries dissolved into a contented smile. Eddie acknowledged a moment of envy for his childish capacity to remain oblivious to the troubles and complexities of the adult world.

"Do you think they'll let me testify?" Samson asked. "I want to, Eddie, I really do!"

"I don't know who else they plan on calling as witnesses."

"But I want to! I want to tell everyone how much I miss Julio and Gideon." A shadow crossed his face.

"I can't promise anything, but I'll ask General Hollenbach if you can speak."

Samson brightened again. "Good-good-good!"

"C'mon, we should head back over. They'll be starting soon."

Eddie hoped they would let Samson testify, along with any other witnesses present or waiting in the wings. All should be called upon first. Anything to delay the inevitable, the moment he was summoned to the stand and prompted to tell the whole truth.

FIFTY-EIGHT

Eddie caught Gen. Hollenbach and Capt. Morozov as they were about to reenter the courtroom. He passed on Samson's request. The captain was skeptical.

"I get that he wants to feel like he's a part of this. But I really don't think it's necessary or appropriate."

Gen. Hollenbach disagreed. "I'm sure we can allow him a few minutes. Just keep your questions short and simple."

"Yes ma'am."

"But Samson will have to wait. Sgt. Boka, you'll be testifying first. It's time everyone heard your story."

Eddie managed a weak nod. At his debriefing, he'd told the truth about what had happened to Nastor. It was probable the general had received a transcript of his interrogation. Because none of the debriefers had ventured any opinions or criticisms at the time, he had a good hunch of what everyone expected of him today. Gloss over the grimmer details, thus sparing himself from prosecution, and maybe save Project Saurian in the bargain.

And should Addi subsequently testify to what she'd seen, they'd likely subject her to a harsh cross-examination meant to cast doubt on her statements. It suddenly occurred to Eddie that grilling her might not even be necessary. Much safer for them if she simply wasn't called as a witness.

Gen. Hollenbach announced the start of the afternoon session and Capt. Morozov summoned Eddie to the witness stand. He glanced at Addi as he took his place. She was no longer avoiding his gaze. Her eyes were locked onto him but her face still betrayed no emotion, at least none he could read.

"Sgt. Boka," the captain began, "would you please tell us, as best as you can recollect, the entire sequence of events on the night of the incident."

Eddie began with getting the summons to report to Col. Marsh. He told of learning the nature of the emergency, encountering Tanya in the OR and Samson near the obstacle course, then tracking the soldiers to where Julio and Gideon tunneled out of the compound. He went on to describe uncovering the nature of the mercs' murderous mission, enlisting the aid of Addi and Billy to escape the compound and entering the ghost town. He told of finding the dino-humans hiding in the church and their subsequent capture, and gave a blow-by-blow description of his fight against the mercs.

He panned his gaze across the assemblage throughout. Everyone was hunched forward in their seats, riveted by his story: the plunge into the sinkhole, the climb to the surface, his final battle with the mercs. Finally he came to the confrontation with Nastor. But before he could describe what happened in the luncheonette, Capt. Morozov interrupted.

"And after dispatching the leader of Col. Marsh's murderous contractors, you went upstairs. Tell us what you found there?"

Eddie matched his steely gaze. "I didn't finish telling you what happened to Nastor."

"As I've come to understand, it was brutal hand-to-hand combat, with nothing less than your life hanging in the balance. But didn't the truly horrifying part of the night commence immediately after that fight, when you and Dr LaTour proceeded to the second floor of the luncheonette. Tell us what you found there."

"We discovered Julio and Gideon in a bedroom, unconscious. A scene was being staged to make it appear that the poison they'd consumed had been by their own volition, that they were committing suicide together. You pretty much know from the earlier testimony what happened from that point on."

"Yes, we do. And I believe everyone appreciates the incredible bravery you displayed in saving your friends."

"Thanks. But now I need to go back to the part we skipped over. It's important everyone hear this."

The captain hesitated, unsure how to continue. He glanced up at the judges, seeking guidance. The general spoke.

"I don't think Capt. Morozov meant to cut you off, Sergeant. I believe he was only trying to move things along and avoid irrelevant details."

"Absolutely," the captain said. "I was just trying to keep us focused on the most important aspects of that terrible evening."

Manipulation. Eddie thought again about how the four of them had been used from the beginning to ensure a successful and ultimately profitable outcome: sell the world on the concept of dino-human armies. He'd been a partner in all that, even hiding and distorting the truth at times to ensure the goal was reached. And now in this room, it was clear that everyone except Addi wanted him to uphold one of those distortions.

Would he be doing the right thing by coming clean and exposing his darkest secret? Did it make sense putting an end to the lies if it meant possibly throwing away his own future, maybe even trading his freedom for a prison cell?

Those questions didn't really matter, he realized. He'd known what he needed to do from the moment Nastor breathed his last breath.

Gasps emanated from the assemblage as he related in vivid detail what he'd done, how he'd savaged the merc like a wild animal. When he finished, some of those faces regarded him with shock. A hush seemed to envelop the room, as bleak as a winter night in Arizona near where he'd grown up. He couldn't gauge Addi's reaction, but it did seem that her features had softened, and that she was glad he'd put it all out there.

Gen. Hollenbach conferred in whispers with the other judges, or whatever the trio were calling themselves. They seemed to reach a consensus. The general rose.

"Sgt. Boka, we need you to clarify something. Upon engaging in combat with that contractor, did you at any time feel there was a reasonable chance of subduing him rather than inflicting fatal injuries in the manner you described?"

They were giving him a way out, one more chance to save himself. But he'd come this far and saw no reason to change course.

"I could have taken him prisoner there at the end rather than assaulting him. All I can say is that I was under the spell of a powerful compulsion. But ultimately, that's no excuse, not really. I could and should have been able to control those violent emotions. I didn't."

The general gave a resigned nod. "While your candor is

admirable, you have just admitted to killing a defenseless enemy combatant. Under both DoD regulations and international law, that is a crime. At the conclusion of today's proceedings, you will be taken into custody pending the filing of charges."

"Yes ma'am, I understand."

"In light of these latest disclosures, I believe it's in everyone's best interests that we adjourn for today. We'll reconvene at 9:00 tomorrow morning."

A postponement made sense. They wanted time to attempt some form of damage control, come up with ways to save Project Saurian from Eddie's devastating body blow. He didn't think it was possible.

As he got up and returned to his seat, he met Addi's eyes. Her expression was finally readable. Sadness, tinged with regret.

As everyone started making for the exit, a booming voice froze them in place.

"Folks, we're not done here. Please remain in your seats."

Eddie was shocked to realize who had uttered the words. His astonishment grew as Samson got up and strode toward the front of the room. Instead of his familiar waddling gait, he moved with a commanding swagger, like some triumphant politician on his way to center stage.

"Good job, Eddie," Samson said, easing his bulk into the witness chair. "I can only imagine how hard it was for you making that admission. But truth will out, or so the classic aphorism goes. Personally, I found your willingness to reveal everything quite inspiring."

Eddie was momentarily speechless. "Samson... I don't understand."

"I know. But I've got things from here. Sit back and relax while I bring everyone up to speed."

Samson's reassuring smile seemed otherworldly. It was as if the familiar Big Guy had transformed into an entirely different person. Puzzled mutterings coursed through the room as everyone resumed their places.

"I'm afraid we're at a loss, Private," Capt. Morozov said. "What's going on here?"

"Transformation. Eddie Boka took the commendable step of emerging from the darkness into the light. What I have to say will continue the process."

The captain hesitated, then turned to the bench. "Whatever is happening is highly irregular. I would suggest an immediate adjournment so that we all may–"

"Sit your ass down, son. It's *my* turn."

The volume and severity of Samson's words reminded Eddie of his drill instructor at boot camp, a man possessing a voice that any within its range ignored at their peril. Gen. Hollenbach nodded to Capt. Morozov to back off.

"Private Samson, I believe it's safe to say that our curiosity has been piqued. You have the floor."

"Thank you, ma'am. I'll start by addressing the first question likely running through everyone's head, namely, 'Who the hell is this guy and what did he do with the real Samson?' But we're going to have to flip that around so the question becomes, 'Why has the real Samson been hiding behind the persona of a lovable doofus?'

"Here's the backstory, the short version. When I awakened from my last series of infusions and surgeries, I perceived the world like never before. For reasons that remain a mystery, the severe modifications resulted in an IQ boost. An *extreme* IQ boost. Not to brag, but I went from a guy of modest intelligence to someone in the stratospheric heights of the profoundly gifted. All things considered, it was a weird and wonderful transformation.

"Within minutes of awakening, I grasped the ramifications and realized what would be in store for me. I'd already been pressured into becoming a physical freak – that's a tale for another day – and although I'd come to terms with being a dino human, I didn't relish the idea of idea of also being viewed as a mental freak as well.

"Had I outed myself, the project would have consigned me to the status of a lab rat. I'd have been studied by well-meaning scientists and researchers, all eager to discern how and why I suddenly could calculate the wave functions of a quantum-mechanical system and had a better grasp of international diplomacy than most politicians. And after determining the extent of my intellectual gifts, I would have been used by the project for whatever tasks the powers-that-be deemed appropriate.

"Those fates weren't for me. So as my physical recovery progressed, I feigned escalating levels of ignorance until I was perceived to have dropped to the emotional level and IQ of a rather dim-witted child. I created the persona you've come to know, someone with the characteristics of a loyal pet. I became good-natured, happy-go-lucky Samson, everyone's friend. That had the added benefit of allowing me a certain freedom of movement around the compound.

"After a while, no one felt the need to monitor where the big friendly doggy was trotting off to, or wonder what kind of mischief he might be getting into. And oh yes, I did get into some serious mischief." His eyes displayed a roguish glint. "*Bad* Samson. But more on that in a bit."

He rose, came out from behind the table and began a waist-twisting exercise, keeping his legs immobile while slowly pivoting his upper torso from side to side.

"Sorry, need to recondition some muscle groups. Been doing that waddling routine for so long that my body sometimes forgot how to move normally. And unfortunately, I also took a few nasty spills trying to sell the act."

Eddie watched with fascination. He still found it difficult trying to reconcile the uber-confident dino-human limbering up in front of him with the gentle simpleton he'd come to know. A glance around the room suggested he wasn't the only one experiencing that problem.

"So, that's the basic outline of what happened to me. I wish I could tell you I'm sorry for having deceived everyone. But the truth is, I'm not. Circumstances dictated my duplicity.

"At this time, it will be necessary to ask most of the individuals gathered here to leave the room. We've now come to a discussion of matters of an ultra-sensitive nature. Only those with the highest security clearances should be permitted to stay."

The judges again conferred. After some back-and-forth whispering, Gen. Hollenbach asked that the room be cleared.

"The stenographer and the MPs too," Samson instructed.

As the chattering crowd filtered out, many glanced wide-eyed at the witness, still stunned by his revelations.

"But not Eddie and Dr LaTour," Samson clarified. "They need to hear this. Dr Steinhauser and Dr Kim should remain too."

Soon only the four named individuals, the three judges and Capt. Morozov remained. Eddie didn't know what fresh revelations were about to be shared. But as Samson finished exercising and resumed his seat, he was certain one long-smoldering mystery had been solved.

Hello, Cwacian.

FIFTY-NINE

"Project Saurian was flawed from the start," Samson explained. "Don't get me wrong, the idea of a dino-human army is probably sound. As long as humans make war upon one another, technological advancements will be incorporated into battlefield weaponry. Genome-electrome alterations to produce super-soldiers is the logical next step.

"No, what I'm talking about is the personality flaws of those in charge, especially the five overlords. Their shortcomings in the form of deep neuroses and egomaniacal behavior introduced corrupting elements, leading ultimately to the present crisis. Selfishness and arrogance are often unavoidable byproducts of creative and intensely driven individuals, and the overlords possess those qualities in excess, particularly Blayvine, Col. Marsh and Dr Quelphius. Still, Dr Kim and Dr Steinhauser also share significant responsibility for the project's deficiencies."

"I resent the accusation," Dr Kim interrupted. "I'm sure Dr Steinhauser does as well. Certainly I admit to character imperfections, like everyone else on the planet. However, I assure you that we joined Project Saurian with the best of intentions. Dr Steinhauser can back me up on this. On numerous occasions, the two of us engaged in private discussions on how to temper and ameliorate some of the more loathsome ideas proposed by the others."

"There's some validity in what you're saying," Samson admitted. "But all five of you were aware of and fully supported a massively cruel deception, namely that our surgical transformations rendered the dino-humans sexually neutered. That was an outright lie. The two of you then participated in the secret administration of those green capsules, libido inhibitors meant to keep us chemically castrated."

"Yes, we did," Dr Kim said. "But that decision was made early on in the project, well before we ever came aboard. We had no choice but to go along with what by then was established policy."

Dr Steinhauser shook her head. "No, Samson's right. I've felt bad about what we were doing to them from the beginning. It's always tormented me, kept me awake many a night. I've been in treatment myself for anxiety, and my therapist and I pegged its origin to that deception." She faced the judges. "As medical professionals, Dr Kim and I should never have allowed such a thing to go on. We should have stood up to Blayvine and the colonel and demanded they find another way."

"Which would have led nowhere," Dr Kim countered. "We would have been dismissed, and doctors with more agreeable dispositions found to take our places. And all the good we were able to accomplish in helping Eddie and Samson, and Julio and Gideon, would never have occurred. From day one, we fought for the best interests of the four of you."

"And I'm sure you did some good," Samson said. "Yet your justification for the green capsules still boils down to,

'We were just following orders'. War crimes tribunals at least as far back as the judges in the Nuremberg trials of the Nazis have rejected that argument, declaring that it doesn't negate culpability."

Dr Kim stiffened. "I resent the comparison."

"Resent it all you like, Doc, but that doesn't make it untrue. I doubt either of you will face any sort of legal consequences for your actions. However, I'd respectfully suggest that you follow Dr Steinhauser's lead and search your conscience. Some badly needed introspection may guide you toward enlightenment."

Dr Kim looked ready to unleash an angry response but instead clamped his mouth shut. Eddie resisted an urge to stand up and clap in support of Samson's put-down of the psychiatrist. Since learning about the libido inhibitors from Gideon, he'd gone through a harsh reappraisal of the two doctors he'd once considered friends.

"The unchecked egos of Blayvine and Col. Marsh indeed led them into some dubious decision-making," Samson continued. "But I want to talk about the third overlord. For some time now, Dr Quelphius has been acting against the dino-humans' best interests in a more fundamental way, by sabotaging the project.

"Months ago, he secretly diluted the libido inhibitors to render them ineffective. It wasn't difficult, considering he's in charge of the labs. Later, when the overlords became curious about why the green capsules no longer seemed to be working and why the dino-humans' sexuality had become an issue, it was Quelph who reviewed the procedures of the compounding pharmacy. Naturally, he lied to cover up his tampering and reported that everything was fine."

"Why would he resort to such behavior?" Dr Steinhauser asked.

"To kill Project Saurian. Surveys have always suggested that public support for dino-humans would be severely weakened should the four of us be perceived as sexually active. Drilling down in the survey data revealed concerns by both males and females. A majority of men exhibited subliminal fears that our powerful animalistic natures would enable us to out-compete them in securing mates. Those same qualities left many women repulsed by us, again at a level operating below that of conscious thought. Bottom line, such apprehensions would reduce support for the project. If that support fell beneath a certain threshold, the project would be cancelled. In Quelph's mind, Blayvine Industries and the DoD would then prioritize what he's desired and worked toward from the beginning, having the retroverts be the basis for a future army."

"That was never going to happen," Gen. Hollenbach said. "Those creatures were never more than an experimental shot in the dark. They turned out to be too dangerous and unmanageable."

"A rational conclusion, but one that not everyone was capable of reaching." Samson faced Addi. "Dr LaTour, what is your professional opinion of Dr Quelphius?"

She hesitated. "He has some issues."

"No need to be coy, Addi. Cards on the table, if you please."

"All right. I believe he likely suffers from narcissistic personality disorder."

"Could that lead to more severe problems, even something as severe as a psychotic break?"

"In extreme circumstances, yes."

Samson faced the judges. "I believe Dr Quelphius may have suffered such a break. Admittedly, that's the opinion of someone with no formal training in psychological analysis. But I unearthed some disquieting information just before this hearing began. I believe Quelph introduced some sort of experimental toxin into that flask Blayvine was always sipping from, the nutrient cocktail he believed would extend his life. The toxin is responsible for Blayvine's illness."

Gen. Hollenbach couldn't hide her shock. "You're saying Dr Quelphius caused his cancer?"

"Yes. Blayvine gave the order to have the retroverts executed. In Quelph's mind he had to be punished. It was a matter of extracting vengeance." Samson glanced at Eddie. "Blayvine's not the only one he might seek retribution upon."

Eddie understood. Quelph blamed him for Dilopho's death.

"You have proof of any of these charges?" the general asked.

"Enough circumstantial evidence to strongly urge that Dr Quelphius be immediately removed from all official responsibilities and interrogated. I'm certain a formal investigation will dredge up proof. One more thing. I realize the turmoil of the past week has postponed the transfer of the retroverts to Leavenworth to be euthanized. I'd suggest an even longer delay, at least until Quelph can be questioned and any notes he made on those cochlear implants studied by an independent research team. I suspect those implants of his can do far more than just mediate the retroverts' levels of aggression. They may enable him to engage in a more direct form of communication and control."

The general again conferred in whispers with the other judges. This time she appeared to get into a heated argument with the woman serving as acting CEO of Blayvine Industries.

"You make a strong case," the general said at last. "But if you're wrong about your accusations, you could further alienate a brilliant scientist, the man largely responsible for both the dino human and retrovert projects."

"Understood. But I'm not wrong."

"Be that as it may, it might be too late to further delay the euthanasias. The retroverts left the compound this morning by copter for Leavenworth."

Samson frowned. "Is Quelph aboard?"

"He is. Part of the agreement Blayvine and Col. Marsh came up with to soften Dr Quelphius' anger over the retroverts' death sentence permitted him to accompany the creatures to their final destination."

"You mustn't think of them as creatures, General. They're Quelph's *children*. By his way of thinking, they're on their way to being *murdered*. I strongly suggest you contact that flight immediately and direct the pilots to set down at the nearest base."

"Whatever your concerns, I can assure you that multiple precautions were undertaken. Soldiers are onboard. The retroverts were secured in predatory-animal enclosures and given a potent anesthetic."

Samson stood, underscoring his urgency. "And did that anesthetic happen to come from the pharmacy here in the compound, the same one Dr Quelphius oversees?"

Gen. Hollenbach got the point. Reaching into her pocket for a phone, she abruptly recalled banning comm devices from the room.

"Capt. Morozov, please have someone contact that copter and get a status update."

"Yes ma'am."

"And order them to land," Samson called out as the captain rushed for the door.

"First things first," the general said. "If it's warranted, we'll bring them down. While we're waiting, how about telling us how you learned of Quelph's tampering. In fact, how you learned about all these matters."

"I mentioned earlier about getting into mischief. Primarily that was accomplished through Wesk. Early on, I discovered Blayvine's means for accessing and controlling the AI. I piggybacked on his work and created my own secret backdoor into Wesk's core, bypassing normal entry procedures. From that point, I had full systems ingress, including comms and surveillance."

Eddie recalled Tom Koplanski's theory about Cwacian, that he'd probably found a way of using Wesk for his own ends, routing those text poems through the AI to hide his identity.

"An unintended byproduct of my intrusion into Wesk's core substructures was that on occasion, my own personality made it seem as if Wesk was experiencing an enigmatic quality suggestive of AGI, Artificial General Intelligence. In reality, my presence deep within it gave that illusion."

Gen. Hollenbach frowned. "You do realize that these admissions you're making likely constitute criminal activity. For starters, illegally accessing classified government information carries severe penalties."

"I'm aware," Samson said. "But I always figured on someday outing myself, revealing the true me. Realizing that such admissions could lead to trouble, I took precautions.

I'll forward you the particulars when we have comm access again. But for now, a quick summary should suffice.

"I used Wesk to penetrate a large number of supposedly secure external networks, including those within Blayvine Industries and the DoD. I've gathered a formidable amount of evidence of illicit activities by numerous individuals within those organizations and others. Not to brag but you might want to think of me as the hacker from hell."

"And you're now flirting with potential charges of treason," the JAG major warned.

"True enough. But nobody's likely to bring me up on charges. If they do, I have thousands of incriminating files ready to be automatically distributed to media outlets. I've documented nefarious activities related to Blayvine Industries and its subsidiaries, everything from money laundering and securities fraud to tax evasion, bribery and embezzlement. I doubt if the corporation could avoid bankruptcy, with the end result having its corporate carcass picked apart by many of the competitors it wronged over the decades. As for the Department of Defense, I've uncovered a number of shady dealings, as well as actual crimes, and a level of systemic malfeasance reaching all the way up to the Joint Chiefs of Staff."

Gen. Hollenbach glared. "Private Samson, are you threatening to blackmail the entire United States military establishment?"

"No ma'am, just parts of it. But as long as cooler heads prevail, none of this need ever come to pass."

Before anyone could respond, Capt. Morozov barged through the door. He looked out of breath from running.

"Ma'am, contact was lost with the retrovert copter. So far, attempts to reach the pilots and crew through normal and emergency systems have been unsuccessful."

"Where is the craft now?" the general asked.

"Its exact position is unknown. After leaving St. Louis airspace, it went off course, turning south. At last radar contact it was approaching the Ozark Mountains of lower Missouri."

"What about its transponders?"

"They appear to have been disabled."

The grim thought flashing though Eddie's mind, that Quelph had taken over the copter, was no doubt shared by everyone. If the craft set down and those three retroverts were unleashed, the death toll could be far greater than when Dilopho had rampaged across the compound.

But would Quelph risk freeing his precious children in the wild only to see them eventually hunted down? Eddie didn't think so. The researcher was shrewder than that. The escape and its aftermath would have been carefully planned.

"Meeting adjourned," Gen. Hollenbach announced, her voice tinged with apprehension. As Eddie and the others headed for the door, the general and her fellow judges began an urgent whispered discussion.

SIXTY

"Pronga to!" Doc hollered. "Stop pushing me so goddamn hard! Want me to fly right off the end of the dock?"

Pierre muttered "mo chagren" by way of apology and eased up on how fast he'd been shoving Doc's wheelchair down the ramp from the house.

Addi had been offering to buy her father a motorized chair from the beginning of time. And since the med team had assumed much of his daily care, they'd been showering him with brochures of the fanciest models. No matter how many bells and whistles those chairs boasted, Doc gave them a thumbs down. Pierre couldn't tell whether his refusals were due to his natural stubbornness or because he enjoyed having someone at his beck and call when he grew too tired to wheel around on his own.

"Guess you're pretty excited about seeing her, huh?" Pierre offered, guiding the chair off the ramp and pushing it slowly toward the far end of the dock.

"Now why the hell would I be excited? We talk most every goddamn night, you know."

"Not the same as seeing somebody you love in person."

Doc managed a grunt, which was as close as he'd come to admitting that after months of calls and video chats, he was looking forward to being with his daughter. Pierre knew it was true from the way he'd been acting over the past few days. He'd even ordered a new dress shirt and tie for the occasion, the former extra-large to accommodate the BAM.

Pierre remembered how appalled the med team had been at Addi's use of the collar. They'd assured Doc they'd never employ such a cruel and primitive method to control his water-guzzling urges and demanded it be removed. But a curious thing happened. Doc, who in the past often had been more ornery than a penned-in gator about being made to wear the collar, put his foot down.

"Understand something," he'd warned the team. "Nobody but *nobody* other than my daughter gets to say when I take off this caca contraption."

They'd wisely backed down. However, Doc didn't realize one of the nurses had figured out how to deactivate the BAM, rendering it little more than a fashion statement. Best of all, they found a new drug cocktail for controlling his polydipsia; the insatiable bouts of thirst had been brought under control. Erring on the side of caution, the water-bottle cabinet remained locked.

But nothing could slow the deterioration of Doc's mind. His episodes of dementia had increased and now occurred daily. He might ask Pierre when dinner was being served right after finishing the meal, or wonder where Addi was just after he got off the phone with her.

"Right up to the edge but not a frog's leg farther," Doc ordered as they reached the end of the dock.

Pierre cocked his head, hearing something in the distance. It sounded like the whirring blades of another spy drone dispatched by those rich brats from town. He was tempted to dash inside for Doc's shotgun and fire a warning shot.

But the drone sounds disappeared, outamplified by the approach of a boat. Addi's familiar craft rounded the bend in short order, and there she was in the flesh, her new friend beside her. Pierre felt like he knew Eddie Boka already from all the publicity.

The boat drew close enough to see Addi smiling and waving. Pierre waved back, noting that Boka no longer wore a DAM. Addi had assured them he was OK and wouldn't go all Rougarou on them and feast on their flesh.

"Your girl looks good," Pierre offered.

"She does," Doc agreed, his voice surprisingly tender.

Boka hopped out of the boat as it docked and secured it to a cleat. Addi ran the last few feet to her father and threw her arms around him.

"Papa," she whispered, her eyes tearing up.

"Hey there, Tour Tot. No need for a wet face."

"I know, Papa. It's just… it's so good to be home."

She finally released him and turned to Pierre. "And you! I couldn't have made it all this time away without knowing you were here helping care for him."

"The med team did most of the work. They always made sure your Papa had–"

She cut him off with a crushing bear hug. Pierre squeezed her back, feeling guilty. Part of that deal she'd struck with Blayvine Industries had included doubling his salary and enabling him to choose however many hours he wanted to work. He'd made good use of that generosity. The extra money had enabled him to quit his other part-time jobs last month, having saved enough for a full year's tuition at the culinary school.

He wasn't looking forward to telling Addi he'd be moving to New Orleans in January to begin the next available term.

It felt like a betrayal, especially with the med team's contract also ending soon. Caring for Doc would again become her primary responsibility.

Addi released him from her grip and motioned for Boka to step forward. He shook hands with them both, and although Pierre had seen plenty of videos, the dino-man up close was still a freakish sight. Doc, never known for holding his tongue, expressed what was running through Pierre's mind.

"You must scare the caca out of 'em at Halloween."

"Papa!" Addi scolded. "Mind your manners!"

"I haven't gone trick-or-treating in a while," Eddie admitted. "But I know what you're saying. Next year, I was thinking of wearing a pink dress and pearls and going as Dino-Barbie."

Doc's hearty laughter rippled across the swamp. A pair of startled loons took flight from the canopy.

SIXTY-ONE

Eddie's delighted expression announced he was enjoying Pierre's dinner even more than Addi. Although she'd eaten Cajun chicken fricassee numerous times growing up, this one was Pierre's own recipe. Tantalizingly unfamiliar seasonings accented the creamy sauce of bell peppers, onions and celery. The meal paired nicely with the dry champagne Eddie had brought for the occasion.

She sat across from him, with Papa and Pierre occupying the oak table's other quadrants. Dusk had come upon the bayou. Skies morphed into pink and purple streaks, infusing the main room where they dined with a soothing glow from the picture window. December temperatures enabled the screened side windows to be left open, and the breeze was a pleasant change from the early snow they'd endured on the drive from Axton to the airport. The soundscape of crickets and frogs amid the mangrove trees was intruded upon only by the generator's faint hum.

"Out of this world," Eddie offered, lending support to the compliment by ladling a third helping onto his plate. "I don't think I've ever had such delicious chicken."

"Pierre's a fantastic chef," Addi said. "He picked a lot of it up on his own. He's thinking of going to a culinary school to get formal training, maybe someday becoming the chef at one of those fancy New Orleans restaurants."

"Someday," Pierre said quietly.

"Maybe they'll teach him the right way to make shrimp remoulade," Doc grumbled.

"Papa, that's not fair. Just because he makes it a different way than what you grew up with doesn't mean his isn't just as scrumptious."

Doc was about to respond but Pierre jumped in, shifting the topic by directing a comment to Eddie.

"So I heard those other dino-humans, the ones you saved, are doing better."

"They are, after a bunch of surgeries."

"It was scary for a while," Addi said. "But Julio and Gideon are expected to make full recoveries."

She and Eddie had paid another visit to the pair just before flying down here. They were no longer confined to hospital beds and were able to walk the corridors, although they had to wheel around IV poles with a conglomeration of medicinal drips. Julio had even thanked Eddie for saving their lives, hopefully putting an end to the bad blood between them.

"Doc, I really want to thank you for having me here," Eddie said. "This is a fantastic home. It's so peaceful down here."

"Living this far out looks easy but it's not. House takes a goddamn heap of work. Ain't no hardware stores nearby."

"I'm sure it's a challenge. Still, a dreamy place. You're a lucky man in more ways than one."

Addi locked eyes with Eddie as he stared at her from across the table. She found herself smiling, as she often did since they'd reconciled.

Still, their relationship remained something less than wine and roses. Visions of Eddie's assault on Nastor popped into her head at unexpected moments, which in turn ignited memories of her own savagery in killing Glose. She'd initially tried mentally separating the two incidents, telling herself that what she'd done had been necessary to save her life, whereas Eddie's cannibalism – compulsion or not – was an act of cruelty.

A more nuanced view took hold after an online session with her long-time psychiatrist. Addi came to realize that her revulsion toward Eddie's behavior, although justified, also served to camouflage her own pain. She finally was able to admit that coming so close to being horribly violated and murdered had left her with post-traumatic stress.

Allowing the psychiatrist to guide her into reliving that terrifying night – literally expressing the screams and tears she couldn't let out while it was happening – put her on the path to recovery. Integrating the trauma not only brought a degree of self-healing but allowed her to see Eddie from a fresh perspective. Her formal resignation as his psychiatrist lowered the final barrier, allowing her long-gestating feelings toward him free rein.

They'd had sex for the first time on Eddie's sofa two weeks ago, one day after the extraordinary revelations in the courtroom and the disappearance of Dr Quelphius and the retroverts. It had been fast, weird and crazy. Addi had gone to his house that evening just to talk. After a long and mutually heartfelt exchange, they'd agreed it would be best to take things slow, let their relationship develop naturally. Moments later they were entangled in one another's arms, shedding clothes with little regard for buttons and zippers. Wild humping followed, devoid of foreplay.

That accounted for the fast part. The weird part came during the actual sex act. She'd studied dino-human physiology enough to know that Eddie's genitalia were no different than that of the average male. But what she hadn't been prepared for was her nipples rubbing against his scaly torso, creating a fusion of pain and pleasure that induced a heightened level of stimulation she'd never come close to experiencing.

The crazy part occurred after their bodies separated. Energies spent, brain functions slithering back to normal, they came to the mutual realization that two raging hot libidos had overwhelmed common sense. Neither of them had thought of using protection.

Addi had tested herself several times since that night and was relieved not to be pregnant, although she intended peeing on sticks a while longer just to make sure. But her foremost concerns came from looking ahead. What if some far-off day came when she and Eddie decided to start a family? Could they even have children? And if so, what would their offspring be like?

She'd felt uncomfortable exploring the subject further with him, not wanting to spook him with the idea she was contemplating such a future. Dr Steinhauser and Dr Kim weren't good prospects, given her rocky relationship with them. Billy Orb, having worked closely with Dr Quelphius, might have answers, but she didn't feel she knew him well enough for such an intimate conversation. That left only one possibility.

She'd finally worked up the courage to knock on the door of Samson's quarters. Since his spectacular coming out, he'd embarked on a very public mission to display his dizzying expertise to the world. He seemed to know, or claim to know, something about every imaginable subject on the planet.

When the door opened, she realized Samson had been ready to leave. His movements no longer restricted, he'd been making regular jaunts to a trendy Axton nightclub. Although he sometimes wore his familiar coveralls around the compound, in the evenings he went into flash mode, dressing like a football or basketball star. That night his ensemble consisted of silky black pants, a cheetah-print sports jacket, aviator shades and enough jewelry to open a bling store. Rumors swirled about his sex life. The most repeated one said that he preferred two or more women simultaneously.

He'd greeted her warmly and invited her in, chuckling as she hesitantly revealed that she and Eddie were dating.

"Seriously, Addi? You thought your mutual attraction was a secret?"

"No. Of course not. I knew some people suspected."

"I realized from the day we met that you and Eddie would become a thing."

"How could you have possibly known that?"

"Same way I know why you're here. You want to ask about the two of you having a baby."

Addi gave a sheepish nod. She normally wasn't intimidated by super-smart people. But she sensed Samson was in a category of his own.

"There's no medical reason it shouldn't be possible," he said, his concentration divided between talking with her and texting someone on his phone. "Still, it is unexplored territory, so no guarantees. Do you want to get pregnant?"

"No, no, this is all theoretical. And I'm hoping you won't tell Eddie that we're having this conver–"

"Privileged communication, strictly between lawyer and client." He unleashed a smile. "I'm working on my online law degree. Figure it might come in handy someday should the powers-that-be ever try judicially restraining my so-called blackmail threats."

"Uh-huh. So, my next question is—"

"You want to know that if indeed your eggs and Eddie's sperm are compatible, what junior will be like. A knockout like mommy? A freak like daddy?"

She nodded.

"I'd been curious about that too and had Wesk run some simulations a while back. I concur with its conclusions. The xenotransplantation surgeries account for our scales and other external distinctions to a greater extent than the genetic infusions. Translated into the numeric, that means you'd have about a sixty-five percent chance of your offspring looking human and a thirty-three percent chance of them being born with dino-human characteristics."

"And the other two percent?"

"A fetus you might choose to abort rather than bring into the world."

His phone buzzed. Delight grew as he read the text.

"Listen, I have to go. Meeting a friend for dinner."

Recalling Samson's final remark snapped Addi's attention back to the present, to the four of them at the dinner table here in the bayou. The discussion had shifted to the fate of Dr Quelphius and the retroverts.

"It hasn't been announced to the media yet," Eddie was saying, "but searchers finally found the missing copter in northwest Arkansas. It was intact but the flight crew and the guards are dead, their injuries consistent with carnivorous animal attacks. No sign of Quelph and his unholy brood."

"You'd think they'd have been spotted by now," Pierre said.

"It's mostly mountainous wilderness so lots of places to hide. But thousands of troops and regional authorities have been mobilized to hunt them down. It's only a matter of time."

Addi didn't share his confidence. Quelph had vowed retribution on Eddie, and after what he'd done to Blayvine, she doubted he was ready to let bygones be bygones and be content to lie low. Still, although Arkansas and Louisiana were contiguous states, the copter site was hundreds of miles away. And Quelph wouldn't know they were here.

Eddie finished his final serving of chicken fricassee and raised his champagne glass.

"If I may, another toast. To three special people. A fine chef, a loving father and an extraordinary woman."

Addi and Pierre clinked glasses with him. Doc declined and scowled at Eddie.

"Who the hell are you?"

"Papa, this is Eddie Boka. Remember?"

"What's that scaly crap on your face? You look like something straight out of the swamp!"

"Papa!"

"What are you doing in my home? I didn't invite you. I want you outta here now!"

"Papa, enough!"

As quickly as Doc's dementia had come on it disappeared. His features crumpled into an expression halfway between confusion and sadness.

"I'm tired," he muttered. "Want to go to bed now."

"Sure, Doc, sure," Pierre said, guiding his wheelchair out from under the table and toward the narrow stairs. Helping him to his feet, Pierre gripped him firmly under the shoulders and half-guided, half-carried him up the steps.

"Sorry about that," Addi offered.

Eddie reached across the table, took hold of her hand.

"Nothing to be sorry about."

SIXTY-TWO

Eddie sat on the porch swing gazing over the swamps. The sun had gone down. Waters shimmering under the glow of a half moon lapped gently against the boathouse. Two crafts were tied up at the far end of the dock, Addi's and her father's. Pierre had departed for home after Addi assured him she'd manage Doc's care until the med team arrived for their morning shift.

Eddie felt more relaxed than he had in a long time. The bayou gave off an amalgam of scents that triggered an olfactory memory from months ago, of trekking through the jungle to rescue that kidnapped CEO from the guerrillas. A memorable day and a pivotal one. Had he not succumbed to the bloodburn and ravaged that guerrilla, he never would have met Addi, never would have ended up here. Fate could be a nasty bitch. But it also could portend the most phenomenal of futures.

Footsteps sounded from inside: Addi descending the stairs. Emerging onto the porch, she joined him on the swing and rested her head against his shoulder.

"How's he doing?" Eddie asked, putting his arm around her.

"Down for a little while, I hope. I gave him a mild sleeping pill. Hate using those strong sedatives the med team employs."

"Worried about side effects?"

"Mostly unknown drug interactions. They've been pumping him with a shitload of medications. Don't want to chance it."

He felt a familiar stirring. "Want to chance something else?"

"What'd you have in mind, Sgt. Boka?"

He couldn't see her face but felt her smile. He gestured to the boathouse.

"How about in there? Sedatives or not, won't risk waking your father in the next room."

"You want to do it in some grungy shed?"

"Right here on the porch works too."

"The grungy shed it is." She leaped to her feet and dashed down the ramp. He raced after her, playfully swatting her butt. Giggling, she wrenched open the boathouse door. Inside, an old rowboat floated in the drink. On the deck above the waterline was a dilapidated wooden canoe with a missing bow seat.

"Perfect," Addi said, removing a pair of old oars from the canoe and casting them aside.

"Doesn't look so comfy," Eddie said, noting that the canoe's narrow belly of cedar strips were chipped and cracked. "Want me to grab a blanket from the house?"

"No need." Grinning, she hopped in and kicked off her pants. "I'm getting used to prickly things rubbing against me."

"Kinky you."

She grabbed his arm, yanked him down on top of her. The rest of their clothes came off fast, as usual. But recent extensive practice had taught them that everything else was best taken slow.

SIXTY-THREE

Eddie awakened with a start, senses alert. He sniffed the air but detected nothing unusual. Addi was gone. They'd fallen asleep facing one another, crammed into the canoe's narrow belly, an inherently uncomfortable position made bearable by body warmth and tenderness. He'd left his phone upstairs but sensed he'd been sleeping for several hours.

He slipped on his pants and shoes, opened the boathouse door and was greeted by the swamp's familiar sounds. Nothing looked wrong, nothing smelled wrong. Yet he had the feeling something was amiss.

He headed briskly up the ramp toward the house but froze halfway at the sound of a loud splash. He whirled. It had come from the end of the dock; expanding ripples glimmered in the moonlight. The splash was too loud to have been caused by a fish or bird. Something much larger, no doubt. An alligator?

He kept staring at the spot. All remained quiet. Turning back to the house, he'd barely taken a step when another splash came. This time, the circlet of ripples was closer, halfway along the dock. Whatever was causing it was approaching.

Moving with stealth, Eddie headed back down the ramp, tiptoeing toward the disturbance. He didn't know much about alligators but had heard they weren't as aggressive as crocodiles. But crocs weren't found in the bayou; southern Florida was their nearest habitat. And even a hungry gator was unlikely to leap out of the water to snatch at an arm or leg. Still, he played it safe, maintaining a center path on the planking and staying away from the edges.

He reached the spot of the last splash, peered into the water. A shiny round object was rising from the murky depths.

The object broke the surface. Bright yellow, it appeared to be one of those helium-filled balloons used at birthday parties. Scrawled across the mylar in black marker was a single word.

Murderer!

Something popped the balloon, dispersing an invisible pheromone cloud. The air turned rich with a scent he'd detected only once before, in that fight with Dilopho:

Retrovert!

He realized the danger just as a massive splash came from behind him. Scaly fingers locked around his ankles, yanked him off his feet. He fell face down, his chin slamming the dock.

The second retrovert emerged from under the popped balloon, vaulting out of the water like a torpedo, its seven-foot form a dark silhouette. As its face passed through a swath of moonlight, he glimpsed Julio's countenance in its features, knew it was the one called Spino. Its clawed feet smacked the boards as it landed.

The creature gripping Eddie's ankles pulled hard, dragging him backward off the dock. He had just enough time to fill his lungs with air before he was pulled under. Spino dove in and grabbed hold of Eddie's wrists. All he could do was twist his torso and flail as the duo stretched his arms and legs out until his body was at its full length, all the while taking him deeper.

The third retrovert appeared, its face close. Even in the submerged gloom, enough light filtered down for Eddie to recognize his own monstrous doppelganger. It was Rex, his genetic cousin of sorts. The creature stared dispassionately as he kicked and writhed and struggled to break free from the other two. Whatever thoughts streamed through that primordial consciousness remained impossible to fathom. Yet he had the impression of intelligence, of curiosity.

If so, it was a curiosity unhinged from compassion. Rex darted away, disappeared into the aquatic dark. An instant later, Eddie felt it grab hold of his legs just above where the other retrovert – Gideon's doppelganger Cerato – maintained a vise-like grip of his ankles.

The three creatures propelled him forward. Rex swam around in front again and wrapped a wide leather strap around Eddie's wrists. The retrovert pulled it tight, then looped a strap around the center of the makeshift cuffs, securing the other end to one of the wooden dock pilings.

The retroverts released him and swam away. He yanked hard and tried pulling free but it was no use. He was trapped, his extended arms anchored to the base of the piling, at least six feet beneath the surface. His increased lung capacity enabled him to hold his breath longer than most humans but there was a limit. He was already feeling the strain. And when he reached the point where he needed to take in air...

He rotated his body face up. He could just discern the outlines of the three retroverts above. They'd hopped from the water and were lined up on the edge of the dock, gazing down at him, watching and waiting for his breath to run out. Their means of attack had been clever. By swimming underwater, they'd negated Eddie's strongest natural form of detection, his sense of smell.

He resumed pulling on the strap without success. The pilings were old and eroded, but being afloat in the water deprived him of any leverage. He tried digging his heels into the bottom but it was too sandy and his feet kept slipping. He switched tactics, tried undoing the strap from where it was secured to the wood. But Rex had triple-knotted it, and Eddie's violent yanking had only served to make it tighter. He wasn't undoing it without a screwdriver or similar tool.

He paused in his efforts when a new vibration disturbed the waters. A boat, electric-powered judging by the muffled hush of its engine, drew near. His mind entertained the notion that rescuers were coming to save him. But the fantasy vanished as the boat nestled against the side of the dock.

The motor shut off. A figure stepped out onto the planking. It had to be Dr Quelphius, no doubt the mastermind of the attack, as well as the sick joke of the helium balloon. Eddie's thoughts turned to Addi. Even considering the boat's near-silent approach, it seemed likely that from inside the house she would have heard the commotion of the retroverts dragging him under.

Yet even if she realized what was happening to him, what could she do? The only rational means of escape was by boat, and the one they'd arrived in was effectively unreachable. Quelph and the creatures stood in the way. Besides, she'd never abandon her father.

One of the retroverts disappeared from view, leaving Quelph and the other two to continue monitoring his drowning. Had the other one been sent inside?

He told himself they wouldn't hurt Addi. Quelph's rage was directed at Eddie for the killing of Dilopho. There was no reason to extend that vengeance to others. Yet the researcher had passed far beyond the borders of reason. Addi too could suffer a terrible fate.

SIXTY-FOUR

Addi had awakened in the boathouse needing to pee. Slipping carefully out of the canoe so as not to awaken Eddie, she'd tiptoed up to the house. She hadn't intended taking a shower. But after using the bathroom and checking on Papa – still peacefully asleep – a desire to wash away the day's grit and grime took hold.

As the warm liquid cascaded over her flesh, she found herself contemplating a future with Eddie. It would be a complicated one, no doubt. She was in love with him, without reservation, and could no longer imagine a life where they were apart. But Gen. Hollenbach had a new group of overlords coming in whose goal was picking up and restoring Project Saurian's shattered pieces. Would they permit Eddie to move here to the bayou, so far from the compound? Samson might be willing to use his influence, aka blackmail, to help. Yet even if Eddie was granted permission, he'd have to be willing.

Addi hadn't broached the idea to him yet, at least not in so many words. She'd been hoping this visit would inspire him to reach the conclusion on his own. Judging by how he seemed to have adapted thus far to the environment, she was encouraged. But if official authorization and his own approval weren't secured, the situation would become more complex.

He'd already hinted about her moving into his home in Axton. No way could she abandon caring for Papa, so the only way that scenario worked was if she put her father into a nursing home in West Virginia, one with a good dementia care unit and close enough for frequent visits. An alternate idea, and probably one even harder to sell Eddie on, would be for her father to move in with the two of them. Whatever choices were made, it was a dilemma that needed sorting.

An endless shower wasn't producing any solutions. If anything, it was amplifying her worries. Turning off the spray, she stepped out of the stall and wrapped herself in a bath towel...

And froze. There was movement in the house from downstairs. Moments later, she heard heavy footsteps ascending the stairs.

She relaxed. Eddie likely needed to answer nature's call as well, although being a guy, she was surprised he wasn't pissing right off the dock into the swamp. She was about to call out to him and say she'd be done in a minute when a more inviting thought took shape. Opening the bathroom door, she let the towel drop to the floor. Leaning against the portal, she struck a provocative pose, eager to see his surprise as he reached the top and entered the dimly lit hallway.

"I'm having a bit of trouble in here, Eddie," she offered as he neared the final steps. "I sure could use a helping hand to–"

The remainder of her come-on ruptured into a scream. The shadowy figure of the retrovert stepped into view, made even more terrifying by a countenance with an eerie resemblance to Eddie. Rex froze too, staring down the hallway at her nakedness, its intent unimaginable.

Addi recovered her wits. Slamming the door, she threw the slide bolt, locking it. For an instant she considered reaching into the vanity beneath the sink for a bathrobe, then realized covering up wasn't the priority. She had to escape. But the sole window above the toilet was too narrow for anyone larger than a child to squeeze through. She was trapped.

She heard the creature bounding down the hallway. It body-slammed the door, hard enough for one of the hinges to splinter away from the wood. A new worry surfaced. The noise might stir her father, bring him limping into the hall to investigate.

"Stay in your room, Papa," she whispered to no one. "Please just stay there."

Silence followed. Maybe he hadn't awakened. But she drew a sharp intake of breath as the retrovert started tapping its clawed finger sharply against the wood, three times in rapid succession. The sequence repeated over and over.

A new sound was added, a primitive vocalization eerily similar to a human baby learning to speak.

"Wah-ah... wah-ah... wah-ah."

The guttural voice grew more incessant, almost mournful in its intensity. The bathroom's air, warm and humid from her shower, couldn't prevent goosebumps from dancing along her bare arms and a chill creeping up her spine.

SIXTY-FIVE

The strain of Eddie holding his breath was becoming more dire. Deadly carbon dioxide would be starting to build up in his bloodstream, and when it reached a critical juncture he'd black out. When that occurred his mouth would wrench open, lungs involuntarily gasping for oxygen only to receive a pressurized torrent of swamp water.

He could just make out Quelph and the two retroverts on the dock, gazing down at him, waiting for his death throes.

Do it, he told himself. *It's your only chance.*

He began thrashing again but this time deliberately, intending the violent flailing of his appendages to serve as evidence that his lungs had given out. Opening his mouth, he expelled more than half his remaining air, hoping the eruption of bubbles to the surface would be mistaken for the final act of a drowning man. Then came the hardest part, feigning that the struggle was over and that he'd succumbed.

Releasing all the tension in his body, he allowed himself to go limp. As his motionless form settled back-first into the mud and sand on the bottom, he kept his eyes open just far enough to make out the trio of figures. He dared not blink. It could give away the deception.

He waited, hoping against hope they would leave. But they just stood there. Either Quelph remained unconvinced he'd breathed his last or was enjoying Eddie's termination and didn't want it to end. They had to leave, and quickly. What little oxygen remained in his lungs was needed to power the final step in his plan.

At last, Quelph's distorted voice came through the water. Eddie's depth muddied some of the words but his mind remained acute enough to fill in the gaps. It was Blayvine's favorite phrase.

"Unveil the beyond with eyes wide open."

Quelph stepped back from the edge. The retroverts followed. Eddie forced himself to remain still, giving them enough time to presumably make it up to the house.

He could wait no longer. He was ready to burst. With what strength remained to him, he hooked his shoes around the submerged root of a mangrove tree he'd spotted earlier. It should provide leverage so that he wasn't floundering at the same time he was trying to break his arms free.

Concentrating every iota of remaining strength, he pulled and twisted the dock piling. It didn't budge. His thoughts again turned to Addi and what they might be doing to her.

Anger resurfaced. The bad yen grew. Together, those complementary forces provided his pained muscles with the fuel needed for one maximum effort. He pulled and twisted with all his might, body screaming in pain against the exertion.

The piling broke at its juncture with the underside of the dock. The sudden release sent him somersaulting backward, producing an expulsion of his remaining air. Dizziness from depleted oxygen took hold.

Black out and you drown! Swim! Swim for your life!

He kicked his legs and somehow reached the surface. Bursting free he gulped down clumps of air while noisily thrashing his way onto a muddy bank next to the boathouse. If Quelph and the retroverts heard his struggles and reappeared, he would be at their mercy. He could only lie there, lacking the strength to do anything other than dig his still-bound hands into the sticky gumbo and hang on.

SIXTY-SIX

Addi sat at the table in the main room, trying to keep her fear under control. Once again she was a prisoner, this time with hands behind her back and bound to the chair's cross rail. But instead of a single sadistic mercenary, she faced three inhuman monstrosities and their equally inhuman master.

Dr Quelphius was seated across the table from her. The retroverts stood off to the side like a trio of sphinxes, Rex in the middle, Spino and Cerato flanking. Quelph smiled at her. His serene manner made it easy to forget she was dealing with a sociopath.

He'd arrived in the hallway outside the bathroom where she was trapped and whispered something to Rex. His words were too faint to make out but they prompted an end to that infernal tapping. Samson had been right about those cochlear implants – somehow they enabled Quelph to control the creatures.

She'd managed to don a bathrobe moments before Rex bashed through the weakened door. The creature threw her across its shoulder, carried her kicking and screaming downstairs and bound her to the chair.

"You must believe me," Quelph began. "Involving you and your father in these distasteful necessities was never my intent. However, the situation has changed."

Addi gazed past him at the front door. Any moment now, Eddie would whip it open and come to her aid. Quelph read her hopes and adopted an expression of faux sadness.

"I'm afraid a last-minute rescue by the mighty Eddie Boka isn't in the cards."

Pain knifed through her. She kept telling herself it wasn't true. *Eddie's OK. He's a survivor.* Considering any other scenario would plunge her into a well of despair.

She forced herself to concentrate on her predicament. "How in the world did you find us?" She didn't really care but appealing to Quelph's ego and keeping him talking might give her precious time to come up with an escape plan.

"Did you really think it would be difficult? Boka is not exactly able to travel incognito and his notoriety continues to draw media attention. The two of you were seen entering the airport shortly before a scheduled flight to New Orleans. Your ultimate destination was obvious."

His next words riveted her attention.

"Rex having seen you au naturel has awakened in him certain... desires." He turned to the retroverts. "Rex, please tell her your thoughts."

"Wah-ah... wah-ah... wah-ah."

"No, Rex, sound out the word like I taught you. You can do it."

"Wah-ah... wah-ah... wah-ah."

Quelph flashed disappointment but covered it with a smile. "It's all right, my child. You'll learn to speak eventually. All of you will." He turned back to Addi. "More human than you imagined, aren't they."

Not in the slightest. The chill she'd experienced in the bathroom returned as she sensed what the creature was trying to say. *Want... want... want.* In some twisted way, she'd become the object of its desires. She flashed back to the last time she'd experienced such fear, at the hands of that sexual predator Glose.

No! It's not happening again! She pulled frantically at her bindings. But rather than another zip tie she might slip out of, a tightly knotted cord secured her wrists. Quelph rose, leaned across the table and laid his palm gently against her cheek. Addi flinched and jerked her head back.

"You'll never get away! They'll hunt you down wherever you go!"

"Tomorrow we'll be flown to a new home, a nation with no qualms about the direction of my research. America's failure to accept the retroverts will be this other nation's gain, allowing them to catch up on years of xenotransplantation technology."

"You're out of your mind, you sick fuck!"

Quelph darkened and nodded to Rex. "She's all yours."

The creature came toward her, its slitted eyes locked onto her face. Spino and Cerato, heretofore as immobile as statues, reacted to Rex's movement with sudden aggression, inching forward and emitting angry growls. Rex whirled toward them, crouching into a fighting stance and snarling back.

"No, no," Quelph said, holding a hand up to restrain Spino and Cerato. "No need to fight. You two will have your treat too. Remember what I taught you about being patient, about controlling your desires. After Rex is done, you may have the father."

Addi had assumed that the creature seeing her naked had awakened its sexuality. But Quelph's words made her realize its desire was more basic. It took all her strength to hold back a torrent of screams. She and her father were food!

Spino and Cerrato continued growling, incensed at Rex's preferential treatment. Quelph turned to Rex. "Perhaps it would be better to enjoy your treat in a more private place, out of sight of your brothers. Why don't you take Addi up to her room."

The retrovert picked up her chair, easily hefted it to chest height. The creature's warm breath blew across the back of her head, carrying with it a potent stench that somehow filled her with even more terror.

"Just a suggestion," Quelph said, "but maybe better to untie her from the chair first. I believe it may be too wide for the stairs."

Rex seemed to mull over his words for a moment. Finally, it lowered the chair and undid her bindings. Once again, she was tossed across its shoulder like a sack of animal feed. Stifling panic, her thoughts raced ahead. Being alone with the creature gave her a fraction of a chance. Her Glock, recovered from the mercs, had been reloaded with a 15-round magazine after its trip down here as checked baggage. It was in her room, in her dresser.

Yet even if she was able to reach the gun and shoot Rex, Quelph and the other two would be up here in a flash, and extra-wary knowing she was armed. Attempting to escape out a window wasn't an option. No way could she abandon her father to such a horrific fate.

SIXTY-SEVEN

Eddie's strength returned, enough to crawl farther up the muddy bank. He needed to risk a glance into the house, hoping the retroverts weren't gazing out into the darkness at the same moment. Courtesy of Samson's access to classified material, he'd read up on their augmented faculties, including eyesight better than 20/20 human vision and an expanded spectrum that could see partly into the infrared and detect heat signatures. They also possessed improved auditory and olfactory senses, but those weren't as concerning. Addi had closed the windows after dinner as the night air cooled. It was unlikely they would overhear his movements or pick up his scent. He hoped.

He popped his head just high enough to see over the porch swing. Quelph stood with his back to the window along with two of the retroverts. But the third one, Rex, was hoisting Addi from a chair and throwing her over its shoulder. Seeing her helpless ignited his rage and threatened to bring on the bad yen. He wanted to crash through the window and tear Rex apart.

A dose of cold logic enabled self-control. Bursting in without a plan would be folly. Even in these circumstances, he recognized a certain irony. Addi's training with the shock collar had given him the ability to use rationality to deter the bad yen before it reached the breaking point and brought on the all-consuming bloodburn. Total mastery hadn't been achieved, considering what he'd done to Nastor. Still, the rationality she'd helped impart now might be the only way to save her.

Those insights coursed through him as Rex carried his captive toward the hallway stairs. Whatever the creature had planned for her, he didn't have much time. Even against the two retroverts and Quelph he needed some sort of advantage. Doc's shotgun? Was it still hanging in the kitchen or had Quelph moved it elsewhere? His limited viewing angle into the main room revealed no weapons.

He waded back into the shallower waters ringing the cinderblock stilts and made his way to the back of the house. Grabbing the railing's lower rung, he pulled himself from the swamp and onto the porch. The kitchen was dark but enough light spilled from the hallway to reveal the weapon hanging in its place above the doorway.

He'd ventured onto the back porch this afternoon and recalled the door being unlocked. Hopefully, that hadn't changed. The closed windows weren't latched but getting through the screens would be noisy and time consuming.

He gripped the knob, gingerly turned. The door opened. So far, so good. He slipped through the narrowest of openings, knowing he had to move fast. The retroverts' acute hearing and sense of smell might detect him now that he was inside.

Tiptoeing across the kitchen, he pulled down the shotgun. Pierre had casually mentioned that Doc always kept the magazine full. That meant five shells were available. The first one needed to be pumped into the chamber, a sound likely to give him away. No way around that. He'd have to wait until the last possible moment, then pump and fire.

Dilopho had been gunned down with concentrated rifle and pistol fire from those soldiers who'd stormed Med. Head shots, specifically to the face, had done him in. The shotgun gave Eddie an advantage over their weapons. Even a chest hit from a 12-gauge shell at close range would deliver a high-energy punch, maybe enough to blow a hole in the retroverts' scaly armor. The creatures also had those vulnerable skin patches on their thighs and upper arms. Secondary targets, Eddie surmised. Crippling but probably not fatal.

Ideally, he'd use no more than three shells dealing with Spino and Cerato, leaving the final two for Rex. He figured he could take Quelph out by hand.

Eddie eased into the dark hallway. Just ahead on the right was the main room, and across from it, the stairs. He heard no footsteps from above. By now, Addi and Rex were likely in one of the bedrooms. What was it doing to her?

Don't think about that! Concentrate!

He heard Quelph speaking in a calm voice as he inched closer to the main room, something about self-restraint. But the researcher paused abruptly in mid-sentence.

"Cerato, what's wrong? What do you smell?"

It had Eddie's scent. *Now or never.*

He bolted the final few steps, pumped a round as he lunged through the portal. Cerato came at him. Eddie caught a glimpse of Spino and Quelph deeper in the room as he pulled the trigger.

The blast caught Cerato in the chest from less than a yard away. The creature let out a screech of pain and tumbled backward over a chair. Spino came at Eddie like a raging locomotive. Eddie chambered the second shell but Spino knocked the barrel aside as he fired. The scattering pellets blew a hole in the window.

And then Spino was on him, knocking him hard against the wall. One scaly hand grabbed at the rifle, the other closed around his neck. Fingers squeezed like a vise. If he didn't want to be choked to death or have his neck broken, he had to release the rifle.

Dropping the weapon freed his hands. He grabbed Spino's wrist with his left hand, yanked the creature's upper body toward him and plowed his armored knee into its guts. With his right hand, he simultaneously elbowed Spino in the mouth, bloodying the lip. The double blow forced the stunned creature to release his neck.

Eddie grabbed its forearm, twisting the retrovert's body and pushing it away, then landed a brutal kick to its right thigh. Spino fell, hissing, writhing and grasping the injured leg.

Movement, behind him. Heavy footsteps, rushing down the stairs. Rex! Eddie dove for the shotgun, which had skid under the table. Quelph was closer and got there first. Awkwardly hoisting the weapon, he fired. Eddie jerked sideways, dodging the brunt of the blast. A few scattering pellets clipped the side of his waist. He hardly felt them.

Quelph must not have fired a shotgun before. He hadn't braced himself. The violent recoil hurled him backward. The shotgun sailed from his hands as he tripped over a chair and landed on the floor.

Eddie made another grab for the fallen weapon. Before he could reach it, Rex smashed into him from behind, sending him sprawling onto his chest. He tried getting up but Rex leaped knees-first onto his spine, eliciting a gasp of pain.

Fists pounded the sides of his head, each sledgehammer blow driving him closer to unconsciousness. He tried twisting around and pushing himself up from the floor but Rex's weight on his back was too much to lift.

From the corner of his eye, he glimpsed the other retroverts. Cerato remained down, thrashing and moaning from the gaping hole in its chest. Spino was struggling to stand on its injured thigh.

A boot heel was suddenly inches from Eddie's face, stomping the floorboards.

"Kill him!" Quelph shouted, looking like a mad toddler consumed by a tantrum. "Do it! Do it! Kill him!"

Eddie couldn't take much more. He couldn't do anything about Rex but he could end Quelph's racket. Grabbing the madman's ankle, he wrenched it hard enough to snap the bone. Squealing, Quelph again crashed to the floor.

A pistol barked, three shots in rapid succession.

"Get off him!" Addi hollered.

Eddie could tell from Rex's jerking movements atop him that she was firing rounds into the creature's back.

Rex leaped to its feet, whirled toward the new threat. The release from that crushing weight and those pummeling fists restored Eddie's vigor. Flipping himself over, he scrambled into a sitting position.

Rex was coming at Addi, its arms raised to protect its head from her steady array of bullets. It was closing in on her, slowly and inexorably. In seconds it would be close enough to strike.

From the corner of his eye, Eddie glimpsed Spino limping toward him. With a howl of rage, the creature lunged. Eddie snatched the shotgun, pumped as he whirled and fired point blank. The blast blew away half of Spino's face.

He tried pivoting the weapon toward Rex but the creature grabbed hold of the barrel and twisted it toward Addi. He couldn't stop its scaly finger from snaking into the trigger guard and firing.

Addi recognized the danger in time, dove to the floor. But in one horrifying instant, Eddie realized the fifth and final shell had found another target, the figure who'd been standing in the hallway behind her.

Doc's cane had been severed, its splintered halves lying on the floor beside him. The commotion must have been enough to rouse him from his drugged sleep and bring him to the bottom of the stairs. The blast had caught him in the chest.

Addi's tortured shrieks filled the room. She ran to her father. Eddie longed to comfort her but first had to survive Rex. He whipped the shotgun downward at a sharp angle, trapping Rex's forefinger in the trigger guard.

Rex howled as its finger snapped. Eddie continued arcing the shotgun, twisting until the retrovert's entire arm was forced back. Rex countered by grasping at Eddie's neck while kicking him in the shins.

One of the blows broke Eddie's tibia. The leg collapsed under him and he dropped to his knees. Rex freed itself from the trigger guard and wrenched the weapon from Eddie's hands, throwing it across the room. The creature grabbed Eddie around the middle, lifted him overhead and hurled him into the hallway.

Eddie crashed into the wall beside Addi, landing on his back. Pains too numerous to isolate blended into one throbbing body ache. Addi hardly noticed, her attention riveted to her father. Tears streamed down her cheeks as she dabbed frantically at his gaping wound with the sleeve of her bathrobe.

The Glock was still clutched in her hand. Eddie raised himself to a sitting position, propped his back against the wall and snatched the pistol from her grasp as Rex charged.

He was too dizzy from the pain to attempt a face shot. The best he could do was put a couple bullets into Rex's chest, slowing the creature but not stopping it.

Rex lowered its shoulders, preparing to plow into him like a battering ram. Eddie dropped the gun, snatched the two splintered halves of Doc's cane and stabbed them into the skin patches on Rex's upper arms.

Eddie's thrusts and the creature's closing speed combined to drive the makeshift spears deep. But its momentum couldn't be halted. Eddie grunted as Rex head-butted him in the chest. He felt ribs cracking, adding another level of torment.

Rex jerked upright, raging and howling. The shards of the cane protruded from its blood-soaked arms like a pair of antlers.

Eddie found the strength to overcome his pain and stagger to his feet. Grabbing the Glock, he rammed the muzzle into Rex's open mouth and fired upward, into the brain. Rex fell. If it wasn't dead before crashing to the floor it would be soon.

The battle was over but not its devastation. Three unsettling sources of noise continued filling the house. Addi was hunched over her father, crying bitterly while dabbing her bloody sleeve to his wound, unwilling to accept he was beyond saving.

The other two noises emanated from the main room: Quelph's endless squeals from his broken ankle and Cerato's tormented moans. As near as Eddie could figure, one bullet remained in the Glock. He staggered over to the last retrovert, stared down at a face that was clearly intelligent enough to know it was going to die. Its helpless expression was one Eddie suspected would haunt him for the rest of his life.

He put the gun in Cerato's mouth and fired, putting it out of its misery.

"Kill him!" Addi shrieked.

Eddie whirled. She was standing over Quelph, consumed by her emotions, wailing and raging with a madness that struck him as a kind of mirror version of what he experienced in the clutches of the bloodburn. She rushed toward him, reaching for the pistol in his hand.

"Empty," he said.

She either didn't hear him or didn't understand. Snatching the Glock, she took aim at Quelph and pulled the trigger over and over. Her effort thwarted, she threw the gun against the wall and spun back to Eddie.

"Do it! Kill him! Do it the way you did Nastor! Do it!"

He couldn't. Maybe the explosion of violence had satiated that part of him. Maybe if he was really lucky, that part was gone for good.

"I can't. We can't. Better that Quelph spends the rest of his days in a prison psych ward, knowing that–"

Addi turned on him, pounding her fists against his face and chest, enraged beyond the point where anything he said could penetrate her grief. He raised his arms, fending off her blows until the madness finally subsided. He pulled her tight against him.

He wanted to tell her it would be all right, that she would get over this, that they still had a bright future together. He didn't know if any of those things were true, so he settled for gently stroking her back as she sobbed, knowing the only thing he could do for her was not let go.

"Could the source of most human troubles be the realization that, despite their best efforts, they are fated to repeat their errors?"
— Wesk: Algorithmic Speculations

SIXTY-EIGHT

The most notable differences between Project Saurian's original Executive Committee, the overlords, and this new group – renamed the Executive Consortium – were its size and composition. Instead of five core members, the consortium had eleven. The rationalization for the larger group was based on the idea that spreading decision-making authority among a greater number of individuals would lessen the likelihood of a recurrence of the interlocking corruptions that had brought down the original overlords. Wesk, analyzing that assumption, concluded it had only a twenty-four percent chance of success.

Twelve people had gathered in Admin's secure conference room, which had been modified to accommodate the expanded membership. Gen. Hollenbach was here in a guest capacity, probably to make sure the group got off to a good start at its first official meeting. The eleven regulars consisted of three representatives from Blayvine Industries' corporate side and three from the DoD, including a JAG attorney tasked with monitoring the legal implications of anything discussed. There was a new medical director and a new staff psychiatrist replacing the fired doctors Steinhauser and Kim, as well as two scientists serving as co-representatives of the research contingent, replacing the imprisoned Dr Quelphius.

The eleventh member of the Consortium was Samson. Wesk had been updated on his mental transformation, and informed that he was here to represent the interests of the present dino-humans as well as any future ones. Samson was tasked with making sure the consortium never again fell into the clutches of abusive overlords. Wesk assigned a high probability – ninety-four percent – that Samson would achieve that aim, although it lacked a clear data trail on how it had come to project such a conclusion.

A Blayvine Industries vice-president, a woman named Spears, opened the meeting. It had been decided that in order to maintain equitable power-sharing, the eleven Consortium members would take turns running meetings.

"To start, I propose that our mission statement be expanded," Ms Spears began. "We should no longer limit Project Saurian strictly to military applications, although that certainly will always remain a primary function. But developing enhanced humans to serve in other functions – civilian, governmental, corporate – will enable the project to tap into multiple outside sources of seed money, ultimately leading to profitable initiatives while making this country safer and stronger."

Wesk could not have said how or why, but listening to her detailed pitch that followed proved captivating.

SIXTY-NINE

Eddie suspected the new policy toward dino-human sexuality that granted the four of them the same freedom as humans to pursue erotic desires was due mainly to Samson. Likely also having an impact on the change were the stories by Misty Garrison and other high-profile media personalities in defense of that freedom. And it didn't hurt their cause that the latest polls revealed that falloff in support of Project Saurian was far less than initially projected, the better numbers due to outrage over how their natural sexuality had been so cruelly repressed. The issue had even sparked some rare agreements between the left and right sides of the political spectrum.

"So, should we celebrate?" Eddie asked.

"Celebrate what?" Addi countered. She was sprawled across his sofa, wielding the TV remote like a weapon, mowing down one muted channel after another, giving each of them only seconds to snare her attention. None succeeded.

"How about dino-human emancipation being made official? That's worth some recognition. Or, how about me becoming an officer?" He'd gotten word late this afternoon that he was being promoted to lieutenant.

She didn't react to either suggestion and continued her listless channel surfing. Eddie gestured out the front window.

"OK, what about celebrating something more visceral, like the first snowfall of the season."

That finally prompted her to crane her head away from the TV and out into the early evening dark. The streetlamp in front of his Axton house illuminated a swirl of white flakes.

"Doesn't look like much."

"Not yet but they're calling for six inches or more. We could go out for a walk. I've never felt snow crunching under my boots."

"Me neither. Sounds incredibly boring."

"We could spice things up with a friendly snowball battle."

"Had enough battles to last a lifetime," she said, returning her attention to the screen.

He grimaced. "Sorry, Addi. Not my best suggestion."

She put down the remote and sat up. "No, I'm sorry. I know you're trying." She patted the cushions beside her. He planted himself there and put his arm around her.

"It's just really hard," she said, cradling her face against his shoulder. "Getting through it, getting past it."

She'd lost her father nearly a month ago, and her engulfing sadness had shown few signs of retreat. He wondered how long it would take her to get over her grief and return to being the strong, confident woman he loved. He worried that the answer might be never.

"Your shrink have any fresh advice?" She'd been doing remote sessions with her psychiatrist three times a week.

"Pretty much the same old same old." She sighed. "Addi, you need to start climbing out of the well you've fallen into. Addi, you need to change your daily routine. Addi, take up a new hobby, blah blah blah."

"The hobby idea sounds kind of promising. What about knitting or crocheting? I hear they can be pretty relaxing."

She dismissed the notion with a grunt.

"OK, how about painting or photography? What about pottery? They say there's something organic about shaping clay on a potter's wheel that can lead people toward a more optimistic outlook."

"Sounds tedious."

"Something more dynamic then. Wait, I've got it! An action-based hobby, plus one we can do together."

"I'm listening."

"Two-person speed sledding!"

She laughed. It was the first authentic amusement he'd heard out of her since that awful night. He was instantly encouraged. Hopping from the sofa, he pulled her gently to her feet, determined to take full advantage of the moment before it could pass.

"OK, we're doing it! Adelaide LaTour, put on your booties."

"What?"

"We're not actually doing it tonight. We don't have a sled or any of the right gear. But what we can do right now is walk around town and scout the best hills."

"You're crazy."

"No doubt. But according to my favorite psychiatrist, I'm getting better by the day."

She scowled. He quickly released her hand, worried the remark had somehow offended her and killed the moment, and that she'd now sprawl back into couch-potato withdrawal. But she surprised him with a giggle, revealing that the furrowed brows were bogus.

Eddie felt himself brightening into a carefree smile. It was the sort of expression he'd been deliberately holding back over these past weeks, fearing that any display of a good mood would somehow make her feel worse.

"I think the steepest hills are west of Gordon Street," he said.

"No, they're even steeper out by the old ice pond."

"The old ice pond it is."

They slipped into their boots and donned their coats and ambled out into the snowy night, armed with warmth against the cold.

EPILOGUE

Fernanda had done a six-month nurse residency program at a hospital in El Paso, but she wasn't fooling herself. Someone of her youth and inexperience would never have found such a well-paying job at the Nullenberg Care Institute without the help of la familia. Aunt Isabella was a staff physician here at the nondescript, two-story building in an unremarkable Houston neighborhood, and that connection had paved the way for Fernanda's light resume to reach the top of the pile. She would be forever grateful to her tía for the opportunity.

The work wasn't difficult. As the newbie, she'd been assigned the least desirable shift, but had adapted quickly to arriving after dark and finishing at daybreak. Her chief responsibilities were making the rounds and administering medications to patients who came through the walk-in clinic but were diagnosed with conditions serious enough to require short-term stays. The clinic closed overnight and the modest, eight-bed hospital was rarely full. Sometimes, she and the duty nurse had the entire first floor to themselves. With patients asleep, there was little to do but catch up on nursing journals, watch YouTube videos and speculate about the institute's mysterious second floor.

It was off-limits to all but the most senior staff. The parade of visiting doctors and well-dressed business types entering the restricted elevator made it that much more of a tantalizing puzzle. Aunt Isabella, so helpful in countless ways, shut down when Fernanda posed questions about upstairs, reminding her of the non-disclosure agreement she'd signed as a condition of employment. Her dreamy paychecks were making a dent in her student loans, so however grudgingly, she accepted the limitations.

Some details had filtered down to Fernanda and her first-floor coworkers. The second floor was dedicated to caring for a single individual, Patient X, an invalid man whose great wealth paid for such extraordinary care. Patient X was suffering from an unusual condition that required him to be kept in a special room with a decontamination airlock portal. Anyone entering had to wear a biohazard suit. The rest of what she knew was based on rumors, the most tantalizing one from a maintenance worker who'd overheard two suits chatting as they exited the elevator after a second-floor visit. One man was speculating that perhaps Patient X's "extraordinary augmentations" enabled him to see into the afterlife.

One night, near the end of her shift, the duty nurse received a priority call. Someone upstairs realized their latest batch of vancomycin, an antibiotic used to treat staph infections, was tainted and had to be thrown out. Their supplier wouldn't be able to deliver a replacement until the next morning and they didn't want to take the chance of Patient X needing the drug overnight. The second floor knew the first floor got its medications from a different supplier. Did they have any on hand?

They did. The duty nurse procured the vancomycin from the locked refrigerator but wasn't supposed to leave her station except for emergencies. She tasked Fernanda with the delivery, handed her the drug and gave her the elevator code, which was changed daily. Fernanda would be met at the top by a security guard. She couldn't help feeling a little excited as the compartment whisked her up to the second floor.

The door swept open, revealing a long corridor with a series of closed doors. Halfway down it was the airlock portal and just beyond, a viewing window into the sealed room. But no guard.

She took a tentative step out of the elevator and was about to call out for assistance when a beeping siren signaled some sort of emergency. A door opposite the airlock opened and a middle-aged woman in a biohazard suit rushed out. An air tank was strapped to her back but she hadn't yet pulled the airtight hood over her face. She spotted Fernanda and frowned.

"Who are you? What are you doing up here?"

"I'm the night nurse, from downstairs. A security guard was supposed to meet me." She held up the drug case.

The woman's frown turned into a full-blown scowl and she muttered a curse. Fernanda picked up just enough of it to conclude the guard was on a bathroom break.

"If that's the vancomycin, bring it to me."

She did as instructed. The woman moved into the middle of the corridor, blocking her from stepping past the airlock entry, an obvious ploy to prevent Fernanda from getting a look through the window.

The woman snatched the case and opened the outer airlock door. Before she could step into it, she gazed past Fernanda and hissed, "Goddamn security protocols!"

Fernanda turned. The elevator door had closed.

"I have the code to–"

"Won't work, not up here. You need the card key. Mine is under my suit. You'll have to wait for the guard."

"No problem."

The woman hesitated, apparently reluctant to enter the lock while leaving Fernanda unattended. But when the emergency siren escalated into a more urgent beeping, she snarled a curse and dashed through the portal.

"Stay here!"

Those were the woman's last words before donning the hood. The outer door closed, leaving Fernanda alone, only steps away from the window.

She knew she shouldn't do it, put her job at risk just to satisfy her curiosity. *Atiende a tu tejido* – stick to your knitting – was one of her madre's favorite sayings, meaning she should mind her own business.

No security cameras were visible in the corridor. Fernanda could hear a gentle hissing from within the airlock, indicating a decontamination procedure, maybe a disinfectant spraying the suit. That meant the woman was still in the airlock. Fernanda had the impression that the woman and the guard were the only ones on duty up here. No one else should be inside the sealed room.

But what if Patient X was awake and looking in her direction? What it he spotted her? What if...?

Just do it.

She took three quick steps. The window revealed a spacious bed flanked by intensive care equipment and other electronics she didn't recognize. Several of the monitors were blinking, indicating some kind of minor emergency. Patient X was on his back, naked except for an adult diaper. IV needles and tubes protruded from various parts of his body. Even though a narrow blindfold covered his eyes she recognized him from the news. But it wasn't his face that caused Fernanda to emit a loud gasp, followed by a stifled shriek.

She backed away from the window in horror, trying to process what she'd seen. Retreating to the elevator, she found herself anxiously pushing the down button. Nothing happened, of course. The slot below the button required the key.

The beeping sirens finally ended. A door at the far end of the corridor opened, disgorging the security guard. Fernanda had seen him on the first floor a few times, summoned when a patient needed restraining.

"Sorry you had to wait," the guard said, rubbing his stomach. "Had something for dinner that didn't agree with me."

Fernanda nodded nervously as he keyed open the elevator. She was relieved to be deposited back downstairs and glad her shift was almost over. She just wanted to go home, snuggle under the covers and try forgetting what she'd seen.

She awoke from a troubled sleep to a mid-morning phone call. It was a man from the institute whom she didn't know, requesting her presence there in one hour, well before the start of her shift.

Fernanda was a nervous wreck by the time she arrived in the office of the clinic's director, who apparently had been asked to make himself scarce. Aunt Isabella was there too, sitting off to the side. Behind the desk was a slight-figured man, obviously the one who'd summoned her.

"I'm Mr Kerns," he said pleasantly. "Have a seat. Do you know why you're here?"

Lying would only make things worse. Fernanda figured her only chance of not being fired was owning up to what she'd done.

"When I delivered the antibiotic to the second floor, I glanced through that window. I guess I wasn't supposed to."

"Indeed. And thank you for being honest. One of the cameras inside the room caught you. You were quite startled. It's a familiar reaction of anyone encountering Patient X for the first time. Do you know who he is?"

"Reginald Blayvine." She didn't know what to do with her hands, finally tucked them under her thighs.

"Relax, Fernanda, you're not in any trouble. The guard should have met you at the elevator and kept you away from the window and the nurse had a mild emergency related to the patient's vitals. Our review of the incident concludes it was an unlikely sequence of circumstances with no one at fault. As for your peeking through the window, we would have been surprised if you hadn't.

"That said, we must extract one promise from you, that you do not share or discuss what you saw with anyone. Only a select group of people know about Blayvine and his condition and we need to keep it that way. I think you can imagine what would happen if word were to get out. Everyone would want to see. The clinic would be overrun by the media, gawkers and god knows who else. If that happened, we might be forced to relocate the patient and possibly have to close the Nullenberg Care Institute."

"Jobs could be lost," Aunt Isabella added.

"I won't tell a soul," Fernanda said, relieved she wasn't being fired. "I swear on my life."

"And we're confident you'll keep that promise," Kerns said. "We've received excellent reports on your work, and not just from individuals with a vested interest in your success." He nodded toward Aunt Isabella. "The institute is part of a much larger organization that is always on the lookout for skilled and dedicated people with the qualities necessary for advancement. I'm certain you have a bright future with us."

"Thank you," Fernanda said.

Kerns smiled, rose from the desk and shook her hand. "Although I know you'll adhere to your promises, you may become tempted to try learning more about Patient X's condition."

"I swear I wouldn't do that."

"Nonetheless, curiosity is a powerful driver of behavior. Some mysteries can eventually become an itch we become desperate to scratch. To ward off that possibility, I've authorized your aunt to answer a few of your questions."

With a final smile, he left the office. Fernanda faced her tía.

"Blayvine's condition is the result of a mishap," Aunt Isabella began. "Foul play, actually. A twisted act of vengeance by an unstable researcher who contaminated his drink with an experimental substance."

"And those things on his body, they really are–"

"Yes, exactly what they appear to be. Human eyes. Each is fully functional. Each has its own optic nerve conducting visual impulses to his primary visual cortex."

Fernanda shuddered as she recalled the sight of all those eyes, seemingly staring at her from all over his body. In her brief time at the window, she had the impression there were more than a dozen of them: on his torso, his arms, his legs, even one on his chin. Some were horizontal like regular eyes, but others sprouted from his flesh at odd angles.

"The extraocular count is up to nineteen," Aunt Isabella continued. "Twenty-one including his natural pair. Some are on areas of his body you weren't able to see. On his back, his buttocks. One on his penis even."

"Santo Dios!" Fernanda whispered.

"No new eyes have appeared for several months so there's hope his condition has stabilized. Time will tell. For now, all we can do is keep him under observation."

"And there's nothing that can be done for him?"

"They've tried surgically removing some of the eyes but they always grow back. Did you notice none of them have eyelids? In the early days, opaque patches were put over them, thinking that might help him rest better. Instead, he became highly agitated. Eventually, it was realized that covering his natural eyes rendered him calmer, indicating they'd been rendered superfluous. His vitals remain stable as long as the majority of his extraocular array remain unimpeded." She shook her head. "We can't even imagine the nature of his visual field, what he's able to perceive from so many optic sources simultaneously."

"Is he conscious of what's happened to him?"

"We're not sure. According to the monitors, he's in REM sleep most of the time and dreaming heavily. When he is awake, he appears to be in a dissociative fugue state." Aunt Isabella paused. "The amnesia is probably a blessing."

Fernanda recalled that rumor about Patient X, that he could see into the afterlife. She was suddenly grateful for her own visual limitations. Whatever Blayvine was able to perceive, it was not a realm she had any desire to explore.

ACKNOWLEDGEMENTS

Kudos as always to Etan Ilfeld and the entire team at Watkins Publishing and Angry Robot Books, a dedicated and eclectic band whose editorial and promotional acumen elevates this writer's efforts. Essential voices helping *Scales* reach fruition include Eleanor Teasdale, Desola Coker, Caroline Lambe, Amy Portsmouth, Melody Travers, Dan Hanks, Andrew Hook, Paris Ferguson and Sneha Alexander. And a special shout-out to another light behind the scenes, industrious agent Mark Gottlieb of Trident Media Group.